HEART TO HEART

Still weak-kneed, Marianne lowered herself into a chair. *He's going to ask me to marry him.* His kisses, his hand actually on her breast—hadn't he as much as announced his intentions? He was not toying with her as he had with those other girls, she was sure of that.

I'm going to say yes. Staring out the window, she watched a bluebird take flight, her heart soaring with it. *I'm going to marry Yves Chamard.*

BOOK YOUR PLACE ON OUR WEBSITE AND MAKE THE READING CONNECTION!

We've created a customized website just for our very special readers, where you can get the inside scoop on everything that's going on with Zebra, Pinnacle and Kensington books.

When you come online, you'll have the exciting opportunity to:

- View covers of upcoming books
- Read sample chapters
- Learn about our future publishing schedule (listed by publication month *and author*)
- Find out when your favorite authors will be visiting a city near you
- Search for and order backlist books from our online catalog
- Check out author bios and background information
- Send e-mail to your favorite authors
- Meet the Kensington staff online
- Join us in weekly chats with authors, readers and other guests
- Get writing guidelines
- AND MUCH MORE!

**Visit our website at
http://www.kensingtonbooks.com**

Ever My Love

Gretchen Craig

ZEBRA BOOKS
Kensington Publishing Corp.
www.kensingtonbooks.com

ZEBRA BOOKS are published by

Kensington Publishing Corp.
850 Third Avenue
New York, NY 10022

All Kensington titles, imprints, and distributed lines are avail-
able at special quantity discounts for bulk purchases for sales
promotion, premiums, fund-raising, educational, or institu-
tional use.

Special book excerpts or customized printings can also be created to fit specific needs. For details, write or phone the office
of the Kensington Special Sales Manager: Attn. Special Sales
Department. Kensington Publishing Corp., 850 Third Avenue,
New York, NY 10022. Phone: 1-800-221-2647.

Zebra and the Z logo Reg. U.S. Pat. & TM Off.

ISBN-13: 978-0-8217-8020-6
ISBN-10: 0-8217-8020-4

First Printing: May 2007
10 9 8 7 6 5 4 3 2 1

Printed in the United States of America

For my husband,
Rogers Stephen Craig

Acknowledgments

Thank you to my friends
Julie Williams and Hurshel Farrow
For reading and critiquing the whole endeavor.

Donna Gimarc and Kathleen Baldwin
gave me wonderful suggestions.

The GDWA critique group—
Randy Thompson, Bob Dean, Dee Stuart,
Donna Gimarc, Cindy Sandell, Barb Blanks,
Darrall Brinlee, and Sandy Yeo—
offered valuable insights, especially
with the dueling scene!

All my wonderful pals at Lone Star Night Writers—
I appreciate all of you and your encouragement.

Chapter 1

Scared he'd lose sight of his brother in the night, Peter followed close on John Man's heels. They were in new territory now, miles beyond the boundaries of the Johnston plantation.

John Man reached a hand behind him and Peter stopped. "You hear that?" John Man whispered.

Hounds. Peter grabbed his brother's arm. "John, what we gone do?"

"Likely they's two, three mile away yet. Keep you head."

They ran, the dark pressing in on them. Then the fear pushed them faster and they thrashed through the brush, heedless of the noise they made—the hounds followed their scent, not their clamor.

They struggled up a hill and the woods ended. Headstones gleamed in the moonlight and Peter trembled, dreading the white shadows of ghosts emerging from the graves.

"This way," John Man said, turning right to skirt the cemetery.

Peter's breath came ragged and shallow. "They's

louder," he gasped. He could hardly breathe, his chest was so tight.

John Man paused. The hounds were closing in. He stared at the heavens, at the cold, indifferent moon. "We not gone outrun them dogs."

"John, they tear us up, they get us."

"I ain't going back, Petie. They axe my foot, I go back again."

Peter clutched at his brother, the fear sucking at his courage. "I's scared, John."

"Petie, let 'em catch you, take you home to Grandmama. Hear? Climb up dat sycamore so the dogs don't get you 'fore the men come up behind 'em."

"Don't leave me, John."

John Man pried Petie's fingers loose. "You ain't a man yet, they don't be too hard on you."

"They thrash me, John."

John Man gave him a shove. "Petie, get up dere, now. I's going on."

John Man ran. Peter climbed. Higher and higher up the trunk, the branches smaller and thinner. *Dey stop to catch me, dat give John time.* Peter kept climbing.

His heart began to steady, his breath to slow. He'd be safe once the men caught up with the dogs to hold them off. Then he'd climb down, go back to Grandmama. After the man cut him with the whip, she'd tend him.

The treetop bent over from his weight. Peter scrabbled for a better handhold, grabbed on to a branch. It snapped, and he grasped at the next one. He missed, his body now tipping farther out, away from the bole. Hands seizing on outer twigs, Peter crashed down and down through the leaves. He bounced when he hit the ground, the breath knocked out of him.

He tried to suck air, but his lungs were stunned. *Keep you head. It come back. Wait for it.* At last, air. He gulped it in, and sound returned to his starved brain. The hounds were coming. He ran headlong through the gravestones, too frightened to heed the ghostly rising vapors.

John Man had run east, like they'd planned. He'd go the other way, find another tree. Hurry. They coming.

Nothing but brush now as he ran down the hill. Too late to turn back to the trees.

Peter plunged into briars. The baying of the hounds so close now, so close. Thorns clawed at him, cutting and slicing and snagging as he scrambled for the swamp. No thought of the briars, nor of the snakes and gators in the bayou, he knew only flight.

Moongleam on water. He threw himself into the black soup. Too shallow. Running, thrashing and splashing, giving himself away. Panic had him, and he couldn't stop, couldn't think.

A quick look over his shoulder. The dogs roiling the water now, their eyes gleaming yellow in the moonlight. That dream, he lived the dream that haunted him since childhood, his legs churning but going nowhere.

They were on him. The lead hound dragged him down for the others to snap and snarl and tear at. Slashing, gnawing, crunching as teeth found bone. His brain shut off the pain—but not the horror, the terrible keen knowing as teeth ripped at his clothes, at his flesh.

Over the growling and snapping, Peter heard his own scream, far away, high, and without end.

By the time the men caught up to the dogs, Peter's blood thickened the dark water and he had ceased to struggle.

Warm hands pulled him out of the water and laid him on the ground in a circle of lamplight. A man with a shotgun over his shoulder nudged him with his boot. "You boys may as well take him on back. See if somebody wants to try sewing him up, but I reckon it won't do no good."

Two black men, barefoot and ragged as Peter, knelt down. One of them took off his filthy rough shirt and wrapped it around Peter's neck before they lifted him.

"Let's see can we catch us the other'n," the lantern-holder said. "The bloodhounds'll pick him up 'fore the blueticks, whatcha bet?"

Marianne Johnston rose easily at first light. Not for her the drowsy mornings waiting for coffee to be brought to her in her rose-silk canopied bed. She had too much to do, and much of it was best done before the sun burned off the morning mist.

Freddie, Marianne's tiny King Charles spaniel, bounded from the foot of the bed to demand a kiss, then jumped to the floor and carried off one of Marianne's satin slippers before her feet hit the floor.

After a merry romp retrieving her slipper, Marianne gave her long hair a quick brush and pinned it any which way. She had already pulled on her gardening skirt with the big pockets when she heard the commotion outside.

Throwing her blouse on, she opened the balcony door and leaned out. A cluster of slaves knotted around a spot below her. When someone shifted, Marianne saw the bloody mess they tended. They'd come for her.

She tied her shoes, pulled her medical bag from a shelf—"Stay, Freddie"—ran down the grand staircase, through the polished parlor, and out to the courtyard.

"What happened?" she called, still running.

Pearl, a slender young woman with delicate features and big doe eyes, righted the rag on her head with a trembling hand. "Dogs got him, Miss Marianne. But he still breathing."

Pearl stepped aside so she could see the boy's mangled flesh. Marianne crossed herself and closed her eyes. *Dear God, help me.* She breathed deeply, opened her eyes.

Little Annie, the house's favorite, stood gaping. "Go tell Evette we'll need hot water, Annie, and to clear off her big table. Run on." To Pearl, she said, "We'll wash him in the cookhouse."

Marianne had sewn up gashes and applied poultices among the slaves since she was thirteen, but this poor boy—she had never seen such wounds.

When did we start setting dogs on our people? she thought.

She and Pearl kept pace with the men carrying Peter. Whenever Marianne needed an extra hand for nursing, it was always Pearl she sent for. Pearl had gentle hands, and she didn't carry on at the sight and smell of blood.

Marianne wiped at the boy's face. "Who is it?"

"It be Peter, Miss Marianne."

Not one of them she knew. He couldn't be more than fourteen, and he'd tried to run. The awful risks they take, she thought. His head lolled when they put him down. He'd lost so much blood, she doubted he'd ever regain consciousness.

She and Pearl bathed him first with warm water, then with witch hazel. Marianne watched to see if he felt the sting on his wounds, but he neither blinked nor groaned. Better he was out now, anyway, while she worked on him. Lacerations all over his body, from ears to ankles, even chunks of flesh torn clean away. And they said he'd been in the bayou. He'd have fever for sure.

Marianne set hot pads on the puncture wounds so they would bleed and cleanse themselves. The rips and gashes she cleaned with witch hazel, making sure there was no debris in them. They were ghastly, but not deep.

From a vial in her bag, she dribbled sweet oil on a length of black silk thread and set to work with her needle. With sure hands, she began with Peter's ear, nearly torn from his head. "Was he alone?" she asked.

"He run wid his brother, John Man."

Marianne didn't ask anymore. If they caught John Man, she'd hear of it soon enough.

Evette and her helpers worked around the grisly tableau. There were people to feed, bread and corn and beans to cook, whether Peter lay on the big table or not. The aroma of salt pork and beans, soon to be carted out to the fields, mingled with the smells of blood and witch hazel.

While Pearl kept hot compresses on the punctures, Marianne sewed the other wounds. After an hour, Evette handed the mistress a tin cup of sweet coffee and she drank it down. Marianne paused long enough to dab the sweat from her face, then picked up her needle.

Another gash, and she was finished with the sutures. She packed a poultice of crushed pewterwort stems around each puncture wound, which she left unsewn. The other wounds she covered with comfrey poultices.

Marianne plunged her arms to the elbow in the bucket of warm water Evette had ready for her. Only then did she realize she'd forgotten her canvas apron. Her maid Hannah would shake her head—another skirt and blouse ruined.

Peter cried out, still not really conscious, and clawed at the poultice on his neck. Marianne took his hands to quiet him. At least he showed some strength. *Only God knows if he will survive.*

With Pearl's help Marianne wrapped Peter in linen so that he seemed more bandage than boy. Then she said a silent prayer as the men carefully moved him to a stretcher to take him to his cabin. "Stay with him, Pearl. I'll come down in a while."

Drained, Marianne retreated to her room where she

pulled off her clothes and slipped into her peignoir.
Freddie wanted to explore the bloodstained heap, but
Marianne pulled him into her lap. She could have cried,
from nerves and pity for the boy, but Marianne believed
tears had little use in this world. She nuzzled Freddie's
soft fur and took comfort in his adoring kisses, holding
him close until he wiggled to be let loose.

While she waited for Hannah to heat a bath, she sat at
her rosewood desk, which Hannah had graced with a
crystal bowl filled with gardenias. Freddie settled in, his
tiny mug on her foot, and Marianne opened her medical
log. Writing the particulars of the morning's surgery
helped her put some distance between her feelings and
that poor boy. Next she pulled her leather-bound journal to her and dipped her pen again.

During her sixteenth year, Marianne had gone to fin-
ishing school in New York. Everyone was reading *Uncle
Tom's Cabin*, and Marianne cried her way through it, horrified. A terrible, heartbreaking story. But slavery wasn't
like that, not in reality. She knew no one like that
Legree, no one so desperate as Eliza. Yet the city had
been full of men and women preaching in strident
voices on street corners, filling churches and halls with
their ringing indictments of slaveholding. Earnestly, pas-
sionately, the abolitionists reasoned and railed against
slavery and the evil men who profited from it. They were
very convincing, except that her own father profited
from it, and so then did she, and everyone she knew
back home.

Certainly Father was a good man. Marianne's father's
friends, some of whom owned more than two hundred
slaves, were good men. *These people in the East*, all her
Southern friends assured her, *they simply don't understand
the Southern way of life*. Her friends must be right. Slavery

was not a simple thing. The truth was much more complicated than the abolitionists claimed.

Thus with the innate human capacity to hold two conflicting ideas at once, Marianne returned to Louisiana, where life resumed its comfortable rhythms. Magnolias was a happy plantation, she was sure of it. Father was good to his slaves. She herself ministered to them, wormed their children, treated their earaches, and brewed the potions that cured their fevers.

And so Marianne filled her journal with the many ways her family took care to run a compassionate plantation. Yet, as she matured to a woman of twenty, doubts increasingly nagged her. The ringing voices of those stirring abolitionist orators Julia Ward Howe and Henry Stanton lingered in her mind; the pages of her journal reflected her growing unease.

And now—here was Peter.

Bathed and dressed, Marianne ate a hurried and solitary dinner. At Hannah's insistence, she donned cuff guards and a heavy apron. She checked her pocket for the Keys to the Realm, as she called them, and took the path through the garden to her personal storeroom. Here she had herbs drying from the rafters, pots of salve and the makings for more, and her well-used mortar and pestle.

She chose the bark and leaves of the willow to grind small enough for an infusion; willow tea would do well to fight the fever she knew would come. She cut down more witch hazel leaves and ground them to a powder that she mixed with lard to make a greasy salve. Peter was going to require quantities of both. Reaching overhead, she untied a bundle of comfrey, then shredded and pounded the roots and leaves into a gluey mass to use for additional poultices.

With her pots of medicinals, Marianne walked down to the quarters. The reek of witch hazel and pewterwort coming through the open door led her to the cabin.

Pearl sat on the only stool, fanning the flies from Peter's face.

"Has he wakened?"

"Yes'm, he in and out."

Marianne put her hand to Peter's forehead. Already he was hot to the touch. "Who are his people?"

"He old Lena's youngest grandbaby."

Marianne nodded, but in truth, she didn't know which one Lena was. Nor what had happened to Peter's mother. She felt ashamed of herself for not knowing, but there were so many slaves on the place.

"I reckon she know Petie caught by now," Pearl said, "but de overseer, he don't let her come."

Marianne's mouth tightened. That was cruel, to keep the woman away. With Father in Saratoga and her brother Adam at the lake, she'd have to deal with Mr. McNaught herself. Well, she'd handle him. Later.

She handed Pearl the pot of crushed willow bark. "Tell Evette to make a tea out of this, let it steep a good while. Then go on to the house and ask Charles to bring me paper and pen."

While Marianne waited for the aged Charles, who'd been in charge of the house even when Father was young, Marianne unwrapped the bloody bandage on Peter's maimed foot and washed the wound again. Peter groaned and opened his eyes.

"Lie still," she told him. With the witch hazel salve rubbed into a gauzy cloth, she layered the bandage over the flesh to stop the oozing. Then she tied linen strips round and round his foot. There'd be no flies lighting on these wounds if she could help it.

Charles came in, elegant as always in his butler's livery. She wrote a note, much more polite than she felt, asking Mr. McNaught to send Lena in from the field to sit with her grandson. That taken care of, she cooled Peter's hot skin with astringent until Pearl returned with the willow bark tea.

Marianne lifted Peter's head and held the tea to his lips. He sputtered at the evil taste. "I know it's foul, but you need to drink it all," she told him.

To Pearl she said, "You can clean up now. Then go on back to the kitchen. I'll stay until Lena comes."

Pearl left Miss Marianne with her hand on Peter's forehead. *She a good mistress,* Pearl thought. *Petie have a chance of living through dis wid her tending him.*

Pearl still wore Peter's blood on her hands and arms and dress. At the well, the sand at her feet turned pink as she washed. *My Luke,* she thought. *I make sure he see how Petie all chewed up. John Man all de time talking, make it sound easy to get away. Now maybe Luke think on it some mo.* She checked, her nails were clean. *Till I gives him a baby. A baby on de way, he stay put here wid me.*

Pearl drew another bucket and took it to her and Luke's cabin. When had she ever been alone in the middle of a day? Sunlight through the window caught the dust motes and cast shadows in the corners. She stilled herself to listen to the quiet house. The peace bled the tension from her shoulders. A body could rest, alone, with nothing to hand. *If Luke could rest like dis, find a little peace in de day, he not be so ready to run.*

She stripped off the faded gray sack dress and sluiced the cold water over her belly, as flat now as the day she and Luke first loved each other. *Lord, I needs a chile,* she reminded Him.

Every day she drank the concoction Mammy Lewis made for her. Squaw vine and chaste berries, dandelion and nettle leaves—"It shore to give you a baby," Mammy promised her. But her flow came just the same.

How long Luke gone stick wid me widout no chile? He say he gone stick, but mens want babies much as womens do. She tilted her head as if she could see through the roof to God's domain. *Lord, don forget me down here praying for a baby.* She crossed herself the way she'd seen Miss Marianne do, and the master's wife had done it too back before she died. Maybe that made the prayers stronger.

Pearl pulled on the only other dress she had, threadbare and too tight across the shoulders, but it would do while the other one soaked. She hurried on to her work in the cookhouse.

In the other cabin, Marianne put her fingers to Peter's throat where the pulse pumped under the brown skin. Should it be that fast? She pressed her own throat until she found the pulse. Peter's vein throbbed so much faster, she was sure it couldn't be good for him. She roused him and held the cup to his lips. She'd added peppermint to sweeten the bitter willow brew, but he still grimaced at the taste. "I'll try some honey in the next batch," she promised him. "Go back to sleep."

She checked each bandage to be sure blood wasn't still oozing from his wounds. His limbs were so thin. She wiped his face. Thick dark lashes curled against his cheek, fine brows arched across a smooth high forehead. A handsome boy, this Peter. Or he had been. She wondered what he was like. Did he sing in the evenings with the others? Did he make jokes and tell stories? Did he follow some girl around and pick daisies for her? She dabbed the healing salve on his dry lips and wished she knew more medicine. She'd reread *The Mistress's Essential Medical Book* and see if there was another remedy she should try.

This poor boy won't run away again, not with his legs and foot like they are. But his brother's still out there. God protect him.

Why had these two run now? This new man, she thought. McNaught. He was too harsh. She didn't remember having any runaways when Mr. Smythe had been in charge. But abolition was in the air; the slaves were bound to be roused. *And who can blame them?*

Marianne dipped her cloth into a pan of water and wiped the heat away from Peter's brow. *There can't be, there mustn't be, any more boys brought home like this.*

But Father wouldn't listen to her. He loved her and spoiled her, but he took no counsel from his daughter. How could she do anything more?

Chapter 2

Gabriel Chamard stepped from the gangplank onto the wharf and took in the first breath of home. Not the lemon-scented air he remembered, nor the rich aromas of Creole cooking—the docks smelled of the fetid river and mules and sweating men. But it was home.

Gabriel moved through the hive of working stevedores, a head taller than everyone else, to gain the soil of Louisiana. He arranged for his trunk to be delivered, then shook his head at the for-hires, eager to stretch his legs after weeks on the sailing ship. With long-legged strides, he set out to reacquaint himself with New Orleans.

The streets around the wharves were mucky, laden with trash and filth, the leavings of dogs and horses. Watching where he placed his fine Parisian shoes, Gabriel bumped into a yellow-haired man with shit on his hobnail boots and dried blood on his apron.

"Beg pardon, sir . . ." the man began. Gabriel prepared to offer his own apology, but the fellow looked into the liquid dark eyes of Gabriel's African ancestors. "You a damn colored," he said. He reached out a filthy hand and fingered Gabriel's velvet collar. "Dressed up like your betters."

Gabriel settled his shoulders, ready if the man should touch him again. He was as tall as Gabriel and broader across the chest. But Gabriel noted the softness in the belly, the lines in the man's red face. He could take him.

"Excuse me," Gabriel said and moved to the side.

The man's little pig eyes lit up. He grabbed Gabriel's right arm. "You think you a mighty fine gentleman, don't you? But you just a ni—"

"Release me." Gabriel looked at the butcher's beefy hand on his arm and then into the bloodshot blue eyes.

A couple of working men stopped to watch, their arms crossed, ready for a show. The question was, could he take the three of them and stay out of the muck on the street? Probably he'd ruin his jacket, but if that was the price of being a man in New Orleans, so be it.

The big fellow grinned now that he had an audience. He probably expects to enjoy this, Gabriel reflected.

The butcher yanked the lapel of the fine wool coat.

Gabriel drove his left fist into the man's gut. From the corner of his eye, he saw the two gawkers move in on him, both on his left side. Gabriel whirled, took the nearest one with his right. The second man got in a blow near Gabriel's eye, but paid for getting too close— Gabriel caught him under the jaw with his fist.

The butcher was up, coming for him, but first Gabriel had to fell the first spectator who was still standing. A powerful, well-placed punch, and the man went down.

Gabriel turned his attention to the pig-eyed butcher. The big blond had assumed the fighter's crouch, but he hadn't the discipline to wait for the moment. He lunged at Gabriel, arms spread to grapple him to the ground.

Gabriel stepped aside, put out a foot, and the man's

own force landed him in a sprawl facedown in the filthy road.

Gabriel glanced around. No more takers? The Paris Région's champion in fisticuffs three years running shot his cuffs, straightened his collar, and proceeded on his way.

Unfortunately, by the time he strolled through New Orleans and into *Le Vieux Carré*, his eye had swollen from the second spectator's blow. What a nuisance. His mother would no doubt make much of it and resume the lectures she'd delivered so many times in his youth: Don't look for trouble. Don't look those people in the eye. Walk away. You get yourself killed, you don't settle down. Thus the three years in Paris to better his manners and his disposition, or so his mother thought. And here he returns with a blackened eye. Gabriel smiled. It'd be a pleasure to hear his mother carrying on once again.

Number 24, Rue de Royale. The door robin's-egg blue. The brass knocker polished and gleaming. Gabriel knocked. Footsteps clattered down the staircase inside. Not the butler, but his own mother threw open the door and rushed into his arms.

He held her tight until she drew back to gaze at his face. "I've been watching out that window the livelong week expecting you any minute. Let me look at you."

Gabriel watched his mother take in the bruise and grinned at her. Her eyes darkened. Here it comes, he thought.

"Why'd I do without you for three years and you still getting into trouble?" she said.

Gabriel took her in. Still a beauty, her face unlined, her brown skin clear and bright. She could pass for a woman half her age, though she'd grown a little plump. "You going to let me in?" he teased her.

"Cleo, that him?" a man called from within.

"Come in and meet your stepfather, son."

Gabriel's smile faded. He knew his mother had married, of course, but he didn't know the man and he had no need of a stepfather. Bertrand Chamard was all the father he'd ever needed or wanted.

A tall, slender, very dark man met them in the hallway. He smiled, showing beautiful white teeth, and taking Gabriel by the shoulders, he kissed him on both cheeks in the French Creole way. "*Bienvenu*, Gabriel."

"Monsieur LaFitte," Gabriel returned.

"Come in, come in," Pierre said and gestured to the parlor.

Gabriel's mother clung to him, smiling and blinking at tears as she sat with him on the golden yellow settee. Cleo touched his bruise with one finger. "He's already been in a fight, Pierre. Can you believe it?"

"It was nothing. Just a butcher looking for some amusement." Gabriel took his mother's hand and held it.

Pierre nodded and offered him a Cuban cigar. Gabriel gave him credit for not pursuing the matter. His mother's husband had likely had run-ins with white men in his time. He sized LaFitte up as a man who didn't step aside easily. There'd been iron in the man's grip.

"Where is Nicolette?" Gabriel asked.

"At the lake, staying with Pierre's family. Your sister is a great success, Gabriel, singing at Chez Louis four nights a week."

"Tante Josephine and the cousins?"

"Waiting for you at Toulouse."

Gabriel nodded, eager and apprehensive at seeing Simone. After three years, she had not married.

"And now you're *un médicin*," Pierre said. "You don't know how proud your mother is to have an educated son."

A knock on the door called the butler, and a moment

later Yves Chamard strode into the room, his hand outstretched. "I heard there was a French boat in!" Gabriel took his younger brother's hand and pulled him into a bear hug. They kissed cheeks, laughed, and hugged again.

Yves broke away to bend down to Cleo. "*Bonjour, ma belle.*" Cleo lifted her face to be kissed and beamed at him. Pierre had his hand out and the men shook hands genially. Yves was no stranger in this house, Gabriel observed.

"So tell me everything," Yves said.

"He's been in a fight this very morning," Cleo reported.

Gabriel smiled, a little rueful, but Yves grinned. "So you haven't changed? Wonderful."

"What about you? Papa wrote the ladies follow you around like flies on honey." Gabriel winked at Cleo. "Like father, like son?"

Gabriel realized he had been indelicate. Yves' and Gabriel's white father had kept Cleo, a quadroon, for many years, had loved her in fact, and Bertrand Chamard too had had to fight the women off, not always successfully.

Gabriel's family was a tangle: His father had two children, Gabe and Nicolette, with Cleo; Papa also had two sons, Marcel and Yves, by his two wives, both deceased now. And then there was his mother's white Creole half sister, Tante Josie. A complicated family, though not uncommon in Louisiana.

Unoffended, Gabriel's maman laughed, smiling at Yves. "He is like the hummingbird, flitting from one flower to the next, never settling on one for more than a taste. You can't deny it, Yves."

"No, Cleo, I can't. And what of you, my monkish brother? No wife in tow?"

Gabriel had indeed come home to New Orleans as he

left it, a bachelor, his heart as firmly bestowed now as it had been when he sailed for France. "That may have been a mistake," Gabriel said. "You've no doubt ruined all the ladies in New Orleans for anyone else."

As the foursome passed an hour catching up on news, Gabriel watched his brother. Yves had been, what, twenty, when Gabriel left for Paris? What kind of life was Yves making for himself? Did he while away his time with the usual pursuits of wealthy young men, gaming, racing, and hunting? It's not what he would expect of Yves.

Yves had always had a streak of passionate idealism. Whatever he read, he espoused vigorously to his brothers and to Papa. One month it would be Emerson's essays on transcendentalism, the next, Thoreau or Oliver Wendell Holmes. Even that radical Shelley and his tracts on social bondage. Gabriel wondered if his intellectually inclined, morally astute brother had read Charles Darwin's scandalous treatise on the origins of species. In their devoutly Catholic family, the book would be branded wicked, heretical, and blasphemous. Not that that would stop Yves from reading it.

Gabriel shifted his attention to his mother. She had gained a little weight, just enough to soften the lines of her face. Clearly, she was happy with this man Pierre. She'd been happy with Papa, too, and miserable as well. *May Pierre be the man she needs.*

Cleo rang the bell and asked for mint juleps before dinner.

Gabriel Chamard leaned back into the settee and sighed. A mint julep. He was truly home.

Chapter 3

The fever consumed Peter's flesh, in spite of every remedy Marianne concocted from the plantation's medical books. Corruption seeped from his wounds, and he wakened less and less.

Afraid to leave him, Marianne spent the afternoon, the evening, and the night at his bedside. In the hours before sunrise, she lay down on the dusty boards to rest a few minutes. She didn't dare lie on one of the four other cots in the room, fearing bedbugs. This was a bachelor's cabin, she realized. Where did those other young men sleep tonight?

She woke to find Lena had removed her shoes and rolled up a feed sack to make a pillow for her. The candle still burned, casting a yellow glow over the bent old woman kneeling at Peter's bedside, her hands clasped in desperate fervor as she prayed.

As Lena's entreaties to God whispered through the cabin, Marianne felt Peter's skin. Hot and dry. They'd used all the water and brews made up for the night. Marianne pulled her shoes on, picked up the bucket, and stepped out.

A snore from the moon-shadowed corner of the porch startled her. "Who's there?"

With a snort, the man wakened and let his tipped chair fall back to the floor.

"Charles? What are you doing here?"

He ran a hand over his face. "Master wouldn't like you being down here by yourself all night." He rubbed the kink in his neck. "Strangers coming through here this time of year."

"Strangers?"

Charles stood up, dwarfing her he was so tall. An imposing man, even now with gray in his short kinky hair. Marianne waited for him to explain, but he stared out at the moon-soaked yard, then shook his head. He took the bucket from her hand.

"Who are you talking about?"

"Just an old man dreaming, Miss Marianne. I'll get you some water."

When Charles returned with the bucket, she woke Peter to drink from the gourd. Lena sat on the floor with her head and arms on the corn-husk mattress, sleeping a little at last.

She's too old to stay up all night like this. And her other boy gone too. John Man, they said. Marianne wondered if Lena had daughters to take care of her, other grandchildren to help her bear the loss of two grandsons. *No, Peter isn't gone yet,* she reminded herself. *He might pull through.*

As the sun rose, Peter moaned and turned his head from side to side, the fever roiling his brain with delirium. Eyes staring wide, he screamed, "Dey gone get me! Lawd help me!"

Marianne tried to speak over him—"Peter, you're safe! It's just a dream." She couldn't get through to him, but his grandmother could. Lena held his head and kissed his face. "Petie, boy," she said softly. "It's all over. Dem dogs cain't get you no more."

Peter's eyes cleared. Marianne could see he knew his grandmother, knew where he was again. His face contorted, pain and grief wrenching sobs from deep in his chest. Lena pulled him to her bosom and rocked him.

Marianne put a hand to her mouth, fighting sobs. The delirium, Lena's cradling Peter like this brought back the day her little sister died. Mother had held three-year-old Elizabeth just like Lena held Peter, clasping her to keep her from going. But nothing old Dr. Benet had been able to do could save her. And only months later, Mother. Losing Mother still hurt, even after seven years.

On the porch, she leaned against the post and gave herself to the grief welling up. She hadn't cried for Mother in such a long time, and now the loss seemed as fresh as Lena's fear. That was part of her grief, too. Fear for Peter. And rage. His foot, his leg, and the poor mangled hand. What the men had let the dogs do to his poor body—he'd never be the same, if he survived.

Straightening her shoulders, she stanched the useless sobs. There was nothing else she could do for Peter at the moment. By the gray and yellow bar of light on the eastern horizon, she walked through the quarters to the garden, to be among her roses and camellias.

This, the dawn, was the best time of day, every leaf and stone bedewed, the tiny drops needing only the rising sun to gleam like pearls. The moisture in the air kissed her skin, and the river breeze cooled her after the breathless, hot night in the cabin.

She rested on the cypress bench in the center of the garden. This had been her mother's favorite spot, and Father had had *Violette* carved into the back of the bench. Mother had plotted the paths and laid out the original beds.

Marianne's passion was the search for the perfect crossbred rose. Monsieur Vibert, the noted cultivator of roses in Europe, had corresponded regularly with Mother, and out of kindness, Marianne presumed, he continued to do so with her. She would write him soon to tell him what her latest crosses had produced. A Chinese descendant red and one of her hardy European pinks had yielded blooms with a curious white streak.

Joseph appeared across the garden. Dear Joseph. His hair was grizzled and his black skin deeply wrinkled from a life spent in the sun. She knew his gnarled hands hurt him too.

Joseph was a partner, not just a minion, in this tending of the garden. He had been among the slaves Mother directed in setting out the original garden paths. Now, illiterate as he was, Marianne was sure he knew as much about crossbreeding as she did.

"Morning, Miss Marianne." He stopped in front of her bench and squinted at her. "You been up all night with that boy Peter, look like."

Marianne glanced at her rumpled clothes. She put a hand to her hair and discovered it was more down than up. "I'll sleep later. Right now I'd rather transplant those seedlings."

They consulted Marianne's markings about each bush's parentage and decided which canes to pot together. The roses would pollinate one another when the time came, and then she and Joseph would see what qualities the new bushes inherited.

"They tell me that boy bit up pretty bad," Joseph said as he mixed compost into the black soil they used in the pots.

"I never saw—" Marianne began.

"Missy!" Hannah called. She trotted through the garden waving Marianne's hat at her. "You forget Mr. Adam bringing company in a few days? You be red-faced and ugly as a turnip you don't put you hat and gloves on."

Father often chided Marianne for letting Hannah talk to her like that. Too familiar, he told her. No way for a slave, or a mistress, to behave. But how formal can you be with someone who once wiped your snotty nose and who now launders your pantaloons?

"Thank you for the compliment, Hannah," Marianne said with a laugh. She tied the hat ribbons under her chin and pulled on the gloves. Too late, really, for the gloves. She already had dirt under her fingernails and a thorn scratch on the back of her hand. "Run me a bath, will you, please. I'll be up in half an hour."

With Hannah gone, Joseph picked up the conversation. "Petie gone be able to work?"

"This place here," Marianne said, showing him her own Achilles tendon, "is nearly torn through on one leg. I don't see how that'll ever be right again."

"No'm, I don't reckon it will."

Marianne pushed hair off her face. "Joseph, I don't remember Mr. Smythe having dogs to hunt slaves."

"Das right, honey. Dese dogs come wid dis new man."

Marianne scooped rich loam into another pot. Finally she said, "At least I could get rid of the dogs."

"Mr. Adam, he planning to use dem hounds hisself in deer season. Das what I heard."

"Even dogs that have tasted slave blood?"

Joseph looked at her. Not as a slave looks at, or rather avoids looking at, his mistress. But, as one human being looks at another.

Marianne set her trowel aside. "I better do it today before Adam comes home."

After she'd bathed and breakfasted, Marianne dressed in her brown silk day dress. She put up her wavy hair and surveyed herself in the mirror. She was aiming for an authoritarian look, not easy for a young woman of twenty. *I still look too young*, she thought. She added a lace cap, which she detested, and a crocheted shawl. Hot, but she did seem older.

When Marianne entered Father's office, Mr. McNaught rose from the leather chair and took his hat off.

"Good morning, Mr. McNaught," she said.

"Morning, miss." The man had shaved and slicked his hair back. His shirt was clean enough. But she noticed he hadn't trimmed his nails in some time. What Father had seen in the man, Marianne didn't know. He struck her as rather slow and stupid.

She assumed an air of confidence and walked around Father's big desk to his high-backed chair. "You may sit down," she said. She herself remained standing.

"Father will be away for some weeks yet," she began, "and so I have the responsibility for Magnolias until he returns."

Mr. McNaught cleared his throat. "I understood Mr. Adam had the running of the place."

Marianne tilted her head to one side and looked the man in the eye. "My brother is also away, as you know." Certainly he knew. McNaught shifted in his seat. *Uncomfortable, is he? Good.*

"The dogs you used the other night. The ones who attacked the boy they call Peter. How many are in that pack?"

"Thirteen. Didn't use but eight or nine of them, though."

"And you have trained them specifically for hunting down slaves, Mr. McNaught?"

"It don't take much training to switch from game to slaves, miss. They take to it quick enough. The trick is to have the best scent hound you got to lead the pack. A bloodhound's the best. The redbones and the blueticks, now, they—"

"Yes, I understand about scent hounds, Mr. Mc-Naught. I wish you to disperse the pack."

He looked at her for a moment and again Marianne wondered how bright the man was.

"Disperse the hounds?"

"Yes. I don't like to see the dogs killed. Spread them among Father's various properties. Cane Haven could take one or two, maybe the produce farm another pair."

McNaught stood up, his hat crumpled in his big fist. "Now hold on, miss—"

"I don't care how you do it, but the pack must be broken up. We will not keep dogs that have run down a man and bitten into him like he was an animal."

"Some of them dogs is my own. Mr. Johnston never said—"

Marianne interrupted him again. Standing behind the big mahogany desk gave her power, she realized. She was going to win this battle.

"Mr. Johnston isn't here, as I've said. But you will be compensated for the loss of your dogs. And I will inform my father how well you have cooperated." She looked him in the eye. "How well you have complied with my orders."

Marianne watched McNaught struggle to contain himself. The man's blue eyes darkened with anger, and his fair skin flushed. She could just imagine what he was thinking: Who does she think she is? Well, she was, for the moment at any rate, the one in control of this plantation.

Without the courtesy of a farewell, McNaught donned his hat and turned his back on her. *That's done. No more murderous dogs on Magnolias Plantation!* she thought, congratulating herself in spite of the man's pique.

Marianne sat down in Father's big chair. Yes, it was a powerful position, sitting behind this desk.

Chapter 4

Nicolette Chamard's voice lacked the husky sensuality of her mother's, but the lightness of her soprano suited the humor and wit she infused into her singing. The crowd tittered when she winked and chuckled at her sly delivery of innuendo. *And this is my baby sister,* Gabriel marveled. *A beautiful, talented performer who already knew how to mesmerize a roomful of sophisticates from New Orleans society.*

The French doors open to the night air, Gabriel nevertheless felt trickles of sweat underneath his jacket and starched white shirt. He ran a finger around his stiff collar and nodded to the waiter to approach.

"Gentlemen, another round?" Gabriel asked. Marcel and Yves Chamard agreed, but their friend Adam Johnston did not seem to hear. Gabriel held up four fingers to the waiter, and sat back to watch Mr. Johnston admiring his sister.

The room demonstrated the strange relationship between New Orleans white society and its less privileged tier of well-to-do coloreds. Had the occasion been at the American and Creole resort on Lake Pontchartrain, Nicolette would have sung to an exclusively white audience. Her brother might have heard her only if he waited tables. Here, however, white gentlemen of liberal inclinations, or perhaps of libidinous pursuits, mingled with the freedmen and women. And so it was that Gabriel sat with his white Creole half brothers Marcel and Yves, listening to their sister sing.

Bertrand Chamard, their father, had always acknowledged his colored children, and he'd encouraged his white sons to accept Gabriel and Nicolette. His wives—Marcel's mother who had died rather young, and his second, Yves' mother—had both pretended ignorance of Bertrand's other family, but he arranged for his children to know one another.

Gabriel smoked his cigar and observed his brothers' friend Adam. Marcel's cousin, actually, though not Yves'. Adam Johnston's face in the candlelight fairly glowed with delight. He had not taken his eyes off Nicolette from the moment she'd begun to sing.

Gabriel caught Yves' eye and they smiled at Adam's obvious infatuation. The thunderbolt, Gabriel had heard it called. The instant when a man knows his heart, soul, and body belong to a woman he has only just that moment seen.

Nicolette finished her performance. As the applause rolled through the room, she opened her arm to include Pierre LaFitte, who'd accompanied her on the piano. They bowed to the left, right, and center, and finally retired, applause following them from the bright lights of the stage.

Gabriel, host of their table, whispered in the waiter's ear to invite Nicolette to join them. She soon wound her way through the tables, her satin gown gleaming in the candlelight, the matching blue *tignon* on her head accenting the shape of her lovely long neck. Several gentlemen stopped her to offer congratulations, accolades, and invitations, all of which she responded to sweetly and deftly. She'd had a full year as a professional chanteuse; she knew her role on- and offstage.

The gentlemen stood to greet Nicolette, her brothers each delivering kisses of fraternal pride. Adam Johnston waited for his moment. He seized her hand and kissed it, too fervently, Gabriel thought.

"Mademoiselle, I'm honored," Adam breathed. The man is transparent as glass, Gabriel thought. He might as well have announced, *Je t'adore, Mademoiselle.*

"Monsieur," Nicolette murmured.

A smile played around her lips. Accustomed to being admired, Gabriel surmised. He seated her safely between Marcel and Yves.

"Mr. Johnston is a cousin of sorts to you, Nicolette," Marcel explained. "Albany Johnston, my late mother's brother, is his father."

"How do you do, Monsieur?" she said. Gabriel wondered if Nicolette would make the connection through their own Tante Josephine. Josephine and Adam's mother, Violette, were cousins also. *What a jumble*, Gabriel thought. *One needs a chart to keep it all sorted out. It would help if we didn't call anyone who ever shared a connection with a connection a cousin. Not a drop of blood between most of them.*

"We've waited supper for you," Gabriel said. "Hungry?"

"Famished. Do they have ice, do you think? I'd love chilled shrimp."

The waiter took their orders: oysters, shrimp, étoufee, turtle soup, peaches, a feast of what Louisiana had to offer.

Conversation at table focused on catching up with Gabriel after his three years abroad. He entertained them with his observations of Parisian society, careful to skirt the issue of race in front of his brothers and their friend. The acceptance a man of color found in Paris had altered his view of himself and the world, but that observation would not fit the present company. Gabriel was fond of his brothers. No need to make them uncomfortable in this pleasant setting.

Mr. Johnston seemed oblivious to Gabriel's stories of *ducs* and *comtesses*. He neither laughed when the others did nor remembered the courtesies of nodding and making eye contact with his tablemates. His eyes were fastened on Nicolette.

Gabriel wished his little sister's gown revealed not quite so much shoulder and bosom. Nicolette herself, however, seemed unperturbed. Beauty learns to be observed, he supposed.

"Mr. Johnston," Gabriel said. "Have you been to Paris?"

Adam tore his eyes from Nicolette. "Paris? No, not Paris." He adjusted his wineglass and seemed to make an attempt to gather himself. "Have any of you gentlemen been there?"

For a moment the table was silent. *The man's made an ass of himself now*, Gabriel thought. *Poor fool. If it weren't my sister he's ogling, I'd feel sorry for him.*

Yves smirked. Marcel, ever the kind one, rescued him. "But you have been to New York, haven't you, Adam? How did you find the theater there?"

During dinner, the host announced Madame Cleo Tassin, accompanied by Monsieur Pierre LaFitte. The audience welcomed their old favorites, and Gabriel's mother stood before them in her trademark red gown and elaborately folded *tignon*. Pierre seated himself at the piano and riffled the opening notes.

Cleo's smooth sultry contralto filled the room. Unlike Nicolette's saucy sexiness, Cleo's sexuality oozed across the stage in waves of a darker-flavored sensuality. The music became sinuous and insinuating in Cleo's bosom, and the men in the room, every one of them, put down their forks.

Her first number finished, Cleo stood a moment with her eyes closed. Listening to the silence, she'd told Gabriel long ago when he'd asked her why she did that. The silence is part of the song, she'd explained. As much as she loved the applause, it interrupted the silence, and so she closed her eyes to hold it back until the song was truly finished in her mind.

There's no one like her, Gabriel thought. *Not even the chanteuses in Paris have the soul to sing like she does.*

At the end of the evening, Marcel and Yves kissed Nicolette and promised to see her later in the summer.

Adam Johnston bent over her hand once again. "May I call on you, Mademoiselle?"

Gabriel tried to see the man as Nicolette might see him. Tall, well built. Sandy hair. Blue eyes. Women liked blue eyes. Handsome, he supposed. *But he's such a puppy.*

"That would be . . . *charmant,*" she said.

She seems to like him, though.

"I must absent myself tomorrow," Adam said, "but I will return later in the summer, if I may."

Nicolette bowed her head slightly.

A lily to his dandelion, Gabriel thought.

Gabriel cautioned Marcel and Yves, Adam too, to look alert as they returned to their lodging. Times were strained. With the division in Washington over free states versus slave states, with the strident speeches from abolitionists and politicians from both sides of the issue, dealings between the races had become tense. His guests were not on their own turf here, and resentments flared at the merest slight. Except for himself, Gabriel doubted his brothers were accustomed to dealing with freed men who felt no obligation to step aside on the walkway.

On the morrow, Gabe took a carriage back to the Mississippi to catch a steamboat going upriver. He'd not yet seen his father, nor Tante Josephine and the cousins. Well, these actually were cousins of a sort. Their mother and his were half sisters. That made Simone, Musette, and Ariane half cousins, he supposed. Another reason to avoid the one person he'd missed the most while he'd been away.

An hour from home, the boat passed by the Johnstons' Magnolias Plantation. The trees were laden with saucer-sized creamy blooms, their scent wafting through the muggy air. Gabriel inhaled deeply. No place else like this patch of God's earth, he thought.

And this was Adam Johnston's home. Gabriel knew the outline of that family's story, knew where Adam Johnston came from.

He paced the deck now they were nearing Toulouse. From his sister Nicolette's letters, he knew Simone had turned down two offers of marriage in his absence. Two. Because of him? He didn't know whether to hope or to despair.

The whistle had alerted Toulouse the boat was stopping, and the ancient and venerable Elbow John met Gabriel as he disembarked. At his side stood sweet-faced Onkle Thibault, Cleo's simpleminded but beloved brother.

"Welcome home, Mr. Gabe." Elbow John took off his hat in greeting, started to raise a tentative hand.

Gabriel brushed John's hand aside and wrapped him in a bear hug. This old man had been like another uncle to him growing up, taking him out in the bayous, showing him how to bait his hook.

"I's glad to see you, son," Elbow John wheezed.

Gabriel turned to his beaming Onkle Thibault and opened his arms. Thibault grinned and laughed aloud.

"I 'member you. You belongs to me," he said. "I knows you do."

"Yes, I do, Thibault, and you belong to me." He draped an arm around his uncle's shoulders. "John, it's good to be home."

"We's glad to have you, M'sieu Gabriel. Yo Tante up at de house. Dey tink you coming tomorry."

Gabriel walked on alone while Thibault and Elbow John dealt with the mail and the valises. The massive trees from the levee to the doors of Toulouse mottled the grass with green and gray shadows and funneled the cooler river air to the front gallery. The mighty oaks awed him as they ever had, yet the oaks did not distract him from the tension in his neck, now spreading into his shoulders the closer he came to the house.

The double doors flew open and Ariane DeBlieux clattered down the stairs. Petticoats flying, she ran full tilt down the alley to Gabriel. He caught her and used her momentum to swing her in circles.

"Who can this be?" he teased as he set her down. "No gaps in her front teeth, no freckles, taller than a belt buckle—this can't be Ariane?"

She twirled in her nearly full-length dress to show him how grown she was and smiled at him with no more shyness than if she'd seen him only the week before, for Ariane had written him long misspelled letters while he'd been gone, and he'd taken the time to write her about the Paris a child could love.

"And you're how old now? Sixteen?" he said.

She laughed at him. "I'm almost twelve, you silly."

Gabriel cocked his elbow for her to take his arm and they bantered their way to the house, up the stairs to the gallery, and into the parlor.

"No one else saw you get off the boat," Ariane whispered. "They don't know you're here yet."

"Shall we surprise them?" he whispered back.

With a grin and exaggerated tiptoes, Ariane led him to the back gallery where her maman and sisters sat with their sewing. At the doorway, she held a hand up for Gabriel to stop. Then, with all the flair of a Creole and Cajun offspring, she leapt onto the gallery, arms spread wide, and said, "I present to you . . ."

Gabriel stepped out, eyes searching for Simone.

Tante Josephine yelped and let her rocking chair bang against the wall as she reached for her darling Gabriel. A little gray showing at her temples, he noticed, but she'd leapt from her chair with the vigor of a young woman. He opened his arms for her, and she hugged him and laughed and cradled his face in her hands. "*Mon cher Gabriel*, home at last."

Gabriel held his aunt to his side as he turned to Musette. She hung back a little, though she smiled at him.

Sensitive to the shyness of a fourteen-year-old girl still uneasy in her womanhood, Gabriel held out a hand. Musette took it, relenting gladly when he pulled her to him with his free arm and kissed the top of her head.

With Ariane dancing around them all, Musette and Tante Josephine on either side, Gabriel looked to the remaining cousin. Simone stood beside her chair, her hands at her sides. Not shy, as Musette—was, nor delighted, as her mother was. Was that determination he saw in her eyes? Or anger, after all this time?

Simone's eyes locked on his as she stepped off the distance between them, no smile at all on her face. Would they ever have peace between them?

She stopped only inches from him. He tried to still the tremble in his limbs, to pretend his heart didn't thud inside his chest at the sight of her. She stood on her toes, placed a hand on his arm for balance, and kissed him firmly on the mouth.

"Welcome home, Gabriel," she said.

He couldn't take his eyes from her. His aunt had let go of his arm and was staring at the two of them, but all he could see was Simone, the high cheekbones and arched brows framed by her dark hair. And in the depths of those eyes, Gabriel found the other half of his soul.

Simone broke their gaze. She looked at her mother, an unspoken message in her eyes, and then returned to her chair, picked up her sewing, and sat down.

Gabriel turned to his dear Tante. The joy had gone out of her face, and he grieved at that.

He had accepted Father's offer to send him to medical school in Paris in order to spare the family the combustion of his attraction to Simone. Medicine had called him, too, but he would have been content to finish his schooling in the States.

Honor, and love, had decided him. Simone was seventeen when he left. During his years in Paris, he planned, Simone would forget her infatuation with him, move on with her life, marry, perhaps even become a mother before he returned. Why else had he exiled himself from his home?

Gabriel leaned over and kissed his tante Josephine's cheek. As complicated as their family was, white, colored, half sisters, half brothers, all of it—there had never been any doubt his aunt loved him as she loved her own children. It pained him to see the pleasure at his homecoming fade from her eyes.

"Mother sends her love," Gabriel said. "I've met my stepfather, heard him play, heard Nicolette sing."

"Tell us," Ariane burst in. "What did Nicolette sing? What did she wear? Did she do that number with the naughty lyrics?"

"Ariane!" Musette scolded. Showing grace beyond her

years, Musette said, "Sit down, please, Gabriel. I'm sure you have many things to tell us about Paris."

"First about Nicolette, though," Ariane insisted.

Gabriel told all. What she sang, how she made the audience laugh by raising a single eyebrow. He even remembered what she'd worn. Through it all, Ariane sat rapt, Musette and Tante Josie asked pertinent questions, and Simone stared at him mutely. He would have to leave as soon as decently possible. He hadn't the nerve for a private confrontation with the woman whose touch made him burn. Three lonely years spent abroad for nothing? He wanted her as badly as he ever had.

All through noon dinner Gabriel amused the ladies with his store of tales about life in Paris. Josie was particularly interested in hearing about the places she and her husband Phanor had visited two years before he died. What of the Tuileries, the Louvre? Did they still display the *Mona Lisa* in the great hall?

Sated with all the favorites Tante Josie had asked cook to prepare, the crawfish pie, the stewed okra—delicacies not even Paris had to offer—Gabriel pushed his chair away from the table. "No more, please," he groaned as Tante Josie offered him pecan pie.

They sat together on the front gallery and watched the tall stacks of the steamboats plying the river. So much traffic nowadays. When he'd been a boy, they might sit for hours without a boat passing by. He and Nicolette had used to run to the levee from Maman's house to see them trailing black sooty smoke, hoping the pilot would toot his horn for them.

Gabriel savored his cigar, responded to his cousins, and laughed when he should, yet all the while his mind and heart were in turmoil. Simone sat not six feet away, her slippered foot tapping the floor. Her pale yellow dress fit her bosom closely and the summer neckline revealed an expanse of dewy skin. The fingers she rested on her chair arm sometimes gripped the wood, sometimes drummed. Beautiful fingers, the nails rounded, white tipped, buffed. The last time he'd kissed those fingers, they'd smelled of jasmine.

Simone's unblinking eyes bored into him every time he looked her way. Soon he guarded his glances, but the heat of her gaze brought the blood to his face.

I've got to get away from here. Coward I may be, but I don't know what to say to her. His hand trembled as he ground his cigar butt in the crystal ashtray.

"I must be off," he said rising.

"You'll come to supper tomorrow night?" Tante Josie asked.

"I will. And I'll bring the baubles I've brought from Paris."

"Oh, I love baubles," Ariane breathed. She held her cheek up for Gabriel's kiss and followed Musette and her mother inside.

That left him alone with Simone. She stood close enough he could have reached out and grabbed her, but he willed his hands to hang uselessly at his sides.

"Well, until tomorrow," he said.

Simone crossed her arms. "Afraid to be alone with me for even a moment?"

Gabriel measured the angry tilt of her chin, the bitter note in her voice. "Yes," he said. But he did not leave her.

She leaned against the porch rail. "You've not brought a wife home with you."

"No." Gabriel felt pinned, as if he could not move until she took her eyes from his. "Nor have you married."

"My choice turned me down," she said. "Perhaps you remember."

"Simone." He could only whisper her name. "I had to go."

"No. You didn't. I would have gone away with you. We could have made a life in the North, in Canada, even France."

"You were—"

"Too young, yes, so you said."

Gabriel swallowed. Behind her resentment, he read the hurt still burning. If he could only hold her, kiss her, tell her he loved her. But that was why he'd gone away. He must not love her, and she must find a suitable husband, not a colored man who would never be accepted in her world.

"You can't forgive me?"

She dropped her arms and walked past him into the house.

Gabriel walked the short way to his mother's home. Tante Josie, Maman's half sister and onetime owner, had deeded her ten arpents on the edge of Toulouse, enough for Cleo to build a bungalow and keep a garden. This was where Cleo brought her family in the summertime when New Orleans all but closed down. Her paramour, Bertrand Chamard, his plantation on the other side of Toulouse, wore a path from Cherleu through the back fields of Toulouse to his heart's home with Cleo and their children. And so this was Gabriel's true home, where mother and father, Gabriel, and baby Nicolette were a family together, where they picked the sweet warm scuppernongs in the evenings, where Father put them to bed and Maman played her piano and sang softly as they fell asleep.

Gabriel stopped at the old oak with the branch hanging far out over a strip of river cut off from the main current by a wooded sandbar. A rope, now darkened and frayed, hung from the branch and swayed in the wind. One July morning, Gabriel had tied that rope to a stone and, a hero to his younger brothers, had tossed it impossibly high, up and over the branch. The three of them, Gabriel, Marcel, and Yves, spent the summer swinging out over the water, dropping, yelling and whooping and splashing. The world had been smaller then, and simpler.

As Gabriel approached the bungalow Cleo's caretaker, Old Ben, was in the front yard scything the grass, wielding the blade with enviable strength. Ben's aged wife Claire shook a hook rug over the gallery rail and saw Gabriel first. She cried out and hurried down the stairs to grab him and hug him. Another warm and wonderful homecoming for Gabriel. So many loved ones here, so many connections.

At twilight Gabriel propped his feet on the gallery rail and watched the summer sun leave the sky, the aroma of his Havana cigar discouraging the mosquitoes. When his father rode up on the latest of his fine black stallions, Gabriel hurried out to meet him.

Father and son embraced, trying to express three years of love and affection.

"*Mon Dieu,* it's good to see you," Chamard said.

"Come sit with me, Papa. I've brought a fine brandy home just for you."

The two put their feet up and listened to the crickets, drank their brandy, smoked their cigars. Chamard inquired about his neighbor Josephine and her children and received Gabriel's amazed report of girls grown into young ladies.

"And your maman?" Chamard said into the dark.

Gabriel knew from Nicolette's letters that their father had not let go of Cleo willingly. Papa was still in love with Maman, she wrote, but what could he do? Maman was her own woman, freed by Tante Josephine, made independent by her own talent and perseverance. And, Nicolette added, Pierre LaFitte would belong to Maman alone. They shared a life in music, and Cleo would never have to wait for Pierre to come to her from his other family.

"She's well," Gabriel said.

Chamard shifted in his chair, drank his brandy. "What did you think of LaFitte?"

I hardly know the man, Gabriel thought. *And what does Papa want to hear? That he beats her, that she's sorry she married him?* "He seems a good man," Gabriel said. "He'll take care of her."

Chamard nodded. "You must let me know if she ever needs anything."

Talk turned to the years they'd been apart, what Chamard had done with Cherleu, how his pony had run in the last race. And then they explored all the deeds and exploits, and even the studies, of Gabriel's years in Paris.

Late in the evening, Chamard put his brandy snifter down. "Son, you could have remained in Paris," he said. "It would be easier there for you. You could even pass for white, I think, if you wanted to. Yet you've come back."

"Father, I'd rather be here on this river than anywhere else on earth. I'm home to stay."

Chapter 5

While Marianne tended to Peter, his grandmama Lena sat on the floor, her hand on her grandson's foot, her head on his bed, asleep. Charles dozed on the porch in a rawhide chair tilted back against the wall.

When Peter had intermittent spells of peace, Marianne's tired mind wandered. Moonlight beamed between the boards of the walls, making silver bars on the floor. When a wet wind blew from the northwest, this house must be nearly as cold as being on the levee. At least it had a floor. Over at the Morgans', she understood, the slave cabins had packed dirt instead of board floors.

Six pegs in the wall for the slaves to hang their meager belongings on. One stool, a few cots. Not a scrap of paper, not a picture on the wall. No crystal vase filled with roses. No books on a polished table.

But of course the slaves couldn't read. She had heard some of them could learn to, but it was against the law to teach a slave to read. *Ridiculous law.* Maybe, if Petie survived, she'd try him with chalk and slate. No one would have to know.

Has Petie ever dreamed of being able to read? What might a slave do if he had leisure? They worked most of the daylight hours, more than that at harvest time. *But everyone has a dream.*

When Lena woke, Marianne lay down on the swept boards. Hard as the floor was, she fell asleep instantly. Late in the morning, when the sun beamed through the window and warmed her face, she sat up, stiff and sore.

Lena smiled at her, showing the three or four teeth she had left. "Petie better, miss. Feel fo yoself."

Marianne put her hand to Peter's forehead. Cool. Almost as cool as her own.

Peter watched her with big black eyes as she unwound a bandage. The gauze stuck to the wound and Peter flinched as she peeled it off. "I'm sorry. I'm trying to be gentle." Peter steadied himself and endured the rest without a murmur. *He's got grit,* Marianne thought.

She checked all the wounds. The festering had been drawn out. The discharge had ceased. Marianne rewrapped the wounds in clean bandages. "You were very brave, Peter."

Lena wiped the sweat from his brow. "My Petie not gone complain when you workin' on him like one o' God's angels, miss."

Marianne, light-headed with relief, laughed as she repacked her bag. "My mother used to call me an imp."

"Naw, miss. I knowed yo ma'am. Miss Violette, she tink you an angel could she see whut you done for Petie."

Annie, short spiky pigtails covering her head, peeked into the dim room.

"Whut you want, chile?" Lena said.

"Miss Marianne." A smile big and bright as a new moon lit her face as she found her mistress. "You brother and his friens be here. Dey drinkin whiskey while dey waits for dinner."

"Oh." Marianne looked down at her soiled apron. Her

shoes were filthy, too, and she hadn't done anything with her hair. "I'd forgotten they were coming."

"I comb out dem rats' nests for you, Miss Marianne," Annie offered.

Marianne laughed again. "That's very kind of you, Annie."

After a long hot ride to Magnolias Plantation, Yves followed Adam and Marcel from the stables to the house. The ride from the lake had been tedious and hot, and he looked forward to a glass of something wet.

The gentlemen stopped to clean their boots against the iron scraper at the edge of the back verandah. Yves made a thorough job of it, but, ever the observer, he noticed his host made only a halfhearted attempt to scrape his boots before he led his friends into the house.

Charles took their hats and riding gloves, then went to fetch the decanter of single malt whiskey for the gentlemen.

Adam took the chair nearest the open parlor doors and propped his feet on the splendid damask ottoman. Yves winced at the marks his friend's boots left on the fabric. Among the things one learns from one's mother, is to have a care for the furniture, he supposed, thinking of Adam's having lost his mother years ago.

Familiar guests in this house, Yves and Marcel settled into their equally luxurious chairs without ceremony. As Marcel spoke of a certain lady who had caught his eye at the lake, Yves admired the long oval room that stretched from the front of the house to the back.

Adam's late mother had created this room with an artist's eye, and it was a marvel of light and shadow. Above the wainscoting, the walls were paneled in pale green Chinese silk. The same cool green damask cov-

ered the heavily carved mahogany furniture, and the
matching drapes puddled at the floor in an excess of
fine fabric. The paintwork on the elaborate ceiling and
door carvings was brilliant lead white, the Flemish carpet
heavy wool, deep green with large rosy peonies woven in.
With its tall windows bringing in the light, the cool shadows faintly green, Yves thought it one of the finest rooms
on the river.

"Where is your charming sister?" Marcel asked.

Adam looked an inquiry at Charles, who was circulating once more with the decanter.

"Miss Marianne doctoring in the quarters, Mr. Adam."

Marcel examined the color of his whiskey through the
cut crystal glass. "I believe she was 'doctorin' last time we
were here."

"Might have been," Adam said.

"You disapprove?" Yves said to his brother.

"Not at all. I simply marvel that the young ladies we
meet at the balls in New Orleans, powdered and rouged,
in satin and lace, come home after Lent to work in the
quarters, getting their hands into God knows what. In-
congruous, that's all."

"I think Marianne is as fond of satin as the next girl,"
Adam said. He'd had enough to slur his speech a little,
Yves noticed. *Have to watch what I say.* He'd known Adam
to turn surly and mean with too much whiskey. *He's probably hungry,* Yves thought. *I certainly am.* Maybe dinner
would cut the whiskey.

As if reading Yves' mind, Charles announced, "Dinner
be soon. Quick as Miss Marianne get herself back from
de quarters. Oh, and Mr. Adam, Mr. McNaught say can
he see you? He waiting in de office."

Adam sighed. "Send him in. Let's see what the man
wants."

McNaught presented himself to the gentlemen, his

hat still in his hand. Yves, leaning against the mantel, thought him the picture of a brawny blond Scot. With his face close-shaved that morning, and his coat brushed and aired, he seemed a respectable man.

Adam remained slouched in his chair. "Mr. Mc-Naught. What can I do for you?"

McNaught glanced at Marcel and Yves and back to Adam. "It's about the hounds, Mr. Johnston. Miss Johnston says get rid of them."

"Does she?" Adam sat up. "And why is that?"

"Miss Johnston I guess is softhearted," McNaught remarked. He turned his hat in his hands. "She don't like it that the dogs messed up a runaway. But I need them hounds, Mr. Adam. If the nigras don't think the dogs'll be after them, we'll have a runner every week. And most of them dogs are my own."

Yves watched his fastidious brother pull out a handkerchief reserved for the task and remove a spot of dust from his boot. As for himself, he was intensely interested in the Johnstons' runaway and was curious how his friend would handle the overseer's complaint.

"I see," Adam said. "Most precipitate of her, I agree."

He's not going to back his sister? Yves wondered.

"So, what have you done with the dogs, Mr. Mc-Naught?" Adam asked.

"I got them bedded back behind the cane, two mile and more from here. Till you come back and tell her the place needs them dogs."

When he was growing up, Yves reflected, if his mother had told the overseer to do something, didn't matter what, paint all the cabins blue or sing the slaves to sleep at night, Papa would have backed her up. He might have had a word with her later, but they were a united front, always. Of course, Papa had kept Cleo all those years over his wife's protests, and Yves knew that was a grievous wound to his maman. But in the running of the plantation, Papa and Maman had been a team right up until her death.

Yves wondered if his rather diffident friend could resist siding with a strong-willed man's man like Mc-Naught.

"Well, Mr. McNaught, I—"

"For myself," Yves interrupted, "I'd find it enlightening to hear Miss Marianne's telling of the events over dinner. Wouldn't you, Marcel?"

"Hm? Yes. I'm sure she'll be all afire about something, as usual."

During the winter social season in New Orleans, the brothers often attended the same soirées and balls as Marianne. Marcel adopted the role of an indulgent older brother when they were together. He never failed to ask her to dance, and was ever courtly. Yves, less involved with his brother's relations, was nevertheless acquainted with Miss Johnston. At various functions, sometimes he would ask her to dance and sometimes not. She often seemed remote, he'd thought, even difficult, and he imagined she might be as bored as he. Nevertheless, Yves endeavored only to pass a pleasant evening at these affairs, not to labor in amusing a lady who seemed uninterested in the usual idle chitchat. Besides, manners were not Yves' strongest suit.

"Well," Adam decided, "I suppose it would be a courtesy to consult with my sister before I rescind her order, Mr. McNaught. Come around again tomorrow."

Yves saw the flicker of—triumph, contempt?—in the overseer's eyes. *The man has little respect for Adam, it would seem. But I notice he took the trouble to hide the dogs from Miss Johnston.*

"Yes, sir. I'll come by in the morning, then, 'fore I go to Blackwood Farm," McNaught said.

Marcel and Adam engaged in desultory conversation about their racing ponies. Yves wandered out the French doors, glass in hand, to admire the grounds. Ambling through the formal beds into Marianne's experimental garden, he found a path he presumed led to the quarters. *How do the Johnston slaves fare?* he wondered.

One of Yves' peculiarities, according to his brother, this looking into other people's slave quarters. Yes, he supposed it was peculiar. But he learned something about the families he knew along the lower Mississippi by the way their slaves made out, and since they'd had two runaways here at Magnolias, he was especially curious about the Johnstons' slave quarters.

Last season, he'd had an interest in Lindsay Morgan, a lovely girl with skin as smooth as cream, hair as yellow as buttercups, and who'd actually read a book or two. He'd accepted her father's invitation to tour the plantation, including the quarters. A hungrier, more sullen group of slaves he'd never seen. And Mr. Morgan had boasted of how he kept his people in line with short rations and swift punishments. Yves had avoided Lindsay Morgan and her family the rest of the winter.

He emerged from the shade of the pecan grove into the central alleyway of the Johnstons' quarters. Nearby a set of stocks stood for confining miscreants, but weeds grew thick around it. The whipping post, not so overgrown, stood like a silent sentinel beyond the stocks. He fingered the rope hanging from the crosspiece. It was unoiled and frayed, but the weeds around the post had been stomped down. Evidently it had seen use, at least in the last weeks.

The cabins were typical enough, most of them one room, a few doubles. They all had generous porches, a door and a window front and back for cross ventilation, and a brick chimney. Behind every house was a well-kept garden of okra, crookneck squash, onions, garlic, yams. Even a vine of honeysuckle here and there scenting the air with heavy sweetness. Not many people about this time of day—most of them were probably in the cane hoeing weeds.

The Johnstons seem to run a humane plantation, he mused. *Better than most. Yet a kindly treated slave is still a slave.* He stared at the flogging post and pondered why the runaways had not waited for him to take them to the next safe house. He had scheduled the run for this coming week.

The overseer was new to Magnolias. Likely they were frightened of what McNaught's reign promised. Some men believed they'd get more work out of slaves by threats and whippings than by simple human decency. Anyway, this Peter and his brother John Man had run without his help.

A shepherd, Yves was called, for his work as a clandestine guide on the Underground Railroad. And a stockholder, for his financial support. The people who lived at the stations did what they could, but they hadn't the resources to feed and clothe everyone who needed their help. And his brother Marcel wondered why Yves seldom bet on the horses anymore. He simply couldn't chance losing money he could send to the stations.

An old woman with eight or nine little ones trailing behind like so many chicks emerged from behind one of the cabins. She stopped short when she saw him.

"I hep yo find somebody, Master?" she said. The little ones piled up behind her and peeped at him from behind her skirts. They were all barefoot, and mostly naked from the belly down, but then it was summertime. Most of them had a finger or two in their mouths, and all of them were smooth skinned and bright eyed. None of the huge bellies he'd seen on children who don't get enough to eat.

He was about to answer, but then he heard Marianne Johnston's voice coming from a nearby cabin. At least he thought it was hers. "Oww," she'd said. And then, "Leave it, Annie. I'll just cover it up with a cap."

Yves forgot the old woman and the children when Marianne appeared in the doorway, her back to him. *Does she have no crinolines on at all?* The limp gathers of her skirt allowed him to discern the actual shape of her hips before she turned around.

"Annie, stay here," she told the little girl. "Lena's going to need a fresh bucket of water."

Marianne clattered down the steps, her eyes on the ground. He'd never seen a woman, a white woman, so disheveled. The impeccable Marianne Johnston looked like she'd slept in her clothes, and her blouse was pulled loose from her skirt. Dark circles under her eyes spoiled her complexion. A lock of hair near her ear seemed hopelessly tangled, but the rest of her red-brown hair fell about her shoulders, loose and swinging with her gait.

The real Marianne Johnston, completely unaware she was observed. Yves had never seen a more captivating woman.

"Mr. Chamard!" Marianne stopped. She put a hand to her open collar and flushed red. She looked at him as if she wished him at the bottom of a well.

"Miss Marianne." The sun shone on the chaste muslin of her summer blouse, shadowing her breasts, outlining her nipples. This was far more interesting than seeing her at some ball with every hair in place, her bosom bedecked with ribbons and ruffles.

Marianne fingered the snarl in her hair, then touched the button open at her neck. "What are you doing here? I mean, here in the quarters?"

"Just stretching my legs." He gazed in inquiry at the cabin she'd come from as if trying to see through the walls.

Marianne's lips tightened in a straight line across her lovely face. Anger darkened the blue of her eyes to nearly purple. *Fascinating*

"The dogs attacked a boy. He'll never be the same again. Ever."

The set of Marianne's jaw and the fire in her eye were altogether absent from the social scene in New Orleans. Certainly, the lovely Lindsay Morgan had never shown herself to be angry, or flushed, or anything but properly pleasant.

"A runaway?" he asked.

"Yes, but that's no excuse to tear a body up like this. That's no reason to——"

Yves held a hand up to stop her. "I can't argue with you," he said, intending to show her he agreed.

Somehow, rather than calming her, his words fanned the flame of her indignation. "No, oh no," she snapped. "You won't argue with a mere girl."

"I merely meant . . ."

She lifted her skirts, showing at least one lacy white petticoat, and strode away from him, her hair flouncing with that ridiculous tangle, her boots muddied.

He thought she was magnificent.

Marianne Johnston, he mused. Not the haughty, bored belle he'd seen last season, yawning behind her fan as some young swain tried to amuse her.

Yves leisurely followed his hostess back to the house. His stomach grumbled, but there was no need to hurry. The lady would require an hour or more to prepare herself for dinner.

In the parlor, Adam and Marcel had the chessboard out. Yves found the *Times Picayune* and tried to forget his empty stomach. Hardly thirty minutes passed, however, before Miss Marianne Johnston, late of Quarters Row, appeared.

Yves could hardly believe it was the same girl. She'd put her hair up, no tangle in view, and tilted a lace cap fetchingly to one side. Her face, though a bit pale, was scrubbed and lightly rouged. Her day gown, a blue muslin with embroidered white vines and leaves, carried the scent of fresh flowers. One might have supposed the young lady had spent the morning preparing for this moment.

Miss Johnston's dog scampered along beside the bell of her skirt. *What do women see in these ridiculous pets? Useless creature, not big enough to chase a rat.* Freddie stopped when Marianne stopped, but as his mistress divided her attention among the three men, Freddie sat on his haunches and stared at Yves. *And it reads minds too.*

The gentlemen stood to greet her. Adam kissed her cheek, Marcel her hand. With a bit of frost, Marianne held her hand out to Yves. The warmth of his own hand might have melted hers had she been disposed toward him. However, she was not.

Freddie had made up his mind, contrary to Marianne's evident feeling. He marched over to Yves and sat as close to his boots as he could get, then gazed up at the tall wonder he had chosen to adore.

Yves made no move to encourage the pest, much less to pet it, but Miss Johnston added this to his list of offenses, he supposed. She snapped her fingers and Freddie returned to hover around her skirt. Yves suppressed a sigh. *I have not pleased the lady, no, I have not.*

Marcel held his arm out to escort Miss Johnston into the dining room where they were served chicken, new potatoes, pole beans, tomatoes, crawfish, ham, and lemon tarts—enough food to feed a dozen. Yves spotted Marianne slipping morsels to Freddie from her plate.

Ordinarily, Yves found this a silly feminine habit, but Miss Marianne at least did so without baby-talking to the offending creature.

When they'd finished their *poulet fricassee*, Marianne rose to leave the men to their tobacco.

"Ah," Yves said, before she departed. He knew very well the matter of the dogs was none of his business, but he did want to hear how the dispute came out. Not that he cared a piaster about the dogs, but one of his vices being curiosity about the character of his friends, he was willing to risk offense by reminding Adam about the hounds.

With a match poised unlit in his hand, he said, "I wondered how Miss Johnston came to banish the hunting dogs." He watched her backbone stiffen and her lovely mouth tighten. This would be very interesting indeed.

"Oh yes," Adam said. "McNaught came to see me about the dogs." He lit his cigar and puffed until it drew. "They're prime hunting hounds, Marianne. Father and I plan to put them to use next season. Whatever possessed you to ban them from the place?"

"You wish to discuss this now?" Marianne raised her eyebrow to remind him they were in the presence of their guests. She glanced at Marcel, who courteously repocketed his smoke. She favored him with a smile.

Yves waited for her gaze to fall on him and kept his features neutral. When she did look at him, the smile was gone and her eyes flashed. *My poor mild friend must have a time of it with his little sister.*

"Very well." She turned back to Adam. "This man McNaught has trained his hounds to hunt slaves. He also allowed the dogs to tear a poor boy to shreds before he called them off. We don't want such dogs on Magnolias."

"I understand the boy was a runaway," Adam countered.

Steel in her voice, Marianne answered, "Whether he was a runaway or not, we do not allow a slave to be torn into as if he were just another raccoon or possum."

Yves admired the firm line of her jaw as she spoke and her perhaps instinctive advantages. She stood, Adam sat. She looked directly at her brother; Adam's eyes were on the snowy-white tablecloth. Adam didn't have a chance.

"You and Father can buy another pack of dogs," Marianne went on. "Ones that have not been taught to sink their teeth into human flesh."

Marcel cleared his throat. "Would be a pity if one of those hounds got hold of a child."

Marianne looked at Marcel, appreciation in her eye. *Ah, the women all love Marcel,* Yves thought.

"Most of them are McNaught's own hounds," Adam said.

"You can write him a draft for the cost of the dogs this afternoon. That's fair enough, I think." Marianne lifted her voluminous skirt to sidestep the chair behind her as if the matter were settled.

Yves noted Adam's glance at Marcel. Adam's pride needed some assuagement in front of his friends, of course.

"I'll think about it," Adam said. Marianne swept out of the room as serenely as if she had won his complete approval. No doubt she knew her brother better than anyone else.

The lady and gentlemen having retired from the table, Pearl collected the pickle dish, the preserves, and the salt cellar to put in the sideboard. Next she listened for Charles' footsteps. No one coming. She picked the plates clean of a half-eaten chicken breast, a biscuit, and a yam and stuffed her skirt pocket, the one she sewed in the middle so her apron would cover it.

Pearl herself ate well. The women working with the cook had all the food they wanted, some of it just the same as what they served in the big house. What Pearl stole was for Luke. His rations kept him going, but a man big as he was, tall and broad across the chest, doing the work of two men in the field all day, he needed more.

Maybe by tonight he be over his mad at me, she thought. *I give him a good dinner, and he be calm down. We talk it over.*

When Peter lay so sick like to die, Pearl had taken Luke late in the night to see what the dogs did to him. Miss Marianne slept, dead to this world, and Luke got down on his knees next to Petie and whispered to him, told him be strong, they try again.

So full of fear and fury, Pearl didn't see how she could hold it in till they got back to their own cabin. She closed the door and lit into Luke. "How you tell dat boy he run again? You eyes don' tell you nothin? You don't see what dem dogs do to him?"

"Pearl, keep you voice down." Luke tried to take her hands, but she yanked away from him.

"You not gone run, you tell me dat. You not gone put youself out so dem mens take you down wid a pack of hounds. What good it do you be free, you dead?"

Luke sat on the edge of the bed and ran a hand over his sun-scorched hair. "McNaught after me, Pearl. He say I look at him one more time, he have me at de post." He held his hand out for her, but she wouldn't take it. "Pearl, a man can't be beat but so much 'fore he turn into something else."

"Why can't you keep you eyes down, like you sposed to? He don' bother you, you mind yoself."

"You want a man, Pearl? Or a mule?"

She fell silent, but the set of her jaw betrayed her stubbornness.

"You got to have hope," he said. She wouldn't look at him. Exasperation tinged his voice. "Dey givin' away land, woman. Out West, Joseph say. I try to tell you dat. Why you don' listen?"

Her voice quavered. "Land don' do you no good, you end up like Petie."

"I'm not Petie." Luke spoke slowly, reasoning with her. "I'm a man grown, and I gone get away."

Pearl heard the determination, the absolute certainty in his voice and leaned her forehead against the wall. "You run, I never see you again."

In a quieter voice, Luke told her, "Joseph say dere a new station on de railroad now. No more dan thirty mile from here. I get dere, I make it to de next station. Good folks all de way to de free states, all de way to Canada."

"Canada be in de West? You don' know nothin but here. How you gone find Canada?"

"I find it, Pearl. I find it, and I send for you."

She let him take her in his arms now and hold her close. "We had a baby, you wouldn't run," she whispered against his chest.

"You think I want my chile be a slave?"

"Don' leave me here alone, Luke." She turned defeated eyes on him. "Give me a baby 'fore you go."

Luke kissed her eyes, her lips, her neck. He laid her on the corn shuck mattress and proved to her once again he loved her. She clung to him, shaking. *Please, God, don' let him leave me here alone.*

Chapter 6

The deep red roses seemed nearly black in the twilight as Marianne walked in the garden, her hands on her bronze taffeta skirt to ensure it didn't snag on the thorns. Freddie tagged along, sniffing at the warm fertile earth.

Soon Annie would fetch her to supper with Adam and the Chamard brothers. Such a contrasting pair. Were she and Adam as different as Yves and Marcel?

Of course, the Chamards had different mothers. Marcel, her true first cousin, had his father's dark good looks with soft brown eyes and sweet manners. His mouth, she blushed to recall, invited kissing. Not that she had ever kissed him. Of course not. The only kisses she'd experienced, so far, had been with Martin Milkstone and Albert Prud'homme. Martin's kiss had been most unpleasant; he'd mashed his teeth hard against her lips and then had apologized profusely. As indeed he should have. And poor Albert. After a very pleasant kiss, he'd fled. Not at all the man for her.

Indeed, she had decided there was no man for her. None of the young men in her circle really drew her to him. They were all rather silly. Shallow. Not a one of them ever asked her opinion of anything more weighty than the prospects for fine weather. Not a one ever offered to speak with her about what he'd been reading or thinking. Mother had yielded to Father on every point that Marianne had ever seen rise between them, but Marianne simply could not imagine a lifetime of ladylike submissiveness for herself.

She would not marry. Father would just have to get over it.

Yves Chamard, really, is no different from the others. Well known to be a pursuer of women in a rather superficial way, he certainly had never asked a belle to discuss, oh, Stephen Douglas' candidacy, for example. Dear Cousin Marcel, he at least was courtly and gentle and had the most beautiful eyes of anyone in her acquaintance, male or female. Yves, no blood relation to her at all really, had a sharp nose, piercing hazel eyes, and manners that came and went as the mood struck him. Marcel carried himself with ease, relaxed and at-home everywhere. Yves seemed always a coil of energy, alert and observant, ready to act.

"Miss Marianne!" Joseph appeared from a side path, shuffling as fast as he could, his breath ragged.

"Joseph?"

"Dere been a terrible thing. Some o' dem dogs loose. A littl'un got scared and run, and dey chase her. She hurt bad."

"Oh God." Marianne reached for Joseph's arm and they steadied each other. "I'll get my bag. Wait for me."

She ran into the house and up the stairs, Freddie at her heels. At the head of the staircase, she met Marcel going down for dinner. "Tell my brother I'm called away. Don't wait for me," she said.

Marianne burst into the bedroom where Hannah was hanging the blue muslin dress in the armoire. "Someone's hurt, Hannah. I need my bag."

Hannah stepped in her way while Marianne reached for her medical kit. "Wait, Miss Marianne. Stand still and I take that new dress off you."

"There isn't time. Hannah, no."

Before Marianne could get away from her, Hannah attacked the buttons at the back of the taffeta gown. "Yes'm. I knows you hurryin'. Just lift yo arms."

Marianne yielded in order to hurry things along as Hannah replaced the gown with one of Marianne's older muslin frocks.

"See how fast? Now you run on," Hannah said.

Marianne, the top buttons still open, collected her bag and hurried to the door. "Stay, Freddie," she said over her shoulder as Hannah reached for him.

Adam stopped her at the foot of the stairs. "You're not going to miss supper? We have guests."

"Those damned dogs have attacked a child, Adam."

Adam stepped back. She'd shocked him with her language, she knew, but he should be more shocked about what the dogs had done. She rushed across the polished cypress floor in her taffeta slippers and out into the night.

The child was no more than three years old. She lay on a coarse corn-husk mattress, her black eyes big and full of fear. She whimpered and clung to her mother. Marianne recognized Irene, who worked in the laundry.

Someone brought in extra candles. In the greater light, the blood all over the child and the bed shone darkly red. *The color of the roses in the twilight,* Marianne remembered, her mind fastening on the arbitrary while she steeled herself to deal with the wounds on this small body.

"I need Pearl," she told Joseph. "And tell Evette we'll want lots of hot water."

The child's mother shifted without letting go her little one's hand so that Marianne could kneel at the bedside.

"Hello, sweetheart," Marianne said. "What's your name?"

The child stared at her. "She be Sylvie," her mother said.

"Sylvie, you're such a brave little girl. I'm going to look at where the dogs bit you, all right?"

Sylvie pulled away from her, crying now. "I just need to see, honey. Be still."

Marianne took scissors from her bag and cut away the ragged, bloody shift Sylvie wore. The bites on her arms and legs looked like straightforward punctures, little of the tearing and gnawing as there was on Peter's body. One bite had gone clean through the flesh on Sylvie's thin arm, the four punctures lined up in perfect symmetry.

What worried Marianne was the deeper wound in her belly. How had the hound got a grip on her there? And how deep had the fangs gone into her body? This really was more than Marianne knew how to heal. A body cavity wound—who knew what complications might arise from that?

Pearl came in, straining with the weight of a bucket of hot water. "Evette said she send mo water soon as she can.".

Marianne left Pearl to finish the bathing while she went to her storeroom for the herbs to make poultices and tea. She would pack all the wounds, but on the tears and more open rips, she thought she'd hold off on the sutures. *The pus needs to flow first, I think. I wish I knew more.*

When she returned with the astringent witch hazel to bathe the child again, Marianne placed her hand over the wound in Sylvie's abdomen. Already it was swelling, the purple lividity spreading. Sylvie needed a doctor even more than Peter had.

Old Dr. Benet certainly would have come, but he was long dead. His replacement, Dr. Clark, had let it be known he had no time to treat slaves. Not anymore. His Hippocratic oath and his politics lodged in harmony in his breast. He was a staunch advocate of the state's right to choose its own path, and slavery was the heritage, and the future, of Louisiana. He had little sympathy for those who whined and fussed over the plight of their chattel.

Marcel Chamard appeared at her elbow and raised her up. "A moment, Miss Johnston."

He escorted her to the darkened porch where the mosquitoes buzzed.

"I understand you are quite an accomplished nurse," he began. "However, the child's wounds are quite grievous?"

"Yes." She waited. What did Marcel want here in the quarters? These Chamards and their wandering about. She was ready to return to Sylvie when he touched her arm.

"I know a doctor. Trained in Paris. He'll come if I send for him."

"You know a doctor who will treat a slave?"

"His mother was once a slave. Gabriel Chamard."

The love child of the famous affair between Bertrand Chamard and the celebrated chanteuse? "Your . . . ?"

"Yes. My half brother. He's at his mother's place near Toulouse. I'll fetch him myself."

Marianne put her hand on his sleeve. "Thank you, Mr. Chamard. Ask him to hurry."

Gabriel, asleep in his bed at Chateau Chanson, wakened to the sound of footsteps in the house. Not Ben's shuffle nor Claire's slippered feet. How long had it been since the pistol in his bedside table had been fired? It might at least serve as a deterrent—the intruder wouldn't know it was unloaded.

Gabriel stood in his bare feet, listening. The steps reached his bedroom door and the knob turned. He raised the pistol as the door opened and a tall figure stepped in.

"Gabriel?"

"Marcel!" He put the pistol back in the drawer. "You could get yourself shot sneaking into a man's room like this."

"I didn't want to waken the old folks. You're needed across the river, Gabe. At the Johnston plantation."

Gabriel dressed as Marcel explained what had happened. In five minutes, the two were ready to leave.

"I left the boat at the Toulouse dock."

"Fine." Gabriel picked up his bag.

At Toulouse the house was dark. Gabriel sought the window of Simone's room. What were they going to do, the two of them? Tied to each other, and yet . . .

"Over here," Marcel said.

Only a sliver of moon lit the river and the churning current. Four men, black as the night, waited in the boat to row them across. Gabriel stepped in, dreading the rocking under his feet. Traveling by river was bearable on one of the big steamers where he could stand on an upper deck and contemplate the water from a distance, but he'd always hated the little boats, the ones where the lap of the water came up to the very oarlocks. He knew it was irrational. He swam happily enough, but that was only in the sleepy bayous or along the river sheltered by a sandbank. Crossing the shifting currents in a boat this small, in the dark—he broke out in a cold sweat.

He tried to think of other things. Not Simone. He'd be in no state to help anyone if he let his heart loose now. His future. That was a conundrum to occupy his mind. If he wanted to make money, he needed to minister to the wealthy clients in New Orleans in the winter and on their plantations in the summertime. Would the white planters accept him? He was nearly white, but he made no attempt to pass. He wished to be accepted for what he was, an octoroon, a free man of Louisiana, a doctor.

Gabriel cursed the fog hanging over the river, though a better sight of the black water would do nothing for his nerves. The air hung heavy with the scents of wood smoke, fecund bayous, rot, and rampant growth.

The four slaves pulled across the current at a slant. Marcel's face caught hardly enough moonlight to show his features, and he too sat in silence.

It might be, Gabriel continued his line of thought, that he would have a lucrative practice tending to the ailments of the other free coloreds only. It was a growing population, and some of them were quite well off. Furthermore, in the political climate of the times, if he came to be known as a slave healer, it would no doubt affect his reputation, and his empty purse. Yet here he risked crossing the treacherous currents of the Mississippi River in the dark to treat a slave.

But of course there was no question he would treat slaves. A child, Marcel had said. How did Adam Johnston justify keeping dogs like that, ones that would attack a small child?

A drifting log caught the boat broadside. Gabriel gasped and grabbed hold of the gunwale, wishing it were daylight so they could at least see where they were going. Finally the perfume of magnolias wafted across the water and the light on the Johnston dock beckoned them.

Ashore, Gabriel and Marcel followed the lantern past the big house and through the pecan orchard. As they approached the quarters, Gabriel's spirits sank. Any slave quarters, no matter how "good," overwhelmed him with the poverty of hope and opportunity. He felt sympathy for the slaves, yes—and always, that nagging guilt, and fear: *It might have been me living here.*

Marcel led the way into the cabin, he and Gabriel both ducking their heads to enter. Marianne Johnston sat dozing. Everyone else in the cabin slept, too, even the child. Marcel touched Marianne's shoulder and she roused with a start.

"I've returned," Marcel said in a low voice. "The doctor is with me."

Gabriel made his bow absently as Marianne greeted him. His eyes were already on the little girl.

He turned to the man with the lantern, who was about to leave them, and said, "I'll need that light."

"It's the wound in her abdomen that most concerns me, Dr. Chamard," Miss Johnston said.

Gabriel lifted the loose bandage and held the lantern close. Sylvie did not stir, though her mother stared at the doctor with hope in her eyes.

He placed his palm over the wound with a gentle hand. Then he palpated the surrounding area, probing, his fingers sensing what his eyes could not. Many, perhaps most, of his colleagues did not indulge in the laying on of hands to make their diagnoses. Gabriel, however, had been trained by the most progressive doctors in Europe; there was much to be learned through touch. Next he felt the other bites, comparing the heat in them with the heat of the punctures just to the side of her navel. Sylvie whimpered in her sleep.

"What have you given her?" he asked.

Marianne detailed all she had done, and he nodded. This time he really looked at the mistress of Magnolias Plantation. "You've done well."

"How bad is it?" she said, indicating the wound that might have reached into Sylvie's inner body.

"She's so small, my guess is the teeth penetrated the peritoneum. We'll know more in a few hours."

He looked for Marcel outside the circle of lantern light. "Miss Marianne should go to bed," Gabriel told his brother.

Marianne looked at Sylvie's mother. "I can't leave," she said.

Gabriel smiled at her, at the circles under her eyes. "You will allow me to sit with the child now. In the morning, I will need you fresh if we should have to open the wound." He turned to Sylvie's mother and placed a hand on her arm. "You won't be distressed to let your mistress go to bed for a few hours?"

Irene, her faded, threadbare dress hanging on her thin frame, hung her head. "No, sir," she said. Then she cast a shy glance on her mistress. "I be glad Miss Marianne get some rest."

Marcel stepped to Marianne's side and offered his arm. She hesitated, looking at Pearl.

"I be here, Miss Marianne, he need anything," Pearl reassured her. Marianne took Marcel's arm and let him lead her to the house.

By dawn, the draught Marianne had given Sylvie no longer soothed her. She groaned and thrashed and called out in pain. Her abdomen swelled, hard and hot, and Gabriel feared the worst. If the dog's fangs had pierced the peritoneum, that was very bad and likely fatal. If they had torn into the intestine, there would be only hours before she succumbed.

"I bathe her again, Doctor?" Pearl asked.

He nodded. Once the child was cooled, Gabriel fed Sylvie a draught of laudanum. When Miss Johnston returned, he would consider opening the punctures to drain them. Better Sylvie be unconscious.

The sun hardly up, the mistress of Magnolias appeared at the cabin door. She'd pinned her hair back neatly but plainly. She wore a brown homespun dress and a canvas apron. Her face was pale, but she was alert. And calm. Gabriel valued her equanimity most of all.

Gabriel read her face as her eyes sought Sylvie. She was truly frightened for the child. He made room for Marianne to kneel next to the bed. She felt Sylvie's forehead, judging the dry fever. Irene's eyes sought her mistress's, craving reassurance. She had sat on the floor at Sylvie's head all these hours, never ceasing to touch her, caressing her cheek, stroking her hair.

To Gabriel's surprise, Marianne reached out to Irene, and they clasped hands.

Most of the mistresses Gabriel knew up and down the river nursed the slaves on the plantation. Some of them did it willingly, some not. Some of them were competent, some not. But Gabriel had never known one, in the years he'd studied under Dr. Benet before he went to France, who involved herself to the degree that Marianne Johnston did.

"Pearl, go on to bed," she said. "Sleep awhile before you go to the cookhouse."

To Gabriel, she said, "What will you do now?"

"I've given her a draught. When she's fully under, I'll drain what purulence I can from her belly." He palmed Sylvie's tight swollen abdomen again. Very hot.

"I believe," he said to Marianne, "you have another patient? While we wait for the laudanum to take effect, I could look at him. The same dogs?"

Marianne nodded. "The same pack, anyway." She turned to the older man standing in the corner. Sylvie's grandfather, Gabriel assumed. "What has been done with the dogs who attacked Sylvie?" Marianne asked.

"Dey chained up at de whipping post last I knowed, miss. Lessen Mr. McNaught do something 'wid em.'"

Gabriel saw her jaw tighten, anger clearly stamped on her features. *This McNaught*, Gabriel thought—*He's in for a hard time. I'd not want this woman angry with me.*

Gabriel followed Marianne outdoors. They passed by the whipping post where two hound dogs slept in the morning sun. They were each chained around the neck. They didn't seem very dangerous at the moment, but Gabriel knew they were never to be trusted again after what they'd done to little Sylvie. Adam would surely have them destroyed.

Marianne stopped just out of the dogs' reach and simply stared at them. Gabriel saw her shoulders tremble. *Is it fear or fury she's feeling?* He offered his arm to support her, but she shook her head. "I'm quite all right, Dr. Chamard. Thank you." *No, I don't imagine this young woman is afraid of much.*

They found Peter awake and propped up in his cot. His grandmother Lena still sat by his bed. Gabriel introduced himself and then asked to examine Peter's wounds. Thoroughly and gently, he unwound the bandages and tested for morbidity. He palpated and sniffed, noting the color and firmness of the flesh around each wound.

"You've an excellent constitution, young man," he said to Peter. "And you've been most fortunate in your nurse."

Peter glanced at his mistress, shy in her presence. "Yessir. I be lucky."

"Miss Marianne a angel," Lena added.

Marianne smiled, and Gabriel winked at the old

woman. "You may be right, Mammy," he said. "She may be an angel on earth."

He turned back to Marianne. "Do you have slippery elm?" She shook her head no. "Well, then, continue with the witch hazel solution and the comfrey poultices. Watch the wounds do not become blackened around the edges. You must send for me at once if that happens. Otherwise, you have done all that needs to be done. He's very fortunate to have come through the fever with no more corruption than you've described."

"Praise the Lawd," Lena interjected.

"I'll look in again before I leave," Gabriel promised. He followed Marianne out and walked alongside her on the way to Sylvie's cabin.

"You're to be congratulated, Miss Johnston. Those were ferocious bites that young man sustained."

"He's going to live, isn't he?"

Gabriel nodded. "I believe he will recover very well, except for walking. That tearing of the left Achilles tendon will never heal properly. Add to that the toe missing on his right foot, his gait will be awkward in the extreme." They walked a few steps. "His hands will be badly scarred, but he should have adequate use of them."

"I'll have to find a task he can do," Marianne thought aloud.

Gabriel glanced at her. Many plantations sold off anyone who didn't carry his weight. "Yes, he needs to be useful."

They came again to where the dogs were chained. One of them stood, then growled and bared its teeth at them. The other dog joined in, both of them snarling and straining against their chains.

"They were not to have been on the place," Marianne said, her voice husky, broken. "I'd already told the overseer. And now . . ."

"Yes."

They moved on toward the cabin where Sylvie lay, and then Gabriel stopped. "Miss Johnston, what I propose to do with Sylvie will be most unpleasant. You need not assist if you prefer not to."

"I will do whatever you require."

He studied her a moment. No evidence of hysterical heroics, no hesitation. Here was a woman to be reckoned with. She might have made a doctor, had she been born male.

Sylvie was deeply asleep from the draught of laudanum. Gabriel asked everyone but the mother to leave the cabin. To her, he gave the task of holding Sylvie still should she rouse or twist in her sleep.

He began by bathing the child's abdomen with witch hazel. From his bag he retrieved the scalpel he kept sharper than any razor he'd ever used for shaving. The sun coming in through the window glinted on it, and Gabriel noticed Irene's eyes fix on the blade.

"Perhaps you had better look only at Sylvie's face," he advised her. "Or out the window."

He checked that Marianne had at hand the absorbent cloths and the witch hazel to cleanse the wound once he'd drained it. "Ready?" She nodded, and he began.

The punctures had nearly closed of themselves with so much pressure around and under them. Gabriel chose the point nearest Sylvie's navel and gently touched the scalpel to the skin. A thin line of red appeared, and he pressed just slightly harder. The blade reached through the layers of the epidermis, through the muscle, and—pus welled up around the knife, nearly foaming to escape the cavity too small for its mass.

He let it flow, mopping the purulence as fast as it emerged. The matter decreased to an ooze and Gabriel gently pressed the abdomen to expel more.

Not a pretty sight, this. Sylvie's mother, Irene, had taken his advice at the first cut and kept her gaze out the window. Miss Johnston, he noted with admiration, though her hands were as gory as his, held up well.

He removed a hollow glass rod from his medical kit. Perhaps ten inches long, it was in effect a straw. He wiped it with a fresh cloth, then inserted one end of it into the wound. Gently, a finger at the ready to put over the hole, Gabriel sucked at the pus remaining inside Sylvie.

As Gabriel lifted the rod and emptied its contents into yet another rag, he glanced at Marianne's face, noted the tinge of green around her mouth. "It isn't necessary for you to observe this procedure closely, Miss Johnston. Perhaps you'd like to cleanse your hands. We'll soon be ready to wash the area and close the wound."

"I'll be fine," she murmured.

Gabriel finished his machinations, and Marianne once more assisted him. They closed the wound and dressed it.

"Irene?" Marianne said. Sylvie's mother's body was rigid and she had not once taken her eyes from the window. "It's all over."

With a huge exhalation, Irene bent over Sylvie, and Gabriel touched her shoulder.

"There won't be so much pain now," he told her.

"She gone be well, Doctor?" Irene said through her tears. "You make her so she be well?"

Gabriel looked at Marianne. Surely she understood. The child's body was corrupted; she'd seen it for herself.

"She'll sleep until late this afternoon, I think," Gabriel told the mother.

"I'll send Pearl to sit with you, Irene. The doctor and I will return in a while. Dr. Chamard, please. Let me show you where you may wash."

Gabriel accompanied Marianne to the house where she turned him over to Charles with instructions to take very good care of the doctor.

In her room, Marianne moved as if she were half asleep. She untied her apron and rolled it into a ball to keep it from soiling anything else.

"No, Freddie," she told her pup when he began to sniff it. She lifted him to her lap and let him lick her face until at last she smiled a little. She stroked his silky hair and caressed him. He was the only comfort she knew when she was lonely. Or frightened. And she was very frightened. How could Sylvie live with such a wound inside her body?

Hannah bustled in and bullied Marianne into undressing. She made her a bath, adding a palmful of rose petals to scent the water. Once Marianne had sunk into the tub, Hannah scrubbed her until she was rosy, yet still Marianne did not relax. Instead, she lost the lethargy of fatigue and horror with which she'd entered the room, and as her energy returned, she burned to *do* something.

Dr. Chamard had done all there was to be done for Sylvie and Peter at present. What remained was to ensure nothing like this ever happened again.

Hannah held up two frocks. "You going back down dere?" she asked. Marianne nodded. "Den you wear dis one," she decided.

Marianne truly didn't care. She hurried Hannah with the buttons, brushed her own hair, and put it up out of her way without fuss. Downstairs, she inquired whether Dr. Chamard was ready for breakfast.

"He's on the verandah, Miss Marianne," Charles informed her. "I give him a glass of lemonade to start him off."

"And Mr. Adam? And our other guests?"

"They's all out to the pond with they fishing poles. Been gone since sunrise."

Not a one of them had bothered to stop in the quarters to see how the child did. Her anger, that shapeless force pressing on her heart, grew to encompass her brother and Yves. *But not Marcel*, she thought. *He'd volunteered to fetch the doctor, and that had cost him a night's sleep.*

"Mr. Chamard," Charles said, "he ask 'bout de little girl dis morning 'fore he went off."

Yes. Marcel, she assumed, *at least Marcel cares.*

"The doctor and I will have breakfast on the terrace, please. And send word I'd like to see Mr. McNaught in an hour."

"Remember, he gone for yesterday and today," Charles said. "He over to the other farm checking the cane."

And left the slaves to catch his brutes and chain them. Where is McNaught keeping those dogs? She marched toward the terrace. *He certainly has not dispersed them as I ordered. No wonder the man doesn't listen to me when Adam plays right into this Men Know Best foolishness.*

She greeted Dr. Chamard with as much of the gracious hostess demeanor as she could muster. They breakfasted on melon, fresh trout, corn grits, and plenty of dark coffee. And discovered in each other a kindred spirit. Marianne asked him every question she'd had for months, even years, from the medical books she'd read, the doctoring she'd done. No topic was too indelicate for the two of them to discuss over fresh beignets and strawberry preserves.

They talked again of the possibilities for Peter's working life, what he could do and what he could not with his maimed extremities. Marianne traced a design in the tablecloth. She surely could trust this man. His own mother had been a slave, and the story was that Cleo

Tassin had been educated right alongside her mistress, Miss Josephine.

"I was thinking I might teach Peter to read."

Gabriel Chamard raised an eyebrow. "You would teach a slave to read?"

"You think it wrong? Too difficult?"

"Neither," he said. "Your neighbors would not approve, however."

She smiled at him. "I do not intend to inform them."

With breakfast and coffee in her, hope returned. Surely the doctor's ministrations would save Sylvie. As they walked back to the quarters, Marianne held up a sugary beignet she'd brought from their table. "Maybe I can coax a smile from her with this."

They were in the shade of the pecan grove when the sound of keening, high and long and desolate, filled the air. Marianne seized the doctor's sleeve. The hair on the back of her neck stood up, and she felt her blood turn cold.

Marianne lifted her skirts and ran pell-mell through the trees, down the path, and into the crowd gathered at the cabin door. Inside, Irene lay across the bed, her arms draped over Sylvie's lifeless little body. Sobs had overtaken her and drained her, but in a moment, she rose and again wailed her grief to the rafters.

Marianne stared at Sylvie. She'd never get used to seeing death, never. The body so obviously an empty vessel, the vital spark gone, and yet the features the same.

Marianne began to tremble, then to shake. Vaguely she knew the doctor took her arm, drew her out of the stifling cabin.

Once outside, Marianne shook him off and began to run. Through the pecan trees, over the lawn, and across the verandah. Her intention was a mere picture in her mind, words unnecessary for an aim so elemental. In Father's study, she fumbled with the ever-present keys from her pocket. Once she had the gun case open, she grabbed Father's shotgun, broke it and loaded two shells, then snapped it shut.

Charles appeared in the study door. "Miss Marianne, what you doing? Here, let me take dat from you."

She brushed past him without explaining. She wasn't yielding the shotgun to anyone. She marched back to the quarters, unaware of the tears that flowed over her face and of the looks of alarm from the people gathered in the alleyway.

At the thrashing post, the murderous dogs, made mad by the sounds of grief, pulled at their chains, snapping and snarling.

Trembling, her face flushed, her eyes the color of steel, Marianne stopped ten feet away, raised the heavy shotgun, and aimed. She pulled both triggers at once.

The impact knocked her backward onto the ground. The roar seemed to come from everywhere, its echo going on and on.

Gabriel knelt beside her. The doctor didn't immediately try to raise her, but let her breathe, let her realize it was done. When she was ready, she let him help her stand. The shaking was gone. She was steady and calm again. She didn't look at the dogs.

Father's shotgun lay in the dirt. I'll have to clean it now. She bent over to pick it up. Father didn't tolerate careless treatment of his firearms. She wondered if she remembered how to break it down and put it back together.

Strange, the silence. Maybe her hearing was gone from the roar of the blast. The people watched her. With McNaught away, they had come in from the fields, those who were close in, when they heard the death wails.

Gabriel Chamard handed her over to Charles, who'd

followed her from the house. "Come on, honey. I take you home."

Marianne let him take her arm and lead her away. She cradled the shotgun. Is this how Father told me to carry a gun? She couldn't remember. It didn't matter. It was empty now. Like Sylvie's body.

Chapter 7

Yves Chamard didn't like fishing. Too damned idle, sitting with a line in the water, waiting for some action. And they'd been out here since just after dawn. He'd seen a gator in the bayou a while back, but he didn't have his gun with him.

He glanced at his brother. Marcel had the gift of stillness. What did he think about during the hours he was content simply to sit and muse? Probably writing a poem. Yves could guess what Adam thought about. He hadn't spoken of Nicolette since they left the lake, but he'd obviously fallen hard for her. *My little sister, knocking them down like flies.* But Adam Johnston was not the man for her, Yves thought. *My brother's cousin, my friend, but not the man for her.* But would she know that?

A fish tugged at his line and then leapt from the water. "About damn time," he muttered. He worked the pole, let the fish fight as long as it would, and then pulled in a fine bass. "Two pounds, what do you think?"

"If you say so," Adam teased. He put the catch in the keel with the others. "What say we fry some fish before we head back?"

Marcel grinned. "Who's going to clean them?"

Yves hated cleaning fish. But it was his turn. "Anybody bring meal? A pan?"

"Yep."

"Oil?"

"Yes, that too. Get to it," Adam said, "and I'll build a fire."

The gentlemen saw to themselves this morning. Free from the constraints the presence of women required, they'd left their frock coats at home and were comfortable in collarless cotton shirts with the sleeves rolled up. Yves gutted and scaled their half a dozen catch, his the biggest, he noted with satisfaction. He smiled at himself. *Still trying to outdo my big brother.*

Adam gathered the wood and built a fire. Marcel, by consensus, was the best cook, so he dredged the fish and slipped them into the hot oil.

Breakfast over, the sun was up high enough to punish them with the heat, and they gathered their gear to head back. But Yves had another motive for having come out this morning. He wanted to know where McNaught had moved the pack of hounds.

Marcel had told him all about the little girl and about going after Gabe. Clearly, the overseer had not taken care of the dogs.

They mounted their horses. "I don't believe I've ever ridden to the far reach of Magnolias," Yves said to Adam. "What kind of property do you have on your eastern border?"

"It's good back there. Higher than the land west of the river. We should ride back there some time."

"How 'bout now?"

Adam and Marcel looked at each other. Yves knew they'd no interest in prolonging the expedition in the coming heat. "Unless you're too tired?"

A very mild challenge, but of course they couldn't

admit to being tired from a morning's fishing, not even Marcel, who'd spent the night crossing and recrossing the river fetching Gabriel. It was simply part of the rich young man's code to be ready for any and all amusements. "All right, then," Adam said.

They followed a pair of wagon ruts through woods and past fields until they stopped on a high knoll. "Wonderful country." Yves hadn't spotted a likely place for McNaught to have hidden the pack. "Let's go back this way," he said and gestured to a more southerly path back toward the river.

As they rode through a shady copse, warning barks fifty yards away told the location of McNaught's dogs. Yves, leading the trio, looked back at Adam, who merely shrugged.

At their return to the mansion, they found the house quiet. They cleaned themselves up and met in the parlor, ready for noon dinner, but it seemed a long while before Charles called them to the dining room. Miss Johnston did not join them.

Adam gestured to Charles, who leaned over to hear the young master. "Is my sister ill?" he asked.

"In a manner of saying, yessir," Charles said, bending near Adam's ear. "The child died this morning. Miss Marianne took it awful bad."

Yves watched his host receive the news. A line appeared between his eyes, but was Adam vexed that Marianne did not appear to play hostess or that the poor child had died from her injuries?

"How old was she?" Adam asked.

"She 'bout three," Charles said.

Adam nodded, his eyes downcast. After a moment he opened the napkin over his lap. Yves thought, *He does care. But not enough.*

Charles ladled a cold soup into Adam's bowl and

leaned over again to his master's ear. "She kill dem dogs, she did. Wid Master's shotgun."

Adam looked up sharply. "The devil she did."

Charles' face closed down. "Yessir."

Yves ended the charade that he could not hear the exchange. "Bad news, Adam?"

"Domestic matters. Please, help yourself to the wine."

Just as Charles had hidden himself behind a blank face, Adam too allowed the mask every slave owner wore to slip into place. The death of a child, a slave child, was simply a "domestic matter." What ownership did to the owners—Yves felt it in his soul. The twisting of reason, of compassion and morality—deforming the minds and hearts of the people who lived by the labor of their fellow man. Soul killing to be a slave; soul killing to be the master. Though the master's soul rotted in comfort and self-satisfaction.

The gentlemen amused themselves throughout the afternoon. Adam had accounts to look at; Marcel sought the quiet of his bedroom, no doubt to write down a poem he'd been composing. Yves gathered the *Times Picayune* and the *Bee,* both from New Orleans, and the most recent *Natchez Courier.* He even found an old paper from Richmond in the library. He sat down to digest the conflicting accounts of the Republican nominee, Mr. Lincoln.

The election was not six months away, and the country was in turmoil. The issue of slavery and the states' right to practice it had even split the Democratic Party. Mr. Lincoln remained strangely silent on the issue of slavery.

Yves wished he had a *New York Tribune.* His own clandestinely written essays often appeared in the *Tribune* and other Northern papers. The Southern publications he had regular access to made little effort to print a balanced picture of what was happening in the North, nor even in Washington. Just how seriously did the Northern pols take the persistent rumors and threats of Southern secession? And how committed were the Southern movers and shakers to the sovereignty of the state?

He heard steps in the grand hall. Lowered voices, but Yves had no compunction about listening in. Why on earth not? Curiosity was no more than a healthy interest in one's fellow man, as long as one didn't engage in sly talk. And Yves never gossiped.

"Where you want I should put the doctor?" Charles said.

A pause. Adam's voice. "Hm. He's octaroon. Nearly white." Another pause while Adam wrestled with the finer points of the culture's racial policies. "What does Miss Marianne think?"

"I tell her the room under the back stairs be ready for the traveling men dat come by. He could stay there."

"And what did she say to that?"

"She say put him in you father's, Master Johnston's, room." Charles didn't make any attempt to hide his disapproval.

"Yes, well. Perhaps that is going a bit far. No more guest rooms, are there? No. I'll speak to Yves. He'll share a billet with his brother."

"Yessir," Charles said.

Adam walked into the library. "Ah, there you are," he said, spotting Yves behind a held-up paper, apparently engrossed in the news.

"Your brother is staying the night," Adam said. "Perhaps he could share your room?"

"Certainly," Yves said. "We've shared a bed before now." He stood up. "I believe I'll stretch my legs."

Adam glanced at the gilt ormolu clock on the mantel. "Then I'll finish my correspondence. See you at supper."

Yves crossed the wide verandah and walked into the garden. Marcel might be the poet, but Yves appreciated the beauty of a rose as well as the next man. Besides, he'd like to talk to the gardener again. Joseph, his name was, his underground contact here on Magnolias. Yves walked with his hands behind his back, his mind on the politics raging through the land. He feared there would be war before it was over.

He came to a nook off the path and would have passed right by it had he not spotted a slippered foot peeking from a tent of skirts. He paused, and Freddie gave a sharp yelp of greeting.

"Miss Johnston," he said. "I believe you are hiding."

Freddie squirmed and wiggled in her arms, thrilled to see him. Marianne, however, did not greet him with a coquette's assurances and wiles. She really had been hiding from him. "Would you like me to pass on?" he offered.

She stepped out from the camellias and sat heavily on the bench behind her. She was dressed for the evening in a blue silk gown that managed to do justice to her bosom, Yves noted, at the same time it covered the deep bruise he knew must be on her shoulder from the shotgun's kick. She moved her skirts aside. "Excuse my appalling manners," she said. "Please, sit down."

Not a sincere invitation, but enough for Yves. He had hoped he might come across this newly discovered, intriguing person. Marianne Johnston had twice the allure now that he'd seen her in a role besides that of belle of the ball. Here was a woman of spirit, of muscle and tissue and fire.

Her hoops afforded him a seat near enough to breathe in the expensive scent she wore. The blue silk brushed his leg. He'd have preferred the feel of her thigh next to his, but quite enough stimulation, Yves thought, considering the circumstances.

Marianne set Freddie down, and he promptly came to attention at Yves' feet, panting and staring in adoration. One conquest, at least, he thought.

He touched his pocket.

"Yes, you may smoke."

"Among your many attributes I now must count prescience?"

"If only that were so."

Yves examined her profile as he lit his cigar. "You'd have prevented what happened to this child."

"Yes."

Yves was no fan of small talk and clearly Marianne was in no mood to banter. He merely kept her company. If she wanted to talk, she would.

His cigar was half smoked when Marianne broke the silence. "You visit other plantations. Who else keeps dogs that track down slaves and attack them?"

He tapped the ash off. "There are some. You probably know most of them."

"Father would not have approved, had he understood. But most of the dogs came with this man McNaught, and Father thought he was getting the value of a trained pack of hunting dogs along with the overseer. He couldn't have known they were for slave hunting. He didn't know."

Yves hoped she had herself convinced. It was a sad thing to find one's father was no more noble than other men.

The heat, even at this hour, brought a fine sheen to Marianne's complexion. Moisture beaded her upper lip, outlining its curve. He liked a full mouth, especially a salty one, and Miss Johnston's looked luscious.

Her face was a bit tanned, rather careless for a lady of marriageable age, Yves thought, but he wasn't like the dandies he consorted with during the season in town. They expected flawless white skin, a perpetual shy smile on a reddened mouth, a submissive and attentive demeanor. How boring the belles were. He'd seen Marianne Johnston play that role, though without much enthusiasm. Clearly it was not her true character.

So tempting to gently wipe her lip, to trace its shape with his thumb. But she would no doubt never forgive him. It wasn't lovemaking she needed. At least, not today.

"Do you follow the news, Miss Johnston?"

She nodded, her eyes on Freddie as he explored around their feet.

"This may all change in the next few years." He gestured with his smoke to indicate the plantation. "How would you feel about that?"

"To the end of slavery?" She surprised him with her directness, and again with her answer. "It is an evil. It cannot go on."

"Few slaveholders would agree with you." They were on dangerous ground now. She had no idea of his opinions; another man might spread the word of her radical declaration, might blacken the Johnston name up and down the river. She really must not speak so freely.

He took her hand to caution her, neither of them protected from skin-to-skin contact by the requisite gloves. Marianne started at his unwarranted familiarity and, did he deceive himself, with something else? And she looked at him, so strangely. With . . . could she be aroused merely by his touch? He'd be delirious to find a woman so responsive.

Marianne had been mired in her own thoughts, of Sylvie, of Peter, of Father. The grief and the rage of this day had left her feeling bruised, convalescent, and vulnerable. As if all her nerves were raw, her defenses depleted. She had not been prepared to be touched. She had not been prepared for that touch to rush through her body, warming her, disturbing her.

She looked at Yves, expecting him to laugh off her start. Make some pleasantry. But he didn't. He met her gaze, and what she saw in his hazel eyes brought the blood to her face. Suddenly she was aware they were alone, far from the house, and secluded in the garden. She touched the bare hollow at the base of her throat, and Yves' eyes followed her gesture, reminding her of her low-cut gown and the expanse of bosom it revealed.

Marianne riled at his frank gaze. *He is no gentleman, that is clear.* She grabbed her skirt away from his long thighs and rose to her feet. Her mouth pulled tight, she strode from the bench into the path.

"Miss Johnston." Yves caught up to her in two strides. "Please pardon me. I merely wanted to impress upon you that you should be more circumspect in delivering your opinions. I had no intention of offending you."

Even now, she felt where his fingers had grasped hers. *Outrageous behavior. It's probably true, what Lindsay Morgan boasted about—his stealing hot swooning kisses and they not even betrothed.* The injustice of that thought, in light of her own few stolen, and disappointing, kisses, did not trouble her.

Freddie, his tail waving like a flag, scampered at Yves' heels. Marianne stopped, and Yves nearly barreled into her. She brushed his arm aside and reached for Freddie.

The puppy-faced spaniel reclaimed, she faced Yves Chamard. "As I recall," she said, "you asked for my opinion. I was not aware compliance with your own was required." Marianne pivoted on her toe and strode away from him.

Yves wisely did not attempt to catch her. He followed her at his leisure, content with admiring the tapering V from her shoulders to her narrow waist. No amount of corseting could achieve a waist that small or allow a walk that furious. *Adam's little sister.* He shook his head. Not just a Southern belle bred to be sweetly subservient to the men in her life, not this young woman.

The next morning, Gabriel endured another crossing of the Mississippi in a small boat. The men rowed upstream along the eastern bank to half a mile north of the Toulouse dock. Then they began to cut across and down to their destination. At least the day was sunny and the current propelled no errant logs against the boat.

On the whole, Gabriel reflected, the population of the Magnolias quarters was healthy enough. Far better nourished and no harder worked than most slaves. Good management evidenced by the cleanliness of the place. The privies no more odorous than they had to be, no debris littering the ground around the cabins. Yet, even here, a child died because the man kept dogs to hunt runaway slaves.

The evening before, the talk had turned to politics. Yves was convinced there would be war. Marcel and Adam denied it. Gabriel feared it and hoped for it at the same time.

What will I do if it does come to war? Where will my place be? With my Chamard brothers? Or fighting for the freedom of all my brothers?

The boat pulled up to the Toulouse dock. Gabriel handed the men a few coins to divide amongst themselves, then waved them off. He looked down the alley of oaks to the DeBlieux house and thought of inviting himself to dinner.

But he had no answer to Simone's anger. What could he do? He couldn't apologize for having left her. He'd done it for her sake so that she would forget him and go on with her life. Without him. But she hadn't.

He followed the river road to his own home, to Chateau

Chanson. He'd have to make a decision soon about his practice. Staying next door to Toulouse would only be inviting trouble, Simone so near, as impossible as ever.

Gabriel spent the day corresponding with doctors in Louisiana, Mississippi, and even Alabama. Very likely one of them would welcome him as a partner, a junior partner of course. Even an octoroon associate could bring more dollars into the practice.

Claire killed a capon for supper and fed him chicken and dumplings, which lay in his stomach like so much lead. He chewed a few caraway seeds, secretly, and took himself to the back gallery to watch the sun set. Ben and Claire retired to their room in the attic of the north wing and left him to his thoughts. The stars came out one by one in the moon-washed sky. As he named the few stars he knew, Simone's scent, her voice, her brown eyes would not leave him.

She'd been only seventeen when he left, her face still rounded with youth, her skin as dewy and soft as a babe's. They'd known each other all their lives, and when they were children Simone had trailed after him, adoring him. His adolescence was nearly over when she began hers, and for a time she'd been shy with him. By then he understood their friendship had to change, had to diminish. That was a sadness. But after all, though their half cousinship had no real bearing on their being together, there was the issue of color. What small tolerance there had been for mixed relationships, and then only if the white partner were male, had vanished in these heated times. Slavery and abolition and states' rights and racism—all conspired to make it impossible for Gabriel to speak for her. She would be ostracized, perhaps worse, if she were married to him.

She'd made her debut that season, entered the marriage market, to be blunt. Gowns cut to reveal her charms, scents and colors and hair styles—all designed to entice gentlemen to her side. Gabriel, visiting Tante Josie's town house in New Orleans before the first ball of the season, lost his breath when Simone entered the parlor, ready for her big evening. She wore lavender silk, which rustled and swayed over the hoops and petticoats. There were small pink roses in her dark hair and at her bosom, and her brown eyes glowed with the awareness of new womanhood. She had twirled for him and blushed when he'd admired her finery. Had she known even then how he wanted her?

The season went on, and Gabriel tormented himself with jealousy. He did not attend the balls Simone did. He appeared no more black than many other gentlemen of her social circle, but he had determined at a young age that he did not wish to pass. He belonged more to his mother's people than to his father's, and he took no pride in his lighter skin.

Absent from her whirl of dances and dinners, he tortured himself imagining Simone in other men's arms, listening to their flirtations, returning their banter, fluttering her fan. Gabriel knew she had mastered that art—with arch humor, she'd demonstrated the various uses of a fan to him one rainy afternoon. And as the season progressed, so did Simone's confidence. Her shyness disappeared. She knew early on the power she had over men.

But when she chose Gabriel, she found her power only worked to further draw him to her. It did not make him her slave. He'd said no. Lovingly, painfully, but no.

He could not marry her. And he could not resist her. And so he'd gone away.

Now that she was nearly twenty-one, Simone's allure had deepened. Her womanhood ripe, her sense of self complete, Simone knew what she wanted. She had not accepted any of the admirers who'd courted her. She wanted him.

Gabriel shook his head. He would have to find a practice away from here. Perhaps Vicksburg.

The object of his dreams appeared at the top of the stairs. He hadn't even heard her. He dropped his feet and stood, as awkward as a schoolboy. He looked for her escort, and saw no one.

"How did you get here?" he said stupidly.

"I walked. Are you going to ask me to sit down?"

He pulled a chair up near his and held it for her as if they were at a grand ball. She seated herself and waited for him to join her in gazing at the moon, as if this were any night with any young man of her acquaintance.

"Tante Josie surely doesn't know you're here?"

"I told her I had a headache and went to bed."

"Simone, I—"

"Hush, Gabriel. I'm here. And I'm not a child."

He'd have to understand that. Simone loved his protectiveness, but she didn't want that from him now. She wanted him to see her, really see her as a woman ready for him, body and soul.

A candle glowed from the other side of the glass doors, casting a faint warm light over Gabriel's features. His perfect face, the feminine beauty of his curling eyelashes belied by the strong chin and firm jaw. His shoulders, rounded with muscle. His dear hands, long fingered, delicate, the hands of a healer. Simone could have swallowed him, could have drunk him in hungry gulps.

The anger—she'd let it go. Gabriel was home. He was still hers. They needed only courage to be together in this life.

"Simone." Gabriel realized she could see his face, but he could not see hers. She had always had the advantage in knowing what he was thinking while he was bewildered by her. Bewitched, but bewildered. "Simone, what are you doing here?"

"You know what I'm doing here."

"Nothing's changed, Simone."

She rose from her chair. He stood to see her down the stairs, thinking she was leaving, that he'd made her angry again.

She took a step closer to him. Very close now. He could smell the rose water on her skin. His hands trembled with the need to reach for her, to grab her, and crush her to him.

She moved until her full skirt brushed against his knees, and for a moment all his awareness concentrated on that faint touch.

"I've changed," she said. "I won't take no for an answer. Not ever again."

She moved into him and of their own accord his arms opened to her. All he knew was need, the long pent-up need for Simone.

The feel of her in his arms, under his hands, overwhelmed all Gabriel's senses but touch. He kissed her eyes, pulled his fingers through her hair, loosening pins and combs. Cradling her head in one hand, he found her mouth, open and warm and inviting.

She met his kiss, ready and eager for him. Her hands roamed over his back, slid under his arms to feel his ribs, caressing, exploring. Her fingers tugged at his buttons, opened his shirt, and her hands were on him.

"Wait," he gasped. He swallowed hard and stepped back. "You don't know what you're doing."

Simone smiled at him. "Yes, Gabriel, I do. We've passed the test. We're not going to lose any more of our lives together." She closed the distance between them and wrapped her arms around his neck.

Her kiss told him the waiting was over. Their time had come.

Chapter 8

With only a sliver of moon to see by, the man crept between the row of cabins. A dog moaned in its sleep, and he halted, afraid even to breathe.

There it was. A white rag tied to the porch post. He crossed the alleyway, knelt in the dust, and scratched on the porch floor. Then he poised, ready to run if it was a trap.

An old man stepped barefoot onto the porch.

"You Joseph?" the runaway whispered.

"Come in out of sight."

"Anybody else in dere?"

"My daughter and her grandbaby. You be safe."

Caution in every step, the man climbed onto the porch and entered the cabin. Joseph removed the white rag from the post and closed the door behind them.

"Got you some vittles there. Go on and eat. Dere's mo for you to take wid you."

The man sat on the floor in the dark, a plate of cold beans, corn bread, and ham in his lap. He used the spoon like a shovel and ate like a man would who'd had nothing but berries and stolen raw corn for three days.

"I been expecting you," Joseph said. "You's late. You have any trouble on de way?"

"I heared dogs twicet, but dey wadn't after me. I been in de cane, mostly, since I left de place. It high enough nobody see me, I stay low."

A footstep on the porch, and the man froze. There came a scratch on the porch boards. Joseph cracked the door, then opened it wider for Luke to enter.

"I been watching for him," Luke explained. He came in, sat on the floor. "I be Luke," he told the stranger.

The man wiped his mouth with the back of his hand. "Cat," he said.

"Dey calls you Cat?"

The man didn't choose to explain. They let him eat, then passed him a ladle of sweet water. Joseph's daughter sat up, only half awake. "He by hisself?" she said into the dark.

"Yeh, honey. Jest de one man. We don need you tonight. You get you rest."

She lay down again, the corn husks rustling as she settled.

Luke strained to see the man in the weak light from the window. "You a big man," he said. "You strong, able to run all night?"

"I here, ain't I? I been gone four nights now. Dey ain't catched me yet."

"How far you goin'?"

"All de way. Dey say you got to go to Canada, else dem slavers steal you back."

"You know de way?"

"How I know de way? I find it, though. Every station tell you how to find de next station, dat how it work."

Luke spoke to Joseph. "He got a shepherd?"

Joseph nodded in the dark.

Luke sat with his arms around his spread knees, thinking. "Dis shepherd wait one mo night?"

"What you thinking?"

"Listen here" he said to Cat. "I got thirty-five cents."

"How you get dat money, Luke?" Joseph asked.

"I got it." Luke turned back to Cat. "You rest up here. My woman feed you. Tomorrow night, I come wid you. We split de money when we needs it. We watch each other's back."

"Why you cain't go tonight?" Cat said.

Luke hated to admit he wasn't ready. Pearl wasn't ready. Anyway, it was only two hours till daylight, and Cat had to lie low during the day.

"What about de shepherd?" Cat said.

"He waiting down de road a piece," Joseph answered. "I talk to him." He patted his sleeping great-grandbaby on the back and went out.

The moon had nearly set, and Joseph hurried to the road leading to the northernmost fields of the plantation. Where the road turned east and then sharply north again, he stopped.

Too dark to see anything, and his old heart was thumping hard. "Mister?" he whispered, afraid to speak and afraid not to.

Yves Chamard emerged from the copse by the road, two horses in tow.

"Where is he?" Yves said.

"Mr. Chamard, he say can he go tomorrow night? It late, and a man go with him he wait a day."

"Damnation," Yves said. He'd been in the dark swatting mosquitoes nearly three hours, for nothing. He considered demanding that Joseph go back and get the man. But it was late. Even with horses, riding hard, Yves could never get him to the next station by daybreak, much less have the mounts back in the stable before they were missed.

"You was planning to stay a few mo days, Master?" Joseph said.

Yves swatted his quirt against his leg, too irritated to answer civilly. It wasn't the old man's fault. And his own convenience meant little compared to what this slave was risking. Still, he was damned annoyed.

"So there will be two men?" That meant saddling another horse, sneaking three of them out, and putting them back in decent shape before the stable boy got up. He'd have to borrow one of the Johnstons' horses. Irony, that, using Adam's own horse to help his slave escape. *Hope to hell he never finds out.*

"Have them here no more than an hour after dark."

"I tell 'em," Joseph said.

Yves made out the old man's darkened figure turning to go.

"Joseph," Yves said. "Might as well ride back, save your feet a mile."

"Master, I ain't never been on no horse. And I ain't goin' to tonight neither. Thank you just the same."

Yves mounted and Joseph stood back for the horses to move ahead on the dark road.

When he got to the cabin, Joseph scratched the porch post to warn the men inside. Then he crept in and sat his weary bones on the cot.

"He say tomorrow night, just after dark." He rested a minute. "He a good man to come out again."

"He a white man?" Cat asked.

The men would guess that much even in the dark tomorrow night. "Yeh. From other side of de river."

Luke stood up. "I goin' now. Pearl bring you something to eat tomorrow. You lay low, and we go soon as it good dark."

Cat stretched out on the floorboards. Joseph lay back on his cot. Luke slipped out.

Just as quietly, Luke slipped into his own cabin. He stood a minute, listening. Pearl's breathing told him she was asleep. At dawn, he'd be in the fields. He'd have to tell her now.

She lay in the middle of their bed, one arm stretched across where his body was supposed to be. He lifted her hand and kissed it, then eased onto the mattress and under her arm. He pulled her to him so he could talk into her ear.

"Pearl." She rolled into him and murmured something. Pearl was going to cry and carry on when he told her, he knew that. She didn't have any people of her own on the place. Her mammy and her sister had died right after Master brought them here, and she had only him.

Pearl nuzzled his neck, beginning to waken. He palmed the side of her head and kissed her. She ran her hand over his work-hardened chest, then down his ribs, deepening the kiss. "Pearl," he breathed. He imagined for the hundredth time taking her with him, but he didn't see how she could make it. She wasn't like the women in the fields. She couldn't run all night, huddle in fear all day, starve—in the cookhouse, Pearl was next thing to a house slave. She didn't have the stamina she'd need to run. She didn't have his hunger to be free.

She pressed herself against him, rousing him. Love tore at his heart. He might not make it, might not ever see her again. Fighting the tightness in his throat and chest, he pulled at Pearl's night shift. She untied the strings of his pants. In desperate passion, he rolled over onto her.

When they lay quiet in each other's arms, Pearl said, "You leaving, ain't you?"

Luke didn't answer.

"You make love to me like dat, it 'cause you going."

He kissed the top of her head, stroked her bare hip where his hand rested. He marveled how she knew him, could see him in the dark, hear unspoken words.

She pushed his hand away and sat up. "I know it." Her voice broke. "You might as well say it."

He tried to pull her back to him, to hold her, but she fought him.

"You said you'd stay. You said till I have a baby on de way."

"Pearl, it been two year since we partnered. Dere not gone be a baby. Not fo us."

She cried, heedless of how much noise she made. She wouldn't let him hold her, turned her back to him. But as the sobs shook her small frame, Luke tried again. He touched her with one big hand, then the other, and she let him take her into his arms. He cradled her, rocking her, until she quieted.

"It be light soon," Luke said. "You gone be able to act like nothing happening?"

She nodded her head against his chest.

"Dey's a man in Joseph's cabin gone need food during de day. And we both gone need food to take wid us tonight. You get us something?"

The darkness was lifting. "You coming back for me. Swear it."

He put his hand on her face. "I coming back for you, dere be breath in my body."

"I can see yo eyes, Luke. Swear it."

"Befo God, Pearl, I swear it."

The moon down, Yves returned to the stable in the dark and unsaddled his horse. It had picked up a stone and its foot was sore. Another task ahead of him, he sad-

dled Marcel's bay and guided it to the road that he and
Marcel and Adam had taken the day they'd heard the
hounds in the backcountry.

He didn't know what he was going to do with the dogs.
How many there were, which of them were man-hunters,
would they be guarded? *Damn, it's dark.* He hoped the
horse could see better than he could. As he approached
the patch of woods where the dogs were, he dismounted
and walked on, a hand out to deflect branches he couldn't
see. Through the trees he caught the flicker of fire and
headed for it.

Hidden, he observed the clearing where the hounds
slept. The wind blew in his face, else he surely could not
have come so close without rousing them. A boy perhaps
ten years old lay near a waning fire. Warm as it was, likely
he wanted the fire to keep away the hobgoblins of the
night. The smoke helped some with the mosquitoes, too,
that and the thin burlap over the boy. Yves counted
eleven dogs. Fine-looking brutes, their coats shimmering in the firelight.

He couldn't shoot them. He understood Marianne's
disposing of the two who'd attacked the child, but these
hounds, sleeping peacefully—no, he couldn't shoot
them.

What am I doing here anyway? He hated to think he was
about to interfere so blatantly in another man's business
because he admired Marianne Johnston's high bosom
and fiery eyes. *But here I am.*

He thought again of Marianne in the garden the night
the little girl died. Her eyes, bluer than the gown she
wore, had seemed bruised she was so hurt, so spent. A
woman of feeling, and impulsive, too, blasting shot into
those dogs. Couldn't blame her, however. Spirited, and
she'd shown herself a woman who used her mind—in

his experience, not many young women were accustomed to that activity.

But had she asked for his help? Was it his place to act when her brother did not?

Nevertheless, training dogs to hunt slaves was an abysmal practice. The dogs themselves, however . . .

He entered the circle of firelight and sat down. First one and then another dog scented him and opened sleepy eyes. Just a man, sitting near the boy. Yves cleared his throat, and a few more dogs woke, finding no cause for alarm. Good.

The slave boy slept on as only an exhausted child can. Yves thought of waking him, but it was just as well the boy didn't know who'd taken all the dogs away. He added sticks to the fire for him to make it last until morning.

Yves gathered the lines. They were all tied to a length of chain that snaked among them, but he didn't want the encumbrance or clanking of a chain. He counted the dogs, counted the lines. He had them all.

Amid the stretching and grumbling of the hounds, Yves pulled the lines and had them up. He glanced again at the child. What a sleeper. *Poor lad. Hope he doesn't get a licking for this.*

Yves led the dogs back to his horse. As docile as they were at the moment, it was hard to see them as man-eating beasts. But they'd been blooded; they were a menace, and they needed to be removed.

He rode the horse back toward the river, the pack jostling for position behind him. By the time he reached the banks of the Mississippi some three miles north of the Johnstons', the sky had begun to lighten. Yves led the pack up the river road until he came to the old Nixon place. The dock in disrepair, the house itself hollow-eyed and empty, he decided this was the place to wait for a boat.

He tied his handkerchief to the dock pole, signaling he wanted to be picked up. Southbound or northbound, it didn't matter. He tied the horse and the dogs, then sat on the rickety dock to wait.

An hour after sunrise, he hailed a large raft riding the slower outer current. Flatboats weren't seen much on the river anymore, the steamboats having taken the trade, but Yves thanked the stars for the luck of it. Bargemen weren't likely to inquire too closely about a pack of fine hounds being sold on the edge of the river.

Unwieldy as a flatboat was, the men managed to guide it over to the bank not far downstream from the decrepit dock. They were a notorious lot, bargemen, little more than cutthroats some of them. A rough bunch. Yves was glad of the small pistol snug in the back of his waist. These men, however, merely wanted paying passengers, and so negotiations were quick. The bargemen took the dogs aboard, incurious about the well-dressed fellow's willingness to accept a token sum for prime hunting dogs, and allowed the current to take them back into the stream.

By now Yves' head ached and he wanted his morning coffee. He'd have to concoct some story about why he'd been out so early if he couldn't slip into the house unnoticed. And he'd have to pretend he'd had a full night's sleep. It was going to be a bear of a day.

By the time Yves returned to the Johnstons', a man and a boy were mucking out the stables. He left his horse in the corral, the slave assuring him he'd unsaddle and brush his mount, then give him a bag of oats. Yves walked up to the house and entered the back door, avoiding the dining room where Adam or Miss Johnston or Marcel might be breakfasting.

He reached his room unseen and closed the door

behind him in relief. He washed his face and neck, changed his linen, buffed his boots, and prepared for breakfast as though he had only just risen. Late night with a bottle of bourbon, he thought he'd tell them. Disgust generally dampened conversation.

Downstairs, only his brother lingered with his coffee. Yves ran his eyes over Miss Johnston's red damask chair, disappointed it was empty.

Marcel examined him over his cup. "You don't look good, little brother."

Yves gave him a rueful smile. The headache made it easy to play the part of a hungover wastrel. "Bourbon," he said.

"What was the occasion?"

"Why, the presence of a bottle of bourbon." Yves poured himself a cup of coffee and sat down. "Where are our hosts?"

"Miss Johnston is in her garden. The roses, you know. Adam is dealing with McNaught. Seems someone has taken off with his dogs, and the man is in a fury."

Yves put a hand to his brow, hiding his face. "God, my head hurts," he complained.

Marcel finished his coffee. "Have a quiet day. And finish the coffeepot. I'm off to see the roses."

The roses, or Miss Marianne Johnston? Evil thoughts came to his mind about his brother, poetry, roses, and a certain blue-eyed gardener. He groaned and poured himself another cup of coffee.

Marianne had breakfasted early. On her way to the compost heap, she passed the stable.

Curious, she thought, that the man was unsaddling Marcel's bay gelding. Where had he been so early?

She and Joseph were going to oversee the tending of

the compost this morning, having more muck forked in and water filtered through. An hour later, Marianne had her arms in black dirt up to her elbows. More new rose canes needed potting up, and she preferred to do it herself. When Marcel found her in the bottom of the experimental garden, she had already wiped her forehead with a dirty wrist, and tendrils of hair hung around her face. She was a mess.

Marcel strolled down the path toward her. *Oh no. Here I am hot and sweaty, and he's the picture of . . .*

"Good morning," she answered him.

"I've come to interrupt you, if I may," Marcel said. "I don't know a thing about crossbreeding. Will you instruct me?"

"Gladly." Who else ever showed any interest in her project? Certainly not Adam, and Father had merely listened out of politeness when she'd been excited about the white-streaked petals.

She pulled off her gardening gloves and wiped her hands on her apron. "These are the newest saplings. Seed grown, of course. This one derives from a Damask Perpetual and a Pink Gallica." She went on about breeding extraordinary pinks, hoping for something spectacular.

I believe he's actually interested, she thought. She warmed at his questions, at the simple touch on her elbow as she knelt to lift a pot. *He does have beautiful eyes. And he's a gentleman. No leering at her bosom, no making her blood run hot. Yves Chamard was a rogue. She'd always known it. But Marcel—gentleness itself.*

"You were out riding early, I believe?" Marianne said, simply to make conversation.

Marcel looked at her quizzically.

"I noticed your horse being unsaddled when I came out." She really shouldn't be so inquisitive. He clearly didn't appreciate explaining himself.

"Did you?" He looked at his boots.

Damn, she thought. *Now he thinks I'm nosy and rude.*

He lifted his head and smiled at her. "It was a fine morning," he said.

They strolled through the gardens, Marianne commenting on this bed or that, until they reached the back verandah. "Thank you, Mr. Chamard, for your interest in the roses."

Marcel bowed his head and she admired the sweep of wavy black hair off his forehead.

"My pleasure," he said. "It's a fascinating project."

"Well. I'll go in now. I have a transformation to effect before dinner," she said as she smoothed her rough apron. Feeling shy, she touched her hair where it frizzed from under her bonnet.

He laughed. Such a sweet kind laugh. "I'll look forward to the butterfly, then," he said. He left her to have a look at the river while she turned back into the belle.

Marcel did indeed spare a moment to examine the river. Muddy brown. Running swiftly. Same as yesterday, the day before, tomorrow. Miss Johnston had time to be safely upstairs by now, and he strode into the house to find his brother.

"There you are," he said. Yves was in the library with the newspapers. "Where's Adam?"

"With his overseer, I believe. There's talk of a search for the hounds. Though without hounds," Yves said with a grin, "it will be difficult to track them."

"You did it, damn you. And a guest in this house."

Yves snapped the newspaper, hid his head behind it. "Don't know what you're talking about," he said.

"You had my horse out before dawn. You don't have a hangover at all. The dogs menaced your precious slaves. No. I amend that. Mr. Johnston's precious slaves."

Yves peered at him around the paper. "Circumstantial evidence."

"You admit it then. Yves, by God, the world does not belong to you. When are you—"

"Please, Marcel. Not the 'When are you going to settle down?' speech. 'Get yourself a gal, set her up in a nice little cottage, have a brown baby or two.' Marcel, I do not act out of boredom or because I suffer from lack of female companionship."

"Of course not. But having Lucinda and the boy in my life makes me a contented, cheerful man. If you had a woman, Yves, you'd—"

"If your *placée* keeps you happy Marcel, I'm happy for you, but I want neither a wife nor a mistress."

They heard footsteps in the hallway, and Adam walked in, disheveled and distressed. "Would you believe it? The boy watching the dogs didn't hear a thing. Didn't see a thing. He swears it must have been voodoo."

"Is the child in trouble?" Yves asked. He'd been fretting about having set the boy up for a switching with a stick.

"The boy?" Adam looked puzzled. "No, he's just a child."

Yves breathed more easily. *Then I have no regrets about last night.*

"Valuable pack of hounds like that, the thief, or thieves, must be long gone by now," Marcel said.

"Well, there are tracks leading toward the river. I've just come in to get my hat. We'll follow them as far as we can. McNaught's in a rage, of course. Right under his nose, he says, though he didn't return till this morning." Adam looked anxious, Yves thought. "An absolute rage."

"Would you like me to come along?" Marcel answered.

Adam seemed tempted to accept the offer, but in the end, declined. "I'm sure we'll merely follow the tracks to the river and that will be the end of it. The thieves probably had a boat waiting. At least, if I'd wanted to get rid of the dogs, that's what I would have done."

And should have done, Yves added to himself.

Chapter 9

The following morning, Marianne dressed for breakfast. "It's too hot for a corset," she complained.

"Don't make no never mind," Hannah insisted. "Dey's genlemen in de house, and you make you mama shamed could she see you walkin' round widout you hoop."

"My 'mama' never wore a hoop skirt in her life," Marianne countered. Then she thought how much hotter Mother's six petticoats would have been than a hoop and only two underskirts.

Marianne gasped. "Too tight!" But Hannah did her duty.

Properly turned out in a red and blue plaid cotton dress with jet buttons in a pointed waist, pagoda sleeves, and a ruffled skirt flaring over the hoop, Marianne descended the grand staircase to the hall and entered the breakfast room. Marcel rose from his seat, and once Adam noticed her, he stood as well.

"Good morning, Miss Johnston," Marcel said. The precisely tied cravat above his buff waistcoat and deep green frock coat shone a brilliant white. His cheeks were freshly shaved—Marianne was partial to beardless faces—and his teeth gleamed.

Such a lovely smile he has, she thought. "Good morning. And good morning to you, Adam."

"Morning," he said, barely looking up from his grits and gravy. Breakfast being an informal meal, each member of the household coming down when he or she was ready, Yves did not appear until Marianne had nearly finished her plate of fruit and ham. She and Marcel had carried on a lively conversation about the scientists in France and Germany, her correspondent Monsieur Vibert among them, and their exciting innovations.

When Yves entered, Marianne noticed Marcel's searching gaze on his brother's face. Yves too was freshly shaved and his linen as white and stiff as could be desired. His brown hair waved back from his forehead in perfect imitation of a fashion plate. But there were circles under his eyes. He hadn't looked well yesterday morning, either, she remembered. And his eyes were red. He'd probably been drinking all night again, she thought with disgust.

"Good morning, Mr. Chamard," she said formally. She had not forgiven him for his presumptions in the garden.

He gave her a small formal bow and found the coffeepot. Adam put his cup down and asked, "Good God, Chamard. Have you not slept?"

"Of course I've slept," Yves said. "Why wouldn't I sleep?" he answered with the grumpiness of a man who had not slept.

Marianne excused herself. There was no pleasure to be had in Yves Chamard's presence. She took the path through the pecan orchard to Peter's cabin. Early as it was, the warm humid air carried all the scents of the quarters—the chickens, the privies, the dust, the honeysuckle, and the gardenias. The place was quiet, only a few elderly women about, and the smallest children playing quietly in the shade of a live oak.

The cabin doors and windows were open for a cross-breeze. "Morning, Peter," Marianne said.

When Peter tried to raise himself, she put a hand on his shoulder to keep him abed. "I need to see your wounds again, Peter."

"Yes'm."

She sniffed and palpated around the lesions the way Dr. Chamard had shown her. No whiff of necrosis. The heat was gone from the swellings, and the flesh under her fingers was taut and firm. Peter was healing remarkably well, but it was going to take time.

"Have you had your breakfast?"

Peter didn't answer immediately. She glanced at him. "I ain't hongry, miss."

"Pearl hasn't brought it yet?"

He looked away. "She be in soon."

This was unlike Pearl, to neglect Peter. "Joseph has finished your crutch, I see. Have you tried it?"

He reached for the crutch, and careful of his weakened leg and maimed foot, he hauled himself upright and leaned on the crude support. He grinned at her. "I gone be able to walk, miss."

Marianne clapped her hands once and put them to her lips, her eyes shining with pride. "Yes, I think you are." Though never very well. "Not too much yet. Back into bed with you. In a few days you can walk to the porch and sit. Don't hurry it, Peter."

She took the path to the summer cookhouse, which was hot as blazes even with only two walls. Marianne found Evette supervising the two helpers cooking the noon meal for the field hands. Fatback sizzled and popped in huge skillets, rice steamed, and red beans boiled. Rivulets of sweat ran down the women's faces, and their dresses stuck to their wet skin.

"Miss Marianne, it too hot down here for you." Evette flapped her apron as if to provide some breeze.

"Where's Pearl, Evette?"

Marianne caught the nervous glance Evette gave the other two women. "She must be at de cabin wid Peter. You want I send her to you at de house?"

The cook was hiding something. Was Pearl lying out? The slaves did that sometimes. They'd go off to the woods for a few days, then come back in ready to face the overseer's displeasure. Some of them figured it was worth the punishment to get a few days' rest. Maybe Pearl had had too much, what with cooking in this heat and caring for Peter.

Marianne shook her head. "No. Don't send her." She retraced her steps to the cabins. Joseph emerged from one down the lane. Not his own. She knew which was his from her childhood when Hannah would bring her down to the quarters for a piece of sugarcane. Just thinking of it brought the sweetness to her mouth.

Joseph stopped in the hot dust of the lane and waited for her. He needed a new shirt, Marianne noticed. Both sleeves were torn and thin. His overalls looked all right; they were still dark blue from the indigo dye. His hard feet were bare, but then it was hot now. She'd get him a shirt, though.

"Is that Pearl's cabin? Is she ill?"

Marianne had known Joseph all her life. He was the one had taught her to spit out the hulls of the boiled peanuts, had brought her to see the new puppies and kittens, and now he didn't want to meet her eyes.

"Pearl sick in de heart." When Marianne still looked at him, he added, "Her man Luke, he took to another woman."

Marianne crossed her arms. Slaves did not take a day off from work because they had a broken heart. She waited and watched Joseph's kind face. She knew him so well—he wouldn't want to lie to her, and now he struggled with it. "What is it really, Joseph?"

Joseph stared off over her shoulder. She let him think. She saw it in his face when he made his decision to trust her.

"Pearl's man gone."

"Gone? You mean he's run away?" She took a long minute to digest that fact. "When?"

"In de night."

"But this is a good plantation," she protested. "My father takes care of his slaves. We give them plenty of rations, let them have their gardens . . ." Flustered, she looked at Joseph for confirmation.

"Yes'm. Mr. Johnston a good master."

"I don't understand. Running is a terrible risk, and life here is . . . not so bad."

"Luke a man, Missy. He don wan be no man's mule, he don wan be no man's slave."

Marianne walked to the trunk of the shade tree and leaned against it. Joseph hadn't called her Missy in such a long time. He trusted her, and she was proud of that. "What are his chances?"

"Wid dem dogs gone, he might can make it to de next station."

"Station?"

"Dey's many a places, homes and such, dat take in a runaway. Feed him, hide him, den send him on to de next one. Dat how a man get free."

Her arms folded across her chest, Marianne paced. "So that's how it's done," she murmured.

She stopped and faced Joseph. "McNaught doesn't know he's gone yet?"

"Must not, no'm. Else we'd hear de bell, and he'd be calling up de men for a searching."

Marianne Johnston, daughter of a man who owned two hundred slaves, might not fully understand the despair of being another man's chattel, but she understood very well what was at stake in aiding a runaway. It was against the law, for one thing. It was now against the law in Louisiana to even emancipate one's own slave.

And if she did help Luke escape, or even ignored his running away, she would be undermining the very institution that the South depended on for its monetary and cultural existence. She would be disloyal not only to her heritage, but even to Magnolias. To her own father. She walked through the dust to the chicken coop on the far side of the shade and back again. The consequences of being caught didn't bear thinking about. Men had been shot, their homes burned for what she was considering.

But Luke was not just another faceless field hand. She knew who Luke was, had even been present when Pearl married him. Pearl, so much in love Marianne had envied her, her own slave.

Slavery can not go on. That's what Julia Ward Howe claimed. That's what Henry Stanton thundered. They were right. She knew it. And she *wanted* to do something. But she couldn't fight the whole South. She couldn't even persuade Father to make changes, to offer wages; she'd already tried that.

But she could help one man.

"Joseph, go tell Mr. McNaught I want to see him right away. No, tell him Miss and Mr. Johnston want to see him. He'll come in faster if he thinks Adam is asking for him." She touched Joseph's arm. "I can keep him at the house for one or two hours. Maybe that will help."

"Yes'm. It help. Luke be dat much farther from here by den."

Chapter 10

"No, leave the candle lit," Simone said. "I want to see."

Gabriel's eyes held hers as he pulled off his cravat and shrugged off his shirt. He tossed it aside and stepped closer to her, his gaze dropping to her bosom straining at the thin muslin chemise.

He bent to take her mouth. She wrapped her bare arms around his neck, and he pressed her length against him, shuddering at the heat in her. He wanted to tear away the chemise, throw her on the bed, and plunge into her sweet body in a frenzy of possession. It took all his will to hold back.

She ran her fingers over his chest, rubbed her thumb over his hard nipple. His hands wandered down her back to the hollow below her waist, to the roundness of her buttocks. As her body melted into his, he pulled the chemise above her thighs. She raised a knee to open herself to him.

Gabriel gripped her thigh against his hip and held her still. He looked down into her brown eyes. "You know what this means?"

"We belong to each other. That's what it means,

Gabriel." He waited, her weight held against him. Did she know what she was giving up to be with him?

"Stop thinking, Gabriel." She lifted her face to his and demanded his kiss. Her fingers found the fastening of his trousers and he did as she bade on this, their long-awaited, dreamt-for fusion of body and soul.

The next night, and the next and the next, Simone slipped from Toulouse to meet Gabriel under cover of the magnolia near her gate where he greeted her with hot hands and kisses. They walked through the dappled moon-shade to his house, their arms around each other, stopping when they must for the deepening kisses they craved.

In Gabriel's bed, lying spent in each other's arms, the candle flickering in a soft river breeze, Gabriel tried again to talk to her. So far, Simone had resisted all his efforts to impress upon her the seriousness of their situation. Living as man and wife in St. John Parish could not be. They would be shunned, even assaulted—under the cloaked anonymity of darkness and even in public. If they married, the community would not allow him to make a living here, nor could he keep her safe. They had to make plans. But Simone put a finger on his lips. "Shhh," she told him.

One arm behind his head, the other around his love, Gabriel marked out a course. He would find a priest who didn't know them. Maybe in Donaldsonville. He would marry them, even if Gabriel had to pretend to be white.

But then they would have to tell their families. Simone's mother, Gabriel's mother, his father—they would not be pleased. Tante Josie loved him; she had been a second mother to him. But she had to want more for her daughter than a freedman of color could offer. Surely, though, Tante Josie had suspected Simone's heart was already committed. In her most eligible years,

Simone had dissuaded all suitors for her hand. Tante Josie could not be truly surprised.

Gabriel's father, Bertrand Chamard, should be the least offended of the families. He'd loved Gabriel's mother, a mixed-race woman herself, for more than twenty years before she left him for Pierre LaFitte. Papa should understand if anyone would that the heart does not consider convenience or propriety.

Simone shifted. The yellow candlelight gleamed on her smooth skin and across the rise of her bare breasts. He stroked her arm and she opened her eyes.

"Is it time to go?"

"Almost." He kissed her ear and she turned, her hands reaching for him.

He tasted the salty hollow at the base of her throat. "I want to marry you," he said.

"Yes. But not tonight." She tilted her head back to reveal her long white throat. "Kiss me, Gabriel."

A lazy satiated hour later, he raised himself to his elbow and caressed her face.

"What are you smiling about?" she said.

"You. Who knew you were insatiable?"

She laughed. "I suspected it."

He would have to make her listen to him now. He grasped her hand and brought it to his mouth. "You'll have to give up so much," he said, kissing each of her knuckles. "Society. Position. Wealth. Friends. You know this?"

"Marry me, Gabriel. That's all I want in the world."

The candle sputtered out. "Kiss me in the dark, Gabriel."

"Woman, you are going to consume me." He grabbed her to him and kissed her hard. Then he laughed. "Never thought I'd say this. Get your clothes on, woman."

They walked down the road arm in arm, starlight glinting on the river, the humid air caressing them, making Simone's hair curl around her face. When they reached the magnolia tree, Gabriel stopped. "I'll find a priest today. Is that what you want?"

"It's what I've always wanted."

"After we tell the family, we'll go to Baton Rouge or Vicksburg until I find a position further off, maybe in Jackson. You understand, Simone, we may be very poor for quite some time."

"I have a little money," Simone said. "Papa called it my pin money, and I saved most of it. We can live on that for weeks and weeks if we're careful."

"I don't intend to live on your money."

"Gabriel, stop. I could have married a wealthy man while you were away. Two wealthy men. I waited for you. Don't worry about money. We're going to have a wonderful life together."

They kissed a lingering good-bye. Simone at last stepped away and, still holding Gabriel's hand, turned to go into the house. She started. Someone was there, in the road near the gate. Watching them.

"It's Maman," Simone breathed.

Tante Josephine's slow steps closed the distance between them. "I wish to speak to you in the house, please. Both of you."

Gabriel followed the women up the gallery stairs and into the parlor where his aunt had left a lamp burning. He'd never felt more guilty or lowly than he did at that moment. His dear tante Josie, he'd betrayed her trust and her love. But she could not stop them, not now. *We are going to be married.*

"Sit down, please," Tante Josephine said.

The lovers took the sofa. Simone reached for Gabriel's

hand and raised her chin. "I'm going to marry Gabriel," she told her mother.

"*Oui*, Simone. You are." Josephine burned a solemn gaze into Gabriel's conscience. "And how will you live? Where will you live? There is no place in Louisiana you will be safe. You know that."

Gabriel nodded. "Yes, Tante. I will find a hospital position, or begin a practice of my own, far from here. No one knows me off the river in Mississippi. Or in Alabama. Mobile is a big place. Or Montgomery."

Simone reminded her mother, "Papa was a poor Cajun, you a rich Creole girl, Maman. You married him."

"And I am grateful every day for the years I had with your father." Josephine stared into the lantern shadows as if Phanor might materialize there and take her into his arms once more. He'd loved Gabriel, too. Phanor would not have sent him away even if he'd not already taken Simone's virtue. Though Josephine knew her daughter: Gabriel had not taken what Simone was unwilling to give.

"Do not pretend, Simone, this is about money. Your lives together will be difficult, even dangerous." Josie took a deep breath. "Gabriel, this will not be a clandestine marriage accomplished in the dark. I want everyone here, in this house, for the wedding. Cleo, Pierre, Nicolette." She hesitated. "Your father, if you wish it."

"*Merci*, Tante Josie." Gabriel was humbled that his aunt would bless them, and he felt Onkle Phanor would have blessed them too after they had tried so hard and so long to find another path in life.

"I have a cousin who married into a family in New York," Josie said. "She can make inquiries for you in the North."

"The North?" Simone said.

Gabriel squeezed her hand. He knew she had not thought this through. "It will be safer," he said.

"New York is farther away than I would wish," Josie said, "but, children, these are dangerous times. There will be no tolerance for your marriage down here, not with the slave owners stirred up by the talk coming from Washington. Southerners don't want our ways to change, and you will be an affront to them."

Simone turned her eyes to Gabriel. He saw she wasn't afraid. "I'll go wherever you go," she told him. She looked at her maman. "If the North is where we must go, then we will go north."

The sun lightened the sky and a gray beam penetrated the windows of the parlor. Servants moved softly in other parts of the house. "Stay to breakfast, Gabriel," Josie said. "Then, if you please, ride to the lake to bring your mother home. You and Simone must not defy propriety any longer." Josie frowned and crossed herself. "And let us not forget your disobedience to God. Hurry home with Cleo, Gabriel, and I'll have the priest waiting."

Gabriel kissed his aunt's cheek. "*Merci*, Tante. I love you."

"I love you, *mon cher.*"

Gabriel retired to the *garconniére*; Simone went to her bedroom to prepare herself for breakfast.

Josie walked out onto the balcony and leaned against a post. Below this very spot, she had first met Phanor DeBlieux. He'd brought hearts of palm to sell to Grandmére Emmeline, and she and Cleo had handed over far too many picayunes for them.

Phanor had the most devilish look in his eye, even then, and a devastating smile. She'd felt the thrill of that smile from her head to her toes. And yet they'd wasted all those years, waiting to learn that the difference between Cajun and Creole meant nothing.

Of course there had been Bertrand Chamard. She had been in love with him, too, for a time. Josie smiled to herself. *I know my Simone, because I know myself. I would have yielded to Bertrand in those heady weeks if he had pressed me. And how I wished he would.* Those weeks of Bertrand's ardent courtship had been exhilarating, and his abrupt marriage to the wealthy Abigail Johnston had nearly destroyed Josie. But he had not been quite the blackguard some had assumed. There had been no formal engagement, and he had not taken her virtue. *Almost,* she laughed to herself, remembering that day in the orchard, *but not quite.*

Josie's eldest had chosen a troubled future, but life was not meant to be easy. Trouble awaited Simone, no doubt, but joy too, and perhaps even happiness.

The smell of coffee wafted to Josie on the gallery, and she walked inside to breakfast. *Simone and Gabriel—may God bless them.*

Chapter 11

Adam wearied of the quiet life on Magnolias and proposed they return to the amusements—and the company of Nicolette Chamard—at Lake Maurepas.

Yves would have preferred to stay on the plantation. He had yet to win Marianne Johnston's favor, and it was becoming oddly important to him that he do so. Everything he said or did seemed to nettle her, and the more she displayed her pique, the more he wanted to win her over. She was a challenge, and yes, that was part of the attraction. But she was so much more than that. More committed, more indignant, more passionate—she had depth, this Marianne Johnston.

The way her mouth tightened and her nostrils flared when she was annoyed intrigued him, but he envied the smiles she bestowed on his brother. Who, by the way, had been showing her far too much attention. Marcel's mulatto *placée* Lucinda, whom he'd ensconced in a comfortable cottage in Le Vieux Carré, might have Marcel's affection, but she would not satisfy the getting of an heir. Just as well Miss Johnston not be any further exposed to the considerable charms of his elder brother.

Curious how eager she is for us to be off, Yves mused.

She had assured Adam that his presence was not required at Magnolias. "I will send out the hue and cry for the runaway. You needn't concern yourself," she insisted.

Yves wondered about that. Having shepherded Luke and Cat to the next safe house himself, he had an interest in their success. *She seems uncommonly willing to be left alone in this big house. Is she truly going to pursue Luke's recapture?*

It was decided. The three bachelors were off. On a stifling, muggy morning, Adam kissed his sister good-bye. Marcel murmured au revoir over her hand.

Yves' inclination was to bend her backward over his arm and take his adieu with a deep and lingering kiss. As it was, he chose not even to kiss her hand. He had to get her attention before he could ravish her, here on the verandah or anywhere else he could capture her. Thus, with his mouth in that crooked smirk that could charm, or infuriate, he held his hand out in the American fashion, as if she were a gentleman of his acquaintance instead of a delectable belle.

Marianne accepted his handshake, a bit taken aback at the lack of gallantry implied. *Oh.* She breathed in sharply. His finger stroked her palm. Such a simple touch, and yet it sent a shiver down her spine. She jerked her hand away.

Even a handshake is an opportunity for seduction? He is *a rake.* Yves smiled his good-bye, a gleam in the hazel eyes. She refused to smile in return. If he thought she was that kind of girl, he was mistaken. Surely these feelings he roused in her were improper. Neither Martin nor Albert had upset her equanimity like this. Not even Marcel, and he was far more handsome than Yves.

In her other hand, she grasped the offended palm, still hot where his finger had violated her.

As soon as the men mounted and were on their way, Marianne wiped her palms on her skirt to erase the

sensation. That failing, she tried to ignore the lingering impression and marched into Father's office. She
untied her muslin neckerchief and sat down at the
heavy desk. Her legs safe from observation, she pulled
her skirt up around her knees in a distinctly unladylike
pose to relieve the heat. Alone as she was, she blushed
when an image of Yves Chamard finding her like this
came to mind. Well, he was gone, and good riddance
to him.

Searching for paper and pen in the top drawer, she
considered how to write the hue-and-cry notice for the
circulars.

She decided to state the facts clearly, if not entirely ac-
curately. Luke was, she remembered, a fine-looking
Negro, broad shoulders, tall. Wasn't there a small scar
over one eye? In her notice, she wrote the runaway was
of average height and of an unprepossessing appearance. Joseph said he'd headed north to the next safe
house. "Believed to be looking for a ship bound for England," she wrote. She offered a twenty-five-dollar
reward, respectable, but not enough to inspire a thoroughly intense hunt for him.

Satisfied it was a properly written notice, Marianne
folded it and addressed it to a printer in New Orleans with
instructions it should be forwarded to the *Times Picayune*
from there. She looked around for stray papers, books,
whatever might do for her purpose. There were two yellowed newspapers, a bill from her dressmaker she had already paid, and a periodical about fishing in the gulf.
These she arranged on a corner of the big desk. Then she
inserted the hue and cry amongst the layers.

*That will do. If Adam or Father wonders why no one has seen
a notice for our runaway, I can truthfully claim to have written
one.* She smiled to herself. *Adam at least will have no trouble excusing me as a "poor featherbrained female."*

Marianne's satisfaction lasted through the morning as she went about her duties. Before the sun grew any hotter, she tied her bonnet on and made a quick trip to the vegetable garden where she directed the gardener to harvest some of the tomatoes for drying. The cucumbers were ready, so she walked over to the cookhouse to inform Evette how many vats of vinegar and how many of brine pickles she wanted.

Next she commandeered the household maids to change all the linens from the gentlemen's rooms, to air the pillows and bedding, to sweep and mop and polish. The runner on the stairs bore marks from some careless fellow's boots, most likely Adam's, and she supervised one of the girls in cleaning the stains so that the expensive carpet wasn't damaged.

With Father and Adam gone, she would again have to meet with Mr. McNaught. She had Hannah help her into her most severe frock and sat behind Father's desk. This time, she did not invite the overseer to sit down. After mulling it over, she had decided to discover if it were more advantageous for him to stand while she sat, or for her to stand while he sat. She listened attentively as he went over the current activities and events on the various farms that made up the greater plantation. Then she said, "About these runaways, Mr. McNaught."

His respectful tone became aggressive. "Your slaves have been spoiled, Miss Johnston. A new overseer has to show he's the man in control. Bound to be some discontent at first."

Her impulse was to jump to her feet in order to confront him eye to eye. But she kept to her resolve. She placed her hands on the arms of the chair as if she were completely relaxed, but in truth she hoped to hide the fact that they were trembling.

"Mr. McNaught, Magnolias has been a prospering,

well-run plantation for a third of a century." She had to tilt her chin up to meet his gaze, but her eyes bored into his without any of the submissiveness he seemed to expect. "Brutality has not been necessary. We expect our overseers to manage the property and the slaves without recourse to harsh treatment."

McNaught was not a man who could hide his feelings. His fair skin flushed and his mouth turned down. He knew his place, however, Marianne observed. He stood, bowed stiffly, and took his leave.

Marianne sank back into Father's chair. Thank heavens McNaught had not been more bullheaded. She didn't really know how to run things, not nearly so well as Father, nor even Adam. All she knew to do was try to seem authoritative and tell McNaught to be nice. She wished Father would come home. *I wonder if that widow, Marguerite Sandrine, followed him to Syracuse. If I read the signs right last season, she's definitely set her cap for Albany Johnston.*

In the heat of the afternoon, Marianne retreated to her room for a respite. She began to hear how still the house was with only Hannah and Charles and a few more slaves about. There'd be no conversation at supper. No lovely attention from Marcel. No rudely overt gazes from Yves. The man was insufferable. He made her distinctly uncomfortable. Not nearly as fine-looking as his brother. Why, that faint scar running into his lip completely spoiled his looks. He seemed not so much to smile as to smirk at her. Sometimes it was all she could do not to stare at his mouth, waiting for that little half smile. Marianne ran her tongue over her upper lip. He was an outrageous flirt, and if Lindsay Morgan told the truth, a presumptuous lover. She was glad he was gone.

She threw herself onto her lounge and opened *Jane Eyre* to where she'd left off. Jane was entangled with this man St. John, and Marianne could not like him. So bloodless. Jane would be better off with the arrogant Mr. Rochester. Except for the inconvenient detail of the crazy wife in the attic. There was that. But still. Rochester had passion and vigor and . . . Well. It was fiction. Well-bred young women did not in real life marry such over-bearing, dangerous men. And she had no interest in a man as indifferent to human suffering, and to the opin-ions of womankind, as Yves Chamard. He hadn't any sympathy for Peter, hadn't even asked about Sylvie.

Marcel, however—he was handsome, and he was kind. Nothing domineering in *his* manner. Marcel was the one who crossed the river in the night to bring Gabriel to Sylvie's side. He was the man she should encourage.

Actually, she didn't want to marry. And why should she? She was wealthy herself. She didn't need a man's money, nor his name. And a wedding would mean sub-mitting herself to a husband. No way around it, the hus-band ruled the marriage.

But loneliness did have its weight in this decision. Adam had his own life. Father had his friends and his work. She did not like the vision of herself dried up and virginal and alone. But neither did she want merely to be some man's ornament, some man's breeder. Surely Marcel displayed a mild temperament, was not of a dictatorial nature.

Well, if I do marry eventually, and Father seems to think I've dallied too long already, Marcel would do very well.

The sensual and heavy scent of magnolias, ever pre-sent from May until August, weighed on her. The perpet-ual light sweat from living through a Louisiana summer dampened the chemise between her breasts and made her acutely conscious of her body. Again she rubbed her palm where Yves Chamard had so boldly stroked it.

She shook her head. *I should bestir myself.* She retrieved her sketch pad and began to draw. A quirked smile with

a small straight scar quickly took shape under her pencil.
She tossed the pad aside. She'd go riding. No, it was too
hot. She'd take a bath. Wash her hair.

"Hannah?" she called. And so the day passed, Marianne
as unaccustomed to discontent as she was to idleness.

In the cool of the evening, Marianne wondered what
to do with herself. Her fingers were damp on the piano
keys, so she abandoned the sonatina she was learning.
No one to talk to. She missed Adam. And Father. And
Marcel. But not his brother, she assured herself. Maybe
she'd wander down to the garden. Joseph would be
there and they could talk awhile.

Or she could look in on Peter. That's what she'd do.

With new purpose, she strode across the hall to the
old schoolroom where Adam and she had been miser-
ably instructed in their youth by a series of pinched-
nosed tutors. One very proper, very starchy lady had
even taken a switch to Adam's bare legs. She'd been
trying to teach him how to eat like a gentleman. He'd
gotten the giggles and snorted milk out his nose all over
Madam's best brown frock. To this day, Adam declared
it had been worth a switching to see the look on her face.

Slate and chalk in hand, Marianne marched down to
the quarters. There were no idle hands on a plantation,
not among the slaves. She had to find something Peter
could do with his crippled feet and mangled left hand.
Of course, it was illegal, this teaching a slave to read. But
once he already knew how, what could anyone do about
it? It seemed a small risk. Who would know?

This will be fun, she thought.

The thick horde of buzzing flies had dissipated from
Peter's cabin now that he was healing. What set his cabin
off from the others was that it was inhabited before dark.
This time of year, the slaves toiled fifteen hours through

the long days, and they still labored in the fields in the last hour of daylight.

Marianne heard Peter's voice as she approached. "I's full, Mammy, I keep telling you. You gone make me fat as a hog, you don quit dis now."

Marianne stepped into the room and Lena got up from her chair. "Evenin, Miss Marianne. You come in and set, I'll get you a piece of dis pie Pearl brung over," Lena coaxed.

"My mammy gots to feed somebody, miss," Peter said.

"I'd love a piece. Look here, Peter," she said. "I've brought you a slate. You know what this is for?"

"No'm, I don."

"I'm going to teach you to read, and this is how we start."

Lena and Peter looked at her stunned. "You gone teach Petie to read?" Lena's eyes were huge and alight. "You gone teach him to read?" she said again.

"Yes. What kind of pie?"

"It peach. Don' nobody down here in de quarters can read."

"Evette sent blackberry up to the house." Marianne reached for the thick slice of pie, so dense it kept its shape in her hand. "First, Peter, take the chalk. Try drawing a little to get the feel of it."

Peter held the slate against his knees with his bandaged hand, took the chalk in the other. He looked at the mistress. "You gone let me read?"

She nodded at him, pie bulging one cheek. "Go ahead."

The only drawing Peter had ever done was with a stick in the sand. He pressed down so hard that the chalk broke, and he dropped the slate on his bed like it was hot. "Oh Lawse, Miss Marianne. I's sorry."

"Don't worry. Chalk breaks all the time. Try it again." Lightly this time, Peter drew the chalk across the slate in a smooth curved line. He held it up to show his grandmother, and Lena nodded. The two of them might have been examining the Holy Scrolls, so solemn were they.

Marianne finished the pie and wiped her hands on the cloth Lena offered. "Now let me show you." The first lesson began as she drew a large A on the slate.

It was nearly dark when they stopped. Marianne knew there were no secrets in the quarters, so she didn't ask Peter and Lena to keep this to themselves. They were both exhilarated; they'd need to talk about it.

She stepped across the alleyway to Joseph's cabin to ask him to walk her through the gloaming back to the house. She wasn't afraid, but she too was excited. She'd tell Joseph how smart Peter was. Already he could draw the first five letters perfectly.

Joseph was gratifyingly speechless when she told him what she was up to with Peter, and she chattered on happily. When they reached the edge of the verandah, the gaslights from the house spilling their glow out the parlor doors, Joseph stopped. "You sho dis be all right wid de master?"

She squeezed her old friend's arm. "It distracts Peter from his pain. Anyway, Father isn't here, Joseph, remember? By the time he comes home the end of August, Peter will be reading."

The next several days, Marianne hurried down to Peter's cabin first thing after breakfast to continue the lessons. They broke in the heat of the day for Peter to rest. He was a long way from being whole yet. After supper, Marianne reappeared at the cabin with more chalk and a kerosene lantern. The two of them were nearly breathless at the thrill of this illicit project. Lena sat with them after she'd finished her tasks for the day, marveling that a boy of her own was learning letters.

Chapter 12

After corn cakes and fried trout, Gabriel took leave of Tante Josephine, Musette, Ariane, and his Simone. He was off to collect his mother and sister from the lake, and when he returned, he and Simone would become man and wife.

The others granted the two of them only a moment's semiprivacy to say their good-byes, so Gabriel contented himself with a rather chaste kiss. He walked down the oak alley to the levee and turned back to look for Simone on the gallery. She touched her lips with her fingers and held her hand out to him.

At the levee, he hesitated, suddenly anxious. He wanted to go back, to hold Simone to him one more time, but of course that was nonsense. He'd be back in three or four days.

With two men to row him across the river, he set out for Magnolias Plantation. He'd borrow a horse there, and he hoped Marcel and Yves were still Adam Johnston's guests, and that they would ride with him to the lake to gather Maman and Nicolette. And Pierre, of course.

No sooner was the boat running downstream than the

two slaves, George and Hunter, threw off their shirts. Their dark skin shone with sweat in the heat, and they wiped their faces with their kerchiefs. Gabriel pulled his hat low to shield his eyes from the sun's glare and from sight of the rapid swirling brown water at the boat's sides. His hands gripped between his legs, he began to recite the 206 bones of the human body to distract himself from the incomprehensibly massive river.

Half an hour downstream, the slaves began to angle the boat across the width of the river to reach the east bank. A flatboat riding the central current began to close in on them. George and Hunter murmured to themselves, and Gabriel looked up at the tension in their voices.

He followed their gaze to the fast-approaching flatboat. It seemed typical enough, if not so common these days: a large platform of logs tied into a raft to transport goods and the logs themselves to New Orleans. "What's the matter?"

George and Hunter began to pull hard toward the nearer shore, their own west bank, but they were only two in a small boat with little surface to accept the river's push. "Them's bad 'uns," George panted.

Gabriel looked again. Certainly the flatboat men had a nasty reputation as rogues and rapscallions, but they appeared to be rather idly guiding the boat in the current. What did George and Hunter see that was so alarming?

"Look dere, M'sieur," Hunter said. He nodded his head again toward the raft. Gabriel looked more intently. There, along the back edge of the flatboat, black women and men sat chained together in a row. "Dem's slavers, sho."

"But you're with me," Gabriel began to explain and then stopped as the men on the raft, with surprising efficiency, launched a large rowboat with six men in it over the side. The helmsman pointed the boat right at them.

Hunter and George put their backs into the oars, but the other boat closed the distance rapidly. The pursuers had plenty of river to run them down, it being as wide as four cane fields along here, and the six flatboat men were fresh and determined.

The boat approached and Gabriel stood to his full height. He wore a gentleman's breeches, waistcoat, and frock coat. His boots were fresh polished, and he himself was often mistaken for white. Protection enough for George and Hunter, he was sure. The slavers would go on their way once they understood these men were not runaways but slaves from Toulouse on their mistress's bidding. As he assumed a stern and authoritative expression, he wondered if Tante Josie had remembered to write the men a pass.

"'Hoy there," one of the raft men called. As the larger boat bumped into theirs, Gabriel pushed at it with his foot.

"Gentlemen, you seem to have deliberately run us down. Account for yourselves."

A filthy, yellow-toothed man in the bow grinned and tilted his head at the man nearest him, who jumped into Gabriel's boat without so much as a good morning to you.

"You will leave this boat at once," Gabriel began, but the boarder, shorter than Gabriel and therefore with a lower center of gravity, ignored him and caught a line the grinning man tossed him. The raft man secured the line to the oarlock, ensuring the boats would not drift apart.

"This is no more than piracy. You will disembark," Gabriel commanded.

He simply could not grasp the man's lack of fear, his

total indifference to his authority. When the boarder clapped a hand on Hunter's shoulder, Gabriel at last understood Hunter and George had been right to run for shore.

"Let me go," Hunter hollered. "I don be no runaway. You—"

Gabriel swung the boarder around and ducked as the intruder threw his fist at Gabriel's head. Gabriel then delivered his renowned right punch to the man's jaw. The slaver reeled, falling back on Hunter. With George's help, Hunter heaved the brute up and threw him into the river.

The man's confederates paid no heed to his screams and pleas for rescue as he whirled away into the current, sinking, struggling, and sinking again. Four of the remaining five men flooded onto Gabriel's boat, kicking and fisting and cursing. Gabriel landed many a blow, Hunter and George struggled, and all the while Gabriel was conscious of the swift current pulling the boats along, a current that could suck a man under in less than a minute.

Two of the rafters grappled Gabriel to the bottom of the boat and another trained a pistol on him. The other two had George and Hunter in headlocks, knives held at their throats.

"This is a mistake," Gabriel said, wiping blood from his mouth. "These men belong to my aunt, Mrs. DeBlieux of Toulouse Plantation, not more than ten miles upriver. If you're looking for runaways, these are not they."

"What we gone do with the fancy man?" one of the rafters said. "He ain't worth nothing to us."

The man with the pistol spat over the side. "Let Monroe decide that." He tossed the men a rope. "He's a fighter. Best tie him up. Them others too. They're prime stock."

Gabriel kicked as the man tried to get the rope around him, sending him overboard, though the ruffian grabbed hold of the side of the boat before the river took him. Gabriel seized the other man by the ankle and yanked. The raft man fell, hitting his head on the oarlock, and he was out cold. The odds were better now. Gabriel was up and poised to lunge—

The pistol fired. Gabriel kept coming. The pistol fired again, and this time he was thrown back to the bottom of the boat, hardly aware he'd been shot.

A cold steel barrel ground into Gabriel's cheek. The pistol man grinned. "You got any more fight in you, I'll have to kill you. Monroe won't say nothing about it, neither."

Gabriel lay still. They had him, for now.

The rowboat was taking on water from the pistol shot having gone through the bottom. George and Hunter were quickly trussed. Next the men double-roped Gabriel and shoved him into their own boat. They kicked the rowboat off. It'd likely sink before the current pushed it ashore.

Back at the raft, more men took them aboard. Two kept pistols on him as Gabriel tied a handkerchief around his upper arm where the ball had gone clean through the muscle. Thank God it missed the bone. When he was finished, they cuffed his hands.

A rougher lot of men Gabriel had never seen. The slaves along the back edge of the flatboat were subdued, cowed by the rafters' violence, actual and threatened. With chains threaded through the ankle and wrist shackles they wore, they sat with their hands between their knees, their heads bowed. The women did not dare make eye contact with any of the rafters, fearing they'd be taken from amongst the other slaves to relieve what was no more than an itch to these brutes.

A lanky rafter, dressed in torn jeans and a stained canvas vest over his calico shirt, chewed on his cigar. With a pistol hanging loosely from his hand, he ambled over to examine his latest captives. He kicked at Gabriel's fine boots. "What you got here, Wilson?"

"He talks pretty as he looks, Monroe. Reckon we's among our betters."

Monroe took the cigar out of his mouth. "'S'at so? What's your name, fella?"

Gabriel's hands were bound and he struggled to stand. Wilson shoved him back to his knees. Gabriel was so angry he truly saw these men through a red haze. *Keep your head*, he told himself, his teeth so tightly clamped they ached. *They can't take a white man—and that's what they think I am. Handle it with your wits, not your fists, Chamard.*

His knees might be on the deck, but he straightened his back and looked in the man's startling yellow eyes, as flat and depthless as a reptile's. "I am Dr. Gabriel Chamard. My father is Bertrand Chamard of Cherleu Plantation. My aunt is Josephine DeBlieux of Toulouse. These men belong to Madame DeBlieux, and she will not tolerate their mistreatment."

Monroe seemed not at all anxious about the lady's displeasure. He walked around Gabriel, looking him over. "Fine-looking fellow," he announced to his men. "I seen his type before. Real pretty."

Standing behind, he spat the juice from his chawed cigar onto the top of Gabriel's head. The brown sludge began to ooze into his ear and Gabriel's gorge rose, but he would not give this man the satisfaction of wiping it away.

"Look at that hair," Monroe said, walking back around to the front of him. "Got a little curl to it, don't it?" He used the barrel of his pistol to raise Gabriel's chin. "And got them real shiny dark eyes."

"Know what makes a man that pretty, boys?" He had their attention. "If he got a white daddy and a real pretty brown mama. That what you come from, pretty boy?"

Gabriel tossed his head to release his chin from the pistol. "I am no slave, sir. You would do well to release me and these two men."

"Ooh, he do talk nice," the one called Wilson said. "Don't reckon he's much use to us, though, Monroe. Ain't nobody gone buy a white man."

Quick as a shot, Monroe snaked an arm around Wilson's neck and half choked him. "What you think I been telling you? He ain't white. He got enough blood in him to make him look white, but a haircut and a few days in the Luzianne sun fix that."

He shoved Wilson away. "Chain him up with the rest. We'll have us a lesson in sun browning. If he don't darken up, well, all the worse for him."

The raftsmen hauled the three captives to the back of the flatboat where the others were chained together. "Take the shirt off the fancy one," Monroe hollered across the deck.

The men added Gabriel and Hunter to the chains running through the shackles. The wrist chain reached its length and no amount of crowding would stretch it to include George's iron bracelet.

"He ain't going nowhere, anyhow," a gap-toothed white man said. He pointed a finger at George. "Set there and don't move."

George seemed dazed. He trembled, but his eyes did not focus when he looked at Gabriel.

The unfortunates hardly stirred throughout the blazing hot day. Gabriel was glad there were no children among them. They could not have taken the heat and the thirst. No telling what these men would do to a child who fussed. Every man and woman suffered in silence, sweating until their bodies had nothing left to sweat, and still no one brought them water.

The muddy river only four feet below him, Gabriel eyed it warily. It shamed him to be scared of the water. He could swim quite well, in a bayou, a lake, or a stream—but the enormous mass of this river overwhelmed him. As the hours wore on, however, with his skin burning and the sun sucking the moisture from his mouth, the fear became a small thing. He imagined himself plunging his scorched body into the river, drinking his fill before he drowned.

In the late afternoon, George broke. He heaved dry sobs, and violent trembling shook his body. Likely he has a wife and children on Toulouse, Gabriel thought. And he might never see them again. Gabriel reached for George's shoulder, and pulled two other sets of hands along with his own. He dropped the hands back to their laps.

"George," he rasped, his voice hoarse, his eyes watching the idle raftsmen. "Hold on, man. They'll be looking for us. Madame DeBlieux will send out a hue and cry we've been taken. We'll get home again."

Hunter shook his head. "No, M'sieu. We be on de block in New Orleans 'fore she know we not coming back."

Gabriel darted an impatient look at him. "We have every reason to hope. I am a freeman. I will take you home again."

George did not hear, or did not listen. With despair stamped on his features, he scooted toward the edge of the raft. Gabriel realized his intention and tried to grab him, but the chains confounded him.

George, with bound hands, slipped over the side into the Mississippi River.

Gabriel shouted, "Get a line! Man overboard! Get the boat!" Two of the river men set their playing cards down and walked over to the edge of the flatboat.

"Get a rope, somebody," the one called Wilson said, not even a suggestion of excitement in his voice. A man sauntered over to a supply of coiled hemp and fumbled for the longest one. Meanwhile, his confederates watched George flounder in the water ten feet, then twenty, then thirty feet behind them.

"Save him, damn you!" Gabriel roared. He lunged to follow George into the water—he could swim for both of them—but the human chain held him on deck.

The rope man came back to the edge and began tying a lasso to throw out. George, struggling now to stay afloat, sank below the water, emerged with his hands stretched out toward the raft, then sank again for the last time.

Wilson shifted the chaw in his cheek, spat a stream of tobacco juice into the river, and ambled over to his cards.

Gabriel stared at the swallowing, devouring waves of the Mississippi.

Chapter 13

Marianne came in from a twilight stroll in the garden to be met by Charles at the door.

"You have a visitor, Miss Marianne. Someone from Toulouse. A Mr. Gale."

She looked at him, puzzled. She knew Toulouse, of course. The DeBlieux plantation just upriver. Charles opened the sliding cypress doors for her and she entered the parlor. A young man with sandy hair stood and made a stiff halfbow.

"Miss Johnston," he said. "I'm Robert Gale. Me and my brother Andrew, we're the overseers over to Toulouse."

"Yes, Mr. Gale. Please sit down."

"I come from Madame DeBlieux. She's worried herself sick and sent me over to find out when you seen her nephew last. That'd be Dr. Chamard, Gabriel Chamard. See, Madame thought he'd be back with the family by Wednesday, maybe Thursday latest. But here it is Friday night, and she ain't heard from him."

"Mr. Gale, I'm sorry I have no news for you. Dr. Chamard has not appeared here this week at all. Perhaps Dr. Chamard went to the lake?"

"My brother Andrew's gone down there to look for him. See, the two slaves that was rowing the doctor across the river, they ain't come back either."

Marianne stared at Mr. Gale. Tales of abducting slaves to sell them were common enough. "Surely to God you don't think they've met with misfortune? Dr. Chamard looks like a gentleman, he is a gentleman. He's a freedman. No one would . . ."

"No'm, I hope none of those river rats got him. But we'll see what Andrew finds out at the lake. Likely they's all playing cards and enjoying theyselves."

"You'll let me know, immediately, please, Mr. Gale?"

"Yes'm. Soon's I know something."

Marianne offered the downstairs guest room to Mr. Gale so that he wouldn't have to travel in the dark, but he declined. "I got a crew of men at the dock. We'll get on back across tonight."

Marianne stood on the gallery watching the starlight on the river, far too disturbed to go to bed. She admired Dr. Chamard very much. She liked him; she hoped they could become friends. But there were so many ways a man could go missing. Slavers could have got him. The river could have got him.

At the lake, the very first morning after he'd arrived with Yves and Marcel, Adam called on Nicolette Chamard. She received him cordially though he had come without her brothers. She wore a dove-gray morning gown with blue ribbons on the bodice, a blue *tignon* on her head. Her gray eyes shone when she told him good morning, how kind of him to call.

"Would you care to walk, before the heat claims the day?" he invited.

"I would, Monsieur." She nodded to her maid for her

parasol and accepted Adam's arm. The maid trailing behind them, they took the crushed oyster-shell path along the lakeshore, the mixed pines, magnolias, and oaks shading them.

Adam and Nicolette fell into step and quickly discovered a compatibility of temperament and taste. On not every topic did they agree, but every subject engaged them. They hardly noticed when they reached the end of the path and turned back toward Nicolette's cottage, so intent were they on their dispute about the merits of dramatic plays versus opera.

At the foot of her raised porch, Adam offered his arm to help her mount the stairs. She accepted, and he dared to place his hand over hers. Nicolette smiled at him.

"May I see you tonight? After your performance? We could have supper."

"Yves and Marcel have asked me, Mr. Johnston. Could you not join us?"

Yves appeared in the doorway, as stern a look on his face as Adam had ever seen. "Come in, Nicolette," he said. "You too, Johnston."

Adam bristled. "Miss Chamard and I merely—"

"Gabriel is missing."

The family—Cleo and Pierre, Nicolette, Yves and Marcel—gathered in Cleo's cottage. Yves made Adam and Mr. Gale welcome as well. They would need every head and every body to find Gabriel.

They first dealt with the possibility that the small boat might have been lost to the river. Steamboat pilots constantly watched for shoals and currents and changes in the color of the water. Surely they would see a rowboat in time to avoid it. Yet a big boat ran over a smaller one only a while back, Pierre reminded them.

Cleo, barely holding herself together, shuddered.

"Gabriel doesn't like the river," she said, as much to herself as to the others.

"Maman, that happened in a rainstorm," Nicolette reminded her. "Mr. Gale said the river was clear that day."

Cleo nodded, her hands clasped together in her lap. Pierre wrapped his arm through hers and squeezed her knotted fists.

"They were to have traveled from Toulouse to Magnolias, one dock to the other," Marcel said. "No need, I think, to consider brigands on the road. River rats seem to me the most likely culprits. Two prime slaves at the oars, and no one armed. Or did Gabriel carry his pistol?"

"Madame DeBlieux thought of that. She had me look for his pistol up to Chateau Chanson," Mr. Gale said. "It was in the drawer by the bed."

"They'd have been easy pickings if a crew of slavers happened by."

The thought hung in the air for a moment. "I think we should split up," Yves suggested. "Marcel and Adam, down to New Orleans. The stolen slaves will surely show up at one of the markets, maybe even at the Exchange. If Gabriel, or the slaves, turn up there, you'll be on the spot."

"I reckon I ought to go with them," Mr. Gale said. "Hunter and George are my men. I can recognize them, testify they belong to Toulouse."

"And you?" Marcel asked Yves.

"If they have trouble selling Gabe in New Orleans, they might take him upriver. The market at Natchez is the biggest one between New Orleans and Virginia."

"Perhaps I should go with you," Adam said, "rather than you searching on your own."

Someone knocked on the front door and Cleo's maid let in a boy of perhaps sixteen. "Uncle Andrew?"

Mr. Gale, the co-overseer from Toulouse, stood up. "You bring news, Larry?"

"Yes, sir. Daddy sent me to tell you they found the rowboat. It come ashore way downstream, past the Morgan place. It had a hole in the bottom. Daddy said it looked like a bullet done it."

Nicolette balled her handkerchief in her fist and pressed it against her mouth. Yves did not take it amiss when Adam Johnston comforted her by taking her other hand and speaking softly to her.

"He's taken, then," Marcel said with finality.

"Now we know where to look for him. Adam," Yves said, "you'll be needed in New Orleans to cover all the little auctions, and there are the wharves where the captains grab up any able-bodied man they can to sail their ships. You know the docks?"

Adam nodded. "I know them well."

"Let's go, then," Yves said. The men stood, ready to leave on the instant. Cleo, startled at the suddenness of their move, grabbed at Pierre.

"Sweetheart," Pierre said. "I'm going north with Mr. Chamard."

Yves crossed the room to Cleo's side. The grief on her beautiful face broke his heart.

"Monsieur Lafitte," Yves said. "I would take it as a kindness if you stayed with my sister and Madame Cleo."

"Please, Pierre," Cleo said to him, her eyes wide and fearful. "I don't think I can bear this without you."

Pierre looked at the younger men, all of them white. Yves knew he would realize a dark-skinned freedman like himself would be a hindrance, not a help.

"Truly, Monsieur," Marcel said, "we will cover New Orleans, inside and out."

Yves saw it galled him, but Pierre relaxed his stiff posture and nodded. "Very well."

"Have you a pistol in the house, Monsieur LaFitte?" Marcel asked. "I should like to borrow it, if I may."

Marcel, Adam, Mr. Gale, and his nephew rode south. Yves let them think he rode to Natchez simply to cover all the possibilities. In truth, he had a stop to make first. If anyone had heard about rogue slavers, it would be Joseph and his network.

Gabriel's head ached perpetually from dehydration and the glare of the sun. He'd thought he knew what the life of a slave was like, but nothing had prepared him for the abject subjugation he endured. Chained to more than a dozen slaves, there was no "I" separate from the other miserable souls.

The boss, Monroe, moored to some big trees every evening, and he and a couple of others left the raft to go hunting. They needed meat, but he stalked another prey as well. In the morning, he generally came back with one or two slaves he'd highjacked from the nearest planta- tion. This promised to be a most profitable trip, Monroe boasted. Once in New Orleans, he'd break up the raft and sell the timber like in the old days before the steam- boats. Then he'd take all this chattel to auction. A very profitable trip.

When Gabriel began to tan rather than burn, the boss ceased kicking him. He might make a sale of the dandy Negro after all. "Wilson, strop your razor. Get this girly hair off him, see if it don't grow back kinky like it ought to."

His shorn scalp taking the full brunt of the sun, Gabriel's head pounded. They were all suffering without even hats to protect them, but Hunter, Gabriel thought, shrank every day. His flesh wasted from the short rations and the inadequate water Monroe allowed them. Worse, though, Hunter sat cross-legged on the deck with bowed head and bent back. He had given up.

Marie, a tiny woman farther down the chain, moaned

and babbled. She'd been carrying a basket of eggs along the river road, she'd told them, when the thugs grabbed her. Three children she'd left behind. Now grief and the unrelenting sun made her delirious.

"We need water over here," Gabriel called to the group playing cards on top of a hogshead. His voice cracked, his throat was so dry. The men ignored him. "She needs water, or she'll die!" he shouted.

The raftsmen had already made it clear when Gabriel had protested the slaves' treatment earlier that they would not heed a colored man. The dandy was "uppity," that's what they said, and now they ignored him, studying their cards.

Gabriel turned to Hunter. "Stand up." The man stared at him with glazed eyes. Gabriel pulled at the chain. "Stand up, damn you! All of you, stand up."

He pulled on the chain, reached across Hunter, and yanked hard at the next slave. "Get to your feet. You're men, not beasts. Get up!"

The men and women roused as if coming from hibernation. They raised themselves one by one, each helping the other manage the shackles.

Wilson, twenty feet away, slapped his cards down. "What the hell?"

Gabriel had the slaves on their feet, even Marie, but now what? His head ached so he could hardly think. He stepped toward the men lolling around the card game. Hunter necessarily followed him, and then the others. The line advanced, one stumbling step at a time.

Several of the white men tossed their cards and jumped to their feet, fumbling for their guns and stepping back and away from the hollow-eyed slaves. Wilson drew his pistol and brandished it at the coffle.

Gabriel kept coming. Wilson pointed the gun at his

chest. Gabriel swayed on his feet, but he stopped. The others halted alongside him.

"We've got to have more water. What good are we to you, if we all die before you can sell us?"

Monroe emerged from his tent and assessed the situation. He stepped around the kegs of goods piled on deck and pushed Wilson's gun hand down. "They ain't no use to us dead. Get 'em some water."

"And shade," Gabriel said. "This woman has sunstroke, and the others aren't far from it."

He met Monroe's narrowed eyes. Never in his life had he lowered his gaze because a white man looked at him. And it could be, Gabriel thought, that never in this man's life had a Negro stared back at him.

Monroe finally spoke. "I got my eye on you, pretty boy." He headed back to the shade of his tent. "Rig a tarp, and give 'em a bucket with a line on it," he said to the raftsmen.

Once the tarp was up, Gabriel had the slaves coil themselves under its shade. He managed to keep Marie near him, and their first ladle of water was for her. The second and third ladles Gabriel poured over her head and chest to cool her. Only then did he pass the bucket along to the others. When it was empty, he refilled it himself, pulling two men along with him as he stretched the chain to the edge of the raft. He lowered the bucket into the river and passed it amongst the people again and again. Once they'd had their fill, they poured bucket after bucket over their bodies.

Clearheaded once more, Gabriel began to plan. He did not see how the rogues could sell him in New Orleans. He was educated. His hands were soft, his manners as refined as any white planter's. He had a tongue in his head.

Gabriel shuddered at the image that passed through his mind. There was a way to silence a slave. With sufficient brutality, and a knife, the man Monroe could ensure he never spoke again.

How could Monroe make a profit from a man like him? He could put him out as a boxer. There were arenas for such sport between desperate men. But Gabriel did not intend to show them any more of his physical talents until the time was right for escape.

There were always ships in the harbor at New Orleans. Maybe Monroe meant to sell him to a ship's captain who had lost too many sailors to the yellow jack to be overly nice about whom he took on. Gabriel saw himself jumping ship, swimming through the river, his fear of the deep moving water inconsequential compared to his desire to be free.

But what if they kept him chained until the ship sailed? He might labor for months before he could return. No, once away from New Orleans, Gabriel could bargain with the captain. His father would ransom him for far more than a mere slave sailor could profit him. He'd offer to serve as ship's surgeon until they docked in England or France. Gabriel would be free, eventually.

But he didn't see how he could save the other poor people caught in this trap. This man Monroe would take them to one of the lesser slave markets in and around New Orleans, one where the brokers did not examine the false documents of ownership too carefully. Equally unscrupulous buyers would take up the bargains one by one, enriching Monroe's pockets and gaining for themselves despairing, but seasoned, laborers.

They would need their hope if they were to survive. Gabriel began to talk to the people around him, to ask them where they were from and how they were taken, to remind them they were husbands, wives, mothers, fathers. They were more than this man's slaves.

Chapter 14

Yves retraced his dusty journey from Magnolias, turning over all the possibilities. He knew his brother. Gabriel was proud. And he was a fighter. It would not be easy for anyone to abduct him.

How would a slaver unload a commodity like Gabriel? Too high-toned, too soft-handed to pass as a laborer. Even if you could stop him from talking. Once Gabriel opens his mouth, Yves thought, the slave brokers won't want anything to do with him. Gabriel would be nothing but trouble for the brokers if they were caught with a freedman, a literate, articulate freedman in their auction.

That worried Yves. What will they do with him then? The easiest course would be to knock him over the head and toss him in the river. It was hard to keep his hopes up as he urged his horse back to Magnolias.

Gaslights lit the windows of the lower floor when Yves arrived. He passed by the house, though he strained to catch sight of Miss Johnston, perhaps reading or sewing in the parlor. He left his tired mount at the stables to be looked after. From there, he took a lantern to light his way to the quarters.

People were still about, talking, whittling, tending to

the last of the day's chores in the twilight. Children ran through the alleyway chasing a ball somebody had made for them out of old cowhide and sinew.

Yves recognized Joseph's cabin as the one with the hydrangeas on either side of the steps. He knocked on the door, aware of the slaves' eyes on him. He wondered if they knew who he was, what he did. It was better for him if they didn't, but he couldn't worry about that now, not with Gabriel missing.

Joseph opened the door. "Come inside, M'chie."

Yves set his lantern on the table and quickly told Joseph all he knew. "What have you heard?" he asked the old man. "Any word of a light-colored man taken?"

"Dey's plenty a news. Folks missing all up and down dis river, seem like. And dey ain't runaways. I'd know dat. Dey's been taken."

"Where are they headed?"

"Dey's goin downriver all right, 'cause dat's how the missing word come, one after de other down de river. Must be five or six gone below here. Dey's a bold gang, dey is."

"What about Dr. Chamard? You hear anybody say they've seen him?"

"Nobody say nothing 'bout a white man. Nor a near-white man neither."

They kept their thoughts to themselves a few minutes, and then Joseph said, "What can dey do wid a man like Dr. Chamard?" He shook his head.

"Exactly," Yves agreed.

"Les us go on down to Foreman's place. You wid me, we can use de lantern and it be faster. We talk to Rufus, de butler dere, if we can get him out de house. He know 'bout everthing goin' on, and he likely to tell me more dan he would a gentleman coming to de door."

They lured the butler out with a ruse about raccoons getting into the underhouse. People on the Foreman place, Rufus told them, had sighted a barge, a raft nearly big as the big house, floating downstream a few days back. Don't see many barges like that anymore, he said. It was midday, though, the barge was out in the main stream, and nobody noticed what cargo it carried except a few bales of cotton and some hogshead caskets piled high.

With the days marked out for him in the lantern-lit sand, Rufus connected the disappearance of a slave from the Foremans' and another from the next place down with the night after the barge floated past.

Back at Magnolias, Yves made his decision. Marcel, Adam, and Mr. Gale had New Orleans covered, and Marcel could find willing hands to help them. He'd try to pick up Gabe's trail on the way to Natchez.

The flatboat men used to travel south on the river, and then return north on foot by way of the Natchez Trace. If the slavers had no luck unloading Gabriel in New Orleans, they might try to get rid of him in some out of the way part of the Trace, no questions asked. First light, he'd be on his way.

He left Joseph in the quarters. The lights were still on downstairs at the house. Charles would let him in, fix him a late supper. His boot heel clacked on the brick verandah and a movement in the shadows startled him.

Marianne had not seen Yves' approach. She'd been stargazing, a light shawl over her head protecting her from the mosquitoes. When she heard the intruder's steps, and from the corner of her eye saw his sudden movement, her reaction was faster than thought. She realized it was not a bear or a puma or any other beast—indeed, she recognized Yves Chamard's figure almost immediately—but the yelp was out of her before she could stop it.

Yves strode to her chair and knelt at her side. He put a hand out as if to touch her. "It's me, Marianne."

Flustered and embarrassed, she stood up and drew away from him. "I'm not accustomed to being snuck up on, Mr. Chamard."

Yves stood and stepped back two paces. "I'm sorry to have startled you, Miss Johnston." He made his bow, as stiff a one as she'd ever been offered.

Marianne knew she had been harsh, rude even. But rudeness should not perturb Yves Chamard! Still, she was glad the dark hid what must be a raging blush, for her skin was afire—just from his almost-touch. *Damn the man*, she thought. *And I'll damn well cuss in my own head if I want to.*

She gathered herself and realized Yves' irregular appearance must have some import. "Your brother? You've found Dr. Chamard?"

Even from five feet, she could smell the horse on him, and beneath that, the scent of sandalwood. She took a step closer, the combination of man scents drawing her.

He shook his head. "The others are in New Orleans looking for him. I'm heading out in the morning, to see if I can intercept them headed north on the Natchez Trace. If they don't take him to the docks."

"Take him?"

"It seems likely he has been abducted. There have been a number of slaves who've disappeared the last few days on this stretch of the river."

"Not runaways," she said. Marianne realized she'd made a statement, not asked a question, and she had no business knowing there had been no more runaways in the area. But Joseph could have told her. That's what she'd say if he asked her how she knew. She was unaccustomed to secrets, and she would have to learn to watch her tongue.

"No. We don't think they're runaways."

"Come inside. You've ridden all the way from the lake, you'll need your supper."

Yves insisted no fires be lit for him this time of night, but a cold plate would be most welcome. Charles donned his formal jacket to serve him ham and succotash, corn bread and fig preserves. In front of Marianne he placed a bowl of grapes; very astute of him, as always, she thought, to prevent Mr. Chamard the discomfort of eating alone in company.

Marianne insisted on hearing all the news, and for once Mr. Chamard did not condescend. Yves explained all they knew, all they suspected, and every nuance of their reasoning. One aspect of Gabriel's predicament Yves hesitated to bring up, but Marianne thought of it herself.

"If slavers do have him," she said, "I wonder what they can do with him. He will not pass for a slave, a cultured man like him, with his light skin."

Yves' eyes were on her. Rankled, she raised her chin. "Why is it, Mr. Chamard, that every time I show the least intelligence, you stare at me as if I were a prize pig?"

That crooked smile again. He was infuriating.

"Miss Johnston, you misjudge me completely." Now his eyes swept over her, lingering not on her bosom— that would be unforgivable—but on her neck. Feeling stripped bare by his gaze, she resisted the urge to raise her hand to her throat.

Marcel never looked at her like this, like . . . like he could eat her. He didn't make her blood rush and her body tingle with lewd looks.

"Have you finished?" she said. She meant to be as rude as he. She scooted her chair back to rise, but Yves reached for the little silver bell near her own wineglass and rang it.

"I believe I'll have a slice of that cocoanut cake Charles mentioned."

She sat down and put her hands in her lap. She would stare at him every bite he took.

Charles delivered two plates of cake, as white as cake could be, with thick white seven-minute icing, the whole covered with finely grated, sweetened cocoanut.

"I don't believe I'll have any, Charles," Marianne said. She'd rather punish Yves by watching him eat. *He'll likely end up with icing on his lip, and I shall not tell him.* She found herself gazing at his mouth.

Yves made a show of lowering his fork, downcast, hurt, terribly hurt. "Won't you please join me, Miss Johnston? It has been a hellish long day, and I—"

"I couldn't, really, but please, Mr. Chamard. Enjoy yourself."

Yves stared at the cake in front of him. "It looks like very good cake." With the dejection of a child denied his supper, he slowly pushed it away.

"Oh for goodness' sake." She picked up her fork and cut into the cake.

Yves cheered up immediately. "Where do you suppose this cocoanut was grown?"

"Father or Adam could tell you, I'm sure. I'd guess Cuba."

Yves behaved himself, and for ten minutes they had a pleasant conversation. No leering or smirking or insensitive remarks. He wiped his mouth and pushed his chair back. Around the long table he walked, continuing his remarks about a horse race he'd seen.

When he reached Marianne's chair, she held her skirts ready to have her chair pulled out. Instead, Yves sat down in the chair next to her. He picked up her napkin, dipped it in her water glass, and then wiped seven-minute icing from the tip of her nose.

Marianne blushed crimson. She'd never been so humiliated.

"If you smirk," she said, "I'll never speak to you again."

She watched his mouth. He leaned in closer.

"I won't smirk."

His lips met hers, soft and warm and gentle. He moved his head and kissed her again, no pressure, no insistence, just sweetness.

He caught her lower lip with his teeth, and all the breath left her lungs. This was kissing.

He touched her upper lip with his tongue and she drew back, startled by the surge of sensation, but the next kiss reassured her. It was soft as the first one, and she sat still for another and another.

When he stopped, she let out a long sigh.

"Am I allowed to smile?" He was looking into her eyes, and the smile was definitely there, but not on his mouth. She checked on that.

"A small one, perhaps."

Oh my. Her heart flipped. It wasn't a smirk, though of course his scar pulled on his left upper lip just the littlest bit. *Why haven't I seen* that *smile before?* she thought.

Yves took her hand, turned her palm up, and raised it to his mouth. Marianne swallowed. Warmth suffused her entire body. Something was happening to her, something new and very disturbing.

"Thank you for dessert," Yves said. That teasing look was in his eye again, but this time, this time it was charming.

The next morning, Marianne woke early to the song of a mockingbird outside her window. Yves had escorted her to the bottom of the stairs when they left the dining room the night before. "Please forgive me. I've prolonged your evening, Miss Marianne. But I believe I'll have one of your father's cigars before I retire."

The renewed formality was welcome to her. How else could she have walked away from him? "Good night, Mr. Chamard."

She climbed the grand staircase feeling his eyes on her. At the top, she turned and looked back.

"Good night," he'd said.

After a blissful sleep, Marianne stretched and smiled, kisses and kisses and kisses on her mind. Freddie romped on her bed, grabbed her fingers in his mouth, and slobbered on them. She caught him up and hugged him. Even Freddie liked Yves.

She dressed with more care than she'd taken in months. Sitting at her mirror, she held up her amber earrings and turned her head to judge the effect. No, the pearls, she decided. Turned out in her favorite blue lawn dress, she went directly to the breakfast room eager to tell Yves she would write everyone she knew to look out for Gabriel, to be alert to rumors of a light-colored slave with soft hands.

No one in the dining room. Nor in the parlor, nor the library. She tried the back verandah. Where was he?

Charles was in his pantry polishing silver.

"Have you seen our guest this morning?" she asked.

"Yes'm. I have." He breathed onto the belly of a pitcher and rubbed at it again.

"Well, where is he?"

Charles looked at her, all his sixty-three years seeing right through her. She blushed, but she kept her chin up.

"He done gone. Had a quick breakfast down in the kitchen and lit out."

Marianne dropped her eyes. Of course, he needed to hurry on to look for Gabriel. But he hadn't said he'd go so early, without saying good-bye.

"He left you something."

Her pulse picked up and she looked at Charles. "What?"

"I put it in yonder."

She followed him into the dining room to a side table. Charles picked up a bouquet of wildflowers in a crystal vase. Queen Anne's lace and daisies and buttercups. "Dese here fo you," Charles said, forgetting his careful diction for the moment.

Marianne couldn't keep the big smile off her face.

Charles leaned a little toward her and said, "I likes dis Chamard."

Marianne set the bouquet on the table next to her throughout breakfast. Then she carried the vase to her room. She spent nearly three hours at her desk writing everyone she knew about Gabriel's disappearance. Some of the recipients no doubt would waste no sympathy on a colored man's plight, but many of them would. They would make inquiries along their stretch of the river. Someone might have heard something, anything, that would give them a clue about Gabriel.

With ink-stained fingers, Marianne called Charles to take her letters to the landing and personally hand over the packet to the mail boat himself. Then she paced, Freddie watching her with his big puppy eyes.

"Let's go outside," she told him, and he wagged a sleepy tail. "Come on, lazy."

They walked the garden paths until Marianne, careless of her hoops, plopped down on the cypress bench among the camellias, the bench with her mother's name burned into the back. The one where Yves had rudely taken her hand and chastised her about freely expressing her opinion.

Just what is his opinion? She'd hate to think he was as callous about slavery as most men were. She could not like a man who . . . *I'm being silly. It was just a few kisses. That's all.*

Chapter 15

Marianne found the days long. She worried about Gabriel, she missed Adam. She missed Yves Chamard. At odd moments through the day, and all the hours she lay awake in the hot night waiting for sleep, the feel of his lips on hers came back to her. Such sweet kisses, but a hint there of something else, hotter, more dangerous. She touched her finger to her lower lip. *I want more.*

Another sticky, sweltering day passed. After her responsibilities were met and the heat had abated somewhat, Marianne spent an hour with Peter. He knew the alphabet now, and some of the sounds the letters made. She thought the next step might be to show him a few simple words, like *cat* and *rat*, words that rhymed and showed how the sounds fit together. He was bright. He'd get it.

They worked until dusk when Marianne said good night. Hoping for a few minutes with Joseph before she went back to the empty house, she ambled across the alleyway to his cabin with the bright blue hydrangeas. He opened the door before she touched the step and motioned her in.

"I been watching for you. Come inside, Missy."

A single candle burned, and Marianne could at first barely see the people gathered around the plank table.

"Dis chair for you, Miss Marianne," Pearl said.

Evette, the cook, was there, and her man, Daniel, was it? Marianne recognized Joseph's daughter holding her sleeping grandbaby. The other three people Marianne did not know at all.

She looked her question at Joseph. He sat down on the bench across the table from her.

"Missy, dese folks need you help. We wouldn't ask we knew 'nother way."

"Who are these people?"

"Dis here be Bess and Elvin. Dat's dere boy Clem."

Marianne stared at the strangers. The man did not meet her eyes, but she knew he had been watching her. The woman sat on a cot. Her foot, wrapped round and round with ragging, rested in Evette's lap. The third figure was a boy clad only in stained, threadbare trousers.

"They're looking for a station house?"

"Dey come wid de law close behind 'em. I'd send fo de shepherd, but he gone from here."

What were they asking her to do? She had no idea where the next safe house was, nor how she would get them there. And she was a planter's daughter. What did they want from her?

"I knows it not fair to show you dis, Missy. I knows it. But you got to see why. Pearl, show her de boy."

Pearl guided the child to stand before Marianne and then turned him around. The skin on his back was torn and shredded.

Marianne put a hand over her mouth.

"I done what I see you do wid Petie, Miss Marianne," Pearl said. "I wash it good wid de witch hazel I find in you cellar, and rubbed de salve over it all."

"What in God's name?" Marianne said. "He's just a child."

"Yes'm," Joseph said. "It a tipped whip do dat to him. Dat's why dey run, befo de man at dat place do worse."

"And Miss Marianne," Pearl said, "Bess hurt her ankle bad. It swole up big as a punkin."

Evette began unwrapping the woman's foot to show her. Pearl held the candle close. The ankle was enormously swollen. If it was broken, at least the bone had not penetrated the skin. That likely would have been fatal. Perhaps it was only sprained. Marianne grasped the dirty bare foot and very carefully tried to move the ankle. Bess hissed in pain, but Marianne continued to feel the flesh, trying to imagine what lay beneath the swelling.

"I don't know. I think it's only a sprain, but I don't know. I wish we had some mustard. The kind with the black seeds." She realized she was talking to herself. "Pearl, comfrey is the best we can do. You know which herb that is?"

"Miss Marianne, I go in dere now, Mr. McNaught see me wid de lantern."

Marianne nodded. "I'll get it." She stood to go.

"Missy." Joseph stopped her. "We ain't asked you yet what we gone ask you."

"I thought—"

"No'm," Joseph said. "We need yo help with Mr. McNaught. We need you to lie fo us." Every eye in the room was on her.

"Wh . . . Joseph, you know I won't tell Mr. McNaught these people are here."

He shook his head. "We needs de wagon for dese folks. Bess, she cain't walk. And de boy in bad shape. He likely have fever by morning. We gots to move 'em on out o' here befo dey catched."

"A wagon? But then you'd have to have a horse, or a mule. Mr. McNaught won't—"

"Das why we needs you, Miss Marianne," Pearl said. "If you tells Mr. McNaught to give Joseph de wagon fo de day, we hide de family in de bottom and put things on top of 'em. Joseph drive de wagon away befo de men come after 'em."

Marianne swallowed. They were asking her to actively participate in helping slaves escape. Not just pretending not to know, as with Luke, not simply keeping McNaught occupied to give Luke a chance to get farther on. Actually conniving, planning, and plotting. This was against the law. And the law included even the privileged daughters of wealthy white planters. What would become of her, of her family, if she were caught aiding escaped slaves? She could hardly imagine how awful it could be. Jail? A trial? All Father's friends turning their backs on the Johnstons? Prison?

"Joseph, I can't. . . ." No one spoke. They simply gazed at her. Even Joseph did not attempt to persuade her.

"If I were ever caught . . ." Marianne stood in the center of the room, her hands clasped in front of her. Her eyes lit on the boy's. He sat in the corner where the candlelight barely reached him, staring at her.

"What did the little boy do?" she whispered to the still faces.

"Clem spill a bucket of molasses he was carrying," his mother said, her voice thick with anger and with fear for her child.

The candle flickered, the chimney whistled in the wind. No one stirred.

Marianne closed her eyes, but she could still feel theirs boring into her. Deeper into her than she had ever looked herself. What did they see? A comfortable white lady in a fine dress, with shoes on her feet, with ribbons in her hair? A woman who would not mistreat a slave, but who would stand aside and let another owner whip a child for spilling molasses?

Did they see a coward?

She could leave the cabin. She could walk back through the pecan grove and into the house, climb the stairs to her rose-brocaded room, and shut the door. Hannah would help her undress, unlace her boots, and pull off her silk stockings. She could lay her head on the feather pillow and close her eyes. Somehow, tomorrow these people would be gone. It would not be her problem. She might never hear of them again, might not ever know whether they were caught, whether the boy's back healed or was torn open again by an overseer with a tipped whip.

"It won't work," she said at last. "Mr. McNaught is too suspicious since Luke ran. I'll have to go with you."

While it was still dark, Joseph moved the family into a wagon in the barn. Pearl and Evette met them there with a spinning wheel from the weaving house. With a tarp over the escapees, baskets of flax and cotton and the spinner strategically placed, they waited for daylight.

Back at the house, Marianne told Charles she would be leaving at dawn to visit Martha Madison half a day's drive upriver. The Madisons were small farmers compared to the Johnstons, but she and Martha had known each other all their lives. They were friends. As for taking a wagon instead of the carriage—Martha had lost her spinning wheel in a small fire, and Magnolias had more of the essential devices than it needed. That would be the story.

Should McNaught inquire where the wagon and two of his slaves were, Charles would explain. Not that it was any of the overseer's business, which no doubt Charles would imply in that practiced disdainful way only he could effect without reproach. The plan should work. She really would deliver an unexpected and unwanted spinning wheel to Martha after they'd helped the escapees.

Just before daylight, then, Marianne left her room. She wore her second-best traveling costume, the blue one with the black braid, the skirt supported by multiple crinolines instead of a hoop. Trying to maneuver a hoop would be a nuisance sitting in a wagon all day. Her bonnet matched, of course, and covered the tidy bun she'd made of her hair. If she hadn't been in a rush, she'd have left her pearl earrings in her jewelry case. Traveling was a dusty, dirty endeavor, and pearls were better suited to the confines of the house. When she realized she hadn't changed them, however, she was halfway down the stairs and chose to hurry on.

No one stirred in the house yet. She stopped in Father's den, unlocked the gun case, and chose the same shotgun she'd used on the murderous dogs. Several times she'd woken in the nights since then, the sound and recoil of the gun stunning her even in sleep. She had not looked at the dogs lying dead in the dust. Even so, an image of their bloody carcasses disturbed her dreams.

Carrying the heavy shotgun, Marianne let herself out of the house. The dew-soaked grass darkened the hem of her dress, and she could barely see her way in the predawn gloom. She joined the others in the barn just as McNaught rang the big bell calling the slaves to gather in the yard. From the bell stand, he wouldn't see them driving out.

They traveled the river road north to the sawmill, then turned off toward the interior. Marianne sat on the buckboard next to Joseph, the shotgun at her feet. The desperate family lay under a tarp among the baskets and the spinning wheel. Pearl sat in the back with a bucket of water and a bottle of Marianne's brew to ease the Mama's and the boy's pain.

"You've been this way before?" Marianne said.

"No'm. De shepherd, he know de way and he tell me."

"Who is this shepherd, Joseph?"

He looked at her and smiled. "I not gone tell you dat, Missy."

"Is it someone I know?"

Joseph clucked at the two mules. "Get a move on, boys."

Marianne looked to Pearl. She would know, but Pearl smiled at her too. They weren't going to tell her. She couldn't decide whether it was funny or infuriating. She was, after all, involved in this up to her neck. But they both seemed to enjoy their little game, and she let it go.

Midmorning, a farmer driving a wagonful of melons approached, and Marianne tensed. She checked that Pearl had covered the people in the back and then plastered a smile on her face. "Good morning to you," she said to the farmer. He tipped his hat, wished the lady good morning in return, and drove on by.

Another traveler on horseback passed by without a friendly word, rather rudely in fact, without having so much as glanced at the lumpy cargo in the back of the wagon. They encountered a few more travelers, and each time Marianne breathed more easily; she and her freight evidently appeared unremarkable.

Late in the afternoon, all of them wilted from the sun and sore from riding on hard boards with no springs, they stopped under the shade of a live oak. Marianne had Pearl stand in the road to keep watch so the three escapees could stand up and move their limbs.

Marianne pulled Joseph aside. "How much further? There are only a few more hours of daylight."

"I don rightly know just how far it be. I just knows to look for de house on dis road. It white, two winders in front, wid four magnolias in a row side de house. I reckon it was a nearer ride for de shepherd on his horse. Dese mules be old and slow."

Marianne imagined they would have delivered their cargo and arrived at Martha's by nightfall. She hadn't reckoned on spending the night in the wagon. Weren't there brigands on this road? Highwaymen who'd knock you on the head and take whatever they could get from you? She felt vulnerable and a little frightened at the thought. She wished Yves were here.

That caught her up short. *Yves Chamard? I don't need Yves Chamard.* Just because he had that air of competence or confidence or whatever it was. Arrogance, more like. She didn't need a protector anyway. She was quite capable of defending herself and the others with her shotgun. And with her tongue. She was no shrinking violet.

Besides, if she wanted a champion, she'd choose Marcel. She certainly would.

The rest of the weary, steamy afternoon, she reminded herself of all the things she didn't like about Yves Chamard. Mocking eyes, for one thing. All that restless energy. Marcel lowered himself onto a settee with grace and ease, as if he would be happy to repose on a brocade sofa indefinitely. Yves sat, even sat quite still, but there was that air about him of constant readiness for action.

He does have a manliness about him, and naturally I, well, I feel that. And he kissed nicely. Very nicely. *All right, his kisses are fantastic.* Her palm of its own accord reminded her of his taking her hand, of stroking it. Twice he had presumed to take her hand. And how was it that such a simple thing could light her whole being? The image came to her of Yves' mouth, the little scar running into the lip, coming closer and closer before he kissed her the first time. She closed her eyes.

Yes, I admit it. He excites me. But he condescends and he's insensitive. He's all wrong.

A group of horsemen came up from behind them. Marianne turned at the sound of their horses' hooves on the hard packed road. There were four of them, all armed with rifles and pistols. All of them rode good mounts, though their persons were unshaved and grimy. As they passed the wagon, they tipped their hats and wished Marianne a good afternoon.

They did nothing offensive nor even suggestive, but Marianne was uneasy. What kind of men traveled with shackles? She'd spotted them dangling from a saddlebag on two of the men's mounts. She glanced at Joseph, and his tight mouth told her he'd spotted the irons too. She picked up the shotgun at her feet and loaded it. Then she laid it across her lap.

It was nearly dark and still no house flanked by four magnolias. Few houses at all on this road, in fact, though they had passed half a dozen farms with bare-board houses, some of them little more than shacks. This was not plantation land back in here. People were poorer and did their own labor.

Marianne made her mind up to it. They were going to have to spend the night in the woods. The mosquitoes might eat them alive, but the bears and cats of the forest—well, it was silly to worry about them. There were six people in this wagon. An animal would have to be rabid to approach so many. But it was August. Rabid animals more often appeared in late summer. No. She dismissed the thought. She had better save her worrying for the two-legged predators, like those four men on horseback.

With perhaps twenty minutes of daylight left, they came to another farm. A white house, two front windows, four magnolias alongside.

"I reckon this be it," Joseph said. He began to tch to the mules to turn in, but Marianne grabbed his arm.

"Drive on by," she hissed.

Four horses, still burdened with saddles and saddlebags, drank from the trough at the rail. Those same four men, she was sure, were stopped here.

"You right. Dey no quilt hanging out."

Marianne didn't know what he meant.

"De quilt, sometimes it have a north star on it, sometime another pattern. It hanging out, there be a slave's friend in de house. Dis de place, but dere no quilt."

Half a mile down the road, the twilight forced her to make a decision. The moon wouldn't be up for a couple of hours, Joseph said. And Marianne didn't dare go back to the safe house. It wasn't safe, she was sure of it.

Marianne pointed to a field lane, and Joseph hawed the mules off the main road and through a stand of corn. The stalks, nearly six feet tall, rustled in the slight breeze. Once on the other side of the crop, they were shielded from the main road. No one knew they were there. They'd light no fire, make no noise.

Pearl pulled the tarp off the runaways. They sat up, stiff and sore and thirsty. She ladled out the rest of the water in the bucket for them and Joseph and herself. "Dis yours, Miss Marianne." She handed forward the second canteen of water designated for Marianne. Along with a food bundle, Evette had sent along separate water for the mistress of the plantation.

Joseph unhooked the mules, led them to an open pasture beyond the corn, and hobbled them. As far as he could tell in the gloaming, they'd not be seen from the road.

Elvin helped Clem and Pearl out of the wagon. The three of them walked around the clearing to restore their circulation. Bess sat on the back edge of the wagon and Marianne felt of her ankle. The swelling was as tight as it had been last night. It was going to be a long time healing, and Bess certainly could not walk on it. Perhaps not for weeks yet. *How will she ever make it to freedom?* Marianne wondered.

In the dark, they ate the last of the food Evette had packed them. Then they settled in, Pearl and Joseph and the three runaways sharing the bed of the wagon. In deference to the mistress, they insisted Marianne should sleep on the bench seat, where she was possibly even more uncomfortable than the other members of the party.

She could not sleep. The tension would not leave her body. What kind of men carried shackles with them? Bounty hunters did. Did they know what house that was? Did they have some idea runaways used this route?

The moon rose. It was one of those nights she could practically have read outdoors it was so bright. Trying not to wake anyone, she climbed down from the buckboard, but Joseph raised his head.

"Where you goin'?"

"Just over to the bushes," she whispered.

Once she'd finished in the bushes, she looked back at the weathered wagon in the moonlight. If it weren't for the corn growing between it and the road, they'd be perfectly visible and entirely vulnerable.

She couldn't bear to lie down on that hard seat again. Instead, she walked around the corn. Keeping to the moon shadows, she followed the road back toward the house.

She found a vantage in the deep shade of a tree to watch. A gauzy curtain billowed in and out with the breeze. But there were no lights, no sounds.

I don't know what I thought I'd see. She checked the ascent of the moon. It would be bright the rest of the night, she figured. She should try to get some sleep. In the early morning, she would creep back here and watch until the four horsemen left.

Five minutes back toward the cornfield, she stopped. Was that a bird rustling the high dry grass? Or maybe a possum prowling in the night. She listened, but didn't hear it again.

The cutoff shone plainly in the moonlight. She was far into the field when she heard that noise again. *Damnation! My shotgun is still in the wagon.* She stepped into the corn and watched the way she had come.

A man's figure emerged from the shadowed road into the open lane. He carried a rifle in the crook of his arm. He stopped as if he were listening, and then he took to the line of trees along the field road.

My God. I led him right back to the wagon.

She couldn't cut through the corn to warn them. She might as well scream and shout as run through the dry sheaves. *I can't see him.* She held her breath, listening, waiting. *He's gone back for the others!*

Certain he was gone, she stepped out of the corn and hurried round to the wagon. "Joseph," she hissed. She didn't have to call him again. He raised himself up.

"They've found us. We have to go."

He roused the others silently. Marianne headed for the mules. No, that wasn't a good idea. They'd never outrun men on horseback. They'd have to play the innocents.

She ran back to the wagon. "Pearl, stay where you are.

Joseph, we'll hide them in the corn. Then we'll come back here and act as if night caught us on the road."

The three runaways stood in the lane now, Bess leaning heavily on Elvin. Marianne looked around the moonscape. There was plenty of brush about, but the corn looked far more dense. "In there."

The rustling and creaking of the stalks as the three entered the corn seemed loud as thunder, but twenty or thirty feet in, it ceased. They were settled, hidden.

Joseph hoisted himself back in the wagon. "Look like you sleeping," he whispered to Pearl.

Marianne climbed back onto the hard bench and lay down. She sat up again and reached for the shotgun. It was still loaded. She lay down, arranged her skirt over the gun, and hooked her finger on the double trigger.

What good will this shotgun do? I can't shoot down men. Dogs, yes, I did that. But not men. And there are four of them, and four rifles. God, help us.

Chapter 16

Maybe the man hadn't seen the wagon. Maybe he had no connection at all with those men at the house. He could be out coon hunting. She kept her finger on the trigger, but the tension eased from her neck.

I guess I panicked, that's all. The bench bit into her shoulder blades. It was unbearable, and Marianne sat up.

Four men surrounded the wagon. She hadn't heard a thing.

"What do you want?" Marianne demanded. She was the daughter of Albany Johnston, a planter of substance and influence; she knew very well how to assume a tone of superiority.

"Might as well light that lantern now, Wilson," one of them said.

Before the match was struck, Marianne made sure her skirt covered her weapon. The sudden glow of the kerosene wick darkened everything outside its circle, but she could see their faces now. Her heart thumped in her chest, but she meant to bluff these four men as well as any cardsharp on a Mississippi gambling boat.

"Gentlemen, you are intruding. My servants and I are

passing the night here, and your presence is indelicate and unwelcome."

"That right?" This was the tallest of the four men. Tall and lanky. "Gotta wonder why a lady like you is out here in the fields when you passed a farm not a mile back. Whyn't you stop there for the night?"

"Several horses tied at the trough made it clear those people had plenty of company already."

Another man with a chaw of tobacco in his cheek looked in the wagon, staring at Pearl and Joseph. "Come on down out of there."

"Do not presume to address my slaves, sir."

The man raised his rifle at her. "I presume any damn thing I please, lady. Ain't that right, Monroe?"

She stood, almost certain her shotgun remained hidden in the folds of her skirt. "Joseph, Pearl, please stand down so these men can see you are not the runaways I presume they are pursuing."

"You think we're after runaways?" The tall man, Monroe, grinned at her. "What makes you think that?"

She could have bitten her tongue out. They might merely be robbers. Why hadn't she thought of that?

Wilson, the one with the lantern, held it up to inspect Pearl. "Turn her around," he said to the one chewing tobacco.

"Why else would you disturb us? We obviously are not carrying a shipment of gold bullion nor expensive wines. If it's a spinning wheel you desire, then we can accommodate your avaricious pursuit. Otherwise, please leave us as you found us."

Monroe grinned again, looking at his confederate. "She's feisty, ain't she?"

The fourth man tossed the tarp out of the wagon and shoved the baskets around. "Nobody back here, boss."

Wilson held the light close to Pearl's face. "You belong

to this old man, sugar?" He ran a hand over her breast.
Pearl stood as one frozen, but Joseph moved to protect
her. The man backhanded him, quick and hard, and
Joseph went down.

Wilson set the lantern on the ground. "Keep your
barrel on him, Jack." He grabbed Pearl by the arm and
hauled at her, heading for the dark shadows under the
trees.

Joseph lay with Jack's rifle pointed at his gut. Pearl
struggled to free herself from Wilson's grip, but he
wrapped an arm around her waist and half lifted her as
he kept on. "Miss Marianne!" she yelled. He slapped her
and she cried out again.

Marianne turned her back on her friends. She faced
the leader and raised her shotgun. The man who'd
thrown the tarp stood not five feet from him. She could
kill the two of them where they stood.

"Tell your friend to let her go."

Sight of the shotgun wiped the smile off Monroe's
face. He glanced at the man near him. "You didn't see
she had a gun? You a worthless piece of shit, Sonny."

Monroe looked back to Marianne and held his hands
up in a peacemaking gesture. The smile had returned.
"Now, don't get all upset, miss. Wilson ain't going to hurt
the girl. Just gone give her a little. You know what he's
gone give her, don't you? A pretty gal like you? Somebody give you some of it by now, ain't they?"

God gave her the strength to hold the gun steady,
aimed right between the two of them. "I've already
cocked this firearm. Call your man back."

Monroe stepped forward, his hands still up. "Now,
miss, you don't want to go aiming a gun at a man. That
thing go off, you kill somebody. Why'nt you come on
down here, and I'll treat you good? You treat me good,
too, won't nobody get hurt."

The leer on his face sickened her. Her finger, slick with sweat, tightened on the trigger. The smell of the oil on the stock and the barrel stung her nose, but the heavy weight of the big shotgun seemed nothing to her.

"I'm not coming down. You're going to call that man back and release my people."

He was close enough now she had to shift her aim. She'd only the one man in her sights now. In the lantern light, she could see the color of his eyes. More yellow than brown, like a fish eye.

She swallowed hard. Joseph, on the ground with the rifle pointed at him, hadn't moved. Pearl hadn't called out again. She was likely already raped.

"Tell you what," the leader said. Sonny started stepping to the side out of the line of fire. He could work his way all the way around her, she realized, if she kept the gun on the first man.

"Tell you what. You put the shotgun down, and I'll personally see to it your man and the gal are put back in the wagon. You don't have the ones we was after noway. How'd that be?"

She could pull the trigger. She could kill this one, then shift the gun and get the other one. The tension in her finger intensified. But what good would that do? There would still be two more of them.

"I see your man moving around," she said. "But I can kill you before he gets to me. Bring Pearl back now."

Again the man's humor left him. He glared at her, then nodded to Sonny. "Go get Wilson and the girl. Hurry up, damn you."

"Joseph," Marianne said, "you all right?"

"I be all right."

"Get in the wagon." As if the wagon, with no mule tethered, were an island of safety. She didn't turn around to see if Jack let Joseph up. She kept her sights on Monroe, the tall one. When she felt the wagon shift under Joseph's weight, she knew he'd climbed into the back.

The shotgun didn't waver. "Tell them to hurry up."

"Wilson," Monroe hollered, "bring that gal on back. You had time enough to rut her twicet by now anyways." He smirked at Marianne when he said it, and she could have pulled the trigger just for that. And only a few minutes ago, she'd been doubting she had it in her to kill a man.

She heard the two men approaching, laughing and carrying on, using words Marianne did not understand. She heard nothing from Pearl. Finally, the wagon shifted again. "Pearl?"

"I got her, Missy. I got her," Joseph said.

"Now you and your men leave us. If I so much as see a twig move after you're gone, I'll shoot it. Don't come back."

Monroe had his hands up in conciliation again. "Don't need to get all riled up. We ain't done nothing to you. You keep your spinning wheel, thank you, and we'll be moving on." He backed away from her, palms still out.

"Come on, boys. We bothered the lady enough." He looked around for his men. Sonny and Wilson were there, but not Jack. Monroe picked up the abandoned lantern and held it high. He looked around, the lantern glow on the wall of the seemingly impenetrable corn. "Jack? Jack, where the hell you gone?"

Marianne still had her shotgun aimed at the leader, but she believed now she wouldn't have to pull the trigger. They were going to leave, as soon as this Jack came back.

Damn, she thought. *What if Jack caught a sound or a movement in the corn? What if he's found them?*

Monroe stepped down the lane, calling out. "You piece of bug shit, Jack. Get over here."

The weight of the shotgun began to register with her now, and her arms trembled, but still she kept her weapon up, aimed vaguely toward Monroe.

"Jack!" No answer.

Monroe turned on his heel. "What's going on here?" he called back at Marianne. "You got somebody else with you? Sonny, put your gun on her."

Wilson, not far from the back of the wagon, let out an "umph." He dropped to the ground, his rifle thrown out of his hand.

Monroe ran toward Wilson, who was rolling to his knees now. "Keep your gun on that girl," he yelled at Sonny.

"What the hell's the matter with you?" he roared at Wilson. "Get up, you ass."

Sonny yelped and lowered his rifle, his free hand at the crack on his forehead. He swayed a little, then straightened up. "Somebody's hurling rocks!" Another missile caught him square between the eyes and he went down.

Monroe took cover behind the wagon wheel and fired into the woods. And again. Wilson struggled to his feet and reached for his rifle. Another stone caught him in the shoulder and he howled. "Blow the damn lantern out!"

From the dark woods, an angry voice called out. "Marianne, get down!"

Startled, she sat, then rolled off the bench to her knees, her shotgun at the ready.

Monroe fired at the voice. Then Wilson fired.

With her eyes adjusting to the lack of lantern light, Marianne saw Sonny on his feet and about to climb onto the wagon seat. She swung the shotgun at him and he jerked back. Again she swung and this time caught him on the side of the head with the heavy steel barrel. He fell to the ground, flat on his back, and lay still.

A cloud covered the moon, and for a moment she couldn't see even the end of the wagon. Who was out there?

No one made a sound. No one moved. The cloud sailed on and again the moon lit the scene. Marianne could make out Joseph and Pearl crouched together in the back of the wagon. She saw Monroe steady his rifle against the side of the wagon and aim it toward the woods, at somebody out there, who knew her.

The wagon shifted. Wilson was on the bench beside her, his hands grabbing for her and the shotgun. She twisted away—he must not get the gun. He socked her in the jaw and she reeled, but she held on. He socked her in the belly, then in the chest, and she lost her grip.

Wilson yanked the gun from her hands, but before he could turn it on Marianne, Pearl was on his back. She scratched and tore at his face. Her teeth found his ear, and Marianne shoved herself into his knees. He flailed, fighting for balance with Pearl on his back and Marianne in the tight space at his feet.

Marianne heard Monroe's rifle fire again, saw Pearl's moon-whitened face as she gouged at her rapist's eyes.

Screaming, Wilson reached over his head for Pearl. He grabbed her and pulled her around his body. Her fingers tried again to maul his face, but now he had his hands on her neck. Squeezing. Choking the life out of her.

Marianne found the shotgun at her feet. She shoved the muzzle against the man's ribs. She fired.

A strained endless gasp came from Wilson's chest. His hands let go of Pearl. She fell back into the wagon on top of Joseph, who at the moment the gun went off was tackling the man's legs.

Wilson, his torso a shredded, ruined mass, collapsed on top of Marianne.

More gunfire. Monroe shooting into the dark again. Then nearby, a different gun with a different report. Someone was firing back at Monroe, and not with rocks.

"Joseph?" Marianne couldn't breathe with the dead man on top of her. Suddenly, silence. No shots. No sound at all. "Joseph?" What if Monroe had shot Joseph? The wagon shifted. Fighting panic, she screamed, "Joseph!"

"Here, here. I've got you."

The dead man was pulled off her and she sucked in the night air. She couldn't see for the hot blood covering her face.

Hands lifted her, set her on the bench. The metallic scent of blood and something else—sandalwood? Thumbs gently stroked her eyelids, wiping away the blood, and she tilted her head back. Palms cradled her face, sweet breath caressed her mouth. "Are you hurt?" he said.

She opened her eyes. It was Yves, and that seemed right. Then she had sense enough to wonder: "What are you doing here?"

"Rescuing a damsel in distress, among other things."

Yves Chamard took out his handkerchief and wiped her eyes, her nose. Then as tenderly as if she were a child, he cleaned her lips. She sat as still as a porcelain doll, but not so unmoved nor unstirred as a doll. Her heart and her breath came fast and heavy. When he'd finished with the handkerchief, he slid his thumb across her bottom lip, lightly, delicately. Dazed, she thought he was going to kiss her. She opened her lips, but Yves stood up and leaned in to the back of the wagon.

"How's the girl?"

"She breathing pretty good," Joseph said.

Marianne brushed past Yves to climb into the back. "You really are all right?"

Pearl swallowed and managed to whisper through her bruised throat. "I alive, Miss Marianne."

Sonny groaned and raised himself to his knees. Yves vaulted to the ground and smashed his fist into the side of the man's head. Sonny collapsed again.

"Joseph, can you light the lantern?" Yves said.

"Wait," Marianne said. "Where are the other men?"

Joseph climbed down and toed the body of Monroe, a black hole in his forehead visible in the moonlight. "Here dat lanky one," Joseph said.

"There was a fourth," Marianne said.

"He's dead," Yves told her. "Light the lantern so I can tie this man up."

Yves removed the braces from Sonny's pants and wound them around his ankles. His wrists he bound with the shoelaces from Sonny's boots. Once the thug was secured, Yves held the lantern over him to examine the injuries to his head. Where the first rock from Yves' slingshot caught him, there was a swelling big as a hen's egg. Another swelling the shape of the gun barrel ran into his hair. The other blow to the side of his head hardly showed yet, but it would. "I'd hate to have this man's headache in the morning."

Marianne felt warm wet drops on her hand. "Pearl, you're bleeding!"

Yves brought the lantern to the wagon and held it over Pearl.

"I shot you!" Marianne pulled at the shredded fabric on Pearl's side. "Oh God, I shot you."

Buckshot had torn away the flesh just above the waist on Pearl's left side.

"I be dead, you didn't pull dat trigger."

"How bad is it?" Yves said.

With unsteady fingers, Marianne poured water from her canteen over the wound and dabbed at it with her petticoat. "Thank God! It isn't deep. The shot just tore the skin away." She tore a strip from her petticoat to hold against the wound. "Joseph, I need the medical bag."

He handed it to her, and she saw the blood trickling down his arm.

"Joseph! You're shot too?"

"I don think hardly. Maybe I got one or two pellets is all."

Yves set the lantern on the bench and left her to tend to Pearl and Joseph. When Marianne finished cleaning and bandaging the wounds, Joseph's being hardly worse than he'd said, she saw Yves and the runaway Elvin carrying the fourth man between them. They laid him on the ground near Monroe and Wilson. She sat on the back of the wagon, staring, the corpses not ten feet away.

Three men. They had killed three men. Wilson, the one she'd killed—his ribs and part of the spine shone in the light, his middle blasted nearly clean away. Marianne began to tremble. They'd had to do it. She wasn't sorry.

The trembling shook the wagon. "Missy, you be all right," Joseph said. He wrapped his arms around her. "You done fine." Pearl reached for her hand and stroked it. Marianne whimpered once, and the trembling went on.

Yves left the dead men and strode to the wagon. "Marianne!" She could see him clearly, she knew who he was, but she couldn't understand what he was doing here.

Yves grabbed her shoulders and gave her a shake. "Marianne! Come out of it." He shook her again, and she thought he was about to slap her face the way he raised his hand to her, and she began to cry.

Yves pulled her from the wagon and held her length against his. She held on to him, the sobs racking her. His body rocked back and forth, rocking her with him, and slowly she found herself again.

Steady now, no trembling, no sobbing, Marianne didn't stir from his embrace. She didn't ever want to stir. Her face pressed against his chest, her arms wrapped around his waist, she was safe. She couldn't see the dead bodies, she didn't need the shotgun anymore.

Yves was kissing the top of her head. His hand rubbed her back. Suddenly it was too much, it felt too good. She stepped away. With a long shuddering breath, she said, "Thank you. I am recovered. Thank you. I never cry. I never do."

She wiped at her wet face, embarrassed. Joseph took her arm and helped her onto the wagon. "Sit, Missy. Pearl and you, you stay in de wagon. We gots work to do."

Elvin brought his wife and child from the corn. He helped Bess into the wagon, then boosted Clem up. The three women and the boy huddled together, spent from fear.

The moon still sailed high in the sky. Marianne's mind cleared and her emotions settled. She climbed down from the wagon, trying to gauge when sunrise would come. Not soon.

Elvin had already dragged one body away from the lantern light, and he came back for the next one. Joseph was cutting strips from the canvas tarp.

"What are you doing?" she said.

"Gone tie this fellow to the wagon wheels," he said, nodding toward Sonny. "Don want him getting away from us."

Marianne stared at the remaining body on the ground. "Joseph, we killed three people."

"Yes'm. We did. And dey needed killing."

We'll all go to jail. Or worse. They could hang us. But

not Pearl. Not Joseph. Yves and I. We're the killers. I'm a killer.

Joseph looked at her hard in the lantern light. "Don you go on 'bout it, Missy. You done what you had to do. Pearl be dead you didn't fire dat gun."

Yves and a big man with a full beard and a black hat came up the lane in the moonlight. She watched him, Yves Chamard, who'd held her while she cried. She wished he'd hold her now.

The new man tipped his hat to her. "Ebenezer Rogers."

"This is the gentleman whom you sought," Yves said. "He has agreed to loan us his shovels and a patch of ground."

The men took the lantern, the shovels, and the remaining body through the trees. Marianne waited, watching the moon pass its zenith and begin sinking toward the earth.

Chapter 17

By dawn, they were in the house where the farmer's wife, Eleanor, had hot coffee waiting. With Pearl's extra set of hands, she soon had ham on the table along with hominy grits, biscuits, and red-eye gravy.

Yves took his second cup of coffee onto the back porch to watch the morning mist hovering in the tree-tops. He was in his shirtsleeves, one arm braced high against the porch post. Marianne stood at the door for a moment, watching him. "Beautiful here," he said without turning around.

She stepped on the porch to stand beside him. A day ago, she might have sniped at Yves for interfering when she'd already persuaded Monroe to leave. So like a man, to assume his heroics were needed. After last night, however, Marianne was not so quick to judge, and so, not in accusation as much as in puzzlement, she said, "Those men were leaving, you know."

"No, darlin'. They weren't." He looked down at her. "The first man? Elvin got him because he'd headed into the corn. He'd heard the boy, I think."

Then the slavers would have taken Elvin and Bess

and Clem. And Joseph and Pearl. *I'd likely be in the corn-field, dead.*

"Thank you."

He smiled at her. "You're welcome."

"You're not a stranger here, to these people."

"No."

Marianne had been putting the pieces together all through breakfast. "You're the shepherd."

He gave her that quirky grin. "Don't know anything about a shepherd."

And I thought it might have been Marcel. Yves is part of the Underground!

A light rain began to fall. Their host joined them on the porch. "This keeps up, it'll take care of any signs out in the field."

Their captive, Sonny, didn't get any breakfast. Far as they knew, he hadn't regained consciousness yet. They'd left him locked in the corncrib with the farmer's friendly corn snake, his wrists tied, his ankles trussed so he could shuffle but not run.

"What will we do with that man? Will he take money to go away? To keep quiet?" Marianne asked. How she wished he would ride off, grateful to be alive.

Yves and Ebenezer exchanged looks. "Even if he said he would, I wouldn't trust him any further than I would a rabid skunk," Eb said.

"We aren't finished with Sonny Birch yet," Yves said.

"You know him?"

"I've been following these men for three days. Caught up to them last night here at the house."

"Who are they?"

"They're the ones who took my brother."

Marianne marveled how his eyes, so tender on her a moment ago, turned hard.

"I intend to find out what Birch knows before I turn him over to the sheriff."

And then the sheriff would arrest her for murder. Marianne nodded. There was nothing to be done. She had shot Wilson and killed him. Surely the judge would be lenient since she did it to save Pearl.

"I'll be ready," she said.

"Ready?"

"For the sheriff. He'll arrest me. And you, I suppose."

One side of Yves' mouth curved higher than the other in that odd smile. "You are not going to jail, Marianne, and neither am I."

Ebenezer snorted. "Not a jury anywhere send a woman to jail, nor this fellow here, either, for protecting themselves. Rest your mind about that, miss."

Marianne let out a long breath and placed her hand over her heart. She'd known that, of course, but still . . .

"I seen some head injuries," his wife, Eleanor, said, stepping out on the porch. "Don't rightly know how bad this one is hurt, but could be he won't remember nothing anyway. That's the way it is sometimes."

"He'll remember where he left my brother," Yves said, not just determination but threat in his voice.

"Then they didn't find Gabriel in New Orleans," Marianne said.

Yves shook his head. "I got word from Marcel when I was in Natchez. They were seen trying, but they couldn't sell him down there. He was too conspicuous, we think. Then they were seen on the Trace. I've been trailing them ever since."

The rain came down heavier and Eb handed Yves a slicker. "Let's see if that fella has waked up."

Marianne followed Eleanor Rogers back into the kitchen where a pot of water heated on the stove. "Your girl wants to wash you up some, miss. Sit down here and I'll get you a towel."

Pearl dipped a cloth in the warm water. "You got blood in you hair, Miss Marianne. I gone get it out I have to wash yo whole head."

Marianne touched the sticky mess above her forehead. "I would appreciate that very much, Pearl."

In the barn, Yves shook off the slicker and hung it on a nail. His host was a Quaker, or his wife was, he wasn't sure which. Quakers didn't hold with violence of any kind. That's why Eb hadn't come out to the field until the shooting was over. Yves respected that. The Rogerses took plenty of risk helping slaves keep going on the way north. "Eb," Yves said, "I know how you feel about violence. Why don't I go in the crib by myself?"

Ebenezer shook his head. "We haven't even talked to the man yet, Yves. We'll try Christian patience first. Then, if it's necessary, I'll leave you with him."

They opened the door into the crib and heard the rustling of the snake somewhere in the piled-up corn. Or maybe it was an unfortunate mouse. Sonny lay sprawled on his back, his wrists tied and a foot of rope between his bound ankles. His eyes were closed and swollen. A fly buzzed around his open mouth.

"Looks like he stuck his head in a beehive," Eb said.

Yves squatted next to Sonny and turned his head this way and that, trying to judge how deep the bruises went. He didn't want the man's brains scrambled.

Gently, Yves slapped his cheeks. "Wake up, Birch." He slapped him a little harder.

Birch opened his eyes. One eye, blood-filled and gruesome, didn't focus, but the other eye found Yves' face and beamed malevolence. Looked like he had his wits.

As he realized he was bound hand and foot, Sonny's

eyes lost their meanness. He looked around the corncrib, scared now. "Where's the others?"

"Dead."

"By God," he said. His face turned red and his eyes
teared. "By God, you killed Monroe?"

"By God, I did."

Sonny's face crumpled, his mouth wide and contorted.

Yves hadn't expected this, a hardened man, tuning up
to blubber like a baby. *Man's mood changes fast as you can
drop a hat.* Yves looked up at Eb, perplexed, and Eb
shrugged.

"You sons of bitches, Monroe the only brother I got
left," Sonny wailed.

"You're alone in the world, then, Birch. I don't imagine your own mother would own you, the kind of man
you are."

Sonny gripped his head in his hands, rocking and sobbing.

"A little moonshine might calm him down."

"Eb? You've got moonshine?"

Eb grinned. "Don't mention it to Eleanor, though."

Eb went into his tack room next to the corncrib and
shifted some things around. When he came back, he carried a jug and a tin cup. He poured out a dram for Sonny.
"Here, fellow. It'll ease your head."

As quickly as it had begun, Sonny's weeping ceased.
He wiped his nose and knocked the liquor back, not
even spluttering as it went down. He held out the cup for
more, but Yves intercepted it.

"You can have all you want once you tell me what I
want to know."

Mean now, Sonny snarled, "My head feels like it got a
nest of hornets in it. Gimme the damn whiskey."

"Have a little mercy, my friend," Eb argued. "Give the

man another dram. I'm sure he'll be willing to talk after that. Isn't that right, Mr. Birch?"

Sonny drank it down, then lay back against the hard corn, moaning, his head in his hands again. The orange snake, with its black-ringed red blotches, slithered out from the top of the corn, investigating the ruckus in its lair. It slid down the pile, angling toward Sonny. Yves watched, equal parts horrified and fascinated. He'd never been one to bring a snake home in his pocket as Gabriel used to. He could tolerate one within five or ten feet of him, but he preferred to keep his distance. And now here was a five-footer about to crawl on top of Sonny Birch.

The corn snake paused an inch from Sonny's ear, its tongue darting in and out of its mouth. Sonny was carrying on and didn't know it was there until it crawled over his head, across his hands—Sonny leapt clean off the corn, his scream sending chills down Yves' spine.

The man went berserk. He clawed at the snake, stomped his feet, whirling, screaming. Yves and Eb backed out of his way, out of the corncrib.

Eb laughed so hard he had to bend over to catch his breath, but Yves was spooked. He felt all the little hairs on his neck and his forearms standing up.

Sonny finally flung the snake against the wall and it slithered back in amongst the corncobs. Still in a panic, Sonny tried to charge out of the corncrib like it was afire, the rope tripping him up. Yves grabbed him by the shirt and spun him around, then shoved him down, trying not to hit the man if he didn't have to. It was Eb's barn, and Eb didn't want any violence. Truth was, though, Yves didn't much want to touch Sonny, the snake so recently having been on him.

"Funniest damn thing I ever saw," Eb said.

Sonny hadn't finished his flight. He scooted backward

across the barn on his butt until he came to the wall. With wild eyes he stared at Yves. "What you do that for? You trying to kill me, too?"

"Whether that snake kills you or not is up to you, Birch," Yves said. Sonny hadn't even realized it was just a corn snake, and he wouldn't tell him otherwise. Yves closed the door to the corncrib. "Lot of copperheads this part of the country. You tell me what I want to know, you won't have to go back in there."

Eb held the jug up, tantalizing him. Sonny reached for it, and Eb poured him another cup. "Reckon all the good of the first cups got scared right out of you."

Yves pulled over a nail keg and sat on it. He gave the man a chance to settle down and finish the whiskey; then he began. "You and Monroe made a mistake," he said. "See, one of the men you took down the river was my brother."

Sonny's one good eye narrowed. "Don't know what you talking about."

"Shackles in your saddlebags kind of give you away, Birch. You grabbed slaves along the Mississippi, took them aboard, and floated on downstream. But one of them wasn't a slave. He was a free man. And you kidnapped him. That's a hanging offense, Birch."

"Never picked up nobody but runaway slaves. And that's legal."

Yves shook his head. "My brother's name is Gabriel Chamard. He's a physician. A very high colored free man, my brother. Soft spoken, but I bet he put up a good fight when you took him. Where is he now?"

A muscle under Sonny's eye ticked. He glanced at the corncrib door and looked away. "I don't know nothing about any free man. We just took up runaways. We was a recovery business, that's what we was."

"You left New Orleans eight days ago on a steamboat.

You and three white men and one black man got off at Natchez."

Birch shook his head. "Did no such thing."

"A stevedore said the slave you had with you looked like he'd been painted, he was so black. And he had a bit in his mouth, shackles on wrists and ankles, like you were afraid of him." Yves had to stop and breathe. A bit in Gabriel's mouth. He could taste the metal on his own tongue. *I could tear the man apart for that one thing.*

Eb put a hand on Yves' shoulder to calm him down. Yves unclenched his fists and rubbed his hands on his knees.

"At Natchez, you tried to sell my brother at Forks-of-the-Road market. The broker wouldn't have anything to do with you. Your papers were suspect and your 'slave' tried to butt one of you in the back before he was subdued." Yves took a deep breath. "That 'slave' was my brother.

"You left Natchez with Gabriel. Three days later, you were seen in Vicksburg. But just the four of you. Where did you leave my brother?"

Sonny kept his eyes on the dirt floor.

Yves stood up. Birch would tell him. Whatever it took. And if Gabriel were alive, he would find him. That they might have killed him, simply because he was inconvenient, unsaleable, a liability, was possible. It might even be likely. But this man would tell him what happened to Gabriel before Yves was finished with him.

"Fella," Eb said, "I'd advise you to tell this man what he wants to know. If you don't, I'm going to step out of the barn, and then it's between him and you and God what goes on in here."

"You got the wrong man," Sonny said. Keeping his eyes on their boots didn't convince Yves or Ebenezer.

"Well, I think I'll go have a cup of coffee." Eb lifted a slicker from the nail and went back out into the rain.

Yves grabbed Sonny's wrists and hauled them over his head, looped the rope binding his hands to a hook, and Sonny's upper body was secure. Then he tossed a heavy saddle over his legs and Birch was fairly immobilized.

He didn't aim to pummel the man into talking, not yet anyway. He pulled out a knife from his boot and showed it to Sonny.

"It's not a very big knife, but it's sharp." He leaned over and drew it ever so gently across the back of Sonny's hand, and a red seam surfaced. "You tell me everything, I'll let you live. Otherwise . . ."

Sonny trembled. "I don't know nothing about your brother," he muttered.

"Yeah, you do. So you headed north to Vicksburg. Did you take a steamer or follow the Trace?"

Sonny didn't answer, and Yves pulled off Sonny's boot and then his filthy sock. He touched the knife to Sonny's big toe. "How did you go?"

Sonny swallowed. "We didn't take no boat."

"So you followed the Trace. A few settlements scattered along the Trace. A farmhouse here, a stopover there. You find somebody to take my brother?"

Barely audible, Sonny said, "Don't know your fucking brother."

The knife circled Sonny's toe, leaving a faint red stream behind it. "I do this enough times, I figure the toe will come clean off. What do you think, Birch?"

Sonny tried to lunge, but the ropes hindered him. He whimpered.

"So you took Gabriel up the Trace. Did you sell him to somebody?"

Sonny refused to answer, so Yves ran his knife in the

same shallow cut he'd made before. The toe bled freely now, though still it was only a light wound.

"Did you kill him?"

Yves poised the knife for another cutting, and a foul-smelling stain spread from Sonny's crotch down toward his knees.

"I didn't kill him. Nobody killed him," Sonny blurted.

Yves took a breath and closed his eyes. "Then you left him alive on the Trace?" He kicked at Sonny's other foot. "Is that right?"

"Yeah. We left him. Didn't sell him. Nobody wanted him. But he was sick, so we left him."

"Goddamn you to hell. You left him on the side of the road like a sick dog?"

Yves threatened the toe with his blade.

"No!" Sonny tried to pull his foot away, but Yves held his ankle high. "We left him at a farm. Where they'd find him. They could take care of him if they wanted to. He was alive when I saw him."

"What kind of sick?"

"Fever, I don't know. Just sick."

"Tell me about this farm."

With an eye on the knife, Sonny told him how to find the farm. Off the Trace a mile or two, up a spur. East, they'd left the Trace and gone east. Had a beat-up dovecote out back of the house. Two days out of Natchez.

Yves pulled every detail he could get out of Sonny Birch, and then he was through with him. He shoved the saddle off, grabbed Birch under the arm, and heaved him up. "On your feet."

"What are you going to do with me?"

"In the corncrib." Yves unhooked the rope between Sonny's hands.

"No, don't put me back in there." The man disgraced himself, blubbering again. "Just tie me up here. Please."

"That would be real good of me, wouldn't it?" Yves said, dragging Sonny toward the door.

"Wait! I ain't told you everything."

Yves whirled on Birch, shoved his arm against his throat, and backed him into the wall. "You got one chance to tell it, Birch."

"Don't put me in the corncrib. I'll tell you, just tie me up out here in the barn."

"Tell it."

"Your brother. He got something wrong with his foot."

"What's wrong with his foot?"

"It's hurt. Hurt bad." He tried to pull at Yves' arm. "I can't breathe."

Yves shoved against him again. "What did you do to him?"

"Wadn't me. It was Wilson. The nigger kept trying to run, kept causing trouble. Wilson took his rifle and beat the stock of it on his foot till it was good broke."

Yves smashed his fist against Birch's jaw, and the man slumped to the ground. He tied Sonny to the post once more, then wiped his blade in the straw and sheathed it in his boot, picked up the slicker, and reentered the rain.

They didn't kill him, then Gabe's alive. Has to be. He's too tough to die. He stopped in the yard and held his face up to the rain. He let the cool drops wash away the hate and disgust for Sonny Birch that gripped him. He wanted to concentrate on Gabriel now, on hope.

Yves stepped onto the porch and paused in the doorway. Marianne sat before the fire with her hair spread out to dry. It hung over the back of the chair all the way to Marianne's seat. A vision of her without the soiled blue dress, without the petticoats, without the chemise came to him. Just Marianne and that hair cascading down her back.

He pulled his eyes back to her face; she was watching him look at her. *Does she have any idea of the picture in my mind?* He smiled at her, amused, and she blushed. *I believe she does!*

"You put Birch back in the corncrib?" Eb said, handing him a towel.

Yves blinked his eyes. "Nah. Let him run if he wants to."

"Good move. And poor Andy's had enough excitement."

"You named your corn snake?"

"Sure. What'd you find out?"

Marianne left the fire to hear his account. If she was embarrassed to be seen unpinned, wet, and bedraggled, she didn't show it. Not many women would have that kind of aplomb, he thought. But not many women would have been on the trail with three escaped slaves, either.

Yves told them what Birch said, about the house on the Trace, the fever, the injured foot. Then he tipped his head toward the porch, and Eb followed him out.

The rain still rolled off the porch roof into a deep drip line behind the petunias. There wouldn't be a hint of what went on in that cornfield by now. If Birch wanted to make trouble, unlikely as it was, he'd have nothing to show the sheriff except his own wounds, and who would believe that the Rogerses, good citizens and Quakers as they were, would have had anything to do with a ne'er-do-well like Birch?

"I'm going after my brother. You'll see to our three runaways?"

Eb nodded. "We'll hide them long as we can, give the woman's foot time to mend."

"I'd like to send Miss Johnston and her people home.

You know a man around here would take them back for a couple of dollars?"

Eb thought about it. "I reckon Josh Pendergast might welcome ready cash."

Across the rain-soaked yard, a horse dashed madly from the open barn, Sonny Birch on its back riding the horse he had ridden in on, his ropes left behind, not even a hat on his head.

Yves and Eb leaned against the porch posts. "Good. I didn't want to feed the son of a bitch anyway," Eb said. Then he glanced at the door. "Eleanor didn't hear that, did she?" he whispered.

Marianne heard it. She'd gone back to the fire to dry her hair, but she watched the men on the porch. They were talking about what to do with her. As if she were a child, or a mule to be disposed of. She wasn't going home. She was going after Gabriel.

Yves came inside and pulled the bench out from under the plank table. He straddled it, ready to tell the little woman what came next in her life. Marianne glared at him before he opened his mouth.

"I'll thank you not to run my life, Mr. Chamard. I'm quite capable of making my own decisions about when I will return to Magnolias."

She could hear the snit in her voice, but she didn't care how unattractive it sounded. And she quite enjoyed the surprise in Yves' eyes. He'd assumed she would meekly do as she was told. Of course he did.

"I intend to accompany you to Natchez," she said. "And if you are concerned the wagon will slow you down, I am perfectly capable of riding a horse."

Yves looked at Eb. *Women*, that look said.

She wasn't having it. "I'm not afraid of a little rain and mud."

Yves shook his head. "I'm traveling fast, and I'm traveling now. And it'll be dangerous, on the road and maybe when I find Gabe. You're staying here."

"No, I'm not." She stood up. Pearl and Joseph sat against the far wall, watching them, as they shucked a bucket of corn. "We'll be ready in five minutes."

Yves towered over her. "Absolutely not. Joseph has never been on a horse, and I doubt Pearl has. I'm in a hurry."

"Pearl?"

Pearl smoothed her apron. "I can ride."

Yves looked at the ceiling and then at Marianne. "Pearl is injured."

"No, I's all right," Pearl said. "You brother, he a good man, Mr. Yves. He need our hep, den I goin' wid Missy."

"Her daddy was a stable boy where she come from," Joseph volunteered. "She know horses."

Marianne stepped closer to Yves, so close her skirt brushed the toes of his boots. "Your brother is ill. And injured. You don't know what to do for him, but I do. I'm going with you."

She could stare him down, if that's what it took. She tilted her head back and fixed him with her eye. With a little frustration and maybe a little anger thrown in, Yves' irises were greener than she'd ever seen them.

"It's raining," he said. "Hard."

"Eleanor will loan me a slicker."

"There's no sidesaddle."

"Then I'll ride astride." She said it as if she had often ridden in that disreputable pose with her legs spread apart. She felt her face heat up, but she silently dared him to be the first to turn away.

When his eyes dropped to her mouth, she knew she'd win.

Yves blinked and shook his head. "I'm leaving now."
He headed for the door.

"I'll just get my bonnet. Pearl."

Eleanor, who stood not six feet away watching the con-
test, snatched up the bundle of food she'd prepared and
handed it to Yves on his way out. As he stomped off the
porch into the rain, she threw leftover biscuits, boiled
corn, apples, and a slab of ham in a flour sack, then
grabbed her own slicker from its hook. "Hurry up. You'll
need him to help you with the saddle."

Marianne took three dollars from her reticule and
handed them to Eleanor. "For your friend Mr. Pendergast to please take Joseph home."

"All right," Eleanor said. "Eb will see to it. Pearl, child,
hold on. There's another slicker in the chest."

Marianne draped the slicker over her head. She was
halfway across the yard when she remembered Father's
shotgun, the little tote with the ammunition in it, and
her medical bag. Joseph met her at the door with them,
and she splashed back through the yard and into the
barn where Yves was saddling his horse. Eb was busying
himself mending tackle.

"I'll take one of those men's horses," Marianne announced.

"Then you'll saddle it yourself."

She'd never saddled a horse. "Well, how hard can it
be?" she muttered.

She set her things in a pile of clean straw, chose a
saddle from the rack, and heaved it. She staggered only
a little from its weight, and headed for the nearest of the
dead men's horses.

Marianne opened the half door of the stall and thought
Now what? A bridle hung on a peg. She set the saddle back
on the rack, pulled the bridle down, and offered it to the
mare. The horse deliberately raised its head out of her

reach. She looked around. No stool. The horse lowered its head and she tried again, but the mare had been teasing her. It jerked its head up just as she thought she was about to slide the bridle in place.

If she were to look around and see a smirk on Yves Chamard's face, she'd shoot him. She would. She glanced his way but he had his back to her. She remembered a trick she'd seen Father use on an unruly colt. She held her fist out, fingers down, inviting the mare to discover whether she had an apple or a carrot. By the time the horse knew her hand was empty, it was bridled. *There. I can do this.*

Pearl ran in with a slicker and an old bonnet of Eleanor's. "I do dat fo you, Miss Marianne."

"You take that gelding, all right? I can do this."

Marianne left the stall to retrieve the saddle, ready to meet Yves' amused disdain with her chin up, but he was not smiling. He pulled the slicker on, mounted his horse, and looked down at her. "Stay here, Marianne." He spurred the horse and rode out.

Marianne clamped her jaw and crossed her arms. That lasted no more than a heartbeat. She picked up the saddle and lugged it toward the stall again.

"Going to need a blanket under that," Eb mentioned.

Back to the rack with the saddle. She found a blanket and proceeded with her clumsy attempts. No more than ten minutes later, she had the mare saddled. She tied her bag onto the pommel and led the mare to the mounting block. She was about to put her foot in the stirrup when she realized the shotgun still lay in the straw. She retrieved it and climbed back on the block.

Pearl had the gelding saddled and ready to go.

Now Ebenezer moved. "Hold on."

A little miffed Eb hadn't helped her, she still would be glad of a hand up.

"Doubt you've got her cinched. She's likely blown up

her stomach, and then you end up with a loose saddle and a seat in the mud."

He pushed the stirrup out of his way and recinched the saddle. Then he stood there and looked Marianne in the eye. "You know what you're doing?"

Did she? There was certain discomfort ahead of her. Danger? Perhaps that too. But she had the shotgun. Scandal? Well, Pearl was coming, and how could her reputation suffer if no one knew about it? And who would know? Only those who loved Gabriel and wanted him home safe. She could help.

She nodded to Ebenezer. "Yes, I do. He needs me."

"Yves?"

She swallowed. "I meant Dr. Chamard, of course."

Eb held out cupped hands for her foot, lifted her up, and helped her settle her feet in the stirrups. "You'll find it's a better ride sitting like this, Miss Marianne." He slipped her shotgun in the saddle sheath. "Just remember to keep your knees tight, and you'll have a firm seat."

Marianne watched Pearl mount. She had no idea how sore Pearl was, down there, but Pearl didn't wince when she sat in the saddle. "You all right?"

"Yes'm. Riding wid a saddle, I feeling mighty grand."

Relieved, Marianne held her hand down to shake Ebenezer's. "Thank you, Eb."

"Just don't tell Chamard I helped you." He grinned and slapped the mare's flank to get her moving.

Marianne and Pearl entered the rain and took the road west back toward the river. In this mud, they shouldn't have any trouble following Yves' horse, and he wasn't much more than fifteen minutes ahead of them. Marianne spurred the mare on, amazed at how much more secure she felt without a ladies' sidesaddle under her. She pressed both feet into the stirrups and hurried on.

Chapter 18

Gabriel stewed in his own sweat in a shed of some sort. No windows, one door, but the boards were so shrunken that sunlight beamed through in broad swaths, revealing dancing dust motes. He knew there were pigs nearby; the stench told him that when he was conscious enough to register it.

The woman kicked the door open and came in with a pan and a jug. A halo of white hair surrounded her face, and he remembered thinking an angel had come to take him. How many days ago was that? Now he saw the weathered skin, the sunken age-bleached eyes, the nearly toothless mouth.

"You awake again," she said. "That's a good sign, a good sign."

Gabriel struggled to sit up, but he was as weak as a newborn pup. The woman set the food and drink on the dirt floor and bent over to heave him to a sitting position.

"Can't drink lying down, no, sir," she muttered to herself. "Got to get him fed, he going to be any use."

"What's your name?" Gabe rasped.

"What? You talking, are you?"

Gabriel reached for the jug. Sweet cool well water. He

drank it all, then lay down again on the filthy coarse blanket that had been his pallet all the days he'd been here.

The old woman accidentally bumped against Gabriel's destroyed foot, and his eyes rolled up with the pain. He held his breath, and she pounded him once on the chest.

"You breathe, damn you. You're no use to me dead."

He gasped and sweat broke out on his forehead. The fever had left him, but he was far from well.

She sat down next to him and shoved a pan of corn bread closer. "You need to eat."

Gabriel shook his head. "Who are you?"

She sucked on a brown tooth and shifted the lump of tobacco in her bottom lip. "Ginny. They used to call me Ginny."

"I am Gabriel Chamard. Dr. Gabriel Chamard."

Ginny didn't seem interested. "I'm calling you Caleb. That's a good Bible name."

Is the woman simple-minded? "Dr. Gabriel Chamard."

She leaned over to inspect his foot, and Gabriel said, "Please. Don't touch it." It was hugely swollen still, purple black, the skin split in three places.

"I'm not much for doctoring, myself," she said. "You a real doctor?"

"Yes. I am."

"Well, what you want me to do with this foot?"

"Do you know plants? Medicinal herbs?"

"Got a patch of yarrow growing behind the house. Brought it with me from Pennsylvania when I come out here." She scratched behind her ear and brought forth something that she squeezed between her finger and her thumbnail.

"Maypop vines growing all out in the woods. Real pretty. Purple flowers, sometimes reaching the treetops.

Some people call it passion flower. I call it maypop. It's good for this and that."

"Please. Would you make an infusion for me? Use the maypop. And with the yarrow, a poultice to put on my foot?"

Ginny sighed. "Have to feed the hog. If I have time, I'll see about it." She placed her hands flat on the ground and then pressed her weight into them in order to ease up off her bottom. Once she was on her feet, she shook some of the newer dust streaks from her skirt. Gabriel stared at her feet. They were thick-skinned with blackened, grimy creases around the soles. Her nails were yellowed talons, and the skin was stained red from the Mississippi clay. And yet they were small feet, even delicate-boned. Feet that had known the narrowing of shoes, the squeezing bunion-producing tightness of ladies' boots.

"I got work to do. You eat, Caleb."

The least disturbance of Gabriel's foot sent pain racing up his leg like lightning, hot and searing. As long as he lay still, the pain was bearable, so he lay very still. The tool shed must have been a smokehouse once. The ceiling was sooty, and the faint smell of hickory smoke lingered.

The gray rat who shared his meals crept across the packed dirt floor to the tin pan, and Gabriel gladly yielded the dry cornpone. He knew he had to eat, but he could hardly swallow the stuff. "This pan's all yours, Rat."

He still slept most of the time, but now that he'd survived the fever, he had the strength to think. *Lucky*, he kept thinking. He was lucky Monroe and his men hadn't killed him when they couldn't sell him in New Orleans, or Natchez either. Lucky the old woman had found him and managed to get him into the shed out of the sun. If she hadn't, if she hadn't kept feeding him water . . . well, he'd have died.

And he still might. He hardly dared to look at his foot. Raising his head and shoulders was an effort, and he dreaded what he might see. If the healing didn't progress, there'd be gangrene. He lifted his head and looked down the length of his body. The foot was so swollen his toes looked half their length. Splits where his skin had burst from the swelling were angry red. A fly found the raw wounds and flitted and lit, flitted and lit. If the old woman, if Ginny made the yarrow compress, it would at least keep the flies off.

He lay back, exhausted from even that minor effort. Whatever the fever had been, it had drained him of his strength. He distracted himself from the pain by thinking of Simone, always of Simone. *She's playing her piano, right this minute. She has her hair pulled back behind her ears, the way I like it.* Images of her in the candlelight of his bedroom, her hair loose over her bare breasts, tactile memories of her hands on his body, of her mouth on his—he could have wept for wanting her. *I will survive. I will go home. I'll marry Simone, and we'll move away. Wherever Simone wants to go. France, Italy, Egypt. I don't care.*

He woke at dusk to the squawking of chickens. Ginny must be collecting eggs, or maybe a fox was after them. He tried to sit up, to scoot toward the wall so he could lean against it. The effort fatigued him, and moving his foot was unbelievably painful.

He would eat now if there were anything to eat. The rat had left him nothing, however, not even a crumb. Gabriel resolved to eat every morsel Ginny brought from now on. He would eat all he could and force the rest down. He needed his strength, and the sooner the better.

Ginny did not return to the shed that night. In the morning, Gabriel woke to her kicking the shed door open. She carried a bushel basket inside and set it down. "What you want first? Feeding or doctoring?"

He pulled himself up to lean against the wall. "Food, please, Ginny."

She handed him a bowl of black-eyed peas, stewed okra, and her usual overbaked cornpone. There was fatback in the peas and he ate that first. The more he ate, the more he wanted.

"Well, I'm glad you're eating, Caleb. Thought I was going to bury you yet."

"Ginny," Gabriel said gently, "my name is Chamard. Gabriel Chamard."

"I like Caleb." She unpacked the rest of the things from the basket. "This here is the poultice I made out of the yarrow. Hope I did it right. And this," she said as she pulled out a gray jug, "is the brew from the maypop. My old man used to swear it killed the pain in his hip. Maybe it did."

She handed him the small jug and he sipped at it. *Here's hoping she knows the difference between maypop and belladonna.*

Ginny examined his foot, careful not to touch it. She wrinkled her nose and stroked her chin a moment. Then she plopped the poultice onto his foot, none too gently. He lost his breath a moment from the pain, but she didn't notice. She tied the poultice on with what looked like old leather reins.

"Yes, sir, we get you well, and then you get to hauling and hoeing. That's what I need around here, someone to haul and hoe."

"Ginny, thanks to you, I'm alive. But when I can, I'll go home to my family."

She sat back on her heels, a beam of sunlight making a halo of her white hair once more. She looked at him with narrowed eyes. "You were left on my property, not more than fifty yards from the house. That makes you mine, it seems to me. God knows I need help, and He sent you."

"Ginny, I'm not a slave." He rubbed at the dye they'd smeared all over him down in New Orleans, trying to find a buyer for him. "Look, see? This stuff is darkening my skin. I'm a free man, Ginny."

Ginny spat a stream of tobacco juice over her shoulder. Then she raised herself on creaky knees and left him without another word.

Gabriel spent a long day in the shed alone. He was too weak and his foot too damaged to go out, but he slept less. The poultice dried out and he poured a little from his water jug on it. He sat up a good part of the day and watched Ginny through the open door as she slopped the hog and threw corn to the chickens. There was a garden beyond the chicken yard. He saw her tote a hoe in that direction and come back later with an apron full of pickings.

She likely did need help. No telling how long she'd been working the place alone, barefoot and aging. In a few days, maybe he could stand on his foot and start doing a few chores. But more important, next time she came in, he'd ask for paper and pen. Maybe she'd learned to read in the lifetime that had shaped those once ladylike feet. He'd write to his father to come after him, Papa and his brothers. And he'd send a letter to his maman. She'd tell Simone he was coming for her.

When Ginny came in at twilight, she brought him boiled corn and tomatoes and butter beans with a slab of bacon in it. She also brought in a new poultice and another small jug.

"Go on and eat while I see to your foot," she said.

He picked up the bowl and set it down again when

Ginny peeled the old compress off his foot. It hurt like hell and he hissed between his teeth.

"Can't even tell what's broken and what's not, it's so swole," she muttered.

Trying to steady his breathing while she worked, Gabriel said, "How long have you been out here, Ginny? You came from Pennsylvania?"

"Pittsburgh," she said. "My husband, three daughters, and three sons. They're all buried out there." She motioned with her head toward the fields. "Smallpox."

"You didn't get it?"

She shook her head. "I asked God to take me, too, but He didn't give me a single pox." She looked at Gabriel in the failing light. "Now I ask you. Does God love me more or love me less than the others for leaving me here on my own, struggling, but alive?"

Gabriel smiled faintly. "That is indeed a question."

"I'm through hurting you now. Go on and drink your maypop brew. It'll help you sleep and maybe it'll ease you some too."

"You added alcohol?"

"Thought you might be tired of the pain."

"That I am," he said and took a long draught.

She lingered while he ate and drank.

"Ginny, if you have paper in the house, a pen or a pencil, I'll write my family to come for me. They'll take me off your hands. They'll want to thank you, to reward you."

She shifted the chaw in her cheek and looked into the dusky corner of the shed. "No paper in the house." She picked up the bottle of maypop and alcohol and shook it. It was empty. She struggled with her old knees to stand, then opened the creaky door to fireflies in the dark. "Good night, Caleb."

"Good night, Ginny." He'd find another way to send a

message. When he was up and about, he'd stop a
passerby or walk to a neighboring farm.

Gabriel soon succumbed to the alcohol and the seda-
tive effects of the maypop. He needed the sleep, and he
entered a deep and dreamless state.

The moon rose and lit the yard from the farmhouse
to the shed where Caleb slept. Ginny walked softly, not
wanting to waken the chickens. She carried the bushel
basket in her arms. As she opened the shed door, it
creaked. She stopped to listen. Caleb didn't make a
sound. There had been more than alcohol and maypop
in that brew.

Moonlight flooded through the door, clearly lighting
Caleb where he lay stretched out on the floor. His
breathing was deep, sonorous. He'd been real sick, but
she could tell he was a strong man. She'd get a lot of
work out of him, even crippled up like he'd be.

Have to do it. I know what those black toes mean.

From the basket, she removed a chunk of wood. This
she shoved beneath and behind Caleb's injured foot.
She watched him, and he didn't stir. Then she took a
small axe from the basket.

Chapter 19

Marianne spurred her horse down the road, rain rolling off her slicker in rivulets, mud splashing as high as her skirt. She kept her eye on Pearl, but if Pearl had pain, it didn't affect her riding. She moved gracefully with her horse, her gelding's nose just at the mare's flank.

Yves can't be that far ahead. We should see him in a few minutes. At least she hoped so. Even as she rode boldly down the deserted road, a voice in Marianne's head nagged at her. *What do you think you're doing? Riding astride, only Pearl for an escort, and her injured just last night. I'm selfish bringing her out in this rain, chasing a man who doesn't want me along.*

But it's Gabriel Chamard I'm going after, she reminded herself. If he was sick, she could help him far more than his brother could. *I am not chasing Yves Chamard.*

She began to think about her pharmacopoeia back home. As she kept an eye out for plants she could use if Gabriel were fevered or in pain, her attention was not on the open road ahead of her.

A rider rushed out of the woods, his hat covering his face, a slicker concealing his shape. Marianne's mare reared up and neighed in alarm. She held on, squeezing her knees into the horse's sides to keep her seat. The rogue grabbed for the bridle, and the traitorous horse immediately yielded to his hand. Marianne hauled on the reins with all her strength to pull the horse away.

"Marianne! It's me. Marianne!"

She continued backing her horse away from him, furious. "What are you doing? You could have gotten me killed!"

"Get off the road. Follow me."

Pearl turned her gelding to leave the road, but Marianne was still calming her horse with firm hands on the reins. "I will not get off the road. I have as much right as you have—"

Yves reached for her horse again. "Get off the road."

She could see his face now. He had no business being that angry. She knew he was an ill-tempered, arrogant . . . *Oh. He isn't just angry.* "What's wrong?"

"Follow me." He urged his horse into the bracken and through the trees until the oaks and hickories and brush screened them from the road. He dismounted and quickly helped her down, then Pearl. "Keep a hand on your horses. Keep them quiet."

Rain trickled down Marianne's neck. The mare began to graze. She could hear nothing from the road. She looked her question at Yves, but he shook his head for her to be quiet.

Finally she heard harness and hooves, the jangle and thud muffled by the rain. Through the leaves, she could make out a company of riders filling the road. Eight, nine of them? Some of them were merrily singing a song so bawdy she nearly laughed. She looked again at Yves, who had his rifle out. What on earth?

He held his weapon at the ready until the men were

well away. When he shoved it back into its sheath, Marianne put her hands on her hips.

"What was that all about?"

Rain poured off his hat brim, dripped off his nose. The air itself was sodden and cool and reviving. All the colors of the forest were refreshed and deepened. As deep as Yves' glaring eyes.

"Did no one ever tell you about women traveling alone? About bad men? About—" He looked at Pearl and stopped abruptly. Marianne knew what he'd been about to say. About rape.

Lamely, Marianne said, "I have the shotgun."

He blew out his breath in contempt.

"They were just traveling men," Marianne argued. "Why do you assume they were bad? I could have—"

"You could have gotten yourself dead, you and Pearl both. What do you think they would have done when they'd finished with you?"

He tipped the rain off his brim and drew a breath. "Look. They were rough men. They were drinking. They might have said 'Good day' and ridden on by you, but I don't think that's the way it would have happened. All right?"

Marianne thought it over for a moment. Then she smiled. He was rude, and abrupt, and imperious. But he'd just saved them. Or as good as. When Yves continued to frown, she smiled even more broadly.

"Good grief, woman. Get on your horse."

Pearl put one foot against the trunk of a pine tree and levered herself into the stirrup. Marianne was about to try that when Yves cupped his hands for her foot, his mouth a grim line.

Marianne hesitated, willing him to look at her. When he did look up to see why she hadn't put her foot in his hands, she said, "Thank you. Again."

He shook his head, defeated. "You're welcome. Again."

"We won't hold you back, Yves. I promise."

"Uh-huh." He mounted and led them back to the road. They splashed through the puddles and the mud, making better time than the wagon had the day before. They reached the river road and turned north toward Natchez.

Yves rode them hard. Midafternoon, they passed an inn, and Marianne desperately wanted to stop. By now she was sick of the rain. She was wet, cold, and hungry. She thought about the bundle of provisions from Eleanor tied to Pearl's saddle horn. But Yves hadn't eaten his yet, and she wouldn't give him the satisfaction of breaking into hers and Pearl's before he did. But her stomach rumbled and she imagined those buttery biscuits, the salt of the cured ham, the crispy apples. She stared at Yves' back and hated him.

Before sunset, the rain let up and a patch of blue sky promised better weather. The road led them to a bluff overlooking the Mississippi. A steamboat, gay with its gingerbread and paintwork, paddled far below them. Yves turned in his saddle to look at his bedraggled entourage. "Ready to stop?"

Marianne could have whimpered she was so ready, but she nodded reluctantly as if she would stop only if he needed the rest.

She rode the mare over to a boulder and dismounted by herself. Her crotch ached and her right leg twitched. She moved out of the way so Pearl could use the same boulder and waited to see how stove-up she was. Poor Pearl. *I should never have brought her.* In the privacy behind their horses, Marianne took Pearl's arm and turned her around.

"Pearl, are you in pain?"

"It hurt some."

"Are you bleeding? Either place?"

Pearl pulled up the slicker to see if her side had bled through the bandage. It must have scabbed over. Marianne checked the back of her dress for blood, but didn't find any. She pulled Pearl to her and hugged her. "I'm sorry, Pearl. I should have left you with Eleanor."

"No'm. It not bad. Way I figure, you can't come out alone, and I be sore sitting in de house or on de horse, jest the same."

"Thank you, Pearl. Dr. Chamard will need us, I'm sure of it."

They retrieved their bundle of food and joined Yves on a flat outcrop of rock. It was wet, but Marianne couldn't see it made much difference in their present state. Yves took their bundle and along with his provisions, he laid out their supper. Pearl gathered her biscuits and ham and apple and retreated to a nearby boulder. Yves helped Marianne to settle on their rock.

"What, no candles?" she said.

He laughed. Thank heavens his humor had improved. They watched the paddleboat make its way upriver. What a marvel to have the power to fight the mighty current. "Have you ever been on a steamer?" she asked.

They passed a pleasant twenty minutes over their meal. Then Yves turned sober. "Miss Johnston," he began.

Oh, so we're back to Miss Johnston. "Yes, Mr. Chamard?"

He did not acknowledge the mocking smile on her face.

"We are about to experience nightfall."

"I am familiar with the phenomenon."

"And what arrangements did you have in mind?"

"An inn would be nice. Or perhaps we will find a planter's home along here. Whoever lives there probably knows my father. And yours. We could impose on their hospitality for one night."

Yves sighed. "You really haven't thought this through, Marianne."

She bridled at the insult to her good sense. "Well, I'm thinking now," she snapped. She gathered her skirts to get her feet under her, but Yves put his hand out.

"Hold on."

She sat, waiting.

"Shall we consider your reputation for a moment?"

"My reputation is just fine. Pearl has been with us every moment. We have done nothing untoward at all."

Yves waggled his eyebrows. "Not yet." He grinned at her. She moved to get up again.

"No. I'm sorry. That was rude." She still wasn't smiling. "That was unforgivably rude and crude and I should be hanged for it." Now she smiled a very little. "I should be shot first and then hanged."

"I'd prefer that, the shooting and then the hanging."

"First, however, let's decide how we are to spend the night. I know of no inn for miles in either direction. And as for our finding a home to let us in, I am dubious that we will be received as the innocents we are."

She looked at their sodden clothes. Her hair must be tangled as well as wet. Mud all over her. She weighed her appearance against the desire for a warm fire and a dry bed. The dry bed was winning.

"May I point out that as of now," Yves said, "no one of our circle knows of your present adventure? No one knows Albany Johnston's daughter is traveling in the rain with a man with a reputation, quite undeserved, I hasten to add, as a womanizer." He looked at her sideways. "You know Lindsay Morgan?"

She tipped her chin up and met his gaze. "I do indeed."

He had the grace to look uncomfortable. "Well, as I said, not the womanizer I'm reported to be. However, the planter society is small. If we stop at a plantation, soon everyone will hear that Marianne Johnston showed up at nightfall, wet, muddy, and in the company of that disreputable rake Yves Chamard."

"Um. Yes, I take your point."

"So it's up to you. You can hope to retain your covert status by passing an uncomfortable night in the woods, or you can willfully blemish the reputation required of a young woman of your position." The quirky smile lit his face. "Do you require my advice, Miss Johnston?"

"I do not." She stood up and collected Eleanor's sacks. "The woods it is."

Yves found a clearing far enough from the road that they would not be seen or heard. Traveling at night practically invited ruffians to take whatever you had and leave you with your skull crushed in, so they had no fire; the wood was too wet anyway.

They had one bedroll for the three of them. Only Yves had thought to include that in his kit. The ladies stretched the slickers dry side up and then lay down, Yves' blanket over them. Yves, well, Yves could spread his slicker between him and the wet ground, or he could swelter in it but save himself a dozen or two mosquito bites.

And so they passed a miserable night.

Marianne woke to the smell of meat cooking. *I'm so hungry I'm delirious.* She sat up and there was a spitted hare over a small smoky fire. How had Yves killed a rabbit? She hadn't heard a gun. Then she remembered Monroe and the other men yelling out when the rocks hit them. Yves had a very accomplished way with a sling.

Pearl slept on, and Marianne left her to get all the rest she could. Stiffly, her legs and seat sore, she bent over to check the meat. Didn't look done to her, but what did she know about cooking?

She put a hand to her hair. Why hadn't she brought a comb? It was still mostly up except for those tendrils that would not be tamed. She'd put her bonnet back on later.

She looked for Yves. Thirty yards away he stood on the edge of a pond. She crossed a carpet of pine needles and stopped a distance behind him. He was in his shirt-sleeves, no coattails to obscure the line of his long body. His shoulders tapered down to narrow hips and long legs. Marianne leaned against a pine tree, her cheek resting on the bark, imagining those muscled thighs under the fabric.

Yves had a handful of stones and was skipping them across the surface of the pond, watching the series of plops between throws. Seven, eight! *He's good*. She and Adam had thrown stones all one summer when they were children. She could never make it past the third plop before her stone sank.

She walked over to the pond, picked up a stone, and threw it. Two, three, four!

He smiled. "Not bad. For a girl." He threw another. Only six.

"Having an off day?"

He looked at her, and she knew what he was thinking. He was taking her dress off again, only in his mind of course, but she could feel it. "Stop that," she said.

Yves grinned, tossed a stone in the air, and caught it. "Yes, ma'am."

His two-day beard framed his mouth, outlined his chin. The whiskers would probably be scratchy if he kissed her, she thought. She'd like to find out.

He reached over and plucked an errant caterpillar off her shoulder and held it up for her to admire. "Know what we used to do with caterpillars when we were boys?"

"What?"

"Marcel and I would find all the little girls we could. We'd hold up the greenest, juiciest worm, caterpillar, whatever we had, and then we'd eat it."

"You didn't."

"Yes, we did. The girls invariably screamed and ran. Gabe's cousins lived next house up from his mother's and we managed to entertain them many a summer. Until Marcel couldn't stomach the worms anymore."

"But you never tired of eating them?"

"Nah." He held the caterpillar up. "Wanna see?"

"Oh, please don't. I'd carry that image with me forever."

"And then you wouldn't let me kiss you again?" He moved closer.

"Absolutely not. Never."

He flicked the caterpillar away and stepped closer still. "I haven't eaten a worm in years and years."

"Not even one?"

His mouth was on hers. He tasted of blackberries. He'd been holding out on her. Then she tasted only his lips, his tongue. His shirt was thin over the hardness of his chest. She slid her fingers around his ribs to the tight muscles of his back. *Just like I imagined.* Feeling him with her hands, her own skin came alive under his. He caressed her neck, slowly traced her spine to her waist. Then he spread his fingers and pressed her lower back against his. She opened her mouth. She would have inhaled him if she could.

Yves pulled his mouth away from hers, keeping her body close to his. "You know what?"

Marianne pressed her face against his chest. She could hear his heart, beating as fast as hers. "Um?"

"It's a good thing you brought Pearl along."

It certainly is. Marianne sighed. *Keep your head, Mari-*

anne. It's only kisses. They don't mean anything to him. And I know better than to think otherwise.

He turned her face to look at the bruise where Wilson had socked her. "Hurt?"

"A little."

He kissed the tip of her nose. "Let's eat."

They walked side by side, their hands brushing now and again. Marianne looked at him from under her lashes. "You've been eating blackberries."

He laughed at her. "And I thought you were thinking about me." Back at the fire, he pointed to a giant lily pad he'd filled with berries.

She dropped one luscious shiny berry in her mouth. "Hmm. You are *mon beau idéal.*"

"You speak French?"

"*Mais oui.* Was not my own maman a Creole daughter?"

Sensual, sensuous, seductive. And smart. French and English both. Yves tested the rabbit on the spit. Done enough. He struggled to get it off the stick without burning his fingers. Then he realized what he'd been thinking. *Hell. Most everybody I know speaks French and English. You idiot. Watch out, Yves, before you make a fool of yourself.*

Marianne knelt down to Pearl and touched her shoulder. "Pearl?"

Pearl opened her eyes slowly, clearly befuddled for a moment. Then understanding brightened her face.

"We need to eat and get on," Marianne said. "You sore? Can you get up and walk around?"

She did. By the time she had moved and stretched for a few moments, Pearl seemed all right, and Marianne was relieved. They'd spend another day in the saddle and another as well before they even reached Natchez.

Midday they stopped at a prosperous-looking inn. Marianne took a room for her and Pearl to repair themselves while Yves saw to the horses. The three of them enjoyed a hot meal, Pearl in the kitchen, Yves and Marianne in the dining room. Then Yves purchased supplies and a frying pan, and they were off again within the hour. With good weather and the road drying up, the traveling was easier. And with every mile they were closer to Gabriel.

That night they found another inn. After a luxurious washup with hot water and soap, homemade and harsh as it was, they dined on venison pie and fig pudding, then eased their bones in clean sheets and blankets. Pearl slept on a pallet on the floor in Marianne's room, and Yves was across the hall in his.

Two more days on the road and they began to see signs Natchez was near. Twice they overtook coffles of slaves on their way to the Forks-of-the-Road market. The unfortunates walked in double file, their necks in iron collars, their wrists in chains. Yves watched Marianne, wondering how the sight would affect her. Most of the young women Yves knew would simply have averted their eyes from the unpleasant sight, but Marianne could not pull her eyes from the black men who shuffled along, their heads bent in fatigue and defeat.

Pearl examined every poor soul, and Yves wondered whether she searched for Luke in hope or dread. Surely by now he was farther north than this.

As for himself, Yves labored to keep his face blank as they passed the captured slaves, but anger stiffened his body. Some of those bound in iron might have been sold to the slavers for ready cash, he thought, but likely most of them had been runaways. Brave men, to have dared to run with no money, no map, no horse. Hope, that was what they had run on, and courage.

The trail curved here and cut them off from the jangling harness of the slaves. Only the sounds of their own horses overlay the buzzing of bees.

They rode on, and Yves thought through how to describe the scene in the next essay he would send to Rochester, New York. Frederick Douglass ran a newspaper there, and under its masthead was printed *Right is of no sex, Truth is of no color, God is the Father of us all, and we are all Brethren.* Yves had contributed half a dozen articles over the last year. Marcel composed poetry; Yves wrote accounts of slavery. Under his pen name Daniel Rivers, he had developed a following among the Northern liberals. Of course, no one, not even Douglass, knew his identity. That would be tantamount to suicide, to be known in his home state as an active abolitionist.

Thinking of his own risks reminded him that Marianne needed tutoring in secrecy. She was entirely too open, and too naive to see the dangers. There were people in Louisiana, even people whom she knew and liked, who would damage her and her family if they knew what errand had led her to Ebenezer's cornfield. Not simply snubs and shunning. Assault, murder, burnouts—all were possible, and no recourse to the law, which at this point already favored the slaveholders beyond reason, as Yves saw it.

They reached the bustling city of Natchez and agreed to split up on Main Street. While Yves went to the stationers to write to his father and to Gabriel's mother, Cleo, Marianne was to find the herbs and other medicinals she might need for Gabe, then visit the dry goods store. Pearl's boots had disintegrated in the rain, and Marianne meant to buy her a pair of leather shoes, as well as ready-made clothing for the both of them.

Yves imagined Marianne in an ill-fitting, inexpensive frock. *Bet the mistress of Magnolias has never worn a dress not made and fitted especially for her.*

Once his letters were mailed, Yves found a stable with a full corral out back. He bargained as shrewdly as he knew how and came away with a black mare without having paid any more than he should have. He returned to the corner where he was to meet Marianne and waited.

And waited. Across the street was a fine-looking barbershop. WILLIAM TADMAN, PROPRIETOR, it said on the glass window. *Mr. Tadman has done well for himself,* Yves thought. Yves' father and Tadman's were old friends, and the son, William, was like Gabriel, a freedman with a white father.

Several well-dressed men went in with hair over their ears and came out neatly barbered. Yves considered going in to say hello to William, but as surely as he did, Marianne would wander up. *No need to give her an edge in moral superiority,* he thought wryly. *She already has me where she wants me.* In fact, he was the next thing to ravishing her, and if he weren't careful, he'd blurt out a proposal. He probably would propose, but not yet. Not with war looming and his not having decided what he would do in that event. Too much uncertainty to ask a woman to hook her fortune to his star.

At last Marianne appeared, Pearl hurrying along behind her, brown paper bundles in both their arms. They each wore new bonnets and decent though not fine dresses. Not what Marianne was used to, certainly, this light calico. *But she's as radiant in cotton as I've ever seen her in satin. And all the more alluring, for I don't believe she knows it.*

"You haven't waited long?" she said, out of breath.

He'd meant to scowl at her, but she was irresistible. Her new bonnet, a simple straw with the minimum number of the requisite ribbons, couldn't contain all that unruly hair curling in the Natchez humidity, and her cheeks were flushed, her eyes brilliantly blue. He smiled, the reproach he'd been framing flown from his mind.

"Not long. Are you ready?" he said.

"We're ready."

"Then let's ride." At the stable, he stowed their bundles in satchels, helped them mount, and led them north on the Trace. Only two days, Sonny Birch had said. It was hard not to break into a gallop, so urgently did Yves want to find his brother. But neither the horses nor the women could sustain a gallop for so many hours, so he tried their mounts at a slower but mile-eating canter.

In earlier days, the Natchez Trace had been a well-traveled route for the river men on their return trek to homes in Tennessee, Kentucky, or Ohio. With the rising prevalence of steamboats to get them back upriver, however, those men now saved their shoe leather, and the Trace had become no better traveled than most of the roads in the South.

They overtook a farmer returning from the market in Natchez with a wagonload of flour, salt, molasses, whatever the man didn't make on his own place. It was an hour before they encountered anyone else.

Yves kept his company on the move, glancing back now and then at Marianne's and Pearl's faces to be sure he wasn't asking too much of them at this pace. The trees arched over the road, dappling them with leaf shade, and Marianne's countenance showed she was game. Pearl, too, betrayed no discomfort. Admirable women, he thought.

On they went, mostly strung out in single file except for the fourth horse that cantered along beside Yves. Coming toward them, another group of slavers and their coffle approached, the white men on horseback, their chattel on foot. Tight-lipped, Yves nodded to the head man. He'd already passed the file of shuffling men when

Pearl's scream startled him. He turned his horse hard. *If those blackguards have accosted her—*

"It's Luke!" Marianne shouted.

Pearl was already off her horse and running for the line of slaves. She threw herself against the tallest man in the line and, shaking and sobbing, wrapped her arms around him.

A slaver trotted toward them, uncoiling the whip from his saddle horn.

Chapter 20

For Marianne, the chaos seemed to slow down so that she saw everything all at once, Yves whirling his horse around and spurring it back down the line of slaves, Pearl hanging on to Luke, the slaver bearing down on them with his rawhide poised to strike.

The whip cracked over Luke's head, and Pearl screamed. The slaver drew his arm back to strike again.

The roar of Marianne's shotgun broke the action. Everyone froze, or so it seemed. Strangely coolheaded, the shotgun barrel still pointed in the air, she said, "The other chamber is loaded, sir. I advise you not to whip my slave."

The man struggled with his horse to bring it face-to-face with Marianne's mount. "Get your gal out of my line, lady, you don't want her whipped."

Yves pulled his bay up short. "Pearl, mount your horse." For all the fury with which he'd spurred his horse back to the scene, he too was cool. He turned to the slaver. "We needn't be unpleasant about this. We don't mean to delay you. However, it seems you have one of Miss Johnston's slaves among your trophies."

"Yes," Marianne said, matching Yves' unruffled

manner. She lowered her gun barrel. "That man is a runaway from Magnolias. Perhaps you know of my father, sir. Albany Johnston in St. John Parish?"

The man spat tobacco juice. "Never heard of him."

Pearl, as yet on her feet, put her hand on Marianne's boot. Marianne looked into her desperate eyes, read the silent plea on her face. Pearl loved this man. Pearl had nothing, no future, no hope without him. Marianne tried to imagine such desolation. Her own loneliness had never touched the edge of what Pearl's face showed.

I'll save him if I can. That was the message in her eyes as she returned Pearl's frantic gaze. "Get on your horse, Pearl, where you'll be safe."

Marianne knew enough of humanity to conceal how much they wanted Luke back. "I suppose I could relieve you of him immediately," she said to the whip-wielding man with all the nonchalance she could muster, "and save you the trouble of transporting him all the way to the parish."

The slaver leaned on his pommel and eyed Luke's height, his broad shoulders, his erect stance. "Reckon he's worth more than a few dollars, a fine fella like him. The reward should be 'mensurate with his value."

"Of course." *Damnation, I've spent nearly all my money. And I think Yves has too.* "I'll happily write you a note for the reward. You have paper upon your person, perhaps?"

The man snorted.

A young man rode his horse around the coffle and joined them. He had yellow hair, freckles, blue eyes, and a blue denim shirt. At a second glance, Marianne decided he couldn't be more than fifteen, but he inserted himself into the conversation with authority.

"We don't know if this slave is yours or not, lady," the boy said. "Pardon me for saying so."

"You saw this woman," Yves offered in a reasoning

tone, nodding at Pearl, "obviously Miss Johnston's slave, running for him. That should be proof enough."

The first man interrupted. "How much cash you got on you?" he said to Marianne.

The boy's face turned scarlet. "We aren't taking the money, Horn. Pa told me to bring back twenty, and that's what I'm going to do."

"I assure you," Marianne put in, "I will write you a promissory note for the full amount—"

"No'm. We aren't selling slaves on the road. My pa will get top dollar for every one of them I bring in. They're going to Forks-of-the-Road market. If'n you want to buy that one there, then go talk to my pa. I'm taking all of them to Natchez."

"We ought to be able to make a deal," Yves said quietly. He was not the hothead she'd taken him for. "Our party just left Natchez and are rather urgently traveling north. Surely we ought to be able to—come to an understanding."

Marianne caught the suggestion—Yves was hinting that he'd add a bribe to sweeten the transaction. She was willing. But what did she have to bribe them with?

Her earrings. She was wearing her pearls. They should be enough to buy Luke outright, bribery included.

Horn looked at the yellow-haired boy with a raised eyebrow. "Nothing like ready cash."

"I said no. Pa's expecting twenty slaves, he's getting twenty. For all I know, he's already made a contract out for these here."

"Lots of times, slaves die on the march," Horn said.

The boy's ears were as red as his face. "Horn, you want to work for my pa again, you'll do as you're told."

Horn's face turned ugly. He hawked phlegm and spat, and Marianne's stomach churned. Without looking at

anyone again, Horn rode his horse back to the front of
the line.

"Sorry, ma'am," the boy said. "Can't help you here on
the road. You go on back to Natchez and see my pa.
Harvey Fox. He makes the deals."

"But, Mr. Fox. Please," Marianne began.

The boy turned his horse and the coffle began
moving.

"Luke!" Pearl cried out. "Missy, I won't never see him
again. Please, Missy!"

The chains of the slaves in front of Luke pulled him forward, the iron shackles clanking and rattling. His face
broke Marianne's heart. Love for Pearl, helplessness, and
now new hope dashed. Despair painted his features.

Marianne looked at Yves' grim face. It was so much to
ask. They were no more than a day and a half from
Gabriel. Going back to Natchez would take at least another day.

"Yves?" Marianne said.

"I know."

"Gabriel . . ." She didn't know what to say about
Gabriel.

Yves looked at her. "I know."

He checked that the fourth horse was still with him
and fell in behind the coffle. Marianne and Pearl followed him.

At Washington Road, the ragtag caravan turned off,
but Yves continued toward Natchez on the Trace.

"Mr. Yves!" Pearl pleaded. "Dey going de other way!"
Pearl turned her horse to follow Luke.

Yves spurred his mount the few yards it took to catch
Pearl. He reached for the bridle, then took her reins.
"They're going on to the slave depot," he told her.
"There's nothing we can do tonight. Tomorrow, we'll go
out there."

Marianne pulled her horse up beside Pearl and reached over to touch her. "Tomorrow, Pearl."

Pearl nodded and followed Marianne back to their road.

The three made their way through Natchez by gas streetlamps to an inn on Commerce Street. Marianne and Yves took two rooms and ate in the common area downstairs while Pearl took her supper behind the inn.

"Yves, I have a dollar and a half left."

He nodded and sighed. "I have nine." That would be plenty for their daily needs, but would do nothing to help Luke.

"We only need enough for the reward. Do you know anyone in Natchez?"

"Yes, but we will need more than reward money." He looked at her. "Marianne, did you send out the hue and cry?"

"No," she admitted. She understood: The slave broker would not accept her word that Luke belonged to her when Magnolias had not even cried out he was missing. She looked at the simple, inexpensive dress she wore and touched her poorly dressed hair. She didn't look like a rich planter's daughter either.

Marianne fingered her pearl earrings. They'd been a gift from Father on her thirteenth birthday. "There's a bank in town. They'll advance money on my signature, surely."

Yves shook his head. The Natchez bank was not of the same institution with which the Chamards did business, nor was it Mr. Johnston's bank. Yves explained how long it would take for messages to and from New Orleans before the bank here would release any funds to them.

Marianne removed her earrings. Yves watched her fingers slide the slender wires from her lobes, and she felt as if she were disrobing before him. Her breath came faster as she watched him watching her.

But they had business to settle.

She held out her palm to him. "The pearls then."

Yves closed her fingers and wrapped his hand around hers. "You're a generous soul, Miss Johnston. I honor you for it." They looked into each other's eyes, lantern light bathing them in its soft glow, and Marianne thought, *Yves. He's the one.*

He opened her palm and lifted one of the pearls to the lantern light. "A beautiful thing, a pearl." He looked back at Marianne. "You should always wear pearls."

She hadn't known a man could make love to a woman in a public room. Her breathing wouldn't settle, her heart wouldn't slow. He still held her hand, and his eyes penetrated hers. Did he know she wanted him to kiss her, to show her—

"My friend is an honorable man. He will hold the pearls as collateral. You shall have them back again."

Yves let go her hands and sat back as if newly aware there were people at nearby tables.

"Who is this man?" Marianne asked. She put the hand he'd held in her lap and wrapped her other hand around it as if she could retain his touch that way.

"William Tadman. He's a prosperous businessman here in Natchez. He does a little of everything, I gather. Barbershops, moneylending, farming. My father and his were together in Paris for a time."

Yves wrapped the pearls in his handkerchief and buttoned them into his vest pocket.

"Thank you," Marianne said. "For this delay. I know we have to hurry."

"Yes. As soon as we've secured Luke, we have to ride."

"As fast as you like."

Yves hesitated. "Have you considered that . . . You

should prepare yourself." Yves swallowed. "Gabriel may be dead."

She shook her head. "No. He's alive. I feel it."

Yves looked into the fire. "If he is alive, he's liable to be a changed man. Weakened. Sick. And . . ."

"I know he's been sick. That's why I had to come, to nurse him."

"You don't know him well, Marianne. Gabriel is a proud man. He's had to live his life with the shadow of race over him. He's fought it, and he's risen above it. And now this. I don't know what he will have become."

Marianne nodded. "Angry. That's what he'll have become."

Yves was silent a moment. "I'm white. I love my brother, but he may have forgotten that he loves me too."

If Pearl slept, it wasn't for long. She'd spent the dark hours wondering if Luke was awake, too. Could be he was low. He'd been caught. But what he didn't know was these good people were going to give him back to her.

When she heard stirrings out at the cookhouse, she lit the candle and roused Marianne. Pearl wanted to be at the slave market as soon as it was light.

"Did you sleep at all?" Marianne said around a yawn.

"No, Missy. I don need sleep. I jus needs Luke."

She left Miss Marianne sitting on the side of the bed and stepped down the hall to scratch on Mr. Chamard's door. She entered without waiting for him to answer. Another gentleman shared a bed with Mr. Chamard, a huge, snoring fellow. In the light of her candle, the man's gut was rounded like a great sow's belly. Pearl went around the bed to find Mr. Chamard clinging to the edge of the mattress, so deeply asleep she had to tap his shoulder twice to rouse him.

He woke with a start. "Ahhg," he said. He put a hand to his forehead. "I haven't slept a wink with this fellow's snoring."

Pearl nearly laughed aloud. This morning, Pearl was ready to laugh. This morning, this wonderful man was going to get her Luke back for her. She gathered his trousers, his suspenders, his shirt, his stockings, his shoes.

She held the trousers open for him to step into and began pulling them up his legs.

"I can dress myself," he whispered irritably.

"Yessir. I knows you can. But it be light soon, and I get you dressed quick." She held his shirt up for him to slip his arms in and helped him tuck the tail in his trousers. When she started in on the buttons at his waist, he slapped her hands away.

"Now git," he said. "Your mistress needs you."

She smiled at him. She would have kissed him if she'd been allowed to.

"Wait. Light this candle first."

She did and then hurried back to make sure Marianne hadn't lain down again.

Marianne was still on the edge of the bed, but she had her hair down and a brush in her hand.

"I'll do dat, Missy."

Marianne turned so Pearl could sit behind her on the bed. "Joseph and Hannah, and now you. It's nice when you call me Missy."

"Yes'm. We loves you." Pearl finished the unsparingly brisk brushing. "But you still gots to get dressed fast."

"Yes'm," Miss Marianne said.

Pearl hustled her until she was dressed and out the

door. Downstairs they found Mr. Chamard in the common room.

"We's ready. Let's go," Pearl said.

"Hold on," he said. "The Forks doesn't open for nearly two hours yet." Pearl was about to erupt in protest, but he held his hand up. "And we are twenty minutes from the market."

He pulled out a chair for Miss Marianne. "I've ordered breakfast for us. After we've eaten, I'll walk around to Mr. Tadman's place."

Pearl left her bundle with the mistress and found the cook already scrambling eggs and frying bacon. She helped, if only to speed things along. If they arrived after the market already had opened, someone else might spot Luke and buy him on sight. They had to be the first ones there.

After breakfast, Mr. Chamard left to visit Mr. Tadman. Miss Marianne sipped coffee. Pearl stayed in the kitchen and made biscuits for the cook. She couldn't possibly sit still. Work was the only way she knew to make the time pass.

Finally, oh finally, the innkeeper came for her. Her mistress was waiting for her outside, he said. Mr. Chamard had their four horses, Miss Marianne was mounted, they were ready to go.

The Forks-of-the-Road market, not more than a mile east of town, was far enough out to give the townspeople some reassurance that the cholera and other diseases that plagued the weakened transient population would be contained, yet close enough in to be convenient for those buying and selling slaves. This market was second only to New Orleans in this part of the world. Thousands and thousands of enslaved souls entered the wide gates and passed out again, still enslaved.

Pearl trembled at sight of the dreaded place. All her

life she'd heard stories about being sent to the market, about being stripped and touched and probed by strangers who saw you as another ox or horse or mule to labor in their fields. She imagined a dark cloud of fear and hopelessness hovering overhead.

A carriage and several saddle horses clustered around the entrance to the rough wooden building showed Pearl they were not the first to arrive. She shook off the gloom that had gripped her. Luke was inside, and she had come to claim him. She slid off her horse and hurriedly tied it to a rail.

Mr. Chamard dismounted and called her to him.

"Pearl, this impatience won't do. These traders smell eagerness like it was cinnamon on toast. You'll just drive the price up, and we have only a limited check from my friend. You understand?"

Chamard looked up at Miss Marianne. "Maybe she should stay out here with you. I think that would be best."

"No, Mr. Chamard," Pearl said. "I goin' in. I has to see him. You might not know him. I goin' in." She wanted to grab the master's sleeve. She wanted to plead, to beg, to cry. "I'll be quiet. I will be."

Her mistress and the master decided, exchanging looks over her head. Miss Marianne, still on her horse, nodded. "Let her go in, I think." She began to dismount and Mr. Chamard held her waist to help her down. *Dat man in love with Missy. I see it every time he touch her.*

"I should like you to stay out here," Mr. Chamard said to Missy.

Miss Marianne took a moment to think about it. "My father, and I myself, profit from slavery. I don't have the right not to look at what it does to people."

Mr. Chamard nodded. He held his arm out for her, and Pearl followed along behind them.

The soul drivers expected early morning buyers. They'd already arranged their chattel in a semicircle in the courtyard. In order to entice buyers, the brokers had dressed every slave in new clothes. The male slaves stood with cheap hats on their heads, perfectly still, prepared to be inspected. Equally impassive, the women, some of them with small children clinging to their skirts, faced them across the yard.

When the trader in a fine gray top hat tooted a whistle, the slaves began to parade within the confines of the yard.

"Step lively, there, damn you," the slaver called out. He blew the whistle again and the men and women picked up their pace until they were trotting. At the third whistle, they slowed down and resumed their places around the quadrangle.

The man in the top hat came over to Mr. Chamard and introduced himself. Harvey Fox. That blond boy's father.

Pearl found Luke, the fourth man down from where Pearl stood. His shoulders strained the seams of the thin black cotton coat, and the trousers hardly came to his ankles. His jaw muscles bulged as he stared at the far wall of the enclosure, and she knew he was holding himself in.

Her heart pounded so she couldn't hear what Mr. Chamard said to the trader, couldn't hear what the trader said back. She tried to keep her eyes on the ground, tried not to show Mr. Fox her soul lived in the breast of the fourth man from the end.

Other buyers ahead of them were walking along the lines, stopping to examine this or that one more closely. Mr. Chamard and Mr. Fox moved away and conferred in voices pitched for privacy.

Closer to her at the end of the women's line, an elderly

lady perused the potential maids, her black silk skirt so wide she seemed to float rather than walk on concealed feet. Pearl watched her to keep from gazing at Luke.

With her parasol, the old woman lifted the skirt of a girl of perhaps fifteen. "Virgin, do you think?" she asked the trader escorting her. Pearl thought the girl's face might have been made of wood, but the trader barely bothered to conceal his smirk.

"Yes, ma'am. Her last owner vouchsafed she was untouched."

"Hm," she said. "She has a sour look about her, and I don't care for that scar under her chin."

The lady walked on to stop in front of a woman of perhaps twenty. The boy she held wrapped his arms around his mama's neck as the lady looked them over. A little girl, maybe four years old, clung to the mother's skirt, watching the lady with big, bright eyes. "A pretty child," the old woman announced.

Pearl's attention shifted when a gentleman in a bottle-green coat stopped in front of Luke. She nearly cried out, but Mr. Chamard turned slightly to give her a look, and she tightened her mouth.

The gentleman used his riding crop to pull Luke's chin down. "Good teeth, mostly," he said. "Stick your tongue out. All right. Let me see your hands."

Luke did all he was told, his eyes fastened on the wall some forty feet away. *Please, God, don't let Luke lose hisself.*

"Are you of a pliant disposition?" the gentleman asked.

"What dat mean?" Pearl whispered. Miss Marianne frowned at her to be silent.

"Are you content with your life? I don't want to invest in a slave who's going to be running off every chance he gets."

Now Luke looked at the man. Looked him in the eye.

The man in the green jacket stepped back. He shook his head and muttered, "Not a good risk, I shouldn't think." He moved on.

At last Mr. Chamard began to amble down the line of men. He stopped at number two for a moment, looked him up and down as the other buyers had done. Then he moved on and stood before Luke.

"Feel this fellow's arm," Mr. Fox said, inviting Yves to inspect Luke as if he were a piece of livestock. He tapped Luke's thigh with his whip handle. "See that? Solid muscle."

Mr. Chamard didn't say, I'll take this one. He didn't give any indication he was even particularly interested in Luke. *He's jest trying to be smart, tha's all. He won' leave Luke here. He done got de money dis morning.* Still, Pearl could hardly breathe.

Don look at me, Luke. You look at me, I gone throw myself on you. She kept close behind Miss Marianne's skirt, trying not to let her heart show in her face.

Mr. Chamard walked on, and Pearl thought she might faint at Luke's feet. *How he pass on by?* She wanted to grab the mister, to haul him back. Miss Marianne saved her from yelling out by grabbing hold of her arm. "Patience," she whispered.

I got to have faith, Pearl reminded herself. *Dey gone do it, dey is.*

Mr. Chamard hesitated as if he were considering. Then he strolled back up the line. He tapped Luke on the chest. "I believe this one will do well enough."

The courtyard erupted in wails and shrieks. "My baby!" The young mother the old woman had been inspecting was shouting and crying and struggling with the trader who tried to take her littlest one away from her. The silk-clad lady stepped back, her handkerchief at her mouth.

Another trader rushed over, uncoiling his whip as he went. The older child screamed, the younger one clung to his mother and shrieked in panic. The whip caught the mother across her forehead and blood spurted. The next strike cut her back.

Pearl sank to her knees. "Don't hit dat chile! Lawd, don let 'em hit dose children," she cried out.

The slaver pulling on the toddler yanked him from his mother's arms, and the woman attacked him with all her strength, scratching and clawing and kicking. The other man's whip lashed her again and again, but she wouldn't stop. Finally a third man grabbed her and wrestled her to the ground.

Mr. Fox hurried to escort the old gentlewoman from the scene. "Oh dear," she said as she leaned heavily on the man's arm. "Such a fuss. And I so generously agreed to take the older child." She wiped her eyes with her lace handkerchief. "I do hope this doesn't show an ungrateful nature on her part."

"She'll be over it in a day or two," Mr. Fox said. "They don't feel as much as white folks, you know."

"I suppose you're right." The old woman looked back at her new slave being hauled kicking and wailing from the courtyard. "I really couldn't abide to have a little one around. Not with my nerves."

The man with the whip carried the little girl away under his arm like a bag of potatoes. That child too fought to be free, but she had no chance.

That left the toddler, abandoned in the dust of the square. He cried as loud as a child can cry whose mother has been torn from him, but the slave women in the row behind him might have been deaf. They were statues. They were stones.

Pearl dashed across the yard. She grabbed the little one and held him tight, daring anyone to take him from her. The traders paid her no mind, but Mr. Chamard and Miss Marianne strode to her side.

"Pearl, what are you doing?" Mr. Chamard hissed.

Pearl glared at him. "I's taking dis chile. Nobody else want him. I's taking him."

"They won't let you have this child, Pearl," Miss Marianne said over the baby's screams.

"Nobody else want him."

Miss Marianne looked to Mr. Chamard.

She telling him wid her eyes to give me dis chile. Pearl held the screaming boy against her and rocked him. "Sh, sh, sh," she whispered. *She make him do it. He a rich man, rich enough to buy Luke.*

Yves shook his head at Marianne. "I don't know. I'll talk to him." He met Mr. Fox coming from the holding cells where the mother and child were being restrained. They stopped in the center of the courtyard and talked in low voices.

Pearl crooned and petted the child as she watched the men. They would look at her, look at Luke. One would shake his head, the other would gesture with a hand. *If God love His children, I get dis baby.*

The red-faced boy nearly strangled with sobbing, and Pearl soothed him the best she could. Miss Marianne stood beside her, her hands clenched and hardly moving. *Dat Mr. Chamard, he do it for her, he will. Dis baby mine.*

At last, the men shook hands. Yves came back and took Miss Marianne's arm. "He's yours, Pearl. Let's get out of here."

Thank you, God. Thank you, Jesus, Pearl prayed, hurrying behind the two kindest people on God's earth.

Pearl followed Yves and Marianne out the gate to their horses.

"Stay here," Yves said. "I have papers to sign." Before

he left them, he unsaddled the fourth horse and took the saddle with him.

Pearl sat down under the tree with the baby, who'd begun to snuffle instead of wailing.

"A baby for a saddle," Miss Marianne said.

Pearl thought her mistress was about to break. "Sit down, Missy." Pearl pulled at her skirt for her to sit and Marianne sank down on the grass next to Pearl.

"God in heaven," Marianne muttered and leaned her head against the tree.

The baby's snuffles changed to dry heaving hiccups. "Now, you jest hiccupping. Dat's nothing, is it?" Pearl talked to him, telling him how good life was going to be.

He so little. He forget his mama in a few weeks. Den I be Mama, and Luke be his daddy.

Luke came out striding behind his new owner. *He lost weight, but he look good. He not sick.* Pearl hopped up, so happy, so grateful, her smile promising him everything he'd ever wanted. But Luke wouldn't look at her. He scowled, and kept his eyes on the ground.

Why he not smiling? she thought, her spirits sinking. *Pride, dat what pulling him down. He ain't freed hisself. Men gots dere pride.* She patted the little one's back. *He get over it. He gone be dis babe's daddy.*

"You ride bareback?" Yves said.

Luke nodded, his face closed and sullen. With a fluid motion, he was on the horse's back. Pearl knew he'd never been on a horse, with saddle or without, but he was strong. He'd hold on.

Chapter 21

Simone threw a chemise on top of the items in her satchel, ignoring her sister Musette's protests. She rummaged in her top drawer for her pin money and stuffed it into her reticule, which she fastened into a hidden pocket of her traveling skirt.

"You'll disgrace yourself and everyone in the family," Musette harped. "What about Ariane and me? We'll be ruined, too, you know."

Simone scrambled in her jewelry box looking for the most expensive pieces. Finally she threw them all into a velvet bag and tossed them into the satchel. "Do you have any money?"

"Money? Didn't you hear anything I said?"

"Musette. This isn't about how many beaus will ask you to dance at some ball. This is about Gabriel."

Musette sat heavily on the bed. "I have eight dollars saved."

"Go get it, please." Simone added Musette's money to her own, kissed her sister, then fastened the satchel and headed for the back courtyard where Elbow John held her horse.

"Simone." Josie was waiting for her on the back

gallery. "Do reconsider, sweetheart. His brothers and his father will bring him home. You've no need to expose yourself like this."

"Maman, I can't bear it here another day." She kissed her mother's cheek. "Thank you, Maman, for not forbidding it."

Josie smiled. "You would have gone anyway."

"Yes. And so would you have, Maman, if it were Papa."

Josie handed her an envelope. "A hundred dollars."

A lot of money. Maman loved Gabriel too. "Thank you, Maman."

Simone hurried down the steps. She fastened her satchel onto the saddle, mounted, and rode out of the courtyard. In five minutes she was at Tante Cleo's.

That morning, the mail boat had delivered Yves' notes to Cleo and to Bertrand Chamard. Cleo had rushed to tell Josie and her family the news. Then Simone went directly to Monsieur Chamard. He'd only returned from his search in New Orleans the day before. Now he looked at her as if she'd lost her senses. Of course he would not take a young lady with him. It would not be proper. She was not needed. She would slow him down. He held her mother in high esteem and would not wish to offend her. No, and no, and no.

But Simone did not accept no. She didn't cry. She didn't plead. She simply explained, again, that she was going with him. Perhaps the stubborn tilt of her chin persuaded him, or the fact that she had become so thin her cotton frock hung on her. The interminable waiting, the sleepless nights and restless days had taken their toll.

"I'm leaving within the hour," he'd told her in capitulation. "But if you fall behind, I will leave my man Valentine with you and go on alone."

"I understand."

"Meet me at Cleo's. If you're late, I'm leaving without you."

"I will not be late."

Cleo paced in her front garden, waiting to say good-bye to Bertrand. Whatever else was between them, they loved their children. And they loved each other. That she had left him for Pierre didn't change that.

Simone rode into the yard first, in riding clothes, with saddlebags full, plainly ready to travel. "Simone!" Cleo said. "What does Josie say?"

"What you would expect. But I am going, Tante. Gabriel needs me, and I'm going to him."

"Bertrand won't take you."

"I've already convinced him. He's taking me."

Bertrand and Valentine came into view. The three houses, the Chamards', then Josie's, then Cleo's, spread along the length of the river road, making them close neighbors if not always comfortable ones. But they were a family, all of them, especially in bad times.

Bertrand dismounted for a final word with Cleo.

"Bertrand, you can't mean to take Simone? She has no proper chaperone, no business rushing off—"

"Hush, love. She's dying here, can't you see?" He took Cleo's arm and walked her to the gallery steps. "We've known they would be together for a long time. And they've done all we could ask of them. Three years they waited. I can't deny her this."

"You will find him?" Cleo looked into her lover's eyes for hope. He did not disappoint her.

Bertrand raised her hand to his lips and kissed it. "My darling, never doubt I will find him. Yves may be with him now."

She leaned into him and Bertrand wrapped her in his

arms. She sighed. It felt so right to press her face against his chest, to hear his heart beating. She did love him. And Pierre. As Bertrand had so long ago loved both her and Josie, then her and his second wife, Cleo now found her heart divided. But not her mind. She chose Pierre, and would again.

Cleo stepped away. "Bring our boy home."

Leaving Natchez, Luke followed the same path on which he'd been brought to Forks-of-the-Road market. This time, he was not afoot, not chained to another poor soul. He rode a horse for the first time in his life, bareback, one hand gripping the reins, the other in the horse's mane. The man he knew as the Shepherd led the way, followed by Miss Marianne from home, then Pearl and the child. Luke brought up the rear.

His heart should be singing, he thought. *Why I so down? Dere's Pearl. I out a dat coffle, out a dat place.* He was glad to see Pearl, he surely was. *I should a held on to her a minute 'fore the Shepherd took us off from dere.*

That was it. *The Shepherd de one in control. He de one telling me when to move, where to go. He be a good man, but he own me same as a bad man could he pay de money.*

The weeks Luke had been on the run had been terrifying. Heat, rain, mosquitoes, snakes, even gators—and they were nothing to the danger of soul drivers patrolling the roads. Sometimes too the stations had signals out that meant Don't Stop Here. He and Cat had run on empty bellies, fear and exhaustion pushing them on. But they'd made their own decisions. They'd been free, and the air they breathed had been sweeter for it.

Luke and Cat had lost each other a few nights back, the slavers chasing them with baying hounds. They'd come to a brook. Cat had gone upstream, he'd gone down. Luke had been caught and manacled and chained to his fellows in misery.

The chains were gone now, but he was still another man's property. *I could turn dis horse around, make a run fo it.* But Pearl's heart would break, he thought. *She be so happy, I swear de air around her singing.*

I try running dis horse, I likely fall on my head anyhow. Dere time ahead.

They stopped for a quick break in the early afternoon. Everyone gathered under the shade of an old live oak. Pearl mixed up cornmeal mash for the boy. Miss Marianne and the Shepherd ate sitting right there next to him and Pearl. He'd never seen the like.

"We going north?" Luke asked. He'd learned that much on the road, that Magnolias was south of here.

Pearl explained they were after Dr. Chamard. "Remember he de one tried to save little Sylvie?"

Luke looked at Mr. Chamard halfway reclined in the shade. "I reckon I say thank you for taking me from dat place."

The Shepherd nodded. "You're better off with us."

Yves tore off a piece of the loaf in his hand and tossed it at a squirrel. "Watch this," he said to Miss Marianne. "Ever get a squirrel to eat out of your hand?"

"You can't," she said.

"Is that a bet?"

She stopped eating and waited to hear the rest.

"If I do it," he said, "I collect another one of those items you gave me at the pond?"

The mistress laughed. "A stone?"

The two white people paid attention to each other and the squirrel. Luke turned to look at Pearl's happy face.

"What we gone call dis boy?" Pearl said.

Luke eyed the child. It could walk pretty good. It

hadn't cried all morning. He seemed a likely boy. But it wasn't the time for a child, not when he'd be running again. And soon. "Why'nt you ask de man what give it to you?"

Pearl looked at him, hurt in her eyes. *What she expect? How many time I told her I be leaving?*

"Mr. Chamard," Pearl interrupted the others. "You got another name 'sides Yves?"

Yes, white mens likes naming de little black babies after themselves, Luke thought.

The Shepherd smiled. "Yves Stephen DuPree Maria Chamard."

"Den I's gone call him DuPree."

Luke turned from her, but he listened as she talked to the boy in low tones all the while she fed him mush. When she tried to excuse herself for a private moment in the bushes, the boy clung to her. She glanced at Luke, and he knew she needed him to take the boy, but he looked away.

The boy had no claim on him, and Pearl had no right to push it on him. He'd been a free man once. He would be again, and he wasn't going to set foot in the trap of some other man's child she'd got hold of.

By nightfall, they were deep into the Trace. They'd found one half-overgrown path off to the east and investigated it, but it had petered out two miles into the woods.

They bedded down in a glade. Pearl slept near the mistress. Luke supposed she had to do that to keep the mistress safe from being with two men in the forest. They had their rules, he thought. *But I got mine.*

He lay on his back and watched the stars. *Dat one der, dat's de one.* The North Star. Follow that star, and you reach Freedom Land. He listened for the others to fall asleep. First Miss Marianne. A little later, the Shepherd.

Luke waited. If he tried to leave before Pearl fell asleep, she'd make a fuss. *It gone be hard to leave her again.*

Pearl didn't go to sleep. She left the little one snug beside Miss Marianne and crept across the clearing to where he lay. She knelt beside him and tugged at his hand. He rose and silently followed her deeper into the woods.

They found a small glade among a stand of pines. When Pearl turned to Luke and raised her hands to caress his face, he remembered all the nights they'd loved and cherished each other. "God, I missed you, Pearl." He kissed her, soft as a butterfly on a daisy.

With their hands, their mouths, they told each other how much yearning they'd suffered. The sweetness grew into heat and need, and Luke laid her down on the bed of pine needles.

When they lay quiet in each other's arms, Luke saw the stars had wheeled around their pole. His North Star. His hope. This time, when he ran, Pearl would come with him.

"You hardly say nothing dis whole day," she said, her head nestled on his arm.

He fingered her hand on his chest, but he didn't answer. In a little while, she said, "It wadn't my fault you got caught, Luke."

He shifted so he could see her face in the starlight. "No, honey. It not you fault. But cain't you see? I a slave again."

"But we're together, Luke. And we got a little one to raise now."

Luke disentangled himself. "Dat baby yours, Pearl. He ain't mine."

Chapter 22

Yves led the way up the Trace, all the while looking for a trail off to the east. Surely it would appear around the next bend, he kept telling himself. So close now. With every mile, his anxiety increased instead of lessened. What would Gabriel be like? No longer the sweet-natured big brother, but an embittered, angry man? Yves didn't know how he would handle it if his brother blamed him for his white skin.

Yves had known slaves all his life. Most of them had never looked him full in the face. Many, especially the field hands, never smiled at a white man, never spoke to a white man more than required. They wore masks, he'd come to realize quite young. And though they hid their true selves from him, he felt many of them had absorbed the idea that they were no more than mules. It was only a feeling, and obviously he did not know the hearts of the ones who kept their inner selves closed off from the masters.

But this man Luke, Yves mused. *He's nobody's mule. In spite of being treated like one all his life, he's a man, and he can't hide it. Can't or won't. And Joseph—a tribute to the human spirit. After a lifetime of being a slave, Joseph is a man of true dignity.*

Marianne brought her horse up next to his. "Is that an opening in the tree line? That could be the trail!"

What she'd put up with the last few days on the road, and she was still game. Who would ever have expected the Marianne Johnston of the ballroom to be so tough? She had not complained once about the hours in the saddle, about sleeping on the ground. That, however, had probably been harder for him than for her: He'd imagined her sharing his bedroll, counting the stars, snuggling, kissing . . . yielding. Wispy curls escaped her bonnet and framed her sunburned face. *There's no one else like her*, he thought. They reached the trail and turned in. Wide enough for only one horse, it was quite overgrown. This, Yves reflected, would be just the kind of path Monroe and his gang would look for to dump Gabriel.

The woods closing in on the trail cut off the breeze; the sun directly overhead beat down on their heads. Not even the birds moved in this heat. The creaking of the leather saddles, the clop of hooves, and the hum of insects were the only sounds. No one drove a wagon, no one took produce or beeves to market on this trail. Did anyone live this far into the forest?

Yves took heart when they came to a peach orchard. Beyond that, a row of pecan trees. And then the clearing. Set back from the trail was a large weathered farmhouse with a porch all around. There were hints of old whitewash, but now the boards were gray, and a few shingles from the roof lay in the yard. The front door hung ajar, too crooked to close.

Most important, there was a dilapidated dovecote behind the house. This was the place.

Yves held up a hand for the others to stop and listen.

Bees hummed in the shade of the house where untended rose canes climbed to the eaves. Nothing else stirred in the heat and glare.

Yves dismounted and then helped Marianne down. They were as quiet as the little farm, but watchful.

"Marianne," he said softly, "stay with the horses." He reached for her shotgun.

"I'll come with—"

Damn it. I knew she'd argue. He fixed her with a hard look. "Stay with the horses." Her chin began to rise. "Please."

Finally, she nodded. Yves loaded her shotgun and handed it to her.

He checked his rifle was loaded and walked to the house, stepped on the porch, and knocked on the door-jamb. Through the half-open door he could see the place was inhabited—flies buzzed over a half-eaten plate of corn and beans—but the stillness was too complete for anyone to be inside.

Yves walked around back. Off to the right were a couple of outbuildings and beyond that a chicken yard with a dozen or so scrawny red hens pecking in the dirt. A hog dreamed in the sty, perfuming the air with its sickeningly sweet offal.

Yves stepped through a tangled patch that might once have been a windbreak and came to the garden, a half acre of spindly corn, okra, tomatoes, squash—all of it in need of weeding. The smell of ripening tomatoes and hot dry dust hung like a miasma over the field.

Eerie how quiet it is, Yves thought. *But somebody lives here.* He headed back toward the house. Before he began to search the barn and the shed, he looked toward the horses. Pearl and little DuPree were in the shade on the edge of the trail. Luke was pouring water from his canteen into his hand for his horse to drink. *Damnation. Where is Marianne?*

He scanned the area and picked up a motion in the pecan grove. Marianne was flanking the place. *Good strategy, but does the woman do nothing she's told!*

He whistled low to Luke. When Luke looked up, Yves tilted his head toward the pecan grove. Luke spotted Marianne among the trees. He nodded and followed her.

Yves approached the open-ended barn. From the brightness of midday, he couldn't see into the dark interior. What he did see was the glint of the sun on the barrel of a shotgun. Pointed at him.

A woman no more than five feet tall, her white hair a nimbus around her head, stepped into the light. "Put your hands over your head, mister."

Yves took a long moment to consider just where the shot would hit him if she fired and whether, this close, he'd be able to lunge under its scatter. Even with a rifle, pointed at the ground, unfortunately, his bodily options all seemed lethal, and he raised his hands.

"Sorry if I startled you, ma'am," Yves began, plastering a tight smile on his face, but the woman wasn't buying charm.

"Back on up to the road," the woman said. "You're trespassing on my property, but I reckon you'll leave now you see I got this gun on you."

"Yes, ma'am, I'll leave," Yves said. *She's just scared. She won't shoot. Probably.* "I don't mean any harm. Can I put my hands down?"

"If you want a bellyful of buckshot, go on and put them down," she said.

"I'm looking for my brother," Yves said, watching the woman's hand at the trigger. "Gabriel Chamard. I think he was left here, on this trail. He was sick."

Yves saw the woman's eyes narrow. She knew something. "Gabriel Chamard," he said again. "A big man, colored but high toned. Have you seen him?"

Something banged in the shed thirty feet from them. A hoe, a shovel, something that knocked against the shed wall. Yves kept his hands up, but he took a step toward the shed. The old woman said, "Stay put, mister. That's Caleb in there. He's mine."

Yves didn't believe her. He believed it was Gabriel in that shed. A muffled call came through the pine boards but Yves kept still now. The movement in the deep shadows of the barn behind the woman leant him patience.

Hellfire. It's Marianne. Where's Luke?

Yves struggled to keep his attention on the old woman instead of on Marianne creeping up behind her. "My brother, Gabriel, is a doctor. A freedman. He was kidnapped . . ."

Marianne, a good six inches taller than the old woman, wrapped her arms around her, grabbed the shotgun, and pointed it skyward.

The gun went off— *that woman's going to get me killed yet!* The chickens squawked, the pig squealed, Luke dashed out of the barn and wrenched the shotgun from the four hands wrestling with it.

And the door to the shed banged open. Gabriel stood in the doorway, leaning on a hoe. Alive.

Yves registered the comical sight of the tiny woman attacking Luke, kicking at his shins and trying to reach the shotgun held over his head. Then he ran for his brother.

Gabriel, propped against the wall, reached one arm out and embraced him. Yves pounded Gabriel's back and hugged him.

With a second's warning from the look on Gabriel's face, Yves turned to receive the full force of the old woman's attack. She'd given up on Luke and rushed him instead. "Caleb's my boy!" She pounded Yves' chest with her fists and then as he tried to step away from her, she punched him in the gut.

"Ginny!" Gabriel called.

Yves got hold of her arms and turned her back into his chest, but she still kicked at him with her hard bare feet.

"Ginny, get hold of yourself!"

The old woman quit kicking and wrenched her arms out of Yves' grasp. "This here is my slave Caleb." She was as defiant as if she were the one towering a foot and more over her foes.

"Ginny," Gabriel said gently. "This is my brother, Yves Chamard. I told you I had family."

Ginny was glaring at Yves. "Not your brother," she muttered. Then louder, she declared, "Caleb. His name's Caleb Bartholomew Winston."

"I need to sit down," Gabriel said.

Alarmed at how pale he was, Yves helped him back into the shed and onto the dirt floor. Marianne came in behind Yves and knelt at Gabriel's foot, staring at the bandages. Yves looked too. Something wasn't right.

"Gabe?"

Gabriel pushed his head back against the wall and looked up at the ceiling. "The toes are gone."

Ginny, calm now as if this were a social occasion being held in her shed, explained, "They was black. Had to go."

Yves stared at her with his mouth open. "You cut his toes off?"

"He can still get around to hoe and the like."

Yves looked at his brother. "My God, Gabe."

Gabriel caught the eye of his savior and tormentor. "Ginny, maybe you could fix dinner for these folks. Kill a couple of chickens, make your conepone?"

Her attention diverted, Ginny mumbled something

about lighting the stove in this heat. She left them and headed for the chicken yard.

"Ginny's understanding comes and goes," Gabriel said. "She saved my life, Yves, and she's tended to this foot since she cut it. You won't find her apologizing."

"Dr. Chamard, let me unwrap this," Marianne said. "I have medicines with me."

"Miss Marianne, I've hardly had the courage to look at it myself."

Yves stepped to the door and called out to Pearl, who stood alert and tense with the horses. "Can you bring Miss Marianne's medical bag?" He knelt again at Gabe's side and gripped his hand for the pain to come.

Marianne peeled off one layer of bandage at a time.

Yves knew he'd have to look at it, but he dreaded it. *God, don't let the bones show.*

"Did you have fever?" Marianne asked. "Has it been kept clean?"

"It's a clean cut, and Ginny cauterized it."

Marianne picked at the last layer of wrapping. Yves stared at the far wall and swallowed hard. He'd hate for her, or his brother either, to know how close he was to tossing his breakfast.

With the last bloody strip of cloth off, the amputations were exposed to sunlight coming through the door. Marianne sat back and gazed at the ruined foot. *Where does she get her nerve?* Yves wondered.

"Are we not supposed to pull the skin over the wound?" she asked.

Gabe tightened his grip on Yves' hand at the pain of having the wound disturbed. "It's too late for that."

"You mean you'd—" Yves could hardly bear to contemplate the pain Gabe had already suffered, and now Marianne was going to— He blocked it out of his mind.

"I read about it in one of my books at home," she told

Yves. "You can take the good skin and mold it around the wound." She drew a finger in the air above Gabriel's foot. "You have to—"

Yves stood up abruptly. His forehead dripped sweat and he felt ill. He saw Marianne exchange a glance with Gabe, but his pride was not nearly as strong as his nausea.

"Maybe Pearl is having trouble getting my bag untied from the saddle," Marianne suggested.

"Certainly." Yves was out the door gulping fresh air, but it didn't help. He bent over a dried-up bed of phlox and lost his stomach. *How humiliating.*

As he wiped his mouth, he could hear Marianne quietly confiding to Gabriel, a smile in her voice. "He's my hero, you know."

Chapter 23

Simone crossed her arms to keep from fidgeting. Every hour on the river had brought her closer to Gabriel, but not fast enough. He'd been sick, Yves had written. How sick? Was he in pain? Was anyone taking care of him? Even here in Natchez, they were at least two days away from finding him, two more days to endure the waiting and worrying.

Bertrand Chamard touched her arm. Kindness in his voice, he said, "Your standing here watching won't get the horses unloaded any sooner."

They were in the rough part of Natchez, Under the Hill, where the steamboats docked and the river men cavorted, gambled, and whored.

"Let's go see to the provisions," he said.

She accepted Mr. Chamard's arm, and his man Valentine followed them to the shops along the shore. They bought the essentials for survival on the Trace: cornmeal, bacon, matches, rain slickers, and a frying pan. On the way back to the dock, Gabriel's father stopped to talk to an acquaintance, and it took all Simone's will not to blurt out *Let's go!*

At last, the three horses were saddled. Simone followed Mr. Chamard up the steep hill to Natchez, through the busy streets, and onto the old Trace.

Thank heavens, we're on the move at last. The inactivity on the steamboat had nearly driven Simone mad. She'd paced the decks, watched the shoreline, then paced some more. *Dear Mr. Chamard.* He had been patient and kind with her. A charming man, really. No wonder Tante Cleo had stayed with him so many years.

He's as anxious as I am. He just hides it better. Valentine, Monsieur Chamard's especial man, worried with him. From the upper deck, Simone had seen the two of them, heads together, arms crossed, talking. She didn't know Mr. Chamard well, but she read contained rage in the constant bunching of the muscles in his jaw and in the tightness of the hands clasped behind his back as he stood on the deck hour after hour.

Simone's first reaction had been fear. Gabriel might have met with an accident, after all. But when his brothers sent word they were convinced he'd been stolen, she seethed. Helpless, frustrated, frightened. Angry. Of course she recognized Monsieur Chamard's rage. She wondered she did not burst into flames herself. At least now she was doing something, and she had the energy to travel the seven seas if she had to.

They explored every trail off the Trace. Each one ended at an abandoned farmhouse. They'd looked around, but no hint of a living soul did they find.

The second day they turned into yet another lane. Hoofprints marked the sandy soil. Four horses, Valentine said. Simone's pulse picked up. This could be the one. They rode on, single file on the narrow trail. A peach orchard, then pecan trees. Then a clearing with a farmhouse.

Simone saw a figure stir inside. She slid off her horse and flew, her petticoats like roiling white clouds.

Yves Chamard, friend of her childhood, met her on the porch.

All her hopes centered in the one word, she said, "Gabriel?"

Yves smiled. "He's here."

She brushed past Yves to find him. He was here in this house.

The first room, dim after the sun's glare, echoed with emptiness. Only a bench, a few cowhide chairs, a bottle with wildflowers on a worn table. Not here. Her boots beat across the floorboards. She pulled open the nearest door. Faded curtains flapped in the breeze, spreading a red glow over three empty beds.

The next door stood ajar. Simone swung it wide. "Gabriel?" she breathed.

The open window was darkened, and she could barely see a figure on the bed. The man stirred, rustling the mattress. Then the breeze shifted the curtain, lighting him as he lifted himself to one elbow.

"Gabriel!" Simone engulfed him, touched and tasted and breathed him in. Now, for the first time, she wept. And she could not stop. Gabriel wrapped his arms around her and held her like he would never let her go.

Someone closed the door to the bedroom. She had Gabriel to herself, all to herself. She cradled his face in her long fingers and with the haste of deep hunger, she kissed his eyes, his forehead, his ear, the salt on his skin mingling with her tears. He knocked her bonnet off, grasped her head, and pressed her into his kiss.

Frantic kisses and whispered names. Simone wanted only to hold him and to be held. They fell back, her length alongside his. "I thought I'd lost you."

"No, love. I'm here."

She raised her head to look into his eyes. "I'll never let you out of my sight again. Not even for a moment."

He smiled. "I'll take that as a promise."

The footsteps and voices from the other room reminded Simone that Monsieur Chamard had come as far and as furiously as she had to find Gabriel. She'd have to let him go, for a few minutes. But she'd be with him again, touch him again soon. "Your father is here."

She kissed him. Then once more. She rolled off the bed and smoothed her hair. Her hand holding Gabriel's until the last moment, she stepped to the door, opened it, and smiled at Bertrand Chamard. He went in to his son, and Simone let them have their reunion in private.

Yves grinned at her when she joined him in the main room. "I gather he was glad to see you?"

Simone smiled and blushed.

She heard footsteps on the porch. Yves put aside the rifle he was oiling when Marianne Johnston entered the house, pulling at the strings of her bonnet. Yves stood. "Miss Johnston, I believe you are acquainted with Miss DeBlieux?"

Jealousy flashed over Simone hot and fast. *What's she doing here?*

Miss Johnston had her hand out in greeting. Simone accepted it without warmth. "Miss Johnston."

"Call me Marianne, please. We know each other well enough for Christian names, don't we?" Marianne smiled, but Simone could not bring herself to that. She was watching Marianne Johnston's face, trying to read whether Miss Johnston thought she had some claim on Gabriel. What Simone saw was puzzlement, politely restrained; Marianne seemed to have no idea what Simone was doing here. *If she has designs on Gabe*, Simone thought, *I'll stop that right now!*

"I must admit, Miss Marianne, I'm surprised to find you here with my fiancé."

Marianne's eyebrows arched.

Ah, she didn't know. Simone waited for the frown, the scorn, the disapproval of a white woman allying herself with a colored man.

"I had no idea you and Dr. Chamard were engaged to be married!"

Simone saw nothing but surprise in Marianne. Surely she knew Gabriel was an octoroon?

"Miss Marianne has the highest regard for Gabriel, Simone. And she has been kindly and ably attending him."

"Attending him?"

"His foot," Marianne said.

"His foot?"

"You didn't notice his foot?" Yves said.

"Oh, yes. I remember. In your note, you wrote his foot was broken."

Yves looked at Marianne. "She didn't notice."

Simone frowned. Gabriel had been awkward as he'd shifted in the bed. She had a vague recollection his foot had been bandaged. She looked from Yves to Marianne. "What happened?"

"Well, I'll tell you. Sit down first and let's have a little refreshment. The trail must have been dry and thirsty."

Marianne set out three tin cups and Yves found his flask in his satchel. Simone took one of the rawhide chairs and gripped her hands in her lap, knowing it must not be good news.

From a chipped ceramic pitcher, Yves poured branch water into the cups, though very little in his own, and added a dash of whiskey. He handed it to Simone. "Sip it slowly," he told her.

Between Yves and Marianne, she learned the story of Gabriel's ruined foot. Ginny, they said, had been alone so long she had become "eccentric," as Yves put it, but she was a good old soul. Amputating Gabe's toes had probably saved his leg, if not his life.

"I believe Gabriel has grown fond of her," Marianne added.

The inner door opened. Gabriel leaned on a crutch Luke had made for him, his father supporting him on the other side. He grinned at them all, but the effort of being out of bed made the sweat break out on his forehead.

Simone wanted to take Bertrand Chamard's place at Gabriel's side, but she held back. His father loved him too. *I'll have to share him, for now.*

Marianne yielded her chair to Gabriel and set another close by for his father. "If you'll excuse me, I want to babysit while Pearl works in the garden."

"Where's Ginny?" Gabe asked.

"She's showing Luke where the beehives are out in the woods," Yves said. "She's started calling him Caleb, did you know that?"

Gabe laughed. "Just keep the axe out of her way."

"How can you laugh?" Simone said.

Gabriel took her hand. "The foot, or my life."

"But my God—"

Gabe shook his head. "The method seemed perfectly logical to her at the time. And she saved my life, Simone, before and after the axe."

Bertrand Chamard looked at Yves hopefully. "Do I smell whiskey?"

Marianne tied her bonnet as she crossed the hot yard toward the shed where Luke and Pearl had set themselves up. DuPree toddled in the dust, trying to catch a couple of lazy pigeons. He wore the same long shirt Pearl had found him in, but it was now boiled clean and patched with pieces from the hem allowance of Pearl's new dress.

"Here I am," Marianne said.

Pearl set aside the field peas she was shelling. "He gone be sleepy soon, Miss Marianne. You lay him down, he give you some peace."

"We'll be fine. You go on." Marianne sat on the low three-legged stool and watched DuPree waddle after the pigeons, not at all bothered he couldn't quite catch one. The chase was the thing. Once the pigeons tired of the game and flew up to their deteriorating cote, DuPree discovered Marianne's welcoming lap.

When he was tired, he sometimes cried for his mama, and Pearl would rub his back and sing to him. He was losing that painful, but precious, sense of his mother, Marianne thought. Well, God had sent him Pearl.

She held him in her lap and rocked on her stool while he settled down. Holding one of his perfect little feet, brown and dusty, she wondered if Luke was going to accept this child. Pearl wanted him to, wanted Luke to stay with her and make a family. That much was plain. *I think he's planning to run again, though.*

Marianne thought about Luke dodging the slavers, going hungry, in danger from snakes and dogs and even bears. If he had his free-papers, the risk would be negligible. But Father had, in effect, paid for Luke twice. She herself didn't have the kind of money it would take to pay Father back for reimbursing Yves. She dreaded the thought of Father ever knowing her part in Luke's first escape, much less a second.

On the other hand, in the greater scheme of things, money was not as important as a man's life. *Maybe . . . maybe there will be a way.*

DuPree fell asleep in her lap. She could take him in the house and lay him on a quilt, but it was cool here in the shade, and she was new to the pleasure of holding a sleeping child.

Luke emerged from the wooded path on the other side of the clearing, dwarfing Ginny, who led the way. She carried a smoking tin, he a bucket covered with cloth. When they neared, Marianne asked, "Honey on our corn bread tonight?"

Luke smiled. "Yes'm. We got us three, four combs."

Ginny put her tin down next to Marianne. "Give me that baby, sugar. I haven't held a baby in many a year."

"Take the stool, Miss Ginny." Marianne rose and when the old woman settled, she handed DuPree to her.

His eyes on the baby, Luke said softly, "Miss Marianne?"

Marianne understood the worry line in his forehead. How much could you trust a crazy woman who'd taken an axe to a man's foot? "It'll be all right," she said. "I won't leave them."

He let out a breath. "All right." He set his bucket next to Ginny's. "I go help Pearl in de field."

Marianne watched the old woman rocking DuPree. "You're very good to have all of us here, Miss Ginny," Marianne said. "And now we are three more to feed, I'm afraid."

Ginny didn't show any interest in who the new guests were. "Long as you don't eat up all my chickens."

"No, ma'am. We won't do that."

The chickens and the hog and the straggly garden were all Miss Ginny had. Marianne looked at the place. The barn had gaping holes in the roof. The house had boards swinging loose where the nails had worked out. The dovecote, the shed, the fences, the orchard, the garden—Miss Ginny couldn't keep it up by herself.

"Luke and Pearl are working hard for you, it seems to me," Marianne said.

Ginny rocked the baby, one arm supporting his seat, the other across his back. "Lord, how I miss my babies."

"You been alone here long, Miss Ginny?"

Her faded eyes closed for a moment. "Maybe eighteen, nineteen years. Hard to keep track now I can't see to write, which is no account anyhow seeing as I used up all the paper years ago."

A plan began to take shape in Marianne's mind. She'd have to consider it carefully, though, before she proposed it.

When Pearl came back from the fields, she found Miss Marianne had taken DuPree into the house with her. She knocked on the post of the back porch, and Ginny stuck her head out. "You want your baby."

Ginny brought out DuPree, refreshed from his nap. He held his hands out to Pearl, and her heart liked to burst. *Thank you, Lawd, for dis chile. Luke and DuPree, Lawd, dey be all I want in dis life.*

Back at the shed, she built a fire in the pit she'd dug and lined with stones. When Luke came in from hoeing, she'd have him a fine dinner. They had venison Mr. Yves shot that morning, fresh black-eyed peas, corn, okra, and tomatoes. *They eating the same thing up at the house,* Pearl thought. *Dis place make plenty, it tended right.*

When Luke had washed up at the well, he sat down with Pearl on the other stool and took the chipped flowered china plate she handed him. He'd never eaten off anything but wood or tin. What he appreciated, though, was the abundance of the food. "Lawd, Pearl, I never see so much on one plate." She smiled at him, happy.

DuPree shared Pearl's plate, digging his fingers into the peas and okra. "He eats good, don he?"

Luke nodded, his eyes on Pearl's face. *He see I love dis*

chile, she thought, still smiling at him. *Maybe Luke love him, too, God willing.*

They ate and talked about the farm, what needed doing to it. Pearl didn't know much about farming. She'd been in the cook shed for most of her life, but even she knew the place was run-down, the buildings and the land too. "Woods creeping into the fields," Luke told her. "She had a mule, she could turn the soil over like it need. She got a plow in de barn."

"Dis was a good place?"

Luke nodded. "A good place, once't."

DuPree finished his dinner and climbed off Pearl's lap. A pigeon lit nearby. He toddled after it. Where the pigeon wandered, DuPree followed. If he got too close, the bird hopped a foot or two before it resumed pecking and bobbing.

The pigeon waddled closer to Pearl's fire pit, but the radiating heat turned it back toward its pursuer. Within reach at last, DuPree grabbed, but the bird flapped and fluttered, confusing him. DuPree toppled over, and quick as thought, Luke grabbed his arm and pulled him away from the hot stones and the smoldering fire. DuPree wailed, startled and frightened. Pearl dropped her plate, but Luke had him. He was safe.

Pearl stepped around the fire to take the boy, eager to comfort him and settle him. But she held back. Luke had the child pressed to his shoulder, one of his huge hands cradling DuPree's head. "You all right," he crooned. He rocked from side to side, rubbing the boy's back. DuPree's little arms went around Luke's neck, and Pearl put a hand to her mouth. *Dis look like love, God.*

Chapter 24

Miss Ginny agreed to loan them her wagon, but the wood had shrunk away from the iron at every junction. Yves and Bertrand decided they'd have to do substantial repairs for it to get Gabriel to the docks at Natchez.

The men sharpened all the tools they found in the barn. That done, they chopped down a few smallish oaks. They'd have to use green wood, but the wagon would at least be temporarily sound.

Marianne tied on her bonnet to venture into the sun. She collected the men's water jars, refilled them at the well, then set them in the shade. Monsieur Chamard had a mouthful of nails he'd retrieved from the useless boards. One by one he spat them into his palm to hammer into the new lumber Luke shaped and planed.

Yves worked with the wedge and maul splitting a tree trunk. Marianne lingered, drawn by this uncommon display of masculine power.

Yves' white cotton shirt, so sweat-soaked it was transparent, clung to his body. His back muscles bunched as he swung the heavy maul up and then pounded it against the wedge. How could she not indulge in lustful thoughts watching this sweating, sinewy exemplar of brawn?

Yves worked bare-headed. *He needs a hat in this sun.*
She lost that thought when Yves squatted down to place
another wedge, his thighs straining against his breeches.
Marianne's breath deepened as images of her hands on
those legs flared in her mind. *I should go inside before I disgrace myself. A hat. I'll find him a hat.*

Marianne borrowed an old straw one she found hanging on a peg in Ginny's house. Careful of the swinging
maul, she presented it to Yves. He straightened up and
the happy look on his face surprised her. Yves was enjoying this labor. *Truly a physical creature,* she thought.

The wet shirt stuck to Yves' chest. He caught her looking at him and grinned. "See anything you want?"

She tilted her face up, taking refuge in indignation
since she wasn't sure whether she wanted to run or
laugh. "Oh, for heaven's sake. I was thinking of your
laundry."

"Then the sun has burned your face, Miss Marianne,
for surely it isn't my laundry that makes you blush."

"I am indeed sunburned, Mr. Chamard."

"Then you're asking me to take my shirt off so you can
wash it?"

Would he really take his shirt off? She crossed her
arms. She could play his game. "You think I don't know
how to wash a shirt?"

Keeping his eyes on hers, Yves tossed the maul down.
With deliberate movements, he shrugged off his suspenders. Pulled his shirt out of his pants. Peeled it over
his head. And stood half naked before her.

Oh Lord. She couldn't help it. Her eyes wandered over
his shoulders, then his chest, then his flat belly. When
she could drag her attention back to his face, he was
grinning at her again.

"I do admire clean laundry on a man," she said
soberly, hooked the sodden shirt on one finger, and

walked away. *Well, I have a dirty shirt to wash, but he's bare-chested. Who won that one?*

Yves poured a bucket of water over his head and wished he had a bar of soap. Apparently that was not a commodity Miss Ginny set much store by. More water was the best he could do. He'd watched Marianne hang his shirt to dry across the porch rail, amused and touched and embarrassed she had taken his bait. If she knew what it did to him to see her aroused, she'd never have approached him with that hat. She deserved another bouquet of wildflowers, for the hat.

At the porch, he slipped into the shirt. A little scratchy on his skin after being in the sun, but it felt wonderful to be clean.

In the house Yves sat on the bench and finished buttoning his shirt. Marianne sat cross-legged on the floor with the baby. They were rolling pecans between them, Marianne spending half the time keeping them out of DuPree's mouth. The light in her face was something to behold. DuPree toddled after a pecan and she looked at Yves, smiling. "He's walking really well for his age, don't you think?"

Yves had no opinion about how well a baby should walk at any age, much less a notion of how old DuPree was. "Sure is," he said.

DuPree caromed into Marianne, climbing on her. With open, drooly mouth, he glommed onto her cheek. Marianne laughed and kissed him back.

Yves had never seen a sophisticated young woman enjoy a child like this, without thought of her dress or her rouge or her dignity. She was radiant, loving this child. It seemed that in her bosom, a mother's heart waited for a child of her own.

I could give her that.

Yves' father came in the house, his hair wet from cleaning up at the well. "Another day, I think we'll have it." He sat next to Yves on the bench and held his hands out for Dupree. "Come here, little fellow." It was no surprise to Yves that Papa loved children. He knew every child in the quarters by name, even kept candy in his pockets for them. And contrary to the habits of many planters, Papa had not fathered any of the slave children on his plantation.

And yet Papa has slaves. He loved his father, and in all else, he admired him. As a child of the Louisiana plantation culture, Yves understood building one's life around slaveholding—but he could not respect it.

Bertrand put DuPree back on his feet. "Miss Marianne, how is your patient? Think he could ride in the wagon day after tomorrow?"

Their last day with Ginny, Marianne made up her mind. She would speak to Luke and Pearl first, and then approach Ginny with her plan.

That Ginny appreciated Luke was a given. Once he'd helped her with the honey gathering, she thought "Caleb" was a gem of a man. And she doted on DuPree.

As for Pearl, she spent a lot of her working day in the field hoeing weeds and picking off blighted leaves. No one told her to, no one expected her to. She just did it. Twice, Marianne had seen Ginny and Pearl coming in from the field with the hoes and a basket of beans or squash. They talked. Both of them, not just Ginny telling Pearl this or that. They had a real give and take.

Ginny will want them to stay. But what did Luke and Pearl want? Luke was a runner. A discontent. Could he be happy here?

Marianne had already succeeded with her other plan. As subtly as she could without actually mentioning that she had her eye on a different Chamard, she'd assured Simone she was not after her beloved Gabriel. The two belles began to build a friendship. In earlier years, they had been acquaintances, of course. Their plantations were not so far apart, their parents knew each other, and in town during the season, they often attended the same teas, balls, and concerts. They'd each had their own set, however, and had never cultivated a more intimate acquaintance.

Now they delighted in one another's company. They knew so many of the same people, they'd read some of the same books, seen some of the same plays, and taken care of the same man.

While the men rebuilt the wagon, and Ginny and Pearl saw to the gardening, Marianne tutored Simone in how to take care of Gabriel's foot.

"Be as matter-of-fact as you can," she said. "Like removing a splinter from his finger."

"I'll try," Simone said.

Marianne hesitated. "Is it repugnant to you?"

"Nothing about Gabriel could ever be repugnant to me. I'm just a little scared, I think."

Marianne took Simone outside to prepare her for what she would see. She picked up a twig, and in a sandy patch she scratched a sketch of the human foot. She pointed out the arrangement of the bones, at least as well as she remembered them from her medical books, and demonstrated how the toes had been "removed." By the time Marianne took her inside and showed her how to unwrap the injury, Simone was ready.

"Miss Marianne and I can manage," Gabriel said. *That's sweet*, Marianne thought. *He doesn't want to upset her.*

Simone stuck her hands on her hips. "You think I'm

useless and soft," she declared, "but you belong to me, Gabriel Chamard. And I am going to take care of you."

And she did. She cleaned the wound and rebandaged it, Gabriel watching her silently all the while. When Simone had made the last tie of the white strips from her petticoat, she met Gabriel's gaze.

Marianne suddenly felt very unnecessary. Gabriel's dark eyes practically smoldered, and Simone seemed to be having trouble breathing. She left them quietly and closed the door behind her. *Goodness*, she thought, a hand over her breast. *If anyone ever looks at me like that, I hope we'll already have a wedding behind us!*

The object of her fantasies walked into the house, and she blushed guiltily.

"What's wrong?" Yves said, stopping in midstride.

Now she felt the heat in her face double, and she had trouble meeting his eyes. "Nothing at all. It's just hot in here."

"You know," Yves said, walking slowly to her, never taking his eyes from hers, "there are no grandes dames of society here." He shifted his gaze to the buttons at her neck. With one finger, he touched Marianne's topmost button. "You could open your neckline, just a bit."

His voice was soft, low, reasonable. Mesmerizing.

He took her hand. Without asking leave, he unbuttoned her cuff and began to roll the sleeve back ever so slowly. She watched his fingers deftly handling the fabric, barely touching her. Then he did the other sleeve, only this time he allowed himself to feel her naked skin. No one had ever touched her there, on her inner forearm. He stroked the flesh, and she shivered, goose bumps following the path of his finger.

She expected him to smile, to tease, but he was as solemn as she. He moved his hands to her throat. Unbuttoned the first button. Opened the bodice as far as one unbuttoning could afford. She didn't move. He opened the next button.

He was so close, yet he stepped just a little closer and blew against her heated skin, right below her collar bones. She shivered again, and still she waited.

Yves' eyes were on her breasts. *He sees what he's done to me. If he touches me there . . .* He lowered his head and kissed the skin he had exposed. *Too many buttons.* She raised her chin, opening her throat to him.

His lips were under her jaw, behind her ear, on her cheeks—at last, on her mouth. She met his lips with hers, as hot as his own, as eager as his. She slipped her arms around him, feeling the heat in him. His back was broad, hard, and she wanted to—

His hand cupped her breast. His thumb grazed her nipple, and she felt her knees quake.

"Yves?" she whispered.

He wrapped his arms around her and buried his face in her hair.

"You forget what you come in for, Mr. Yves?" Valentine stepped into the house.

Marianne jumped, but Yves kept her close. "I need to talk to you," he said into her ear.

He took a deep breath and let her go. "I was to find Ginny's lard can."

"Yes, sir," Valentine answered in a hearty voice. "We need the lard can out there. You find it?"

Marianne walked over to the shelves on the wall and picked up the white enameled can. Yves touched her fingers as she held it out to him.

"Those axles waiting for us, M'sieu."

Yves looked at her, oddly, she thought, and followed Valentine outside.

Still weak-kneed, Marianne lowered herself into a chair. *He's going to ask me to marry him.* His kisses, his hand

actually on her breast—hadn't he as much as announced his intentions? Lindsay Morgan never suggested anything remotely as intense or as intimate
between them as what she had with Yves. He was not
toying with her as he had with those other girls, she was
sure of that.

I'm going to say yes. Staring out the window, she
watched a bluebird take flight, her heart soaring with it.
I'm going to marry Yves Chamard.

After supper, Marianne walked out to the shed where
Luke and Pearl shared a bench, watching the trees prick
the orange disc of the sun. DuPree, straddling Luke's
knee, cackled every time Luke bobbed his leg up and
down.

Marianne sat on the stool. She was about to make a
proposition that would change their lives. It was time to see
if Luke was ready to commit to a life here. "I've been thinking," she said.

"Yes'm?"

"This could be a good place."

"Yes'm, it could."

"Miss Ginny doesn't have any family anywhere, and
she needs help. What if you and Pearl stayed here?"

Pearl grabbed Luke's hand.

"But, Luke," Marianne continued, "I do not want to
leave Pearl here unless you plan to stay with her. She
would be better off, she and Dupree, at home with me
than here without you."

Marianne waited while they communicated through
their clasped hands, through their eyes.

Pearl turned yearning eyes to Marianne. "We could
stay on dis place? Me and Luke and DuPree?"

Marianne nodded. She met Luke's appraising gaze. "If you're through with running."

DuPree sat on his knee spitting bubbly drool, and Luke looked at Pearl, the woman who had his heart, a long time. Then he looked to the woman who owned his body.

"You giving us to her? Miss Ginny be our new owner?"

Marianne shook her head. "My idea is that if you'll stay here and take care of Miss Ginny the rest of her life, she'll make the place over to you."

Luke's proud face swelled about the eyes. "You do dat fo us?"

"I tole you she different," Pearl said.

Marianne was embarrassed. "If Miss Ginny agrees, yes."

Pearl stood up. "I go get her." She put a hand on Luke. "Yes? You gone do dis? You stay wid me?"

"Yeah, baby," he said, his voice full of hope and tears. "I stay here wid you and DuPree."

Pearl ran two steps, ran back and hugged Marianne, and then rushed off to find Ginny. She brought the old woman back, nearly dragging her by the arm. "Luke, let Miss Ginny sit dere. You let her have DuPree, too."

Ginny settled DuPree in her lap and leaned back against the wall of the shed. "All right. I'm here. So what's got this gal all fired up?"

"I have a proposal for you, Miss Ginny." Marianne outlined how Ginny needed Luke, and Luke and Pearl needed a place of their own.

Ginny pondered, her chin resting on DuPree's sleepy head. "It would be legal, what you're saying?"

"As legal as I know how to make it."

Ginny absently patted DuPree's tummy and looked hard at Luke. "That other Caleb, he's leaving. You want to stay?"

"Yes'm. I make the place good again. I got no reason to run, de farm gone be mine someday."

Ginny grunted. "Get more work out of you than the other Caleb, anyway, his foot being half gone." Ginny stood up and handed DuPree to his mama. "Well then, that's what we'll do."

Leaving Pearl and Luke to contemplate a future they could only have dreamed of, Marianne and Miss Ginny walked back to the house. Yves sat in a chair leaned against the porch wall. The old woman went inside, but Marianne sat down on the stoop.

"How about a walk?" Yves said. "I found a pond back in the woods. I'll teach you how to skip a stone."

Marianne tilted her head, holding back a smile. "I know how to skip a stone."

"Nah. You throw like a girl." He came down off the porch and they fell into step.

"The wagon ready for tomorrow?"

Yves nodded. "Gabe says if he rides with his foot on a pillow, he'll be fine."

They walked close together on the overgrown wagon path, their hands occasionally brushing. *He'll take my hand*, she thought. *We'll walk together, like people who belong to each other.* When he stepped away six inches, she was disappointed. *Should I reach over and take his?* She couldn't imagine being so bold.

He held a branch back for her, then fell into step again. "What was all that about back there?"

"With Miss Ginny?" She stopped walking, feeling proud, and explained. "I'm giving Pearl and Luke their freedom. They're going to stay on, take care of Miss Ginny and the farm. And someday it will be their own place."

He frowned. "You did this on your own?"

"Why not on my own? There is no one else here with any claim to Luke and Pearl."

"You might have consulted with me. Or my father."

"What are you getting at? You of all people? Why do you object to letting Pearl and Luke have their own lives?"

"I didn't say I objected to their being free. I object, Marianne, to your assuming your wishes make it so."

Marianne crossed her arms and set her face to match the severity in his. "I believe my wishes do make it so, on this occasion."

"What you propose is illegal, and you know it."

Why is he so upset? "Yes, it's illegal to free them in Louisiana, but we're in Mississippi."

Yves paced away and came back at her. "You can't assume being in Mississippi will make any difference. Manumission is illegal here too. You can't do this. You're putting your neck at risk, and it's not necessary."

"It is necessary. Not for me, but for Luke and Pearl. This is a perfect opportunity. No one at home knows Luke was found. I'll say—I can say I left Pearl to help out Martha Madison."

Yves' frown turned into a scowl. "And when your father comes home? And if the other slaves find out you let them go?"

"Why are we arguing about this? You don't like slavery any more than I do, and the way Joseph tells it, you risk the noose every time you play the shepherd."

"Risking my life is one thing. I can take care of myself. But you're a woman, and have your position to consider, your—"

"This is about my being a woman? A woman can't have principles? A woman can't stand up for what she believes?"

"I didn't say that. But you have to live down here, in

the drawing rooms of New Orleans, among the planters up and down the river."

"And that's no different from you."

He stopped arguing and looked at her. "No, it's not the same for me," he said quietly. "I'm leaving Louisiana. I have a job waiting for me in New York."

"A job?"

"I've been writing for several newspapers up North."

Why didn't I know this about him? "But you—"

"It's what I wanted to tell you. That I'm leaving. And to explain. If Lincoln wins in November . . ."

He wasn't going to ask me to marry him at all.

". . . some of the states will secede. We could be in a war in a few months, Marianne. I'm not going to fight for slavery."

Marianne stared at him, at those earnest hazel eyes. A man of principle. A man of strength and purpose. A man who'd won her heart. Who had touched her, whom she'd allowed to kiss her till she could hardly stand—and he had no intention of marrying her. She turned from him, feeling sick.

"When the war's over . . ." he said.

She walked away, leaving him behind.

"Marianne, wait."

Head down, she quickened her pace. He let her go, and that hurt too.

Chapter 25

Seven horses, four riders, one wagon, and six passengers filled the old road from Ginny's to the Trace. Once they reached the Trace itself, they spread out and Yves tried to maneuver his horse next to Marianne's. Marianne, without acknowledging his presence, nudged her mount to ride between the wagon and the forest edge.

Damn that Lindsay Morgan. She's poisoned every female mind in three parishes, and Marianne— It was painful to imagine what Marianne must think. He really had not been as forward with Miss Morgan as the gossip had it. When he'd first heard what was circulating, he'd been astounded. Yes, he'd kissed her. And Lindsay had kissed him back. But they were not the kisses he'd shared with Marianne. And he had not been "trifling" with Marianne's affections, as the saying goes. *Pigheaded woman. If she'd just listen.*

He rode up to join his father and Valentine in the lead. Valentine was practically a member of the family. In fact, Yves suspected there was actually a blood connection between Papa and the valet he'd had since childhood; it was common enough. So when Valentine spoke, it didn't surprise him, but it needled him nonetheless.

"Looks like you made a mess of it with that Miss Johnston, young master." Yves had always hated it when Valentine called him "young master"—an insincere epithet he used only in not-so-subtle irony. "You aiming to break another heart?"

"Valentine, I swear. If—"

"You two," Monsieur Chamard said. "It's a beautiful summer's morning. Can't a man ride in peace?"

"Ya'suh," Valentine said in mock subservience. Monsieur Chamard smiled at Yves, enjoying the charade, and Yves let his irritation go.

The three rode abreast, and he told his father about Marianne's scheme to free Luke and Pearl. Monsieur Chamard heard him out.

"The only way to make it legal would be to petition the legislature," Monsieur Chamard said, "and you know as well as I no body of governance in the South will hear such a request in these times."

"I tried to tell her so, but—"

"But she ain't listening to you," Valentine chimed in.

Yves glowered at him but didn't take the bait.

"In fact," Yves' father went on, "having Miss Johnston's freed-papers in his possession would be riskier for this man than being a slave. He'd have no one's protection should he be accosted, and he surely would be. I doubt anyone here would be generous or patient enough to send inquiries to the Johnstons. More likely Luke would simply be put back on public auction. The woman, too."

"So Luke and Pearl would be better off if Miss Ginny had ownership papers."

Monsieur Chamard nodded. They rode awhile in silence.

"Miss Ginny, she's old," Valentine said. "What happens when she dies? They just live back in the woods hoping nobody comes up on them?"

What a tangle. Marianne won't even speak to me, and here I am trying to save her neck and keep her happy at the same time. Yves twisted around in his saddle and looked back at her. *Ha.* He caught her. She'd been watching him and hadn't turned her head away in time to hide it. *She's mine, whether she knows it or not.*

He faced forward again, a sly cocky smile on his face. Which Valentine did not fail to notice. "You think you got her, do you?" Valentine shook his head. "I don't know. This Miss Johnston got a head on her shoulders. She's no silly debutante like them others."

"Valentine, you don't have to lecture me about women," Yves said, all his pique dissolved by Marianne's furtive look. "I believe Papa covered all that some years ago."

Monsieur Chamard continued as if there had been no break in the discussion. "The most practical solution to Miss Marianne's dilemma would be to have our friend William Tadman agree to hold papers on these two. They could still live out here on Miss Ginny's place, but it'd be with William's official permission—and most important, under his protection. And it'd be legal."

Yves could just hear Marianne's protestations. She wanted Luke and Pearl to be free. But she couldn't have it that way, and neither could Luke and Pearl, not if they wanted to stay on Ginny's place. Living in the South, in this time of increased restrictions, Marianne would have to accept the limits of her power to do as she pleased with her slaves. What's more, she seemed to constantly forget they were her father's slaves, not hers, and Albany Johnston was as invested in slavery as his father was.

Life with Marianne will not be easy, Yves realized. But it's what he wanted. If she had the patience to wait for him. His spirits and his confidence sank again. *I haven't even won her trust enough for her to believe I meant what those kisses promised.*

Yves looked over his shoulder again. This time Marianne was not watching him. She rode beside the wagon and was talking to Simone and Gabriel. *She's not meant to be a poor man's wife, living on a journalist's salary in a cold climate.*

Monsieur Chamard spoke quietly over the creak of saddle leather. "You're too much like your mother, son. All hurry and impatience. Give it time. She'll come around."

It wasn't that simple. "Papa, I'm ready to go. I'm taking that job in New York."

Monsieur Chamard nodded. "I expected it. But if you're going to go, Yves, I'd rather you go soon than wait for the political climate to get any worse. You could be caught down here, and the way you feel—you'll be better off up North."

Yves and Marianne skirted around each other the rest of the day. Frustrated, he once more tried to ride with her. She silently but emphatically would not allow it, reining her horse away from him. Yves found himself red-faced, furious, embarrassed, and bewildered.

I swear, I'll never understand a woman. I've done nothing she didn't want me to do. Even as he excused himself, though, he knew very well what he'd done to Marianne, and guilt did not sit easily on his shoulders. He'd allowed her to think, to expect, that he had intentions. *And I do, damn it. Just not right away.*

With DuPree in her lap, Pearl sat squeezed between Miss Ginny and Luke on the wagon seat, happy to have the three of them elbow to elbow. *We a family now. Miss Ginny our granny, and me and Luke got DuPree.*

Pearl hugged Luke's arm to her. He kept his attention on the horses and the reins, never having driven a wagon before, but she knew his heart. *He glad as I am. He just having trouble believing it.*

They camped out overnight. A light shower passed over them before dawn, and Pearl fretted DuPree might catch a chill. "Hand him here," Luke whispered. He took the little fellow and cuddled him next to his big warm chest, sheltering him from the rain. Every kindness Luke did DuPree, Pearl remembered to thank God for it. *You good to us, Lawd, and I knows it.*

Luke made a grand fire to dry out and cook breakfast by. Pearl mixed up cornmeal and water to fry in the bacon grease while Miss Marianne tended DuPree. Pearl had watched Missy being mean to Yves Chamard all day, and she wasn't any friendlier this morning. *Whatever he done to make her mad, she need to get over it. If she don't come round, I maybe tell her dat.*

At midmorning, they crossed a stream running through a meadow. Pearl was puzzled when Yves led their party off the road and dismounted. His father settled his horse close up to the wagon while Yves climbed in next to Gabriel and perched on the sidewall.

"Miss Johnston, will you please join us?" Yves said.

Marianne stopped next to Monsieur Chamard but stayed on her horse. *Look at dat face she pull,* Pearl thought. *She miserable being mad, but she too stubborn to let it go.*

"We need to settle this before we get to town," Yves began. "My father has confirmed what I feared. In the state of Mississippi, there are very circumscribed laws about how a slave may be freed. And it is no easier in Louisiana."

Pearl took hold of Luke. Her heart started pounding

and she knew Luke could feel it through her arm. *Dey not gone free us after all.*

"In order to free Luke or Pearl, your father, Miss Johnston, would have to submit a petition to the legislature. You know how unlikely it is they would respond favorably in this political climate." Yves looked at Luke. "The government would have to grant your freedom, Luke. The Johnstons cannot do it."

Luke's face was impassive, and Pearl looked only at her lap. *Don know why I believed it anyway*, she thought. *We's slaves and dat's dat.*

Marianne spoke up. "Then Luke and Pearl won't have their freedom papers. They can still stay with Miss Ginny. Who's to know?"

"Let's say," Monsieur Chamard proposed, "that Luke has a fine crop of, I don't know. Corn. He needs a new axe. Pearl needs calico, shoes, sewing needles. Luke goes to the market." He looked at all of them. "He will be challenged immediately, and with no papers, he'll not only be forbidden to trade, he'll likely be taken up."

The party sat in the meadow in silence while the horses munched on sweet grass and a blue dragonfly hovered. Pearl swallowed hard. *I gone lose Luke again. He not gone stay wid me and DuPree.* When Luke squeezed her hand, she felt her throat fill up as if her heart beat there. *He telling me good-bye already.*

"But surely someone on the Trace would trade with them," Marianne said. She looked at Luke. "Or you could—"

Luke shook his head. "No way to live, wondering every minute some neighbor man gone turn you over to de slavers."

He gone run, dat's what he means. Pearl bored into Missy's blue eyes, all the yearning in her heart in the look she gave Marianne. *Dat man Yves love you. You ask him, he fix dis.*

Marianne did look to Yves, her appeal silent but eloquent. She felt connected to him even now, in spite of her disappointment, and Pearl needed him.

"Yes," he answered her. "There may be another way."

Monsieur Chamard explained his plan involving William Tadman. "You'd legally belong to Mr. Tadman, Luke, but you'd live on Miss Ginny's place. When you came in to town with your produce, you'd have your paper of permission from Mr. Tadman. You'd have his protection."

"And if dis Mr. Tadman don want me up at Ginny's?" Luke said to the elder Chamard. "If'n he decides he want Pearl in his kitchen, maybe, and me in some cotton field?"

"I know Mr. Tadman. I trust him. That's all the guarantee I can give you."

"Miss Ginny, you understand all this?" Yves said.

Her eyes flashed at him. "I'm old, not stupid." Gabriel guffawed. "You hush, Caleb, or whatever your name is. This here Caleb and his Pearl willing to stay with me." She turned to Monsieur Chamard. "You make it happen, mister." She looked at Luke. "Caleb . . . all right, Luke then. You take it. It'll be a better life than you ever had."

Pearl could have kissed the old woman. Hope surged again: It would work. *We can have us a life on dat little farm.*

Luke bent his head and Pearl leaned her forehead against his. They didn't speak, but they didn't need to.

Please, Lawd, Pearl prayed, *help him see it gone work.*

Luke raised his head and studied Monsieur Chamard a moment. "All right. I'll stick it."

Pearl bent over her knees, trembling in her prayers. *Thank you, Lawd.* Luke took her in his arms, right in front of all those white people, and pulled her onto his lap. "I got you, honey," he whispered. "It be all right now."

They reached Natchez in late afternoon. Marianne strained her patience as Monsieur Chamard settled Gabriel in the hotel, Simone tending to him. At last, the rest of the party followed Main Street to the home of Mr. William Tadman where Luke and Pearl's fate would be finally determined.

Marianne nodded to Luke and Pearl to wait around back of the house. Monsieur Chamard knocked on the front door, and Mr. Tadman's wife admitted Bertrand and Yves Chamard, Marianne, and Ginny.

"Why, Mr. Chamard, good morning. Won't you come in?" Mrs. Tadman said, casting a glance at Ginny's filthy bare feet. She seated them in her fashionable parlor. "Mr. Tadman is at the barbershop this afternoon." She called her pickanniny. "Run after Mr. Tadman, Susie. Tell him Mr. Chamard is here."

While they waited, Mrs. Tadman served them lemonade and sugar cookies. This was a new experience for Marianne. Mrs. Tadman's skin was dark, her nose was broad and flat, yet she wore a lovely day gown of fine yellow cotton and white lace. Her black tightly curled tresses were free of the ever-present *tignon* the slaves had to wear, and it was arranged much as Marianne fashioned her own hair.

"Yes, sir, the Natchez market is flooded with cotton," Mrs. Tadman was saying. She was as cultured and gracious a hostess as any Marianne had encountered. Free Negroes, educated and sophisticated, who owned slaves. Marianne glanced at Yves, wondering if he dwelt on the irony as well.

Mr. Tadman arrived. The gentlemen shook hands,

introductions were made, and the problem put before Mr. Tadman. Marianne wondered if he still had her pearls. Monsieur Chamard and Yves both trusted him, not only with pearls, but with the lives of two people she'd come to care about. She would have to trust him too; there was no other solution.

Mr. Tadman led his guests to the back courtyard to inspect the two slaves they set such store by. Pearl sat on a bench in the shade with DuPree on her lap eating a fig the cook gave him. Luke stood, the tension in his body making him stiff.

Mr. Tadman asked Luke a few questions, assuring himself the man knew what was expected of him. Marianne breathed easier now. It was all but settled. Tomorrow they would have the papers drawn up to transfer Luke and Pearl's ownership to Mr. Tadman. Then Luke, Pearl, DuPree, and Ginny would drive back up the Trace to the farmstead to begin their new lives.

As Mr. Tadman and Bertrand Chamard conferred, Yves took Marianne's elbow, startling her. "I want to talk to you." She drew away, but he had her arm. "Now."

Yes, he had helped Pearl and Luke, but that gave him no claim on her. She should yank herself from his grip. She should stomp on his foot, she should slap him in the face. But, her mouth sullen and tight, she allowed him to take her around the corner of the house into the alley, away from the others, and place her with her back to the wall.

"Exactly what is it that would cause you to hustle me in this way, Mr. Chamard?"

He smiled at her, but she noticed it didn't quite reach his eyes. He didn't like being defied. *Good*, she thought. She had no intention of pleasing him ever again.

"Miss Johnston. I require your ear, if you please. In the figurative or the literal sense, as you like." He lifted a hand to touch her, but she leaned away, remembering those traitorous nibbles he'd taken from her ear.

"Figurative, then. You did not, Miss Marianne, allow me to finish the other day on the path. I would like you to do so now."

"If I must."

"Fact one," he began. "You are the daughter of a wealthy and influential planter. You are accustomed to a certain standard of living. This you will concede?"

Guardedly, Marianne agreed. Even after two days on the road, he looked good. His hair was mashed flat from his hat, and his nose was sunburned, but his eyes were hazel and his mouth—

"Fact two. We may very well be at war in a few months. States' rights, trade, secession, slavery—whatever cause you wish to attribute it to, the Union may soon be torn apart. I know you are aware of this."

"Yes." *I'm still furious with him, though.* "And what has this to do with me?"

"Fact three. You're going to marry me. But, you see, there are these obstacles to consider."

Marianne's busy thoughts ceased. *What did he say?* She met his eyes. There was a hint of merriment there, but only a hint. He meant it.

"What makes you think I would marry you?"

Now his eyes gleamed with wicked humor. He propped one arm against the wall behind her and leaned close. "Why do I think you will marry me, Miss Marianne?" He touched her lips with his, gently—and for only the briefest moment. "Because I can give you what you want."

Marianne couldn't move. She wasn't giving in. He hadn't won her over. She just couldn't move. "You don't know what I want," she said, trying to sound snappish.

He kissed her again, briefly, softly. "I do."

She opened her mouth to argue, and he took her kiss, hot and hard and insistent. For a count of three, Marianne resisted. Then she let him press her back into the wall and melted under his mouth. *If he thinks this is what I want . . .* She parted her lips and tasted his tongue. Her knees felt weak again, but he pulled her away from the wall and into his arms. She let herself sink into him.

She blinked, her head clearing. She stepped out of his embrace with her hand across her mouth. "What do you mean, give me what I want? I can get kisses anywhere."

"Not these kisses." He took her back and bent her over his arm, his mouth on hers. Every bone in her body went soft. Total submission, this kiss demanded. And she gave it.

When he let her up, she was dazed and breathless. He was grinning. Maybe if he hadn't grinned— *Insufferable, arrogant cad.* "Very nice, Mr. Chamard, but I want more than kisses."

The grin faded. Her eyes insisted he offer more.

"Babies," he said.

He knows I want babies?

"An honorable life—without owning other human beings. A useful life—maybe using your medical skills."

"Yes," she said quietly. "I do want all of that. And one thing more."

He waited. What had he forgotten?

She lifted her arms to his neck. "I want you."

The side of that house might have been an intimate boudoir, so completely did the two of them forget themselves. Yves had one hand low on her back, pressing her into him, the other behind her head. Marianne's hands gripped him, and . . . Monsieur Chamard's calls at last penetrated their heated senses. Yves lifted his head. "Did you hear someone?"

"I think it's your father."

Yves put a hand on either side of her face and kissed her once more. "I adore you," he whispered.

Marianne, undone by his tenderness, swallowed tears and smiled at him as she tucked a tendril of hair behind her ear. Once she had her breath and her wits about her, he offered her his arm.

Chapter 26

Next morning at the attorney's office, Marianne sold Luke and Pearl to Mr. Tadman for one dollar each. In exchange for Mr. Tadman allowing his new slaves to live independently, he asked that Luke deliver one bushel of corn, one watermelon, and a peck of okra per year. "Keeps it on the up-and-up," he said, "if anyone should inquire."

Marianne signed every paper with a joyful flourish, and it was done. Luke and Pearl and DuPree belonged to William Tadman, but they were free to live and love in a place with no overseer, no man taking the fruit of their labor beyond a watermelon, a basket of okra, and a bushel of corn. As close to freedom as they could get.

On Main Street, Monsieur Chamard, Yves, and Gabriel left the ladies to their own shopping. The men meant to buy a mule and harness for Luke to use on Ginny's farm.

Miss Ginny stayed with Luke and Pearl at the Tadmans', so Marianne and Simone were on their own. As they stepped into the dry goods store, Simone declared, "I mean to fill that wagon before they drive back to Miss Ginny's."

Marianne smiled at her. *If it weren't for Miss Ginny, we'd have lost Gabriel, and Luke and Pearl would be headed back to Magnolias.* She fingered her own near-empty purse. "Let me spend everything I have, and then I'll help you spend yours."

Marianne picked out three bolts of calico, needles, thread, and pins. "I don't have another dime."

Then the merchant followed Simone around as she pointed to straw hats, stockings, flour, vinegar, burlap, canvas, tin plates and cups, blankets, rice, beans, a barrel of pickles, a cured ham—whatever caught her eye that she thought would be useful.

"What else do they need?" Simone said.

"Ginny has a shotgun, but Luke could use a rifle and ammunition for deer hunting. And a knife."

Simone turned to the dry goods merchant. "You have rifles?"

"Yes, ma'am. I have rifles, pistols, shotguns, whatever you want."

By the time they finished enriching the merchant, Luke drove the wagon up front. Instead of the two horses that had pulled it from Miss Ginny's, a fine-looking mule stood in the traces.

While the wagon was being loaded, Gabriel leaned on his crutch and took Miss Ginny's hand, and Simone joined him in saying good-bye. Meanwhile, Pearl touched Marianne's arm. "I gots something to say, Missy."

Marianne walked Pearl down the boardwalk a few paces from the others.

"You done a fine thing, Missy, and de Lawd gone reward you, dis life or de next. And Missy, Luke and me? No way to tell you but just say de words. Thank you, Miss Marianne." Pearl kissed Marianne on the cheek, and Marianne hugged her.

"One mo thing," Pearl said. "Mr. Yves. He do dis for Luke and me 'cause he want to please you."

Marianne turned her head to look at Yves arranging the provisions in the wagon for a balanced ride. She loved the long line of his body as he stretched across the bags of flour and beans. At breakfast, he'd repeatedly taken her hand or her arm, rousing her so that all her senses were attuned to him—the breeze rifling his hair, the reach of his arms as he rolled a keg, even the faint scent of soap— most of all, her skin was alive to his every touch.

Pearl pulled her attention back. "He de best man any I seen, and he do it all for you. You leave off being stubborn and don be mad at him no more."

Marianne blushed and laughed. "I'm not mad." She glanced at the others and spoke into Pearl's ear. "He asked me to marry him."

Pearl hugged her. "De Lawd be good to you."

Marianne returned the embrace. "God bless you, Pearl."

Mr. Tadman showed up with a black and white puppy. DuPree struggled in Miss Ginny's arms to reach the puppy, and had his face licked good for his trouble.

"You train him right, Luke, you'll have you a good hunting dog," Tadman said.

"Yassir. I will. And I sure thank you, sir."

"Ready to go?" Yves asked. Luke nodded his head, and Yves untied the reins from the hitching rail.

Luke, Ginny, DuPree, and Pearl shared the bench. Luke picked up the reins and clucked to the well-trained mule, and they were off. Marianne's eyes teared as she waved and then watched them turn off Main Street into Commerce on their way to a new life. She'd miss Pearl, but she was proud, too, proud she had done this good thing.

* * *

They boarded the steamboat *Lucky Lady* for the trip home. Monsieur Chamard invited Yves to the gaming tables in the salon. Gabriel and Simone settled in the library and she read to him. Marianne walked the promenade.

So much had happened in the two weeks since she'd set out with a spinning wheel and three escapees in the back of a wagon. She felt she'd earned a new maturity. Father would not be pleased about Pearl and Luke, but she resolved to tell him all of it rather than to lie. She hated a lie, though she thought it wise not to volunteer information about Joseph or the escape route. And if Father was more displeased than she imagined, and she imagined quite a furious father, she would find a way to pay him back. She could forgo the dressmakers, for instance, for the coming season. Of course, it would be embarrassing to be seen in last year's gowns, but she didn't really care about that. What she'd done for Luke and Pearl made the conventions of the social season seem trivial.

And how much of a season as an unmarried woman would she have anyway? Yves had mentioned obstacles, but she only vaguely remembered that part of their communication. Much more vivid was his touch, his tenderness, his kisses. Forever kisses. She didn't care if she even had a trousseau, much less a fancy wedding, if Father was miffed at her. All she wanted was Yves.

Marianne realized she'd lost track of the days. Was this the twelfth or the thirteenth? Father was due home the week of the twentieth. She hurried back to the library to ask Simone for the date.

"It's the fourteenth," Simone said.

"Dear Lord, Father will be home next week!"

* * *

The *Lucky Lady* docked at Toulouse the next day. Cleo and Josie had had a note from Bertrand they were on their way, and they'd kept vigil on Josie's gallery ever since. As soon as they heard the whistle, they hurried down to the river to stand in the hot sun, waiting for their children.

Simone waved from the upper deck, and Josie waved and smiled to see her firstborn safe and home again. "Look at her, Cleo. She's so happy!"

"Then Gabriel is all right." Cleo worked hard not to cry. Young men did not appreciate their mothers crying over them. She scanned every face looking for her son.

Finally Bertrand emerged from the upper deck salon. Smiling, he raised his hand to her. *Bless him, he's brought our boy home.* She wiped her eyes and waited for Gabriel to follow Bertrand out of the salon. Gabriel used a crutch. He hesitated at the stairs, but he managed to descend on his own.

"He's so thin," Cleo said.

Josie took her arm. "Don't let him see you cry."

Cleo straightened up. "You're right. He's alive, and he's home."

Monsieur Chamard passed a few coins to the captain to stop again at Magnolias, and Marianne stood with Yves on the upper deck as the boat pulled back into the stream. After he delivered Marianne safely home, Yves would travel on to New Orleans to meet with Marcel and tell him Gabriel was safe.

They were alone at last, except for the half dozen other passengers taking the air. They leaned on the rail and Yves pulled Marianne's arm through his. They had so much to talk about, to decide, to plan. They chose rather to watch the water, feel the sun and the breeze, and hold hands hidden from the other travelers.

At Magnolias, the steamboat waited for Yves to take Marianne to the house. He opened the door for her and stepped inside. "Charles!" he called. The butler appeared at once.

"Miss Marianne! Lawd, I 'bout gone crazy worrying bout you." He glared at Yves and lost all sense of his place. "You de one taken Miss Marianne? She been gone 'way from here too long, Mr. Chamard."

"No, Charles. It wasn't Mr. Chamard's fault."

"I like to had the countryside out looking for you. Joseph been back here days ago, and you still missing and—"

"Charles, I'm all right. Really."

"Everything is in order here?" Yves asked.

Charles wiped his face and breathed. "Yessir. Everything all right now."

The steamboat tooted the whistle. "I have to go," Yves said.

"Charles," Marianne said, "will you find Hannah for me, please?"

Charles left them, looking over his shoulder at the last moment. "I be right back," he warned them.

Yves took both Marianne's hands and kissed her fingers. The boat whistled again. "I'll see you soon."

Marianne watched from the doorway as Yves boarded. He waved to her from the lower deck until the boat was far out into the river.

Finally Marianne went back into the cool dim hallway and closed the door behind her. She hardly felt the carpet under her feet as she floated up the stairs.

A week passed, and Marianne reestablished her routine. She was in the garden after breakfast, Freddie nearby sniffing every bush and tuft of grass, claiming it all, all, for himself. Marianne paused with a spade in her hand and listened to the boat whistle on the river. She looked at Joseph. "It's stopping here?"

"I believe dat de whistle for it," Joseph said.

At the well Joseph hurriedly poured water over her hands. She splashed some in her face and tucked a stray tress back in her bonnet, then made her way through the lower garden, into the formal gardens, through the back green, and across the verandah.

She rushed into the central hall and there was Albany Johnston just taking off his hat.

"Father!" Marianne ran to him and he hugged her tight and whirled her around, though not so high as he once had. Freddie barked and jumped deliriously.

"How's my girl?" Mr. Johnston kissed her and held her back to look at her. For a moment a crease of displeasure crossed his forehead. "Your face is brown as a nut!"

Marianne laughed. "I'm not a drawing room kind of girl, Father."

"Well, it becomes you. I've seen enough paste-skinned women up North. I don't believe most of them have ever been outdoors more than ten minutes at a time." He tucked her hand in the crook of his arm and led her toward the parlor. "How are your roses?"

Marianne's father eased his considerable bulk onto the sofa and pulled her down next to him. "Tell me everything."

Well, not everything just now, she thought. She did tell him about her roses and some other details about the house, but she wisely led him to talk about Saratoga. He described the horse racing, the promenades, the social scene.

"Where is Adam?"

"I don't know whether he's in New Orleans or at Lake Maurepas, Father." She told him about Gabriel Chamard's abduction and Adam's part in searching the docks of New Orleans. "Gabriel has only been home again a week, and Adam has not yet returned." Her own part in Gabriel's rescue she decided to explain another day.

"He's left you here alone all this time?"

Father need not know how little Adam had kept her company on the plantation since he'd been gone. Father was angry with Adam half the time anyway. "I've been busy, Father. Not lonely a bit."

"You are one of those fortunate people who enjoys her own company," he said. "Well, do you suppose we could have dinner in half an hour? I'll clean up, and then I'd like nothing better than Lou'siann cooking. Not a single dinner did I have in Saratoga good as what Evette puts on the table."

Annie took her place in the dining room to pull the rope of the great punkah hung over the table, fanning the diners and scattering the flies as the master and mistress ate their dinner.

After buttery corn bread, black-eyed peas cooked with fatback, stewed chicken, red beans and rice, pickled cabbage, red potatoes, pole beans, and fresh-cut peaches with strawberries and cream, Albany Johnston folded his napkin and sighed. "That was good."

Marianne smiled. Her father loved to eat, and she took pride in managing a kitchen that pleased him. *Not that I labored over a hot stove*, she reminded herself.

"My dear, I have some news." He twisted his water glass and kept his eyes on the table.

Father's nervous? It's that Marguerite. Oh, heavens, he's going to marry her.

"You know Madame Sandrine, of course."

Marianne nodded. She allowed Freddie to jump into her lap to be petted.

Her father cleared his throat. "We, ah, we ran into

each other in Saratoga." *Liar*, she thought, and smiled. "She was accompanied by her youngest son—"

"Jean Baptiste?" Marianne interrupted only to tease her father a little. Being of an unflappable disposition, he seldom gave her the opportunity.

"Yes. Jean Baptiste. So it was quite proper that we should spend some time together." He drank from his water glass.

"Yes, Father?"

"Over the course of the summer, we have formed an, ah, attachment." He smiled at her sheepishly, and Marianne grinned at him. "You already know what I'm going to say, you imp."

"I believe you are contemplating marriage, Father."

"You don't mind?"

Carrying Freddie in one arm, Marianne left her chair to hug her father. "Of course I don't mind." *Even though Marguerite Sandrine is a calculating, flirtatious female whose reputation is perhaps not as white as it might be.* "I'm sure Madame Sandrine and I shall be great friends." *As long as she stays out of my garden and out of my way.*

Marianne kissed her father's forehead. "I'm very happy for you, Father. When is the wedding to be?"

"Soon. Marguerite wants the wedding to be the first big event of the season."

Marianne looked around at the furnishings her mother had chosen. The deep red upholstery of the dining chairs, worn thin at the corners, the nicked mahogany table, the stained turkey carpet. All sumptuous, at one time, and now comfortable and familiar, if a little outdated and worn. *I suppose Madame will want to redecorate.*

Well, and when I marry Yves, I won't live here anyway. Where will we live? For that matter, he has said nothing about when. Oh. She was unsettled to realize how little she knew what his plans were. He should have told her. *I suppose he tried, that day in Natchez. I have to listen more and kiss less. Not what I want to do at all!*

Marianne hugged her father again, and they repaired to the parlor where the doors and windows let in the breeze.

The following day, Mr. Johnston took his coffee to his office and began to go through the correspondence. Mr. McNaught was to report to him in the afternoon, and Marianne thought she had better have her confessional time before the overseer brought in all the bad news.

She told him about McNaught's dogs, about Peter and John Man and Luke running away, about little Sylvie's death.

Mr. Johnston shook his head. "I didn't leave Magnolias for my daughter to have to manage on her own. I'll be speaking to Adam about this."

"Adam was here then. The Chamard brothers were too." She took a deep breath. "Father, there's more I have to tell you."

She left out what she could. Father didn't need to know about Eleanor and Ebenezer or the three escapees from another plantation. But she told him she'd left home with the spinning wheel for Martha Madison, Joseph and Pearl accompanying her. She told him they'd met up with Yves, who was on his brother's trail, and that they'd joined him because Gabriel reportedly was sick and injured. She'd sent Joseph back with the wagon. After that, she kept to the truth: finding Luke, finding Gabriel, leaving Luke and Pearl and the baby with Miss Ginny, the agreement with William Tadman.

Mr. Johnston did not interrupt. He watched his daughter tell her story, and he knew exactly when she began to tell him the whole truth. He already knew her sentiments about slavery. Four years ago when she'd

come home from New York, she'd been afire with abolitionist drivel. *I should have known she'd not forgotten that
nonsense. Hardheaded, willful. Amazing she's not given me
trouble before now. Wish Adam had her gumption.*

Marianne finished and folded her hands in her lap.
Her back was straight, but at least, Mr. Johnston thought,
she didn't blaze defiance at him—she kept her gaze on
her lap in imitation of a demure young woman.

Mr. Johnston poured her a small brandy and a large one
for himself. "So. You have run all around this country like
a wanton, risking the family reputation and your own neck,
and you have cost me two slaves, is that what you're telling
me?"

"Yes, Father."

"Drink that," he said. He took his own brandy to the
window and stared out at the lawn and the gardens
beyond it. *What am I going to do with her? She's too old to
send to her room. Too old to shake a finger at. She should be
married by now. That's what she needs. A husband and a
houseful of children to keep her busy. Too much time on her
hands.*

"I can make it up to you, what Pearl and Luke cost,
Father. It might take me two seasons, but I can do without the usual wardrobe expenses. And I can economize
in other ways, I'm sure."

"Very noble-minded, my dear." Mr. Johnston turned
back to the desk and sat down. "I have another idea. This
season, I want you to stop sending all the young men away.
You make yourself unapproachable when you want to, I've
seen you do it. You're pretty as any girl on the river, richer
than most. The suitors come around, but you scare them
off. It's time you were married. You see to it this year, and
I will forgive all the rest, the 'adventure,' and the slaves;
and I will sign and send to Mr. Tadman the paperwork so

we can complete the transaction of turning over Luke and Pearl to him. Is that a bargain?"

Tears gathered on Marianne's lashes and she beamed at him. "I promise to do my best to be married this year, Father. I really do." She left her chair and went to him. He took her on his knee as he had so many times when she was a girl and hugged her. "You're a trial, you know that, Marianne?"

"Yes, Father. I love you too."

Chapter 27

A few leaves began to turn yellow, announcing that once again fall would succeed summer. Marianne treated heat rash among the babies in the quarters, ministered to two cases of poison oak, and resumed Peter's reading lessons. If Father noticed she spent an inordinate amount of time in the quarters, he did not mention it.

After ten days at home and no word from Yves, Marianne was fretful and anxious. She suffered most when she was supposed to be resting and enduring the languid hours of afternoon heat. Annie, her shadow since she'd come home, offered to fan her while she lay on her divan, but the child's head nodded and the fan fell from her fingers. Marianne lifted her onto the day bed and let her sleep. She considered stirring about to take her mind off Yves, but thinking of Yves was a constant anyway, and the slaves needed a respite. Marianne sat in the shady window seat and leaned on the sill.

Fact one, he'd said. She was accustomed to a life of ease and luxury. *Yes, I am. But I know how to work, too.* She could be content with much less, if Yves were with her. As for fact two, the election was nearly three months from now. Mr. Lincoln had not made a significant speech in weeks, and

Father thought he was afraid to rouse the Southerners any further by opening his mouth. Maybe Lincoln would lose, and there would be no need for secession. That left fact three: marriage! *I don't see any reason to wait longer than we're supposed to. Even if there's a war. We'll wait only long enough for propriety*

Marianne knew very well that if one announced one's engagement and then married too quickly afterward, all the scolds and gossips watched a woman's figure to calculate just when she had allowed herself to be ruined. So the engagement had to be long enough to prove Yves had not proposed simply to do the honorable thing. *A New Year's Day wedding would be nice. Everyone will be in town, and Father and Marguerite will be married by then.*

But planning a wedding required a groom. And Yves did not appear. Not the second week, nor the third. As improper as a written communication from her would be, Marianne considered it. But how could she write without sounding like a desperate nag? No. Yves had to come to her. She could do nothing.

Twenty-six days. Marianne thought she'd lost him. He'd changed his mind. He'd forgotten her. He was as bad as Lindsay Morgan said he was. No, he loved her. Or perhaps he didn't. And then the heavy cream-colored letter arrived addressed to Mr. Albany Johnston from Yves Chamard. She could have wept at the sight of it.

He would call on Mr. and Miss Johnston on the morrow if he might. He was coming. Marianne rushed upstairs. She would wash her hair. What would she wear? "Hannah!"

She sat in the window to let her hair dry and imagined rushing into his arms, heedless of her father's amazed disapproval. No, she'd be aloof. How dare he ignore her for nearly four weeks! She'd tell him what she thought of him. She'd fuss and rant—he'd take her by the shoulders and hush her with his mouth on hers.

Marianne kept vigil on the upper gallery, wondering if he was coming from New Orleans or from his father's plantation only a few miles upstream. She spied a rowboat on the river and watched as it rode the current. She could make out the slaves with oars, and another man sitting in the bow. The boat slipped out of the central current and angled toward the east bank, toward Magnolias. Surely it was Yves.

She clattered across the upper hallway, down the stairs, and out to the front porch. Then she stopped. He'd kept her waiting twenty-six days! She peered to be sure it was Yves in the boat. It was. She strode inside and closed the door firmly behind her, then marched upstairs to her room and closed that door too. She meant to take as long as she liked before she descended those stairs again. Let him wait.

She sat at the mirror fussing with her hair when she heard the knocker downstairs, then Charles' measured footsteps, the murmur of his greeting, the closing of the big door.

He's following Charles into the parlor now. He's sitting in the green chair facing the door while Charles fetches Father. He's wondering why I don't come down. He knows I know he's here.

Marianne put her ear to the door. Father's heavy footsteps crossed the hall, and in the parlor his big voice greeted Yves, son of his friend Bertrand, friend of his son Adam. *And beloved of his daughter Marianne.*

Lil' Annie's quick light steps came up the stairs. She knocked on Marianne's door and came in without waiting to be called. "Dat man you likes come, Miss Marianne. You sposed to go down to de parlor, Charles say."

"Annie, you're to wait for me to call you before you open the door, remember?"

"Oh, yessum. I remembers. I jest don see no use in it. You gone tell me come in anyway."

"Go on with you, Annie. I'll come down when I'm ready."

"Yessum."

Marianne left the door ajar, but she could make out only murmuring voices. She went back to her desk and picked up a book, read two pages without any notion of what the words on the page said, put it down, checked her hair again. She tapped her fingers on the dresser. Arranged her neckline.

Finally she pinched her cheeks for color and descended the staircase at a stately pace, Freddie at her heels. Cool and composed, she entered the parlor with her chin slightly elevated. Yves was on his feet as soon as she set foot in the room. She met him with an insincere smile on her face, and took some satisfaction in how his own smile died. Twenty-six days, indeed.

She held her hand out for the requisite greeting. Yves bent over it formally. "Miss Johnston."

"Why, Mr. Chamard. It's been such a long while, I hardly recognized you."

Yves retreated a step, wisely silent. Freddie wagged his tail, wonderfully pleased his idol had returned, and Yves ventured a quick scratch behind his ears before resuming his stoic posture.

With great decorum, Marianne arranged the expanse of her skirts as she sank gracefully onto the green silk chair. She'd chosen a pale blue gown embroidered with apricot and green around the low neckline. *I look damn good in it, too.*

"I've just been remonstrating with Mr. Chamard about turning my daughter into an adventuress this summer," Mr. Johnston said.

Marianne struggled to hide her alarm. If Father

blamed Yves for everything she'd done, then he'd never give his approval to the marriage. Father was scowling. She glanced at Yves. She'd never seen him ill at ease before.

"I assure you, Father, Mr. Chamard did not lead me astray. I insisted on accompanying him."

The scowl left Mr. Johnston's face and he laughed. "Don't look so nervous, Yves. I know my daughter." He stood up. "I hope you will excuse me for a few minutes. I'll join you for coffee as soon as I've, uh, spoken with Mr. McNaught."

Marianne kept her eyes on the wall opposite her. Just as Father had said, she could be silently unapproachable. The tinny ormolu clock on the mantel pinged, the only sound in the room.

Yves propped his elbows on his knees, just that many inches closer to her. "You're angry with me."

"Not at all." The pattern in the wallpaper had all her attention.

"Twenty-six days."

So he'd counted them too. She glanced at him. *If he's smiling, I'll leave the room.*

He wasn't. He looked woeful. *Good.*

"If I could have come sooner, I would have."

That earned him the turn of her head.

"I missed you," he said.

She adjusted the folds of her skirt, rustling it a bit.

"Marianne." Yves left his chair and knelt beside her without touching her. "Look at me."

Umm, he smells good. She looked at him, trying to hide the fact that her breathing changed.

"Have you forgotten me?" he asked.

"In twenty-six days?"

"I thought of you every minute. But I couldn't speak

to your father until I had arranged everything. He would not approve of a penniless suitor."

Not a hint of cockiness in him now. His eyes even held a hint of pleading. Marianne relaxed into her chair. She'd had him worried, and that was all the reassurance she needed. "Are we to be penniless?"

Yves smiled now. "No, my darling, not penniless. But not wealthy either. Can you be happy without silk and satin and servants and carriages?"

She tilted her head as if she were considering it. Then she looked into his gold-flecked hazel eyes. "Will you kiss me every single day?"

"I will."

"At night and in the morning too?"

"Every hour on the hour."

"That may not be enough."

Yves laughed. "I'll do my best." He lifted her from her chair as he rose, pulled her close, and kissed her with twenty-six days of yearning.

After a kiss long enough that Freddie commenced whining, Yves released her. "That's all you get for now." He stepped back to his chair. "You sit over there."

She laughed and straightened her hair. Seated in her own chair six feet from his, she endeavored to play the lady. "How is Gabriel?"

"Very well. He's tossed the crutch and walks with a cane. He and Simone are married! His Aunt Josie had a priest waiting when they got home."

Yves suddenly patted his vest. "Oh, how could I forget?"

He fished in his pocket for a small black velvet bag. "I've been to Natchez." He placed the bag in her hand. "Your pearls."

Marianne spilled her earrings into her palm, the ones

she'd given up to buy Luke. "Oh, Yves." She stood up and kissed him. "Thank you."

Father poked his head around the doorway. "How about that coffee?"

Marianne smiled at him, gloriously happy. "Coffee would be wonderful, Father."

After dinner, Yves raised an eyebrow and Marianne nodded.

"Might I speak to you, Mr. Johnston?"

"Certainly. Come into my office and we'll have a cigar."

Marianne stayed behind in the dining room. It was much closer to the office than the parlor.

Annie and Charles cleared away the remains of dinner, polished the table around her, set the silver candelabra back in the middle of the table, and left her. A few minutes later Charles came back in with a silver cooling bucket and a bottle of champagne. Annie carried a tiny silver tray with crystal flutes. They left her alone again and Marianne stared at the champagne for lack of anything else to do until Father and Yves should emerge. Freddie napped at her feet. The clock in the parlor chimed two. It chimed again on the half hour and still they had not finished.

Men and their cigars. Don't they know I'm waiting out here? What on earth are they talking about?

At last the door opened. Marianne stood, waiting to see their faces. Father wanted her to get married, didn't he? And he knew the Chamards very well. Nothing to worry about, surely. But their footsteps in the hallway were slow. Too slow. He'd said no. *Then we'll run away,* she thought.

Yves entered. Where was his smile? Why wasn't he smiling?

He winked at her and took a puff on his cigar. She breathed out.

Father followed Yves into the room. When he spied the champagne, he grunted. "Charles' idea?"

Marianne smiled uncertainly. "Yes."

"Sit down, Marianne," Mr. Johnston said. "We have some things to discuss before champagne is in order."

She sat. Yves took the chair next to hers. Father faced them both across the broad table.

"Yves has refused his inheritance from his father. Did you know that?"

"No, but I'm not surprised, Father. Yves and I—"

"Spare me the moralizing, please. This is about your financial future, not your principles. He will have a little money from his grandmother Ashford, whose fortune came from the fur trade. He has sensibly decided to keep that. He will have a salary from this newspaper job. And he has liquidated his own assets here, his carriage and the like. Correct, Mr. Chamard?"

"Yes, sir."

"What this means, Marianne, is that you will live a very different life. You will not have a new wardrobe with every season. You will not have a houseful of servants to clean and cook and see to your needs. You may, perhaps, have one maid and a handyman, but no more. You understand?"

"Yes, Father. I know this." *So he is not forbidding it!* Marianne's smile lit the room.

"And he means to take you north. You'll have snow and gray skies and freezing rain all winter. You will leave your family behind . . ." Here Mr. Johnston lost his voice. He cleared his throat and went on. "Your family, everyone you know. You won't have your rose garden."

My roses . . . "Doubtless roses grow in New York." She

reached for Yves and he took her hand. "Father, I will miss you terribly. But I must go where Yves goes."

Mr. Johnston set his cigar on the edge of the table. There were several scars around the table's perimeter where he'd forgotten a cigar before now. He sighed heavily. "I know."

"You aren't surprised, Father?"

He smiled at Marianne. "You are not the same girl I left here three months ago, my dear. And after Yves' note arrived, I don't believe you heard one word I said. That, and Hannah's complaint that you changed gowns six times this morning, led me to think that you had perhaps formed an attachment."

Charles appeared in the doorway looking smug. Marianne grinned at him. He'd been listening. Probably Hannah and Annie were out there in the hallway too.

"Charles," Father called, "uncork this champagne, if you please."

In the shady late afternoon, Marianne led Yves through the gardens to show him her experimental roses. Annie was dispatched as chaperone, and when Yves stopped in a secluded nook to take Marianne into his arms, Annie scolded, "Charles say keep ya'll moving. Le's go."

"She's incorrigible," Marianne whispered.

The heady fragrance of roses overwhelmed her, and the feel of Yves' arm under hers nearly undid her. His smoldering eyes told her he was suffering from the same stimulation.

"Miss Annie," he said, "I believe one kiss would be appropriate in the midst of all these beautiful roses, don't you?"

"You mean kissin' Miss Marianne?"

"I'll be happy to kiss you, too, if you'll allow me to kiss your mistress."

Annie thought about it. "All right. But my sissy say one kiss ain't hardly never enough."

"And she's right." Yves bent down to the six-year-old and gave her a whopping big kiss on the cheek. Then he kissed her on the other cheek.

Annie rubbed at it. "All right, I reckon you kin kiss Miss Marianne twicet, too."

Yves took Marianne into his arms and kissed her the way she'd been waiting to be kissed all afternoon. She leaned in to him, and he accepted her weight as if she were only another part of himself.

Finally, Annie pulled at Yves' jacket. "Dat long enough, mister."

Yves kept Marianne close and grinned. "That was only one kiss, Annie."

"Wail, ya'll best make de next one short. Dese ants round here trying to get me."

They walked on through the gardens, Marianne's hand in his because they belonged to each other now. At her experimental beds, she explained what she was doing with her crossbreeding project.

"Can you take cuttings?" Yves asked. Marianne kissed him for caring whether she had her roses with her.

"Oh Lawdy. Ya'll at it again." Annie teared up. "Charles gone whip me he find out ya'll doin' all dat kissing. He tell me keep de daylight 'tween ya'll."

"Annie, honey, Charles won't whip you," Marianne said.

Annie's big dark eyes aswim with tears conquered Yves. "We'll go back to the house and I won't kiss Miss Marianne once all the way back. How about that?"

At the house, Marianne said, "Come on, Annie. Help me dress for dinner."

"I tie de ribbons. I knows how to tie."

Yves held the door wide for Marianne's bell skirt and Annie both to get through. Then he patted his pocket for a cigar, lit up, and took a seat in the shade. He'd never felt more at peace than at that moment. Marianne was his. He was eager to go north where he'd no longer have to pretend he belonged in a culture that sanctioned slavery, where he could pursue his writing under his own name without risking his family's security. Leaving here without Marianne had become unthinkable. Now he had her, the world was his too.

Footsteps on the path from the stables interrupted Yves' contentment, and Adam Johnston appeared. He wore no hat, his coat was mud-spattered, and his gait was uneven. *He's been riding drunk. Wonder he didn't break his neck.*

Yves stood. "Adam?" He could smell the whiskey on him from ten paces.

With deliberate movements, Adam joined him on the verandah. "What the devil are you doing here?" he said, thick-tongued.

Alcohol has unleashed the brute in him, as usual, Yves thought. He hated to tell him the news about the engagement when Adam was in this state. "Business with your father," he said.

Adam raised the flask in his hand. "Want a drink?"

Yves shook his head and held out a cigar. "How about switching from whiskey to tobacco?"

Adam puffed through his lips like a horse. After a moment's consideration, he decided. He opened the flask and drained it. "I'm going in."

At table, Adam drank wine, but he refilled his glass repeatedly and what little he ate did nothing to sober him. Yves caught Marianne's anxiety, her frequent glances at Adam's wineglass. The bounder had no business coming to table like this, upsetting his sister. *After supper I'll take him outside, see what's set him off this time.*

"Adam," Marianne said quietly, "surely the wine makes you hot. Would you not like a lemonade?"

Adam looked at her, resentment clear in his tone and in the sneer on his face. "No, little sister, I would not like a lemonade."

Yves glanced at Mr. Johnston, who was watching Adam, a line between his eyebrows. He must be aware of his son's belligerence when he was drunk.

The tension at the table was disturbed by the sound of quick boots in the hallway. They heard Charles' murmur, and then a louder impatient voice.

Marcel? Yves put his napkin aside and stood up.

Marcel pushed past Charles and into the dining room. His face was rigid with fury. Mr. Johnston stood in alarm, but Adam remained seated, sprawled in his chair, his wineglass in his hand.

"Ah, the avenging cavalier," Adam drawled, raising his glass as if in toast. "What took you so long?"

"Get up, damn you," Marcel said, his hands in tight fists.

Yves stepped around the table, trying to get between the two of them. "Marcel, what are you doing?"

"Move aside, Yves." Marcel shoved at his brother.

Yves held Marcel back. "Wait."

"Explain yourself, young man," Mr. Johnston boomed.

Marcel reined himself in. "Mr. Johnston. This is between your son and the Chamards. We will take our quarrel out of doors."

"Don't want to go outdoors any more today," Adam said like a petulant child.

Marcel yanked free of Yves and slapped Adam across the face, hard enough to whip his head sideways. "Now, damn you. Name your weapon."

Adam adjusted his slouching posture as if he hadn't just been lethally insulted. "No, no," he answered lazily. "I believe I'll challenge you, then you choose the weapons."

"Marcel, he's drunk," Yves said. "Leave it."

"And he was drunk when he hit Nicolette. He beat her, Yves. He broke her jaw."

"He beat Nicolette? Is she . . . Does she . . . ?"

"She has a doctor. Cleo is with her."

Yves clenched his fists. He advanced on Adam, his head down like a bull ready to charge.

Marianne knocked her chair back. "Yves!"

Yves gave his head a shake, the animal in him suppressed by Marianne's plea. He and she were as much at peril as Adam was. If he thrashed her brother, could she ever forgive him? But Adam had hurt Nicolette—how could Yves forgive that?

He stared into Marianne's eyes, darkened nearly to violet. Did she fear for them? Or only for Adam? He stepped toward her. "Marianne." He had to make her understand, to make her see what he must do for Nicolette, for honor—

"Nicolette Chamard?" Mr. Johnston said. "Bertrand's bastard octoroon? Is that what this is about?"

"Father!" Marianne's face flushed. She looked from her father back to Yves, and he saw her fear, but he couldn't stop the red ferocity rising in him. His vision narrowed to the two men who had insulted his sister, his father, and all the Chamards.

He forgot these were Marianne's father and brother, forgot he was a guest in this house. Where Marcel's anger was hot, Yves' was cold.

"You are speaking of my sister, sir," he said. "You will apologize, or I will demand—"

"Yes," Adam interrupted, lifting his glass, a sneer on

his face, "the beautiful bastard with the constancy of an alley cat."

Marcel lunged, but it was Yves' fist that smashed into Adam's face.

As if time were suspended, Yves saw the wineglass fly gracefully from Adam's hand to shatter in brilliant sparkles against the gleaming candelabra. Broken crystal tinkled against the silver, wine splattered in a fine red arc of disparate drops. Adam's heavy red chair slowly toppled.

At the thump of Adam's body on the floor, time released the moment.

Marianne ran around the table. "Stop it! He's drunk, Yves, can't you see that!"

Yves suddenly saw, all too clearly. Marianne bending over Adam, letting the blood stream all over her blue dress, the one he especially liked, the candlelight on her hair. When would he see her again, after this?

Mr. Johnston rushed round the table and saw blood gushing from Adam's face and head. "My God, you've killed him!" he cried.

Marianne had her fingers under the flow from the gash in Adam's head. "No, Father. He's only cut his scalp on the table leg—"

Mr. Johnston raised a fist at Yves and roared, "Out of my house!"

Yves felt like a stone. He'd bashed Marianne's brother.

Adam was sobbing now, blubbering, snot and blood flowing out of his nose, and Marianne was wiping his face with her pretty dress. "Hush, now," she soothed. "You'll be all right."

Marcel took Yves' arm. "Come, brother. Adam will answer for Nicolette when he's sober."

Mr. Johnston's voice thundered from his massive chest. "Never set foot on my property again!"

"Marianne?" Did she not hear him? "Marianne—"
How was he to reach her across the chasm between their
two families if she . . . ?

Marcel dragged on Yves' arm. "We're leaving, Mr.
Johnston. But I expect satisfaction for what your son has
done to my sister."

Marianne's attention was on her brother, who was
completely undone, his caterwauling filling the room.

Won't you look at me? Yves begged silently. "Marianne?"

She turned to him, her hands and gown bloody, her
face red and furious. "Go, Yves. Just go."

Yielding to Marcel's grip on his arm, Yves left the
house, left Marianne.

"Wait," Yves said. "Marianne—"

"No," Marcel said. "There is nothing more to say
tonight. Come away."

He's right. Her face, looking at me like that. He followed
Marcel through the dark to the stables. *God, what have I
done?*

Chapter 28

The morning after Adam destroyed Marianne's life, she tended to his broken nose and the split in his scalp. The big brother whom she'd adored as a child, who'd shown her where the wild blackberries grew, who'd let her play toy soldiers with him—how could she not rush to him when he lay on the floor, sobbing and hurt? Now, however, she placed the compress on his scalp hoping it hurt like hell.

"Jesus, Marianne." He reached for the decanter at his bedside. Marianne got it first and moved it away.

"I'll give you something else for the pain. No more whiskey, Adam."

"You little prig. Give me that bottle."

"I will not. Drink this, and then tell me what happened at Lake Maurepas." She held up a cup of passion-flower brew. "For the pain. You want it or not?"

He took it. "You can't keep me from drinking."

"I'm aware of that. But you won't drink as long as you lie here being the invalid. Tell me what you did."

Adam flushed. "Men have liaisons. You don't need to know anything about it."

"Marcel said you broke her jaw."

Adam looked stunned. "Broke her jaw?" He stared at her, his eyes wide and horrified.

"You don't remember, do you?" she said with disgust. If she were not so furious with him, she might have pitied him. Adam was stricken to the core. He hadn't realized, then, what he'd done.

Adam rolled away from her and curled into a ball. He would not speak again.

Marianne found her father in his office, brooding, his eyes red and puffy. *He's been crying!* "You didn't sleep, Father?"

"What did Adam say to you? Do you know what happened?"

"No. He won't talk to me. And I don't know how much he remembers."

Mr. Johnston swiveled his chair to stare out the window. Marianne sat down in the big leather chair opposite the desk. Was he going to say he was sorry he threw the Chamard brothers out? That he would make it right with Yves? For her sake? She waited, but he said nothing.

"Father?"

He swiveled back to her. "Don't let this ruin your season, Marianne. There will be plenty of young men in New Orleans this winter. You can have your pick, and you know it, if you'll make the effort to encourage them."

She couldn't speak for a moment. Could he think this engagement meant so little to her? "I'm going to marry Yves."

"The marriage is off, and you can thank your brother for it. He's ruined a friendship between me and Bertrand Chamard going back twenty-five years. And no telling what that girl's mother is suffering. There is no forgiveness coming from the Chamards. You may make your mind up to that."

Does Yves not forgive me?

Mr. Johnston stood up, his massive frame blocking the light from the window so that Marianne had trouble seeing his face.

"What about you, Father? Do you forgive Marcel and Yves? Do you forgive Adam?"

He wiped a hand over his face. "No." He walked heavily from the room.

Marianne sat on in the office, her hands in her lap, her face blank and still. She was torn in two. She felt she would drown in blood spilling from her fractured heart.

Across the river, Yves and Marcel had arrived home in the middle of the night. They woke their father with news of the assault on Nicolette.

"It's my fault, Papa." Marcel paced across the bedroom. "I knew he was a mean drunk."

"How did it happen?" Bertrand said.

Yves, leaden and spiritless, sagged against the post of the bed. His heart felt like it'd been cut out of him by the expulsion from Marianne's house, without a word or a look of encouragement from her.

"Adam Johnston has been courting Nicolette for weeks," Marcel said. "We know the family, I thought it was all right. He was in love with her. He adored her."

"And Nicolette?"

"She liked him. Maybe more than liked him, I don't know. But yesterday, she accepted an invitation to noon dinner with Robert Whittington. Adam must have seen them in the hotel dining room. When Nicolette returned to Cleo's house, no one else was home. Cleo was singing that afternoon, I think.

"Adam knocked. Nicolette didn't want to let him in because he was drunk, but he forced the door. Then he accused her of—the usual words for unfaithful women. She told him to leave. He started hitting her."

"Where was Pierre?" Bertrand said, his voice harsh. "Where were you?"

Yves understood his father's need to blame someone, but only Adam deserved that burden. "Papa," he said, "Pierre couldn't be with her every minute. Marcel either."

Marcel shook his head, soaking in their father's anger. "I should have realized Adam was in too deep with Nicolette. I should have watched him. I should have made him leave the lake."

"Tell him about Pierre," Yves said.

"Pierre. He came in only minutes after Adam left the house and found Nicolette on the floor, unconscious. She roused almost immediately, he said. As soon as he had the neighbors in to stay with her, he loaded his pistol and went after Adam. He knew where he stabled his horse. Adam was there, his horse already saddled. Pierre actually fired at him, shooting to kill, he said, but he missed. Adam mounted his horse and ran."

"And you followed him," Bertrand added.

Yves hadn't told Marcel he'd asked Marianne to marry him. Papa didn't know either. They had no idea how many lives Adam had ruined yesterday.

"I made a terrible scene," Marcel went on. "Mr. Johnston threw us out. But Adam denied nothing. I would have beaten him to death, I think, if Yves hadn't been there. Instead, Yves knocked him down, broke his nose."

"So you're expecting an answer from him for the blow?"

"If he has any honor left."

"Who do you suppose it will be for?" Yves asked. He was only idly curious as he leaned against the bedpost,

too downhearted to care much what the answer would
be. His future happiness seemed now as far from him as
the moon, though Marianne lived only across the river.
Mr. Johnston would not allow the wedding after this.

"Adam's answer?" Marcel said. "I'm the one who
slapped him. But I see your point. You're the one who
broke his nose."

I'll choose swords, Yves thought. *Less likely to kill each other
with swords.*

Bertrand Chamard and Gabriel took the first steamer
downstream to join Cleo and Nicolette at the lake. Gabriel wanted to tend to her himself.

Yves and Marcel waited for Adam's response. They allowed a few days for him to sober up, but even then the
answer to their challenge did not arrive.

"Miserable yellow-belly," Marcel grumbled.

Yves could hardly sort through his feelings. He was dis-
gusted with Adam, had never been overly fond of him,
and this show of cowardice confirmed what he'd always
thought: He was weak and small and worthless. For what
he did to Nicolette, he deserved whatever happened to
him in the coming duel.

But he was Marianne's brother. She loved him. In fact,
she'd chosen Adam over him, there on the dining room
floor. Yves remembered her face so clearly, red and
angry. She'd told him to go. She despised him.

God, the days are long. Yves began to read the papers to find
the racing schedule. The season was about to start. He
would go to New Orleans. If Adam Johnston had a sudden
and unexpected infusion of spine, he would know where to
find him.

With cooler weather, the mosquitoes died down.
Shops, supper clubs, theaters, and concert halls opened.

The well-to-do from all over Louisiana and southern Mississippi flooded into town. New Orleans sparkled and roiled with music and dancing and dining.

The most touted event of the early season was the wedding between Albany Johnston and the widow Marguerite Sandrine. The Chamards were not invited.

Yves absented himself from most of the social scene. If he should encounter Marianne at a soirée or a ball, he couldn't simply walk up to her and say, "Good evening, Miss Johnston. How does the weather suit you?" She would turn her back on him, and everyone in the room would hear his heart break.

Yet Yves did not leave Louisiana. He could not bring himself to go so far from her. He wrote the editor of the newspaper in New York and told him he would be delayed indefinitely.

Yves continued to increase his purse at the racetrack. That's where he'd won enough to buy back Marianne's pearls and accrue a nest egg for the two of them. Now, no matter how carelessly he bet, he didn't seem to be able to lose.

Even with his extraordinary luck, the only thing that actually roused his interest was the election campaign. It was going to be close, with the three democratic candidates splitting the vote against Mr. Lincoln.

After the election, he told himself, *I'll go*. The newspaper wouldn't hold that position for him forever, and there was no point in staying in New Orleans. He looked for Marianne constantly, on the street, at every concert and play, yet she might have been hiding from him as he was from her.

In early November, the people elected Abraham Lincoln the next president of the United States. Yves was convinced the Southern states would secede, and there would be war. Young men of his acquaintance, drunk with the glory of fighting for their beloved South but innocent of the horror of combat, began to make plans to turn themselves into soldiers.

The week before Christmas, South Carolina seceded. Yves resolved to see Marianne one more time. If she truly despised him, then he could go. He sat in the study to compose a note asking if he might meet her. After a few words, he wadded the paper and tossed it across the room. *If her father sees it first, she may never get it. I'll have to find her alone, maybe after Mass.*

I shouldn't have waited so long. I should have sought her out, in the shops, on the street. What if she's been waiting for me, wondering why I don't come? Then the image of her angry face when she'd told him to leave came to him. *Or she never wants to see me again.*

Marcel, looking very fine in fawn trousers and chocolate coat, intruded on his solitude. "Enough of this brooding you've been indulging in, brother. Come out with me to the haberdashery. I need a new top hat, and now that I think of it, yours is a disgrace. Looks like someone sat on it."

Yves turned a long face to him.

Marcel dropped the jovial tone and sat down. "This is not like you, moping around. Nicolette is doing fine. In fact, she's singing at the Peppercorn tonight. What's the matter with you?"

Yves hesitated. "The day you came to Magnolias? I'd just arranged for Marianne Johnston to marry me."

"God, Yves. I'm sorry."

They heard the butler answer a knock at the front door. He led someone into the parlor, and then his steps came to the study. He scratched on the door, entered, and handed Marcel a card. "A gentleman to see you, sir."

"By God, Yves. It's Adam Johnston."

No good can come of this, Yves thought. *Better he should have stayed away.*

Yves and Marcel joined their guest in the parlor. They did not invite him to sit or take a glass with them.

"Mr. Johnston," Marcel said to the cousin who had been his boyhood friend, his mother's own nephew.

"Gentlemen."

Yves observed Adam's natty striped silk waistcoat and the softly folded ascot pierced with a pearl stickpin. The man's fine apparel did not obscure the ruin of his face, however. Adam had aged in the weeks since the scene at Magnolias. His eyes were puffy and red-rimmed. The muttonchops he'd grown did not disguise pale and sunken cheeks. His nose had a pronounced bend in it.

"How does Miss Johnston do?" Yves couldn't stop himself from asking.

Distracted, Adam answered impatiently, "Enjoying the season, I'm sure." He turned back to Marcel. "I will be brief. I beg your pardon for the delay in coming to you. I have been in Baton Rouge for some time." He set his hat on the table between the windows and then faced the men squarely. "I have come to arrange the resolution of your challenge, Mr. Chamard."

Yves' torpor left him. "But it was I who broke your nose!"

Adam dipped his head toward Yves. "My memory of that evening is incomplete, but I believe your brother's challenge has prior claim."

Is the man suicidal? He knows what a shot Marcel is.

"Roland Bonheur is my second."

Marcel raised an eyebrow, and Yves nodded. "My brother will second me. And the weapon of your choice?"

"Swords." He picked up his hat from the table. "At dawn, then." Adam showed himself out.

"I'll be damned. I never thought he had it in him,"
Yves said.

"I had come to doubt him, myself."

Yves leaned against the window and watched Adam
stride across the street. *Marcel may actually be more deadly
with a sword than a pistol. Poor fool.* "He looks god-awful."

"Shame will do that to a man."

And remorse. "You mean to kill him."

"Most certainly."

Marianne's brother. Adam won't have a chance. "Your
papers are in order? Lucinda and the baby are provided
for?"

Marcel turned from the window. "Robichaux and
Goldman have everything in hand. I would appreciate it
if you would look after Lucinda for a time, until she finds
someone else. She won't need money, but I think she
and the babe will be—sad—if I should die tomorrow."

"Adam is no swordsman. You can't seriously be thinking you could lose."

Marcel's small smile was grim. "Well, no. But one does
remember one's mortality at such moments."

"Swords, then. I'll see to them, then talk to Roland.
We'll have an early supper, and an early night, you and I."

Marcel nodded, his preoccupation deepening.

It's not easy, Yves reflected, *to contemplate killing a man
weeks after the offense, when one's passion has cooled.* But Yves
had no doubt his brother meant what he said. He would
kill Adam Johnston for what he'd done to their sister.

Adam returned to the Johnston house in the American
sector above Canal Street. The Faubourg Ste. Marie lacked
the Old World charm of the Vieux Carré where the
Chamards and the DeBlieux had their town houses, but the
American mansions were modern, grand, and extravagant.

Adam entered the cavernous foyer and handed Annie his hat, then made his way to his room as quickly as possible. He felt quite furtive, avoiding his father and Marianne. But neither of them looked at him kindly, and he did not know how to begin to regain their respect, much less his own. As soon as his bruises had begun to fade, Adam had left Magnolias. Father had let him know he'd ruined Marianne's hope of marrying Yves Chamard, an additional grievance for him to bear. Unable to endure his father's disdain nor Marianne's disappointment, he'd fled to Baton Rouge.

I beat her. I did it. This was the refrain of all his days. He could hardly, even now, believe he could have done such a thing. But he remembered some of it. He knew he had done it. And yet he loved her. Hopeless and despairing, he loved her.

Upstairs, he drew paper from the desk and dipped his nib in the bottle of ink. He didn't have to ponder. He had been over what he wanted to say many times. "Dear Father," he wrote.

When Adam had poured his sorrow, his regret, his contrition onto the page, he folded the letter and sealed it with wax. He drew another sheet of the ivory vellum and wrote, "My Dearest Sister."

This was far harder to write. Losing Marianne's regard hurt even more than losing Father's. He'd always known he somehow did not meet Father's measure, but Marianne—for all her spunk, she'd been his devoted, doting little sister. Tears rolled down his cheeks as he assured her of his love and of his remorse.

"After what I have done to Nicolette Chamard," he wrote, "I can never deserve the prize of marital felicity. But you, Dear Sister, have every right to the joys of matrimony. I have asked Father to forgive his old friends the Chamards, all of them, no matter what happens, for any man of honor would have acted as Marcel and Yves did that night. I do not believe Father will stand in the way of your happiness if Yves returns to you as he surely wants to, for beyond a doubt, My Dear, his heart is as constant as yours."

One more letter to write, the most difficult of all. Adam wrote her name, then sobbed and dropped his pen, splattering ink across the creamy paper. He buried his face in his hands, overcome for the thousandth time with grief and shame.

Adam had not touched liquor since the morning Marianne told him he had broken Nicolette's jaw. He would never touch it again. It did not excuse him, however. A man who would beat a woman, drunk or not, had no right to ask for forgiveness. But he must write her. Nicolette must know his heart, his true repentance, and perhaps in the next life, he would find she had forgiven him.

He took a clean sheet of paper and began again. "Mademoiselle Chamard," he wrote. "Please do not throw this missive in the fire when you realize it is from me. For the sake of the happy hours we spent together before I destroyed your trust in me, read on, I beg you."

When he finished, he propped Father's and Marianne's letters on his desk where they would find them after the duel tomorrow. Nicolette's letter he put into his coat pocket. In the morning, he would beg Marcel to deliver it to her. They had loved each other as brothers, he and Marcel. He would not refuse this of him.

Adam kept his room until dark, refusing the supper Annie brought to his door. Dear little Annie. Though everyone else in the house shunned him, Annie fussed over him like a little mother. There must be something, here in this room, he could leave her. His eye settled on a Venetian glass paperweight twinkling in the lamplight.

He wrote a note that the carved glass was Annie's and added it to the letters.

Without seeing his family, Adam left the house and made his way along the gaslit blocks of Canal Street to the edge of the Vieux Carré. At the Peppercorn, carriages let out the fashionable folk, all eager to see and be seen at New Orleans' most fashionable new supper club. The featured entertainer was Nicolette Chamard. Adam found a small table in the darkest corner as far from the stage as possible. He would not be seen.

Chapter 29

Marianne endured another round of the tiresome gavotte with a young man who might have been featureless for all the notice she paid him. She yielded to her father and his new wife in attending the season's balls, but she ignored their admonishments to look lively, to put herself forth—to try, for heaven's sake, to have a good time.

Her satin gown, yards and yards of silk the color of champagne, had cost her father more than she'd paid for Luke at the Forks-of-the-Road market in Natchez. *He probably thinks the dress will catch me a husband.* Indeed, the pale blond silk made the blue of her eyes bluer and set off the rich chestnut of her hair. *But it's just a dress.*

Yves did not appear. He had not appeared at any event this season, not any she had attended. He knew very well where the Johnston house stood, she thought. He could find her if he chose. He didn't want to see her. He did not forgive her for what Adam had done. Nor for what Father had said about his sister.

But I myself am innocent of those offenses! Then he took to heart her father's banishment, his disallowing of their marriage.

He gave me up too easily.

All her days since the incident in the dining room had been a swing from one grief to another. She grieved for Adam and raged against him too. He'd lost everything, it seemed, and had shrunk into himself. Yet he had done a despicable thing and cost her Yves as well. She could hardly bear the sight of him.

And mixed with the ache of losing Yves was the indignation that he had not fought for her. *I'd run away with him if he'd only come for me.*

So she passed through the days of fall hardly tasting the wines or hearing the waltzes. Always, in the back of her mind, she was imagining herself finding Yves, taking his lapels in her fists, and . . . what? Battering him until he loved her again?

The clocks chimed five. The party of Americans and Creoles had danced the night away and it soon would be dawn. Marianne climbed into the carriage with her father and his wife for the drive up Canal Street. Once at home, Father and Marguerite said their good nights to her and leaned into one another as newlyweds do on the way upstairs to their bedroom.

Marianne was restless. Bored. Lonely. She wandered through the empty darkened rooms of the big house, unwilling to go to bed.

Where is he now? At some gaming house? In some other woman's arms? She stared at the deserted street. *I could go looking for him. He's in the Old Quarter somewhere. Smoking a cigar. Laughing. Missing me? I could march into the game room of the Blue Ribbon, ignore the stares and whispers, and demand . . .* Her imaginings always dissolved at the moment of confrontation. What could she say? There was nothing she could do. If he wanted her, he knew where she was.

Marianne climbed the stairs to the second landing. Adam's door was ajar, the lamp burning low. She pushed the door open. He wasn't there, and his bed had not been slept in. The crystal paperweight gleaming in the light caught her eye, two letters propped behind it. One for Father, one for her. With growing unease, Marianne fingered the heavy paper.

Open it. With trembling hands, she tore the seal and read her brother's farewell. "What does he mean to do?" she whispered. The river? His pistols? Where were his pistols? "I should have been helping him, not hating him all these weeks!" She grabbed the letter addressed to Father and tore it open. She quickly scanned through the apology—a duel. He was reclaiming his honor with a duel!

The sun was coming up. They might already be at the Dueling Oaks in the park. She raced out of the room to Father's door. She pounded on it and without waiting tossed the letters on the floor for her father to find. Then she ran down the stairs in her dancing shoes, heedless of the golden gown sweeping behind her.

She grabbed her cape from the chair where she'd tossed it and let herself out the back. In the stable, the slaves had unharnessed the carriage and gone to bed. Marianne saddled her horse and found she could not mount wearing the hoop under her dress. She could not stop to undress, to untie, to unhook. She found a chisel on the tool bench and broke through the tapes holding the hoops to her waist. The dress dragging the ground, she gathered the skirts, climbed on a bench, and mounted the horse.

In the dawn light, Marianne galloped through the deserted streets toward the infamous wood where men sacrificed their lives for honor.

The previous day when Yves had called on Roland Bonheur to arrange the duel—weapons, pacing, physician—

he left the rooms of Adam's second a renewed man. All the torpor and passive inertia of the last few weeks fell away. He was energized. Marcel chose to fight by the American custom, to the death. Then Marcel would not fight. Yves would save Marianne's brother. She would be grateful, and she would forgive him for that dreadful night in the dining room.

He would claim her and take her away, whether her father approved or no. *Hell, I don't care if she approves. I'll convince her later. She's going with me.*

Yves knew where to find what he needed. On Rue de Cherbourg, a tiny, narrow lane off Rampart, was an apothecary of dubious repute. Here respectable vials of laudanum shared a shelf with mysterious potions the voodoo used in their secret ceremonies.

Through a filthy window, he could see the crabbed figure of Monsieur Antoine moving among his elixirs and powders. Yves had not been here since he was a boy of fifteen. Some of his friends and he had bought laudanum and taken it back to Marcel's room to experiment. They'd drunk every drop of the foul stuff and then slept for two days. The sight of Maman's tearstained face when he finally woke was enough to dissuade him from ever repeating his dalliance with opium-laced alcohol.

A little bell tinkled when Yves entered the dank, stale shop. He conferred with Monsieur Antoine, explaining exactly what he wanted, and then left with a cobalt-blue vial in his pocket.

In his own room, he fished in the back of the wardrobe for his sword case. He hadn't had it out in well over a year, though when he was still reaching for manhood, he had ardently pursued its use with an esteemed *maître d'armes*. Unpracticed of late, he was even so an accomplished swordsman.

Papa, unaware of the coming event, was out for the evening. Yves joined Marcel for supper in his room. Marcel had used Yves' absence in the afternoon to visit his beloved *placée* Lucinda and their little brown son. Then he'd returned to the house to write his farewells, just in case, and the five envelopes on the mantelpiece—for Nicolette, Gabriel, Cleo, Papa, and Yves—were silent reminders that this was not an ordinary evening. The brothers talked of this and that, of anything but what mattered.

At ten o'clock, Yves said, "I believe I'd like a glass of port. Join me. You'll sleep better."

Marcel shrugged.

Yves poured from the decanter on the side table with his back to Marcel, who in any event was not attentive. The contents of the little blue vial went into Marcel's glass.

Yves handed the port to his brother. They sipped. "I don't believe I care for this port," Marcel said.

Yves cleared his throat and took a showy sip. "It has an unusual aftertaste, it's true. Give it a chance. I think it's fine."

Indifferent, Marcel finished his glass and yawned. He'd have to rise at six in order to meet Adam by dawn, and he was ready for his bed.

Yves put his glass down. "Sleep well," he said, and closed the door behind him.

Chapter 30

The winter sun still below the treetops, Yves arrived at the appointed grounds. Adam, Roland Bonheur, and the surgeon waited at the edge of the open meadow.

Yves tied his horse to a low branch and retrieved his sword case from the saddle. Striding through the dew-soaked grass, he breathed in the fresh scent of morning and the heady aroma of coffee. The others warmed themselves at a small fire as a servant filled their cups.

"Good morning, gentlemen," Yves said.

"You're alone?" Roland demanded. "Where is Marcel?"

"Indisposed. He'll not leave his bed this day. However, I have come *au lieu de mon frère.* Mr. Johnston, I presume you will consider your debt paid by joining with me?"

From Adam's bleary eyes, Yves guessed he had suffered from more than one sleepless night. *Is he remembering why we're here? Does he see Nicolette's bruised, bloody face in his dreams?*

"Certainly. I accept your proxy."

And you'll live another day for it.

"Coffee?" Roland said.

Yves accepted a cup and observed Adam from the

corner of his eye. Marianne's brother had found his courage at last. Good for him. But he had not yet paid for what he did to Nicolette.

Adam pulled a paper from his pocket. Hesitating, he held it out to Yves. "Would you deliver this letter?"

Yves stiffened at the sight of Nicolette's name on the creamy vellum. His voice was dangerous. "You would insult her further?"

Adam's hand trembled. "I mean no offense. Please."

Reluctantly, Yves accepted the letter. *I need not deliver it, after all.*

He looked at Adam more closely. The man was the picture of misery, all his youth swallowed up by his burdens. *If it were allowed, I believe he would apologize here on the field. Is he prepared to defend himself at all?*

Roland tossed the dregs of his coffee into the fire. "Shall we begin?"

The surgeon took the duelists' coats. Yves opened his shirt to Roland, demonstrating he wore no protective shield over his breast. Adam did the same.

Finely balanced, sharp-edged, Yves' rapier was an elegant instrument designed primarily for thrusting, but it could deliver a deadly slash as well. Grandpère Chamard had defended his honor with it on reputedly twelve occasions in the days when dueling was a daily event under the willows of the park.

Roland verified the opponents' rapiers were of equal length, and Yves swished his once or twice to loosen his wrist. Adam too accustomed himself to the weight of his sword, flexing his shoulders and arms.

Yves knew his adversary. In their youth, Adam had been lazy and undisciplined, no match for Yves when they had on occasion sparred together at the *maison de maître d'armes*. Adam had never won a match against him, and Yves did not expect Adam's skills to have improved.

Perhaps Adam thought Marcel's skills more nearly matched his own, but he was mistaken. If anything, Marcel, for all his careless-seeming nonchalance, was a deadlier swordsman than Yves. *Lucky for you, you poor fool, that Marcel lies in his bed this morning.*

Roland produced a silver dollar, tossed it, caught it, and flattened his other hand under it. "Monsieur?"

"Heads."

Roland removed his hand to reveal the tail side of the coin. "Adam, choose your position."

Adam considered the angle of the sun, the direction of the breeze. In a valiant gesture, he walked to the center of the meadow and faced the sun.

Roland invited Yves to take his place so that with swords extended, two feet separated the points of the weapons.

His breathing is fast and we've not yet begun, Yves noted. *He's scared.*

Yves knew what Adam did not: Adam would survive this duel. The suffering was to be in the fear, and by now the expectation, of death. And so Yves intended to play him, to prolong the suspense.

Rapiers at the ready, Yves skewered Adam with his eye. "*En garde,*" he said quietly. Adam's eye betrayed not the steel one expected of a duelist but a hopeless determination to do what he must.

The man is in no fit state for this.

Roland accepted each man's nod of readiness. "*Allez!*"

Adam opened aggressively with a balestra followed by a lunge, which Yves easily put down. Yves countered with his own assault, and the blades sang as each took the other's measure, the meadow stilled at the flash and zing of the swords.

His wrist is rigid.

Metal screeching on metal in a glissade, Adam's blade

scraped down the length of Yves'. Yves disengaged and flicked his point at the loose sleeve of Adam's shirt, careful not to draw blood. A show of blood would stop the duel. It was too soon for that.

Adam backed two paces, caution in his eyes. Yves advanced. Adam executed a contre-dégagement to break Yves' push, but Yves was not deceived.

Sweat rolled down Yves' face, but coolheaded and conditioned, Yves controlled the fight. He worked Adam, feinting and breaking time in a changement de rythme, keeping Adam off balance and defensive.

Adam flagged, his parries growing weak and erratic, and Yves heard his ragged breathing even over the metallic din of blades striking and sliding against each other. In a sudden, impetuous rally, Adam advanced. He wielded his blade furiously, wildly even, overextending his lunge, and Yves easily sidestepped its mortal point.

He's wide open. Does he want *to die?*

Yves refused the opportunity, intending that Adam feel Death breathing on his neck before he finished it. *An ear*, Yves thought as he pressed Adam back another two paces. *For what he did to Nicolette.*

Thundering hooves and a flash of shimmering gold in the sunlight distracted Yves for a moment, but he quickly renewed his concentration. Adam's now frantic unpredictability made him dangerous.

Yves advanced, ready to make an end of it.

"Stop! You *must* stop!"

"Miss Johnston!" Roland shouted. "Go back!"

Marianne? Yves turned his head.

At that moment, Adam attempted a thrust. Yves quickly parried, but he failed to complete the repulse as he simultaneously tried to watch Marianne stumbling, her skirts dragging the ground.

The follow-through behind Adam's unblocked thrust forced the blade through Yves' defensive range.

With regained focus, Yves raised his rapier and diverted Adam's blade away from his chest, but the sword pierced his shoulder, the wound blooming scarlet on the white shirt.

Marianne screamed.

Adam lost his grip on the impaling sword and backed away. He shook his head, eyes wide. "It wasn't supposed to happen like this."

Yves looked down at the sword still stuck in his body and swayed. Adam caught him and lowered him onto his side, the blade still protruding front and back through the flesh just below Yves' collarbone.

Yves chuckled. Adam had drawn first blood. Marcel would not be pleased, but he'd have to admit the irony was delicious. The more he thought of it, the funnier it got, and Yves erupted in one great peal of laughter.

"He's in shock!" Marianne pushed Adam out of her way, the pale gold gown billowing on the grass. "Get some brandy."

Yves grinned. "Hello, Marianne."

"You fool. Both of you. One of you could have been killed."

She touched the sword protruding from his shoulder. "That's got to come out."

"Wait—" Yves said.

Marianne got to her feet and pressed her satin slipper against his chest—"Just a minute!" Yves protested. "The surgeon . . ."—and she pulled the rapier free.

Yves' world went black. "Yves!" he heard. She slapped his face. "Yves! Do not pass out!" She slapped him again, and he opened his eyes.

Her eyes were bluer than he'd ever seen them. And she was worried about him.

He grinned. "God, woman. I'd hate to see what you'd do to a man you weren't desperately in love with."

"You dunderhead," Marianne said, tears wetting her lashes.

"Miss, allow me to attend the patient," the surgeon said, attempting to dislodge Marianne from Yves' side.

"She's not going anywhere," Yves said and kept her close. While the doctor examined the wound, Marianne helped Yves drink from the doctor's flask of brandy.

"No pulsing to indicate an arterial rupture. He'll live." The doctor took the flask and poured brandy over the wounds, front and back, and let Yves lie in the chill damp grass as he fashioned bandages.

Yves didn't mind the chill. Marianne was here, gazing at him, holding his hand. It was as if all the weeks of doubting himself, and her, had never happened. The morning sunlight reddened her chestnut hair, hanging loose and tangled from the bold ride through the park. "You're beautiful even with twigs in your hair."

Adam touched his sister's shoulder.

"Damn it, Adam," Yves said, never taking his eyes from Marianne, "leave us alone. I'm bleeding down here."

"He could have killed me, Marianne, at any time. But he didn't."

Marianne regarded Yves a moment. He waited, hoping she would understand, that there would be no resentments between them.

A radiant smile lit Marianne's face. "You were going to spare him, weren't you? Because you're desperately in love with me."

With his good arm, Yves pulled her to him and proved to her she was right.

Chapter 31

Marianne insisted on a last trip upriver to Magnolias before the wedding and the voyage to New York. Wearing her gardening boots for the mud and a wool pelisse against the wet wind, she walked down to the quarters. The winter sky was deeply gray, promising another night of rain.

She found Joseph in his cabin sharpening a hoe by the light of the fire. "Mighty cold day," he said and sat Marianne next to the cheery hearth. It was snug in the cabin in spite of the blustery wind, and she let her damp cape slide over the back of the chair. A pot of stew bubbled over the fire, scenting the room with onions and carrots and pork.

"You're never still, are you, Joseph?" Marianne asked, nodding toward the blade and the file.

"Oh, I'se slowed up considerable, Missy. De rheumatiz get me, days like dis."

Marianne grasped her hands and leaned forward. "Joseph, you've labored every day of your life. I want to make it easier now."

Joseph worked the file across the blade, the *rasp, rasp, rasp* filling the little cabin. "I's had de life I has. Dat's all."

Over the rhythmic scraping, Marianne reached out and touched his arm. "I'm taking you with me to New York, Joseph. You and Peter and Annie. You won't have to work hard anymore, and I can take care of you."

Joseph stilled the file.

"We'll leave Magnolias tomorrow. The wedding is Monday in New Orleans. We'll sail on Tuesday."

Joseph's expression made her uneasy. Not a pleased look at all.

"Father says there will be war. You won't be doing the Underground Railroad if there's a war on."

"Long as dere's slaves, Missy, dere be a railroad for 'em." He picked up the beat of his strokes against the blade.

He doesn't want to come with me? "Joseph?"

With small shakes of his head left and right, he said, "Honey, I loves you. But I don belong goin' nowhere. I live mos my life right here. My chilrens is here." He shook his head more firmly. "Missy, I gone stay here till I dies."

Marianne's chest tightened. She didn't want to say good-bye to Joseph. Father would visit her, and write her, but Joseph—she might never see him again.

She hadn't given a thought to his daughter, to all the grandchildren Joseph had on the place. She stared at the fire until she had herself under control. She'd been terribly selfish to think he belonged only to her.

"I understand. Of course you don't want to leave your family, Joseph."

Joseph crossed the floor to Marianne and kissed the top of her head. "I gone miss you, honey. You like one of my own."

Marianne hugged him, blotting her tears on the brown wool of his vest. "How can I leave you?" she snuffled into his chest.

Joseph rocked her in his arms. "You gone have me crying too here a minute," he said, his voice thick.

Marianne found her handkerchief and blew her nose. "It really was awful of me to think of taking you from your grandbabies, Joseph. I'm sorry."

With his rough old hands, Joseph cradled her face. "Missy, you don be sorry. I proud of what you done here wid all you people. Proud as I can be."

Marianne buried her face against him, holding on as long as she could.

Marianne and Yves, joined now in the sight of God and of every soul in New Orleans, marched hand in hand down the aisle to the joyous din of ringing bells.

Outside St. Louis Cathedral, their friends joined them in the cold brilliant sunshine of Jackson Square for an impromptu, informal reception. No one congratulated "Miss Marianne"—she heard only "Madame Chamard," "Mrs. Chamard," and she gloried in her new name.

Yves smiled and laughed with the well-wishers, keeping Marianne close, in spite of the throng surrounding them. He needed his right hand to accept the congratulations of his friends, but he draped his left arm around her shoulders, then slid his restless hand down just below her waist. In a moment, he swept up her back to stroke the nape of her neck. Marianne could hardly do her part in smiling and nodding to the well-wishers, her senses so concentrated on Yves' every caress.

While one tedious old gentleman prattled on, Yves ran his hand down her arm, and while he nodded and said "Indeed" to the old man, he stroked Marianne's palm.

He knows what that does to me! He did it again, and a laugh escaped her before she could stop it. The old gentleman frowned, but she smiled him down. In only a few hours, her husband would do more to her than tickle her palm. Nerves, anticipation, a little anxiety—Marianne seized Yves' hand so his fingers could not undo her in front of all these people.

Marguerite Johnston, Marianne's stepmother, stepped between them. "Time to change into your evening clothes," she instructed.

Marianne did not want to let go of Yves even for a moment, but Marguerite had accomplished an amazing feat, arranging the wedding on short notice and making it the grand affair it was, and would be; the evening's reception and ball were the opening of New Orleans society's rousing New Year's celebrations.

Be gracious, Marianne scolded herself. *Only a few hours until all these people go away and I'm in Yves' own room, in his arms, in his bed.*

Her stepmother hurried her home to the Johnston mansion to change for the wedding supper. Marianne allowed herself to be cinched and tied and adorned for the evening in a robin's-egg-blue gown, dipped low across her chest, pearls scalloped over her bosom. Yards and yards of magnificent satin flounced from a fitted waist and barely concealed her blue satin dancing slippers. A hothouse orchid adorned her upswept hair, and the ransomed pearls hung from her ears.

Marianne endured dozens of kisses from elderly aunts, doddering uncles, cousins, friends, and acquaintances. Yves suffered the same duties, and Marianne discreetly maneuvered closer to him as he did toward her until their elbows brushed as they greeted the guests. The supper tables, clothed in snowy linen and replete with fine wines and the best cooking in New Orleans, glittered with silver and crystal. Cruelly, Marguerite seated Yves across from Marianne. She tried to do her duty to the guests, but Marianne's eyes constantly found his.

Supper came to a close, the orchestra tuned their instruments, and more guests filled the Johnston mansion. At last, the ball began.

Marianne, beribboned, bedecked, besotted, tilted her head as Yves whirled her around the room with a dozen other couples, the gentlemen in their black cutaways and striped trousers, the ladies in taffetas, silks, and satins, their skirts billowing behind them as they danced.

"I hope we always waltz, even when we're old," Marianne said.

"Wear this blue dress, I'll waltz you every night of your life."

With Yves' hand on her waist, Marianne followed him round and round the room and then out the door onto the verandah where potted palms screened wrought-iron benches. Seated in shadowed seclusion, Marianne moved her skirt to make room for Yves.

"Madame Chamard, I have something to tell you."

"That you love me desperately?"

"I fear you may need convincing." He kissed her, a deep and proprietary kiss. Marianne's stays prevented the intake of breath she needed, and when Yves moved his mouth to her throat, she didn't care if she fainted. "More," she murmured.

He whispered in her ear, "On the stroke of midnight, I'm going to ravish you."

He nibbled her neck and she laughed. "In front of all these people?"

He stood up and held his arm out for her. "I've reconsidered. We'll leave the ball first."

"I can wait that long only if you dance with me."

She stepped into his arms and he rocked her to the music for a moment before he waltzed her back into the soft light of the ballroom.

All of society filled the Johnston house. Nearly every-

one the families knew sipped punch and admired the
newlyweds. But Marianne counted the missing, too.
Adam was not here. He had sat with Father and Marguerite through the ceremony and the Mass at St. Louis
Cathedral. Afterward, he found a moment to take her
aside, kiss her cheek, and promise to write. Then Adam
slipped out of the church. By now he was on his way to
South Carolina to join Butler's First Infantry Regiment.
Despite the duel and his reconciliation with Father and
her, he seemed still to suffer. *My poor brother, he may never
forgive himself.*

Marianne's list of the missing included Yves' other
family. The Johnston and Chamard parents had not invited them, and neither Gabriel and Simone, nor Nicolette with her suitor Mr. Whittington, danced among the
guests. Marianne's pleasure in the waltz faded.

"You're frowning," Yves said.

"I'm thinking of the family and friends who are not
here, not white, not welcome."

Yves nodded. "Yes, it is our loss. But in New York, we
will choose our own friends."

"And your family, all of them, will be welcome in our
home."

"For now, sweetheart, we have a waltz playing and our
wedding to enjoy." Yves whirled her in wide circles and
brought the glow back into her eyes.

At last, persuaded by Yves' suffering in his wool coat,
Marianne agreed to leave the dance floor and take a
glass of sillery. Cups of wine punch in hand, they made
their way through the congratulatory crowd to the drawing room.

Yves nudged Marianne toward the settee where
Madame DeBlieux sat with her middle daughter,
Musette.

"Tante Josie," Yves said to his honorary aunt.

"Yves, my darling," she said as he leaned down for her kiss. "Madame Chamard, sit with me a moment." Musette made room for Marianne on the sofa.

Josephine, with a gleam in her eye, offered to tell about Yves' boyhood escapades and Marianne settled in to be amused. Yves bent to Musette, who was nervously enjoying her first season, and whispered in her ear. She blushed as she accepted his arm and Yves led her to the dance floor.

At half past eleven, Monsieur Bertrand Chamard found Marianne in lively discussion with Madame DeBlieux. "Josephine, my darling, you look lovely as always."

Marianne, curious about the half-understood ancient gossip she'd heard about the widow and the widower, watched Josephine respond to the suave and handsome Bertrand's familiarity with a particularly warm smile.

"*Bonne Année*, Bertrand," Josephine said. "I suppose you've come to rescue your daughter-in-law?"

Bertrand took Josephine's hand. "I did, Josie." He spoke very quietly, so quietly it was hard for Marianne to eavesdrop "But I wish to return to you before the stroke of midnight. May I?"

She's blushing!

"At midnight, then," Josephine DeBlieux promised.

Bertrand held his arm out for Marianne. "I thought this might be my only chance for a dance, my dear. Yves has monopolized you scandalously."

"Yes." Marianne smiled. "Hasn't he?"

The ballroom, overheated from the gas lamps and the dancing couples, nevertheless enticed with the strains of the orchestra. Marianne placed her hand in Monsieur Chamard's and he led her onto the floor.

"You've made my son a happy man, Madame," he said.

Marianne thought she might never stop smiling. "And I am a happy woman, Monsieur."

"I'd like it if you called me Papa."

Marcel tapped his father's shoulder. "May I?"

Marianne stood on tiptoe and kissed her father-in-law's cheek. "Thank you, Papa."

Still smiling, she held her arms out for Marcel's embrace and he whirled her back into the dance. "I'm having the time of my life," she said, "dancing with each and every Chamard."

"I'm the best dancer, though, haven't you noticed?" Marcel said.

"Are you?"

He winked at her. "And the best kisser."

She laughed out loud at that.

"Now you've hurt my feelings," Marcel declared with a grin. "And here is your beloved, just in time for midnight, so it will be another New Year before I can prove it to you."

Yves elbowed his brother aside. "I think I saw Lindsay Morgan watching you over there. Go prove yourself to her."

The orchestra brought the music to a close. The clock began its chime, and Yves locked Marianne in his arms and kissed her deeply and hotly, consuming her.

"Scandalous!" Marianne heard an old dowager whisper. *Yes, and wonderful.*

At one minute into January 1, 1861, the orchestra struck up a lively tune and the kissing couples released each other, some more reluctantly than others.

"Can we go now?" Marianne whispered.

Yves kissed the tip of her nose, then spoke into her ear. "Let's make a run for it."

With as little notice as possible, Marianne asked Charles for her blue satin cape and slipped out the side door with Yves where a carriage awaited. They were to spend their first night together across town in the Chamard house while the rest of the families partied at the Johnstons'.

The house was dark except for a single lamp in the entryway. Yves tapped on the door with his cane and the Chamard butler let them in. "I got you a fire up yonder, M'sieu Yves. Good evenin', Madame. Ya'll go on up. I see you in de mawnin wid de coffee."

Yves led the way with a candle held aloft. Marianne concentrated on managing her skirts on the narrow stairs. Yes, she'd been dancing for hours, and her corset pressed on her ribs, but those facts could hardly account for the difficulty she had in breathing. She knew what waited in the marriage bed, of course she did. And she wanted what his kisses and caresses promised her. Still, mixed with desire, she recognized apprehension. It would be more than kissing and petting in that room upstairs.

Yves opened the door. The fire, of oak with apple wood shavings, warmed and scented the air. Dominating the room, the four-poster bed, plush and deep with pillows, stirred Marianne's feelings, all of them, the anxious and the lustful.

Yves closed the door and Marianne turned to face him. Her husband.

Her arms were inside the satin cloak, pulling it tight around her. He drew her into him and rested his chin on her head. "Cold?"

She swallowed. "I'm not cold."

He undid the clasp at her neck and let the satin pelisse slip off her shoulders. He shrugged off his own satin-lined cape, the sensuous slide of it down his body drawing Marianne's eyes. Yves gazed at her bare shoulders, her bosom only half covered by the low-cut gown. He toyed with the pearls draped along the neckline, then kissed her ear, nibbled down her neck.

Marianne waited for the kind of kiss he'd given her in Miss Ginny's cabin, but he touched her mouth lightly, brushing his lips across hers. The tension was unbearable; she couldn't stand it. She wanted to feel what she'd felt that day on the Trace. She pressed her mouth against his, caught his upper lip in her teeth. His tongue ran across hers and she leaned her breasts into his chest, pushing her kiss into his.

"Marianne," he whispered. "There's no hurry, darling. Relax."

"I'm just a little nervous," she confessed.

"We'll have a glass of wine. Enjoy the fire."

Yves pulled chairs closer to the hearth and sat Marianne down. Seated across from her, he pushed aside the voluminous skirt and found her ankle. He pulled the slipper over her heel, her silk stocking smooth under his hand, and kneaded her foot, massaging the arch and the toes one by one. Marianne leaned back in her chair.

"That's heavenly."

"I can make it even better." He ran his hands up her leg to the garter and released the white silk. Slowly, carefully, he rolled the stocking down her thigh, over her knee, and past her ankle until it was off, exposing her naked foot in the firelight. He probed her instep with strong, gentle fingers. Then the other stocking. As he unhooked her garter, he opened his hand and ran his palm over her thigh. In every direction, her skin ached for him to explore further, but he rolled the silk down and kept his hands on her foot.

Yves knew other things he could do to her toes than massage them, but his bride was not ready. There would be time enough for all the things he could teach her. *Her first time, it's too important to rush.*

But he didn't want her to fall asleep on him either. He put the wine away. "Are you comfortable in that gown?"

Marianne looked at him, a smile playing on her lips. "No."

"You'll let me help you out of it? Everyone else has gone to bed."

"I don't need a maid if you can handle the buttons."

She stood up and turned. There were exactly forty-six tiny satin-covered buttons down her back.

My God, there must be a hundred of them! Yves thought. *Patience, man.* He caressed her shoulder, his thumb lightly probing her neck.

Everywhere he touched, she felt the tension leave her body. *Touch me there again.*

The buttons were fastened with delicate blue satin loops. A vision of shiny buttons popping and rolling all over the carpet made Yves smile. *Another time.*

He opened the first button and the second, the touch of his fingers tantalizing on her back. Marianne's breathing quickened as he tasted the newly discovered tender skin down to the next button.

Another button released from its satin loop, and Yves kissed a little farther. More buttons, more teasing kisses, and the corset was revealed, the tapes tightly knotted. He thought of the sharp-bladed letter opener on his desk—when it was time, he doubted he'd have the patience left for untying knots.

Marianne felt his fingers' delicate, liberating touch on each button. His lips against her back, his tongue at the base of her neck—his touch wakened her body far beyond where lips met skin.

She forgot every virginal hesitation. Her breasts rose and stiffened. She wanted out of this dress. And still he took his time.

Her dress slipped from her shoulders. One maybe two

more buttons, she could slide it over her hips. Ah. Admirable man, but so slow.

Yves helped her step out of the hoop and the mass of satin, and Marianne stood before him in her corset and pantaloons. "My God," he whispered. "You're beautiful."

She smiled at him, fearless now, and advanced to disrobe him. Her fingers untied his cravat as she watched the firelight find the gold in his eyes. She let the white silk fall from her hand, then worked the buttons of his stiff shirt. The hollow at the base of his throat revealed, she touched her lips there, tasting him.

Slowly she peeled the shirt off him and ran her fingers over his chest, his ribs, around to his back where the muscles tapered to his hips. Her nearly bare body against his, she invited his kiss.

This time he gave her all his heat and desire, his lips firm and then more and more insistent, his tongue penetrating her mouth, tasting and taking. With hands, lips, tongue, she proved to him she was ready.

He ran his palm across her corseted back, across her lightly covered rounded bottom to the softness of her belly. Lower. His fingers touched her and stroked her. Marianne's sharp intake of breath hurried him on.

Without letting her go, he walked them to his desk, reached for the letter opener, and quickly slipped the blade in the lacings of her corset. A single swift cut through the ribbon and the corset opened, freeing her waist, her breathing, her breasts. He had to look, had to see all of her before he touched her again.

He reveled in the glow of firelight on the smooth skin, the full breasts, the curve of waist and hip—her unabashed rosy body at last revealed. His eyes moved up to her mouth, her luscious waiting mouth, and then into her eyes. She was his, this wondrous woman, and she wanted him.

* * *

On New Year's Day, Marianne stood on the dock hugging her cape to her. The sky was blue, the sun bright, but the cold wind off the river chilled her to the bone. *What a strange way to leave Louisiana, cold and sad. A little sad.*

Father had placed his bride to the lee of his massive frame, sheltering her from the wind. *But Father will not be lonely. He's happy with his Marguerite.*

The last good-byes made a tearful scene on the dock. Gabriel and Simone, too, were sailing, Gabriel having accepted a position at a hospital in New York, and all the aunts, mothers, fathers, brothers, and sisters hugged and kissed and cried.

At the last minute, Marcel leaned down and whispered in Marianne's ear. "I'm the best kisser."

Marianne laughed, the tears spilling over her lids. "You come see us next New Year's, I'll let you prove it."

The coxswain aboard the sloop blew his whistle and called, "All aboard!" Peter, limping but strong, led Annie up the gangway. Annie, dressed in a red wool skirt flounced by white crinolines, gripped Freddie's leash and he scampered up the ramp behind her.

Once aboard, Gabriel and Simone, Yves and Marianne stood at the rail. The schooner let go of the dock and moved into the current. Wind filled the sails, and they waved to their families one last time.

In the gulf, the sun beamed down and dried the tears on her face. Marianne untied her bonnet and let the wind do what it would with her hair. Filling her lungs with salt air, she lifted her chin and drank in the blueness of the sky.

She was on her way, wherever didn't matter, because Yves Chamard wrapped his arms around her, and together they faced the wind.

More Historical Romance From
Jo Ann Ferguson